THE ALIEN'S GIFT

• • • • •

THE ALIEN'S GIFT

• • • • •

A Novel

Bruce M. Smith

iUniverse, Inc.
New York   Bloomington

The Alien's Gift
A Novel

Copyright © 2009 Bruce M. Smith

All rights reserved. No part of this book may be used or reproduced by
any means, graphic, electronic, or mechanical, including photocopying,
recording, taping or by any information storage retrieval system
without the written permission of the publisher except in the case
of brief quotations embodied in critical articles and reviews.

This is a work of fiction. All of the characters, names, incidents,
organizations, and dialogue in this novel are either the products
of the author's imagination or are used fictitiously.

iUniverse books may be ordered through booksellers or by contacting:

iUniverse
1663 Liberty Drive
Bloomington, IN 47403
www.iuniverse.com
1-800-Authors (1-800-288-4677)

Because of the dynamic nature of the Internet, any Web addresses or
links contained in this book may have changed since publication and
may no longer be valid. The views expressed in this work are solely those
of the author and do not necessarily reflect the views of the publisher,
and the publisher hereby disclaims any responsibility for them.

ISBN: 978-1-4401-6405-7 (pbk)
ISBN: 978-1-4401-6407-1 (cloth)
ISBN: 978-1-4401-6406-4 (ebk)

Library of Congress Control Number: 2009933291

Printed in the United States of America

iUniverse rev. date: 8/11/2009

My Special thanks to Susan Bennett
for all the hard work she did pre-editing my book.
To IUniverse whose editorial review was invaluable.
My wife Nancy who first told me my short story would be a novel.
Michael Garrett, what can I say about his advice and editorial skill?
Michael, your advice and guidance were invaluable.
Thank you.

Chapter 1

The morning started like any other. I woke early, around five. It was a habit. One I had never dropped from my years in the military. Since those days I had always loved the morning hours. The day was new, the air seemed fresher. Trees had spent the night cleansing the air. Nature had time to revitalize herself during the evening. I was letting my mind wander through these thoughts as I sat on my patio, sipping my morning coffee. Sitting there, I watched my dogs as they performed their morning patrol. It was part of their morning routine.

That's when I first felt it. I'm not sure what it was; it wasn't anything I could put my finger on. But something was different. Before I could actually focus on it, it was gone. Setting my coffee down, I leaned forward in my chair as if the gesture would help evoke the sensation again, but it was no use. Whatever it had been, it was gone now. I still wasn't willing to let it go. I looked around one last time, as if I might be able to see what had caused the feeling, but it was lost. I leaned back into my chair and took another sip of coffee. My mind pondered the thought for another moment before I finally let it go.

In no time I was back into my morning ritual. Watching the trees, their silhouette swaying in the morning glow—the pool with its dancing reflections from what little light nature was providing. The dogs, satisfied with their morning patrol, returned and took their customary positions by my chair. They would lift their heads from time to time—catching the scent of something.

Something which always seemed to elude me, I thought.

There it was again. I could feel it.

Something felt as if it was enveloping me, my entire body feeling the effects. A touch that was there...but wasn't. This time the dogs were also aware of it. I watched as their heads snapped up. They seemed alert to this unseen invasion into our morning. My senses attempted to identify what it might be. Then it was gone, so quick for a moment I doubted it happened.

But the dogs...the dogs had sensed it, too, and now they seemed to share in my confusion.

They were both standing, walking around uneasily, they too were not sure what was there or where it had gone. They took a tentative step forward as if to confront something—someone.

Looking for the Intruder that wasn't there—Intruder, why had I thought that? Like the last time there was nothing, no one to be found.

Finishing my coffee, I started back into the house. The dogs usually followed me straight in, always more than ready for breakfast. This morning they lingered, stopping to look one last time. There had been something. Their actions seemed to confirm it...something. With a final glance I closed the door. Unaware at the time, that another door had just been opened.

The rest of the morning was filled with my normal routine. By the time I got in my car to go to work, I was starting to wonder if I had just imagined the whole thing.

It was a pretty long commute to the office. But one that I always enjoyed. The time was always filled with planning the day ahead of me. That, or I was still resolving unfinished problems from the day before. Either way the drive was always full. The radio always played in the background, but never doing more than covering the sounds of the highway. Traffic this morning was light, much lighter than usual.

Was today a holiday? I thought almost whimsically, knowing better.

I was almost an hour into the drive. I had just started to change lanes. I was slowly working my way out of the commuter lane. That's when I felt the sensation coming over me again. It felt much stronger this time. More tangible, like I could feel someone.

Someone, why did I have that thought? It was a someone—not a something?

Like this morning it felt like I was being violated. I quickly dropped the thought. Trying instead to focus in on what...or who I was feeling, but it was already gone. Even before I could clear my mind enough to focus, it was gone.

What the hell was that? I thought *who the hell was that, was more like it.*

There was no doubt in my mind this time. Something, *no, not a something...*
it was a someone. Who? Why? What the hell is happening to me? Am I going crazy?
If you can ask that question, you're not. I remember hearing that, but...

I was so deep in thought I had almost missed my exit. I snapped my head
back to my driving.

Maneuver your vehicle, guy. Crazy or not, you can't be killing people.

Minutes later I arrived at the office. I was still pretty shaken. I took a
moment trying to regain my composure before going in.

Thinking I had it under control, I headed inside. As I walked through the
door, Cindy my secretary looked up at me.

"What happened?"

I hadn't done a very good job covering that, I thought. Smiling, or at least
attempting to, I mumbled something about the morning drive without going
into any real details before rushing into my office.

Moments later I came back out to get a cup of coffee. I needed some time
to figure this out. I told Cindy I had to finish some paperwork this morning. I
wasn't to be disturbed for the next thirty minutes. *That should buy me the time*
I need to figure this out, I thought, as I walked back toward my office.

Once back in my office, I sat at my desk. My mind started to retrieve
the details of the morning. It was an attempt to regain my sanity. I was
determined to regain control of my life. To put it back into order. My mind
went into itself. I was trying to find the intruder.

Was he there someplace? Hiding, not showing himself? If he was, could I find
him? What would I do if I did? I had no idea.

It was no use. My thoughts were running in circles. I couldn't make sense
of the morning, no matter how much I tried. I knew I wasn't crazy, I had
put that thought to rest earlier. I was too self aware for that, too aware of my
own nature. I had been assaulted somehow. I knew that. Something from
within—I knew that, too. I needed to try and understand what was going
on. It was no use. I was still too rattled to think straight.

*As anyone would, having an experience like...*I was starting to giggle even
as the thought formed. *Who ever experienced anything like this?* My giggle
caught, and before I could control it, I was laughing out loud. My needed to
relieve the stress. So I let the moment take control, allowing myself to laugh
out loud for a moment before I settled down.

It was only then that I heard the tapping on the door. It was Cindy. I
knew she was probably worried about me. I must have been a sight coming
though the door this morning.

I smiled, thinking *get back to now or they'll put you in a room. Then you'll*
have lots of time to study what's happening.

3

Letting the thought go, I called for Cindy to come in. I watched as the door opened.

"Are you alright?" she asked as she poked her head in.

Alright, I thought, my mind flashing through the morning again in an instant *alright.* I started to laugh again.

At first Cindy looked quite concerned. Then my laughter started to have an effect on her. I watched in amusement as I saw the transition. First, she was showing concern, then I watched as her face shifted to a smile. Before she could contain herself, she too was laughing. *Why does that happen to people?* I wondered.

As I watched her laugh it somehow helped. I knew I wasn't crazy. How could I be? I admit, people have accused me of having a strange mind. Strange, that might be true, but not crazy. With my sanity once again confirmed, I managed to control my outburst of laughter.

"This morning has been kind of strange, and it just struck me as funny." I said. Finally composing myself, I asked if she could bring in the folder I'd been working on the night before. That small gesture reconfirmed that the world had returned to normal.

Returned to normal, but for how long? I wondered before I forced my head into the paperwork in front of me. The rest of the day passed without any further intrusions. My thoughts were the only exception. *What had happened to me this morning?*

The rest of the day turned out to be quite routine, ending without any further incidents. I had even managed to spend the second half in relative peace. Before I knew it, I was getting into my car. I was ready to start the long commute home. A drive I had learned to love. Living in the country is worth the drive.

Today, however, I wondered, *would I be driving home alone?* My mind was just starting to relive the morning again when my phone rang. From that point I was in one conversation after another for the rest of the trip. Before I knew it I was pulling into my driveway. I had driven home, *and I had driven it alone,* I thought. I wondered if being on the phone had kept whatever it was that happened this morning from happening again.

The thought vanished as I got out of the car. It was time to greet my puppies, 200 pounds plus between the two I admit, but they are and will always be my puppies. My next half hour revolved around them—it always does when I get home. I loved this time, usually looking forward to it all the way home. Every day it was the same, always starting with the greeting. Nobody can ever greet you with the joy and happiness of a dog. I truly felt like the center of their universe.

The rest of the evening passed quietly. I fell back into my normal way of life. I had dinner, then spent some time on the computer working on a book I'm trying to write. Before I realized it, the pups were informing me it was bed time. They get their snacks at bedtime, so they always seem to know when the clock strikes ten. I turned off the computer before letting the dogs out for their final patrol. Knowing they would be out for awhile, I went to my room and jumped in the shower.

The shower felt good. I let the warm water flow over me. I was finally starting to feel relaxed as the water melted away the pressures of the day. Everything was as it should be again. I stayed in the shower until the pups let me know it was time to come in. It was time for their bedtime snack. Snacks and then sleep; it was the end of the day. Jumping out of the shower I dried off quickly before letting them in. Once they received their treats, they went off to find a spot to eat, before curling up for the night. Minutes later I climbed into bed, and within seconds I had found the peace I was looking for most of the day.

Something woke me. I looked at the time reflected on the ceiling. It was "two" in the morning. The room was quiet. The only sounds I heard were that of the puppies breathing. They were still in a deep sleep. Whatever woke me hadn't bothered them, it seemed. Confident in the fact that the dogs would be more alert to any danger than I could ever hope to be, I laid my head back down and quickly dozed back off.

There it was again. This time I sat straight up in bed.

It was a little after three. Something was here. Whatever it was, it was aware. I could feel it. I was unsettled by the fact that something aware was near me. Yet except for that sensation there was nothing, no one in the room. The dogs were still in a deep sleep. Only now they seemed to sense it too. They both seemed to be chasing the unseen presence, even as they slept. Soft barks and whimpers coming from them were signs of the pursuit taking place as they slept.

But why wasn't it waking them? Why couldn't I see or hear whoever it was? As I sat in my bed I could feel it starting again, the sensation of being enveloped. It was stronger this time. Whatever was happening was progressing more and more with each attempt. That cold realization came over me as I sat there. Whatever it was, it seemed to be encompassing me. I struggled in an attempt to free myself. I could still move, but the movement was wrong. It felt like I was being encased in a gel like solution. My arms and body felt the resistance.

There it is, I can feel it, the mind of whomever, whatever it was that was responsible for this. I could feel it, sensed it. What was it? What did it want with me?

My mind screamed out, asking what it wanted, then it was gone. I was sitting up in my bed, my heart pounding, my body covered in sweat as if I had just been in a battle. I realized at that point it was. I had been in a battle, but with what—over what? Slowly I regained control of myself, letting my eyes focus back on the room.

As my eyes adjusted, I could see the dogs. They were standing at the foot of the bed looking at me. It was only when I looked toward them that they actually stepped forward. They had kept their distance until that point. *Why?* Instead of being at the side of the bed, with their nose in my face, they had kept their distance.

Realizing sleep was impossible at this point I started to get out of bed. As I swung my feet down, the dogs came over to me, sniffing as if confirming it was indeed me. As I reached out to pet them, they pulled back hesitantly before coming forward. Sniffing me once again, before finally accepting it was me and not some stranger in the room. Now with my identity confirmed, they greeted me. They were upset, I could see that. They hung close to me as I got up, not wanting to be alone. Or was it, they didn't want me to be alone?

We walked into the kitchen. I was up earlier than normal, so the coffee hadn't turned on. Flipping it on, I sat and waited for it to brew. I took the time to let my mind recapture the dream before it could be forgotten. *Was it a dream, the dogs didn't seem to know who I was at first? What was happening?*

Once the coffee was ready, I walked onto the patio. It was Saturday, so the lack of sleep didn't concern me. Not that I could have gone back to sleep anyway. I sat in the dark as the pups ran out into the yard. To them, at least things had returned to normal. I sat sipping my coffee, trying to put the dream into some form I could understand. I had felt trapped as if I was being crowded in my own body. I didn't seem to have control over my movements, or at best, little control. Thoughts were racing around in my head, but nothing was making sense.

I finished my coffee and got up to get a refill. It was a weekend, and I needed to rest. Maybe I was just working too hard, and my brain was telling me to slow down, to take charge of my life once again. You know those subliminal messages they talk about in the books. Well this weekend would be full of nothing but relaxation. That decided, I refilled my coffee and returned to the patio.

I just needed to lie around, soak in the pool for a day or two, and be my old self again. I walked over to my floating recliner.

Might as well start relaxing now, I thought, as I put the recliner into the water. I slid into the seat.

The water felt warm. I let myself float out into the middle of the pool before I leaned back to relax in the seat.

Just what I need, I thought.

The Alien's Gift

I was just starting to feel relaxed when I felt it moving over me again. This time I was prepared. I was focused from the start. I wanted to know what was happening.

What was being done to me?

I could feel the sensation again, something enveloping my body. Reaching out with my mind, I tried to make contact. I could barely move. It felt like I was being incased in a gel solution. My movements seemed restricted by the substance.

There was a presence, someone or something. I knew it, I could feel it. But it wasn't communicating with me. I got the sense that it was totally indifferent to me. It wanted something, but communicating with me seemed to be beneath him. *Him, it was a "him,"* I knew that. I don't know how, but I knew it. I was making headway with or without "his" help. I felt like I was being pushed out of the way and flashing across a distance in the process.

I couldn't see a thing. I kept trying to open my eyes. It took a second before I realized they were. I was in the dark, not just dark—much more, this was black. I had expected darkness; after all, I was floating in my pool, and it was still the middle of the night. But this was black. I panicked. I had the feeling I had to get back to myself. That thought scared me more.

Why get back to myself? Why had I thought that?

I fought harder now. When I opened my eyes again I was floating in the pool. Nothing had changed...or had it? It took a second to realize my dogs were standing at the edge of the pool barking and growling.

What are they growling at? I wondered. What had them so upset?

As I slowly recovered my bearings, I started to realize it was me. My dogs were growling at me! I spoke to calm them; their barks turned to whimpers. Now they wanted me to come to them, to get out of the water.

Saying I was upset would be a mild way to put it. As I got out of the water, the dogs approached me cautiously, noses sniffing as if to confirm it was me. It took a moment to calm them down. Then I went in to get a fresh cup of coffee and sat on the couch. My hands were shaking as I sipped my coffee.

You have to get a hold of yourself, was all I kept thinking.

I didn't know what was happening, but now I knew, whatever it was, it was real. My dogs, the friends who know me better than anyone in this world, knew something had happened. I trusted their judgment more than my own, especially now.

Why didn't they seem to recognize me? Was it affecting them also? There was something happening to me. I had to find out what, but how?

I spent the rest of the morning trying to put my thoughts together. I needed to try and find a sequence of events, some order, some form of rationale to what was happening. How could I? I had no idea what was happening.

7

Putting things into order was impossible without knowing more. I had tried to communicate with him, and that didn't work. I did find out things though. I started to write down what I did know.

There was a "him." He didn't seem to care about communicating. No, it was even less. There was almost a disdainful feeling I received from him. He knew I was there, even that I was aware of him. He just had no desire to communicate whatsoever. He was also in control of whatever was happening. *Wait! Was he?* I did seem to be able to break the... What was it? Connection...I wasn't sure there was any, not really.

That was it. That was all I knew so far. I needed to know more. How come my dogs had reacted to me like they did? What was happening when I had the sensation of travelling? I needed some help. Who? Who could I trust to tell without them thinking I was totally if not unequivocally out of my mind?

It was "seven-thirty" Saturday morning. I knew who I could call for anything, Bill—Bill was more than a friend. It was something only Bill might understand. Bill had been my best friend for twenty of my thirty-five years of life. The bottom line was if Bill wouldn't help, there was no help. That was all I knew as I dialed the phone.

Three rings. *I'm going to be waking him up,* I thought. It was still early, but I couldn't wait I didn't know when whatever was happening would happen again. On the fourth ring he answered. I didn't even attempt any morning pleasantries.

"Bill, I need you to get over here as fast as you can." That was all I said; that was all I needed to say.

His response was immediate. "I'm already in the car."

By the time Bill arrived I had started a second pot of coffee. He didn't knock at the door, he just walked in. He knew by the sound of my voice that something was wrong—seriously wrong. When he walked into the kitchen and saw my face, it confirmed his instincts had been right. Bill didn't say a thing as he came in. He just grabbed a cup and poured himself some coffee. Bill sat there watching me patiently, waiting for me to tell him what was going on. I looked toward him, trying to figure out where to even start.

How was I going to tell my best friend I was going crazy and I was taking my dogs with me?

Then I felt it. It was happening again. Suddenly I was afraid for Bill.

What do I do? What if it gets him, too? Did I just bring my best friend into my hell?

I tried to scream out to him, to warn him. I wanted to tell him to get out of here, but I couldn't. It was happening too fast. It had already started.

The sensations were the same. I was starting to adjust to them now. I felt the sensation of being enveloped, then I was flashing across a distance. He was here again. This time I didn't attempt to communicate with him. Trying instead to sense more of his being. There was coldness, like nothing I had ever felt. Not a cold like weather, more like he had no heart, no soul, and no conscience. I recoiled from the feeling, and when I did, Bill was standing in front of me. I was still focusing back into the world when I heard Bill.

"What the hell just happened? What the hell just happened?" He kept saying it over and over.

Once I had my bearings, I started to talk. For the next thirty minutes, Bill sat and listened while I stumbled through what had taken place in my life over the last two days. I tried to tell him what I knew, attempting to distinguish it from the things I had sensed. Finally I finished by saying I really didn't know a damn thing. The only real things I could tell him were about what had happened with the dogs. I told him how I had tried to discover more about what was happening, and the short comings of that plan. I told him everything I could remember except what had just happened—I didn't tell him about the cold. Not yet! I didn't know how to put it into words. I didn't know how to even comprehend it myself, not yet.

I finished by saying I didn't blame him for thinking I was nuts and that I don't know how to make him believe this was real. Finally I was done, my energy level spent. I was totally exhausted, and at the same time I felt better. Finally, I had spoken it out loud. If Bill thought I was crazy, I was lost and I knew it.

Bill just sat there for several minutes. Then he lifted his coffee and took a drink. He drank as if he was taking a stiff shot of liquor. I was bracing myself as I waited. He set his cup down and looked at me. I realized then that I hadn't looked him in the face as I told my story. Maybe I was afraid of the look I might see in his eyes. Whatever the reason, this was the first time I had looked at him since he arrived. He was pale. All the blood looked as if it had drained from his body. I could see he was visibly shaken. When he finally started to talk, it was slow, deliberate, as if to make sure he made no mistakes in what he was going to tell me.

Bill smiled slightly I knew what he was trying to do. He wanted to lighten the moment, to make bad news better.

Then he started to speak. "You know, if you had just told me that story when I walked in here, I would have called for the wagon before you got to the pool part." He followed it by saying, "You've never been the most stable friend I've had. But what the hell, I was never known for having had good taste in friends."

It was working. I was feeling better. His banter was lightening the moment for me. It gave me the lift I need, if only for a moment. I knew he had more to say and, knowing Bill, it wasn't going to be as good. He was taking too much time, preparing me for something. It was his way—it was our way.

"If you had told me when I got here that is …"

This was it. He was going to say something, and I braced for it. Then he told me what he'd seen during my most recent event. He stuck on one thing.

"The eyes," he kept saying.

"The eyes, they weren't yours, they weren't even human…COLD!"

I almost passed out when he said the word. Cold; he had said it with a passion. I knew then that he would understand what I had yet to say. I could tell him that which I thought was unexplainable. He was the only person I knew now that could or would understand.

I told him what I had felt as I reached out to feel what…whoever it was. About the cold sensation I felt from who or whatever it was, the utter lack of concern for any living thing I felt from it. I looked at Bill as I spoke, already knowing that he understood.

Bill got up and walked to the coffee pot. Turning to me, he asked, "Another cup of coffee?"

I had worked the better part of two pots already, so I declined. He poured two cups anyway. Then, walking over to the bar, he took a bottle of whiskey and poured stiff shots into both.

"Too bad," he said as he walked back to the table.

He set the cup down in front of me. For the next thirty minutes we sipped coffee and just looked at each other.

From time to time Bill would look over and comment, "Son of a bitch," then go quiet again. We just sat.

Chapter 2

More than an hour had passed. We had both had another cup of special coffee before starting to speak in earnest. We had decided I wasn't crazy, at least no crazier then I had been before any of this had happened. Now we had to work on a plan. There was only one problem; neither of us had any idea what the hell was going on. So far our plan consisted of, one, we can't call the police, two, we can't call the police, and "C," we won't call the police. From that point we were at a loss. So far the special coffee hadn't helped at all.

We were just starting to discuss how we can't call the police for the fourth time when it happened again. Just like the other times I could feel it when it started to envelope me. This time I noticed it seemed to form around me almost like an energy field. The sensation of flashing across an expanse was next. I passed "him." Nothing was new. It was just like the other times.

"Passed him…we were transferring," I suddenly realized.

I didn't attempt to contact him as we passed this time. Maybe it was the alcohol calming me, but I ignored him. Then I felt the gel sensation again. I tried to move.

I don't know if I was beginning to adjust or if it was the alcohol in my system, maybe a combination of both. But I was able to move, slowly, but I could move. Having some success with that, next I tried to focus my eyes. I could see light this time. But the lights and colors were wrong. Strange, I had seen lighting like this before; I just couldn't remember where. Then I noticed something in front of me. It looked metallic. I was attempting to reach out and touch it. But before I could reach it, I felt myself being pulled from the capsule. I was flashing across the expanse again. An instant later I saw Bill standing in front of me.

He had seen the cold again. I could tell by the look in his eyes. His expression started to change as he realized he was looking at his friend once again. As soon as Bill realized it was me he started to ramble.

"I'm going next time. You stay here with that cold son of a… "

He stopped himself in mid sentence, " Are you alright?"

I smiled slightly, "I think I'm getting used to this."

It was a lie, but I didn't want to add to his concern.

"Maybe you," he informed me.

We started to exchange information. Both of us wanted to go over what we had experienced while the details were still fresh in our minds. I told him about the metallic surface, or at least it had looked metallic. I hadn't been able to confirm that. I was pulled back just as I reached out to touch it. I realized as I said the words, *I was pulled back,* even though I hadn't freaked or fought this time. The connection must have broken for some other reason.

"He isn't able to maintain it yet," I said.

"What?" Bill asked.

"The connection. He isn't able to maintain it yet."

I went on to explain how I just came back. I hadn't fought this time, hadn't panicked, nothing. We had time to figure this out. But the big question was how much time?

Bill told me about the eyes in my absence. COLD was a word he used again and again, but in between Bill kept saying he seemed to be trying to adjust his sight. "Your eyes don't seem to work properly when he's here."

That's when I remembered the colors. They weren't right while I was there either. I told Bill about it, and we started to discuss what it might be. We were just guessing anything we could think of when Bill mentioned infra-red light. That's when it clicked. Now I knew where I had seen that light. I had to be sure. I ran over to the computer, turned it on, and pulled up objects in space. First I looked at the pictures taken in normal light, then I looked at their infra-red counterpart. That was it. I knew I had seen that light before.

"He's used to infra-red, Bill. That's why he had trouble with my eyes. They see in visible light and he wasn't used to it." He seemed no more familiar with our light than I was with his. We went on for over an hour. We were slowly making headway. We knew it, and it felt good.

We had exhausted everything we knew when Bill looked at me. "What are we going to do?" he asked. "We don't know what he wants, how this works, and most important, how to stop him."

The only thing we knew was we had to stop him. If he was a friendly kind of guy he would have just said, "Hey, don't mind if I use your eyes here for awhile, do you?" No! There was more to it. We just didn't know what it was. It was the not knowing that scared me. Bill shared my fear.

What could we do? How could we fight him? Could we fight him? Then I realized, Bill was the one who was here with him when I was…wherever I was. Suddenly I was concerned for Bill's welfare. Did I screw up bringing him here? Now I wanted him to get away from here, far away. Away from whatever might take place when Iceman was here.

"Maybe I needed to work this out on my own." I started to say, "Possibly call in the police or something like that to help me."

Bill knew what I was trying to do. He wasn't buying it, he was staying. I tried to explain that Iceman seems to be getting stronger with each attempt.

"What if he gains control of more than my eyes?" I asked, reminding him that I had been able to move my arms the last time. I could see the thoughts going through his mind as I was speaking. He didn't look convinced. His next statement proved my suspicions.

"Then I guess I'm going to have to kick your ass while you're gone… sorry." Bill said with a smile.

He said it simply, with a matter of fact attitude. There was no more said about Bill leaving. That was a closed subject, and we both knew it. It was almost noon, and I was starving. I hadn't eaten breakfast. Come to think of it, I hadn't eaten in a couple of days. Bill offered to go get something.

I said, "I can go I'm not crippled…not yet!"

The last words trailing by a second came softly from my lips. Bill didn't think it would be a good idea, reminding me that Darth Vader might not go over so big at the Mc food place. I let him go.

With food in my stomach again, we went back to the task at hand. We were trying to figure out a strategy, something—anything. Then the subject of the eyes came up again. They seemed to be a weakness, at least for now. How could we exploit that? Use it to our advantage? We had decided the only thing we could do at this point was to try and maintain a state of disorientation for our visitor. The one advantage I had was I could tell when it was about to happen. We had estimated there was about a five second window from the time I felt it starting until I was no longer in control. We needed to take advantage of that window. Bill went out to the boat and removed the portable spot light I used for night fishing.

"One million candle watts," he said as he set it down on the table. "That should screw up his night vision."

It was a good start, but we needed more if we hoped to keep him disorientated. We had to keep shifting his environment. Darkness was next; how could we exploit that, and would it work? Bill suggested putting a bag over my head. That led to several minutes of light hearted humor, with me being the target of several off-color comments from Bill.

The break was welcome, but we soon got back to the business at hand. The bag wasn't going to work, I knew that. I could use my hands now, which meant the Iceman probably could, too. We had decided early in the conversation to call him Iceman. We also decided when I felt him coming I should move into the closet. If he saw in infrared that would effectively blind him…maybe.

During my rummaging I had found a black light in the attic. I showed it to Bill, asking, "How about this?" Who knew? We were in over our heads. Neither of us could argue that point. Neither of us were scientists. We were just two guys. I should amend that, just two guys in big trouble.

"Go for it" was all Bill had to say about the black light, "What could it hurt?"

You, I thought, but I didn't say it out loud.

Bill already knew that was a possibility. That was a road we had already crossed. I wasn't going back there. Now we had a different problem to deal with. It was happening again; he was coming. I could feel it as the first stage started. I warned Bill, but the closet was too far away. All I could do was stay in the chair this time. I watched as Bill armed himself with the spot light.

"Good luck" was the last thing I heard from Bill, then I was off.

Going across what to where, I had no idea. I just knew that I was going. I had started to answer Bill, to wish him good luck, too. Deciding not too at the last second, Iceman might know what I'm thinking, and I didn't want to let him know about Bill. Instead I just focused on the sensation of being drawn someplace. Could I learn more?

Once again I felt the sensation of gel closing in around me. I opened my eyes. It seemed to be some sort of metallic structure for sure. Something was wrong, though. The exterior walls didn't look solid. They looked as if they were shimmering, fluctuating. Reaching out slowly, I attempted to touch the side. The wall looked like it was only inches away, but it would seem my mind had still not completely adjusted to this new vision. It was farther away than I thought, much further. As I reached out, my arm kept going.

One foot, two feet, than finally I touched it. When my hand came into contact with the shimmering surface, it rippled like water. No! Not water, more like a pool of mercury. Then as my fingers made contact with the wall, it seemed to solidify. The rippling ceasing abruptly, the surface went rigid. It was solid to the touch. I pulled my hand back instinctively, for fear my fingers would get caught in the material as it solidified.

My fingers! I thought. *These aren't my fingers.*

That's when I looked at my hand. No, this wasn't my hand; it was his hand. It had three fingers to prove it. I started to study it, hoping to learn all I could. As I looked, I wondered if I could even call them fingers. They were long and thin. He had nails that looked like daggers, long and sharp. *How about an opposable digit*? I wondered. Yes! He must be intelligent.

What a breakthrough! That was genius, I thought. *Iceman is moving you across God knows where, not to mention you don't know how. Just know you figured out he's intelligent. Get back to it, stupid. You don't have all day.* At least I hoped not.

His skin looked metallic; it was quite similar to the capsule. I had decided this was some form of capsule as I scanned the surface. *What else? What am I missing*? I wondered.

Then, I was moving again, going back. I felt strong emotions from him as we passed. I could feel anger mixed with confusion and frustration, total frustration. I was just starting to wonder why when my eyes opened. I was looking into the sun.

"Turn that damn thing off," I shouted. Bill hit the switch.

I needed something to drink. What I wanted was a good shot of whiskey, but knew I had to maintain a clear head so I opted for a cup of coffee instead. Bill and I just sat at the table for a few minutes.

Finally Bill broke the silence. "Okay, you want to go first?"

It was a conversation I knew we had to have, but my mind was still trying to assemble the details. Bill could see I needed more time. So we sat in silence for a few more minutes. I was still trying to collect my thoughts.

"Well, I'm not crippled, so I guess you didn't kick my ass." It was a way of asking Bill to start. I still needed more time to collect myself.

Realizing that, Bill started. "First I can tell you the light works. Iceman didn't like that at all. I don't think he like the television either."

I looked over at the television; it had been on all morning. I hadn't even thought about it. To me it was a background sound. When Bill mentioned the television I let my ears tune into the volume. It wasn't loud at all, but then I realized it was silent in the capsule. I don't mean quiet; there was total silence.

I don't think I ever heard silence like that, I thought, still listening as Bill continued his recounting of what took place. From what Bill said, it seemed Iceman could move my body now. But he still seemed to be a bit clumsy and disoriented. Bill was describing how I—Iceman attempted to cover his—my eyes. The sound, it seemed, was too much for him and, for several seconds, he kept trying to cover my ears. Bill seemed to think Iceman was so disoriented he wasn't able to figure out how to block the incoming sound.

Another weapon, I thought. I continued listening.

Bill went through everything fast. He barely even stopped to take a breath. He told me that Iceman had tried to make a sound, possibly even trying to talk, but he didn't seem to know how to operate my vocal cords. Bill thought the sound was just primordial because of the stress and discomfort he seemed to be having adjusting to my human senses.

I interrupted him rather abruptly.

"Aggression." The words just came out. "Was he aggressive?"

It was a question. Bill's safety had been a serious concern to me from the start. We had decided to leave the dogs outside. We couldn't be sure how they would react when Iceman was here in my place. That meant Bill was alone with him, which made me uncomfortable.

Bill answer was almost too casual, "He spent too much time trying to cover up eyes and ears to know I was even here." That said, he let the conversation drop.

Now it was my turn. I tried to organize my thoughts. I wanted to relay them just as they had transpired. "Oh! By the way, I had wanted to wish you luck, too." I had to tell him; I took a second to explain why I hadn't.

That said, I began to tell Bill what I had learned about the capsule. I told him everything I had seen and felt during my time there. The more I spoke, the more memories came back. There are always things we see, but don't realize until we stop and look back. If we just concentrate, we remember so much more. Believe me, I was concentrating.

The interior of the capsule seemed to be approximately ten feet tall and around five feet across. I believed it was almost egg shaped. The quiet; I hadn't noticed it when I was there. I only realized it when Bill mentioned the television. I told Bill about the silence. He kept nodding as he listened. It was all making sense to him. It explained some of the reactions he saw. We both knew we had another weapon. We would use sound or noise in our defense. I continued with my observations. I told Bill about all the little details I could remember, the fingers, the nails. The metallic skin, oh, we weren't dealing with someone from Kansas.

I was telling him how I had tried to make sure I used every minute effectively. Then I began to wonder. I hadn't asked before, mainly because it seemed to me that I had known. Now I wondered if my perspective could be just as distorted as Iceman's had been.

I asked, "How long was I gone?" Bill's answer surprised me.

"Only about thirty seconds."

I was stunned. "Thirty seconds! It felt like minutes; several minutes." The answer reassured me in a way. *Not that long, which meant he hadn't gotten very good control...yet, we have some time.*

I repeated my thought to Bill, adding we were gaining on him. Bill agreed.

Gaining, I thought, but we weren't winning. We needed help. Bill was the one who came to that realization first. For one thing, someone had to be with me at all times. Someone awake! With each attempt the Iceman made, he seemed to get stronger, gaining more control. We both knew that at some point I may have to be restrained. Bill was going to need help controlling me...well, Iceman. But, who? Who could we even tell a story like this to, never mind getting them to believe us? Who could we ask to walk into a... situation? I didn't even know what to call it. Not only could we not explain it, we had no way of guaranteeing their safety if they helped.

Bill broke the tension with his qualification list.

"Okay, first they have to be insane. Second, they have to be dumb enough to help two idiots like us. Three ...you know this should be pretty easy; we don't have normal friends."

Bill had been my first choice. He was the only one I had thought of in my state of near panic. Now we had taken the offensive and felt more in control, okay, control is a bad choice of words.

Then we had a name. Almost as one, we both said, "Stan." That confirmed our choice.

Bill commented, "Well, I guess we both confirmed that Stan is crazy."

We would need at least one more person. That choice had been made when we picked Stan. If Stan helped, Steven would be here with him. They were brothers and inseparable. You don't get one brother without the other. Bill and I both knew that. Now all we needed to do was get them to help. Bill got on the phone. An hour later the four of us were sitting at my kitchen table.

"Who tells this one?" Bill asked.

I took a deep breath. The story was crazy. Telling it was uncomfortable. It was mine, so I had to tell it. I started, hoping the brothers wouldn't think we were jerking their chain. That was a major concern shared by Bill and myself. That fear was soon put to rest. As I spoke, the intensity of the situation must have come through in my voice. I watched Stan and Steven as I told them what had been happening. At first they had been leaning back in the chair as if being told a tall yarn. Then, realizing I was being serious, they leaned forward, arms on the table, their eyes focusing in on my face. Now they were listening intently to every word I said. They would look to Bill from time to time, his expression only confirming my every word.

When I finished, there was no laughing, no "give me a break." This was real, and they knew it.

Stan looked at Steve, before turning back to me. "What do we do?"

They were in. That was the first time I noticed the tension in Bill's face. I noticed it only because it dissolved as Stan spoke those words. My relief was so great his words brought me close to tears.

Steve's broke the tension. "Let's kick some ass." His words inspired a new sense of hope.

I laughed as I remembered Bill's comments from earlier about kicking some ass.

"Careful, we're talking about my ass here," I reminded them.

With that comment the last vestige of tension seemed to fade. Win or lose, Iceman had a fight. We had a team. Over the next hour Steven and Stan were brought up to speed. We told them all we had discovered, all we thought, and all we knew but had no idea what it meant. Everything was all there, on the table for discussion or debate.

Stan and Steven were big boys. When I say that, I don't mean grown up kind of big boy I mean *big* boys. To look at them one would think they were just brawny bulls. In reality they were nothing like that. Stan was an accountant, and Steven a computer programmer, both technical guys. Being big was just a bonus, and a bonus we might need. Stan started, grabbing a pad and pen, wanting to make out a list.

They were both asking questions. Bill and I took turns answering what we knew as Stan made notes. They would go back over something from time to time to cross check some things we said, for accuracy.

Bill looked at me, smiling. "Now why hadn't we thought of this?"

The same thought had run through my mind, too. But I didn't want to tease them. They were taking it serious, real serious.

We were going over the sight thing again. I was saying that it seemed like I was seeing in infra-red. Steven jumped on that. He ran to get his laptop out of the car. Once back, he started pulling up pictures of everything he could find in infra-red. He wanted me to study them. He wanted me to become more familiar with that view so I could judge what I saw clearer. Maybe it would help me understand more of what I was seeing. We were coming together as a team. Iceman was in for a battle, we knew that. He would, too, next time I passed him.

The brothers didn't have to wait long before meeting him. I could feel Iceman coming. I made the announcement. "Okay! Guys, he's coming."

They jumped into gear immediately. I saw Bill move toward the television. Steven had grabbed the light, then I was gone.

I passed him on the way. *Always do,* I thought as we passed. I caught his attention this time. Why? Could he tell I wasn't as nervous as I had been? Did I make him stop and wonder just a bit? I didn't know the answer, but it was almost like he turned and looked back as he passed me. The moment was only fleeting before I found myself in the capsule again.

It wasn't going to be a casual visit for me this time. I had answers to find while I was here. Not knowing how long I would be here, I went right to work. First, I would have to confirm it was a capsule, if I could. I was pretty sure about that, but where was it? Was it in a lab, on a spaceship of some sort? I didn't know. How could I find out? I moved toward the outer wall.

Moving in the gel was getting easier each time. I seemed to be developing a technique for it. I got close to the surface, careful to not come into contact with it. I didn't want it to solidify. I wasn't sure if I would be able to see through it or not. I didn't want to make it worse if it solidified. The metallic surface seemed to undulate in front of me just as it had the last time. It was beautiful, almost mesmerizing. The rhythm was hypnotic, I snapped myself out of it. I had things to learn.

I focused my newly trained vision, trying to make out anything that might be outside this cocoon I was in. Infra-red practice or not, it was no use. I could make out blurs, nothing more. I wasn't able to see clearly enough to identify anything. I touched the surface, thinking maybe if I solidified it that would help. The outer wall went solid and opaque at the same time.

That didn't work, I thought.

I turned my attention to my host instead. I knew about his hands; how about the rest of him? Iceman was a bi-ped. He had two legs, what about... Reaching behind me, I looked for a tail—no tail. For some reason I was relieved.

In the process of reaching around, I had caused my body to start rotating inside the capsule. At the same time the walls were starting to undulate again. As I continued to turn, something was coming into view. I moved to the wall on the other side of the capsule, hoping to get a better look. I was careful not to come into contact with it again. There was something out there, something big, really big, but that was all I could say about it. I wasn't able to see anything clearly, so I turned my attention back to my host.

I used my...its hands and reached for the face. *This was not a pretty man,* I remember thinking as I touched the face. His face was elongated, the nostrils only slight slits, but that meant he probably had to breathe. The mouth was elongated like that of a hound and had an impressive set of teeth. *Ugly,* I thought. *This boy could date a shark.*

Before I could learn anymore I was on my way home again. I don't seem to get a warning when I make the return trip; it just happens. One second I'm there, the next I'm flashing through a portal of some sort. I let my thoughts reach out to him as we passed.

We're going to get you.

I felt his mind again, clearer this time. The cold non-caring consciousness was still there, but something else. He showed surprise. We had gotten his attention.

I got back to find the brothers holding me down in the chair. They had my arms pinned at my sides. The television was loud, but there was something more, the sound was disturbing. Suddenly I knew why. The radio, Bill had turned the television up and had also turned on the radio, loud. The sound was disturbing to me. It had to have been insane for our visitor. Stan and Steven had assisted by not letting him cover my ears. They wanted to be sure the Iceman appreciated the full effect of the sounds played in his honor. I looked up and smiled at Stan, knowing what they had done to Iceman was a pleasant scene that played in my head.

One I would enjoy more once I was free, I looked at Stan. "Mind letting me go."

Stan knew it was me as soon as I spoke. Iceman hadn't been able to talk, at least not yet. I had wanted to tell them about what I learned. But now I had to know what happened in my absence. Stan and Steven just smiled when I asked.

It was Bill who spoke up first. "Well, I can tell you one thing. You sure don't seem to have an ear for music."

Steven chimed in next. "I can't say you sing very well either."

Stan had already sat down. He was jotting down notes of what had transpired during the visit, looked up and said, "You can't call that singing. It sounded more like moaning to me."

I turned to Stan, pretending to be insulted by his words. "That is my singing."

Joke time over, we got down to business. Stan had already been writing away, making notes of everything they had observed. He was asking questions of Steven and Bill a mile a minute. It seemed that when Iceman is in my body, he gets to suffer all the human discomforts that may come with it. That was a major problem for him. Unfortunately it might be for me also. Not being used to something was one thing; what they exposed Iceman to was another. I still remember the din when I arrived, television blaring, along with the sounds of the radio. It was enough to drive me insane.

I was about to learn it hadn't been over for Iceman, not yet. Once Bill made those minor adjustments to the audio equipment, he went on to initiate the light show. I couldn't help but smile. Now I know why he was surprised. Shocked was probably a more accurate way of putting it. That, along with the brothers holding my arms down, Iceman got to fully appreciate the welcome they had arranged for him.

They finished telling me everything that had taken place. Stan had taken down all his notes. Making sure he had recorded every detail. Now it was my turn. I started telling them about examination of the capsule. Steven was especially interested in the fact the walls went rigid, then after a time seemed to gyrate again. Then I told them what I had learned about Iceman himself. When I got to the part about his face, everyone's mood got somber.

Bill spoke first, "Hate to say this, especially since it's your body and all, but I'm sure glad he didn't come in person."

I finished by telling them about passing him on the way back. I told them about the sensation of surprise I had received from him when we touched minds. I remembered back to when I first encountered him, he didn't seem to give a damn about me at all. All that seemed to change now.

Now I could tell them something different. I wasn't sure if it was good or bad. But it was accurate.

"He's aware of us now."

Chapter 3

Those words said, we all knew the stakes had changed. Steven was on his computer. Something about the way the walls were acting was intriguing him, sparking some memory. He was determined to identify it. Then, just as he started looking, the screen went blank.

"Fine time for my computer to crash," Steven was just starting to say.

When the screen lit back up and in large letters appeared the words.

"I CAN HELP."

"What the hell," Steve commented as he re-booted his laptop.

We were going over the different things that took place while we waited for his computer to boot up again. As soon as his computer booted up again, he started back to what he had been reading. Before he could do that the screen went blank again.

Again the words came up on the screen in big letters, "I CAN HELP."

"God damn hackers, now is not the time to play." Steven's reaction was a mixture of both anger and frustration. His fingers were typing in the words as fast as they came out of his mouth. He went to clear his screen and go back to his research when again it went blank.

Again in large letters across the screen came the words "**I CAN HELP**" in bold print to emphasis it. Then the word "**PLEASE**" appeared. Maybe it was an attempt to appease Steven. We didn't know, but it did cause us to pause. We looked at each other, wondering what was going on. Was this some punk who just picked one hell of a time to play? Was it my friend out there in space someplace trying to block our attempt to ruin his plans?

Plans, I thought. *What the hell were his plans?*

Steven sat back in his chair running his fingers through his hair. He looked at each of us in turn he till finally stopped at me.

"Well! This is your party."

It was my call. Steven made that clear. There was only one answer. "We need information." Then, putting my hand on his wrist, I added, "Don't let him get the best of you."

With a grin Steven turned to his laptop. "Let's play," he said as his fingers went to the keys. "Who is this?"

A second later the words came up on the screen, "Someone who can help."

Steven sat back and stretched his arms out. He had the look of a man preparing for a battle royale. I found myself grinning. I almost said "go get him, Steven," but I held it back. I knew that this part of the game was Steven's forte, and I didn't want to make light of it. Besides I didn't have a chance to, everyone was already telling him to type something.

"Ask him…?"

"Who are you really?"

"What do you want?"

Finally having enough of us, Steven said, "Gentlemen, do you mind?" That was all it took.

We all shut up and let him work.

"What do you want to help me with? Why do you think I need help?" Steven fired off the questions fast. We waited for the response. Once again Steven had to remind us that he was doing fine without our help. Not because we had started to talk again. This time it was because we had all been watching to close. We had all leaned forward till all Steven could see was the back of three heads. This time it was funny.

Steven said, "Either sit down or go to your rooms."

We sat down. As we did, the answer flashed on the screen.

"You need help because one of you is Under Attack."

The fun was over with that last remark. We sat silently now, barely breathing. I felt a chill run through my body as I read the words again. "Under Attack!" Those words made it all real once more. We had gotten so carried away with learning what we could, I had forgotten how real this was. I hadn't thought about being "Under Attack." My eyes went back to the screen.

Steven had just asked several questions in rapid succession.

"How do you know that?"

"Who are you?"

"How do we know we can trust you?" He was firing off questions fast, and I for one was focused on the screen, waiting for answers.

"I know that because Gera is one of ours."

I froze in my chair. *Now more of them know where I am,* was all I could think.

Then the second answer flashed on the screen "I am what you would call on your world the local authority."

The cops, I thought, *finally the cops.*

But he had typed "your world," reminding us once again that what had been going on wasn't something your neighborhood magician could do. Reading his words now was making that clear. That reality was scaring the crap out of me—us. I could see it on everyone's face. We turned back to the screen again. If this was a hacker, he had us all, hook, line, and sinker. The words coming up now answered the third and probably the most important question Steven had asked.

"As to how do you know you can trust me, that, only you can decide."

"No! Shit, that's an answer out of a movie, man."

I wasn't sure, but I thought Bill said that. He was right.

Bill was almost beside himself. I felt his frustration as he said, "We're almost there, and he throws philosophy at us."

Steven went back to the keys. "Why are you just contacting us now?"

A moment later the screen came up "We had to learn your language. Until you surprised Gera, we didn't have a location on him or even know about you."

Steven typed in fast, "Where can we reach you?"

"Here, I am called Ari" was his response.

With that answer, Steven shut the computer off.

Stan was the first to speak. "What the hell did you do that for, Steven?"

"They might be zeroing in on us," Steven explained. "Hell, they found this Gera from just a thought. Maybe they could us. I just figured we better decide now if we trust this guy. If not, we need to get the hell out of here now!"

"He's right," I said.

Steven said, "Well, time's up, Do we or not?"

We really didn't have much of a choice, and it didn't take long to realize that. This was our only hope of getting to the bottom of things. The decision was made.

Steven turned the computer back on, then simply typed in the word "Hello."

"Good, you have decided" came up on the screen.

Steven's fingers flashed over the keys. "Not so fast, we have questions, lots of questions."

"I was sure you would" flashed on the screen.

"You said authority. Are you the police?"

"We don't have police as you know them. In your language I would have to say I'm closer to a doctor."

We were all just a little more confused as we read the words on the screen.

Finally I said tell him "Gera doesn't need a doctor. He needs a jail cell. He seems to be devoid of any feelings and has absolutely no concern for life." Steven relayed my message.

The screen came back to life. "That is why he needs a Doctor."

Once again his words stopped me.

Our questions continued for the next thirty minutes. We found out that the pod Gera was in wasn't a prison pod of some kind. Not a cell that had been cast out into space for eternity. It was a medical pod. The gel, was some sort of a DNA fix it kit. Ari had said something was wrong with his mental makeup. *I guess that's one way to put it*, I thought. This Gera, as he called him, still seemed like a psycho to me. Ari told us the pod was a cocoon that the subject is suspended in. It's then put in a non gravity environment for three thousand of our years. During that time the body is repaired.

In Gera case, he had been encapsulated approximately five hundred years ago. His capsule, like all the others, was placed in an orbit around one of their moons. An attendant checked on them periodically. During one of the visits it was discovered that Gera's pod was gone.

Ari said, "We believe a small satellite, probably sent out into space from a young explorer planet like yours had passed through their system. It's assumed it came into contact with Gera's pod and set it adrift into the universe."

His capsule had been lost without a trace. The first break was when we surprised Gera. We had caused him to drop his mental shield. Then they found him and were able to lock in on his mind. Gera, still ill, has not tried to be rescued. He was trying to escape. He went on to explain they had to retrieve him, and that without help I would probably become the occupant of the pod.

How it got to where he was able to transfer with me was even more disturbing. The capsule drifted into our solar system and was being pulled toward the planet Jupiter. The magnetic forces from the planet were breaking down the capsule's force field and, along with that, its structural integrity. This was why Gera's mind was now able to reach outside the pod.

As for the mind swapping thing Gera was doing, Ari explained that. I'll try, although I do have to admit I'm still a little lost on this part. Ari says that our essence, the mind as we call it, is independent of the physical body. The mind is energy. What Gera was doing was swapping our energy field or mind, if you will. However, the mind looks over and is attached to the body on a level I was still trying to understand. Somehow, even though the mind seems to be independent, it isn't. Not really.

Here is where it gets real confusing. According to Ari, the mind spreads itself throughout the body, watching over every cell not just the brain. Gera isn't able to do a complete swap because of the gel he is suspended in. It's inhibiting him from being able to pull his mind energy completely free from the body. That's what keeps pulling him back to the capsule. That along with the resistance my energy force puts up, as it fights to return to its own natural source.

I have to admit I was somewhat pleased to hear I was part of the defensive force. It made me feel a little less helpless. That feeling was short lived. Ari went on to explain that as the pod's field weakens, this will change. Gera will be able to extract his entire mind, and the swap will be total and complete. I would not be able to fight in on mind power alone. It seems our minds are a little on the weak side against theirs. It was at that point I dropped out of the conversation. I was on my way to visit the capsule again. I passed good old Gera at the half way point, then I was up to my—correction, his neck in gel again.

Once more I found myself inside the pod, only this time there was no war to fight, no information to gather. I did have Jupiter out there…someplace. I wondered if I could see it yet. I worked my way to the side of the capsule. The rippling effect was a little unnerving this time. I let the thought go, focusing instead on the shadows. Was Jupiter out there? But as hard as I looked, there was nothing there—nothing to be seen. Was Ari making the whole thing up?

Then I remembered the shadows were on the other side. I slowly worked my way around through the gel. There it was, Jupiter. I could see Jupiter there right in front of me. No, I didn't see a big beautiful planet in space. That would have made this whole trip worth something. All I could see was a blotch, a dark blur on the wall, not enough to hold my attention long.

How long will I be here this time? I wondered, especially now. Jupiter was just a blur, and there was nothing else to do now that my spying days were over. *Spy*, I could still spy. Ari had said part of Gera's mind was still here, I turned my thoughts inward.

Could I find Gera?

I wasn't much of a guru or yoga expert but it was worth a shot. It wasn't as hard as I thought it would be. Actually it was way too easy.

Guess we aren't as weak as they thought.

The Alien's Gift

Gera was easy to find, but not something you should look for. The sensations from his essence were chilling. This was a mind like I had never imagined. His intelligence was beyond belief, but with no moral structure. He seemed completely void of any basis for right or wrong. Something had gone seriously wrong with him. I pulled back immediately and forced myself home with all the will I could muster. The contact with Gera must have strengthened my resolve because as I passed him, the sensation I got from him was pure amazement. I had ripped him free just as he had me all these times. When I got back, Bill was standing in front of me.

Bill, you've been here from the start, I thought.

"Are you alright?" He sounded quite concerned.

"What's wrong?" I said, thinking, *what's wrong? What a dumb question to ask these days.*

Bill said, "When Gera left he let out a yelp like he had been hurt."

Hurt, I was smiling now as I explained to them all what had taken place on my last visit to Jupiter. I use the term trip. It sounds better saying it that way, rather than abduction or anything else one might call it. I found it hard to explain the sensations concerning Gera. I had touched his mind. I wasn't sure I even wanted to tell them. I wasn't sure if my contact with his essence might have damaged my own. So I changed the subject and asked what had happened, instead.

Steven said, "Ari cut the communication just as you were drawn away." He was sure it was, so that Gera didn't find out he had been found. Steven had just managed to turn the power off to his computer before they had grabbed hold of my body. I—Gera—had tried to get up this time. He was much more in control of my body this time. The television, though still on, was muted, and the radio was off. Bill didn't even have time to grab the light before he arrived.

There was more to it than that though. They weren't saying but I could see it in all of them. Something more had transpired during my absence. I waited not sure I wanted to even know.

Stan said it first, "Freaky cold bastard, that's what he is."

It just came out of him as he sat with his head down. Bill and Steven nodded in agreement. He was getting stronger; more of him was coming through. We all knew it. We were running out of time—I was running out of time.

We sat at the table for the next few minutes, each trying to explain the unexplainable to the other. Finally we gave up and decided to get something to eat instead. It was almost eight. Where did the time go? Bill ordered pizzas. Soon after, we were all sitting around the table eating. There wasn't much in the way of conversation. No one even looked up as we ate. We were using the time to gather our thoughts, put things into some semblance of order. Each of us wondered what the next move was going to be. Ari was the only one who had an answer to that.

We had finished eating. Steven was about to turn his laptop back on when I stopped him. We weren't ready yet. The tension level for the last several hours was beyond anything any of us could imagine. I suggested we take some time to relax first.

"Hell, I haven't had any company in forever. None of you ingrates ever come over." I had set the tone. At least, broke the ice.

We were going to be just guys for at least a little while before we challenged the universe. I went to the pantry and pulled out a package of cigars. Beside it was a pack of cigarettes left over from my smoking days. I grabbed them both, then headed out to the patio. I passed out cigars and opened the cigarettes.

Bill was watching me like a mother hen. "You quit smoking last year."

"Yeah, I did, for my health I think it was. Well, if Gera gets this body he'll have to deal with a new problem." I lit up.

For the next hour things were normal. I started to tease Bill, with Stan and Steven jumping right in. Within five minutes the sides changed, then it was Stan being assaulted. Steven got his turn next before they finally ended it with me. During that time the dogs came over looking for some attention. They hadn't received much during this entire event. I was more than happy to play. I hadn't enjoyed myself that much in years.

Friends are rare and more valuable than diamonds. That was a thought I would have to keep near.

Chapter 4

We had our moment. Now it was time to contact Ari. We didn't know what we were about to be getting into and wondered if we'd all be able to ever sit on the patio together again. That said it was time to find out. Steven looked at me, waiting for the signal. I nodded, and with that he hit the power key on his computer.

The screen powered on. Steven looked tense for a moment, then he straightened his shoulders, and typed "Hello."

Nothing happened for a second. The screen was blank. Then Ari was there. We started to go over what was needed and why. Steven asked the questions, Ari patiently answering each question in turn. I still didn't understand why they didn't just come and get Gera. They must be fairly close. After all, Ari had said he was only adrift for five hundred years. Steven thought it was a good question.

He asked Ari, "Where is your planet? You said Gera was only adrift for five hundred years. There are no planets that close to earth."

These were the questions that scared us. The answers had to make sense if we were going to be part of this. Ari explained that his planet was closer to the other side of the galaxy than ours. Gera got here moving through slip streams and worm holes.

Lucky me, he hit all the right buttons, I thought.

"How are we going to resolve this if Ari's people can't get here in time?" Bill asked.

29

"Ask him how long does the pod have before it collapses?" That came from Stan. I had thought of it, but didn't want to ask.

Ari's answer sent a chill through my spine. "Gera has to be rescued. The pod will only last another month."

"Oh, good, I thought this was going to be hard," Bill said sarcastically.

The rest of us agreed. Except for Ari; he was serious. We listened as he explained his plan. It wasn't going to be as hard as Bill had thought. Okay, now I'm being sarcastic.

First, we were going to build a machine that none of us knew how to build. Then, Ari would have to come here. That was going to involve another exchange. The last comment made me nervous. It gets better.

After that exchange there would have to be another one…this time with an astronaut. Oh, not just any astronaut, but one who would be on the next shuttle launch. Then, and this is where it gets really good, the shuttle would be altered so that it can make the flight to Jupiter. All they had to do was pick up the pod, put it in the payload bay, and come back to earth. During that time Ari and Gera would be returned to their own planet.

I looked at Bill. "And you were worried."

It was almost ten when I suggested we contact Ari again in the morning. My head was spinning and we had a lot to absorb. We all agreed, and Steven shut down communications for the night.

Watching Steven flip the switch, I thought, *I wish I could just turn off old Gera with a switch.*

I looked at the guys. "The only suggestion I have now is a drink."

I was already walking to the bar. I poured myself a drink and moved out of the way. With my drink in hand, I walked out to the patio. There I would have my second cigarette of the year.

I sat on the patio in the dark, petting the dogs and sipping my drink. Nobody had come out. I was sure each was dealing with what we had just heard and going over it in his own way. Almost twenty minutes had passed before I heard the patio door slide open. It was Bill. He walked over and sat beside me. He had carried out a bottle and some mixer. I smiled, commending him on what a good idea he had there. We finished our drink in silence before making a second. Bill was going to say something; I could always tell.

I sat back and waited, thinking *okay, it'll either be important or dumb,* which would be something important only with a bad idea attached. We sat in silence for awhile longer before Bill started to say what was on his mind. He began by discussing the exchange Ari had mentioned.

"Ari had said the person exchanging had to be someone other than you." He went reminding me what Ari had said. "If Gera were to exchange while Ari was in your body, he would know."

The Alien's Gift

• • • • • • • • • • •

That would have to be avoided at all cost. I had to agree so far. *Gera couldn't know Ari had found him,* I thought. Knowing where he was about to go now I waited while he finished. Since the exchange couldn't take place with me, Bill had come to the conclusion that it should be him. See, I told you, important or dumb.

I had expected this so my answer was quick. "That isn't going to happen. The exchange would take place with me or not at all."

Bill started to argue. I stopped him. I had spent my time out here thinking this one out. I knew why there was no way it made sense for anyone but me. I began to explain my logic to Bill. First, if this is part of an invasion, why would we give them another person to possess? We didn't know Ari. What if this whole thing was just a way of slowly incorporating their race into our planet?

I had already been compromised so it was me or no one. Tomorrow that will be exactly what we *will* tell Ari. We'd just have to wait until Gera transferred with me again. Then after I come back I could transfer with Ari. I reminded Bill that the last couple of times Gera exchanged our receptions had caused him pause. He'd been taking a long time in between lately. So there should be plenty of time for Ari to do what he has to do.

I had another reason, one I didn't tell Bill. I had touched the face of Gera; it wasn't a pretty thing. Whoever exchanged would be on their world, with them. I felt I was closer to being ready for that. Well, closer to ready than he was; at least I hoped I was. There was a second part to that reason. It was rather childish, I admit, but if this didn't work and I spent my last days in Gera's body, I didn't want Bill or anyone to know what I'll look like when I died.

Bill was still trying to debate me, but he realized it was in vain from the moment I opened my mouth. I might have brought my friends into my nightmare, but I wasn't going to let them exchange places with me. This was my plane ride. I would have to be the pilot.

We had just finished our debate as Steven walked out. He was carrying a bottle and mix too.

"You got to love my friends," I said and started to laugh.

Steven needed to talk. He had decided it would be him who exchanged with Ari. I let out a groan and Bill started laughing.

"Let's wait for Stan so I don't have to repeat myself," I said, then, as if on cue, Stan came out to the patio.

"Did you bring a bottle?" Bill yelled.

Stan missed the joke. He did, however, have something he needed to talk about. I waited patiently till they both finished before I repeated what I had told Bill. That finally settled, we moved on to other matters. We had easier problems to deal with. Things like stealing NASA's Shuttle. Now that should be fun. "Let's have another drink." We spent the next hour working on getting plastered.

Then I was off again. *This should be interesting*, I thought.

The gel was bothersome to my sluggish brain. I planned on just lying back and going to sleep. But before I could, I was back. The guys hadn't even noticed I had gone this time. Why had it been so fast? I decided now wasn't the time to discuss it. We had finished our drinks; it was time to get some sleep. Tomorrow was going to be a big day.

***

The next morning, I woke early my mind already working on the last exchange with Gera.

Why had it only lasted a second? The entire exchange was so quick; no one had even noticed it happened.

I walked to the kitchen with the pups following close behind. There they waited patiently as I poured a cup of coffee before following me out to the patio. Once outside, they started off on their morning ritual. They always had to check their domain after a night's passing. I sat in the dark and listened as they scampered around the yard, looking for any signs of intruders.

I had been sitting there for a few minutes when I heard the door slide open. Bill came walking out carrying a cup of coffee. He just smiled as he sat down. We both sat in silence for several minutes. The dogs, now finished with their patrol, came over to visit Bill before lying down. I began to tell Bill about the exchange that had taken place last night. The news seemed to be disturbing to him. At first I was confused by his reaction. Then I realized he had felt responsible. Bill was there to watch out for me and now he was being told that Gera had swapped with me, and he hadn't even been aware of it. I tried to calm him down, explaining it had happened so fast I almost didn't know. I wasn't having much success.

Realizing that, I moved on. Focusing instead on what happened. We needed to figure out why Gera let go almost instantly. Steven and Stan had joined us just as we were getting into the conversation. I stopped long enough to fill them in.

"You were drunk," Steven said without blinking an eye.

"So what? I've been drunk before." I said, a little puzzled by his answer.

"Gera hasn't," he said before taking another sip of coffee.

It took me a second before the meaning of what he said sunk in. *Well, who needed help now? All I had to do was become a drunk and I was safe.* I snickered to myself at the thought.

After finishing our coffee we all moved to the computer. This was going to be a hard day of negotiating. No, come to think of it, not really. I had already decided on a couple of things. On those there would be no other way.

32

The Alien's Gift

Steven turned on the machine, looking around at the rest of us.

"Well, are we ready?" he asked.

With a simple nod from us he typed "Hello." Ari was there. We had begun. I wanted to set the stage immediately, I was the first to speak.

"Steven, let Ari know he exchanges with me or there will be no exchange at all," I said.

My message was relayed, but Ari's response was negative. He didn't want to take the chance of warning Gera of his coming.

"Ask him why?" I said. "What can he do? He is encapsulated."

Ari's response was unsettling. "He can accelerate his exchange. Now he believes he has plenty of time. He's using that time, valuable time, to learn more about your culture, your language. This will enable him to assimilate better. Also the longer he waits, the easier the transfer will be. The capsule is losing its continuity, and he's starting to figure that out by now, I'm sure."

Bill looked at me, saying, "He's got a good point."

"Point or not, it's not happening," I responded in frustration.

I knew what Bill was doing. He felt it was another chance for his side of the argument. I went back to my questioning.

"Steven, ask how much time he needs to come here the first time?" Steven's fingers had finished the last word I spoke almost as I said it.

I looked at Bill "How does he do that?"

Bill smiled and shrugged. As I looked back, Ari's answer was already on the screen. That answer was what I was looking for. He couldn't debate me. Not on this subject, not anymore. Ari said he would need to be here for thirty minutes.

I asked Steven to explain my plan. It was pretty basic. When Gera comes, we piss him off and he stays back in his little pod for several hours. I told Steven to let him know my plan will guarantee that.

"Oh! Also let him know I won't allow anyone zapping around except me. Take it or leave it."

Stan said, "Well, there can't be many answers to that. You sure didn't leave any room for negotiations."

"That's my plan—not to," I responded.

Ari didn't respond to our last statement. He was taking too much time. I was getting uncomfortable. I was starting to wonder if there was more going on, more than we were being told. I was just about to tell Steven to break the connection when Ari finally came back. He didn't like the idea. He believed it was taking a great risk, but he agreed.

I would say I was relieved, but now I thought, *I'm about to visit a bunch of those ugly bastards, and they're all awake.*

With that point settled, we started to make final arrangements. Ari was

33

going to transport some equipment. He explained his people were capable of teleporting basic material without a receiver, however, something as precise as a being would require a receiver, at least the first time. To do that he would need to assemble one. Once the device was in place, he'd be able to teleport himself here without requiring an exchange. He would transmit the parts for assembly. But first he wanted to make sure I was nowhere near. I could not see the receiver. Explaining that Gera would surely recognize the machinery and know something was happening.

I understood and agreed they were legitimate concerns. I believed that, using my plan, Gera wouldn't be here long and wasn't going to see a thing while he was here. However, to ease Ari's anxiety, I asked Steven to tell him I agreed, "Assure him that Gera won't see a thing." Then I left the room.

Now stage one was in place. Ari was going to stand by waiting for our message to exchange. Once the equipment arrived Ari would come and assemble it. For that stage, we'd have to give him the go ahead to exchange.

"With me only," I reminded him.

Seconds later, machinery started to materialize. Now we could only sit and wait. It was Gera's move. We waited for what felt like an eternity. I was reaching the point that I would have exchanged with him if I could. Another hour had gone by, and I was starting to wonder if Gera had given up. *Had we pushed him too hard, and he picked someone else or had something happened to him?*

I actually found myself trying to reach out to him. *Now I must be going crazy,* I thought. However, the only way to end this was to follow the path we started with Ari. Ari's machine was put in the other room. I would stay out of that room completely. That way we were sure Gera wouldn't see it when he came.

When? Was Gera ever going to call on me again? We waited close to an hour before I felt it starting. Gera was finally coming. In my excitement, I yelled, "NOW!"

No one had moved more than three feet away from me in the last hour, but I wanted to make sure. This was it, no mistakes. I was on my way. I tried to maintain a sense of submission with my thoughts. I didn't want to alert Gera in any way.

Why are you doing this? I projected as he passed me.

That must have worked. I could feel his indifference again. He seemed to have regained his confidence. Arrogance was probably a more accurate word.

Once again I found myself in the pod. It was all up to them now. I didn't bother trying to move around or get over to the walls. If all went as it should, I wouldn't have time. I'd be back in seconds. When Gera arrived at my body he would see nothing.

If everything went as planned, a bag had been placed over my head and secured in place with a collar. My arms would be secured behind me and a pair of headsets on my ears playing static at a volume I was afraid might damage my hearing. I had asked Stan to keep it to where I wasn't deaf when I got back. I planned on being able to use them for several more years. Stan assured me the worst I would be was a little hard of hearing. My grin told him to do better than that.

"Don't worry," he said.

Okay! I'm not worried. Bring me back now. I was counting the seconds. They were turning into minutes. Something had gone wrong. I tried to help. I willed with everything I could to pull myself back. Still, nothing was happening.

I was on the verge of panic when I felt that now familiar sensation. I was back, the sound in my ears loud and chaotic, in total darkness. I had readied myself for those. The smell wasn't something I had planned on. We hadn't planned anything like that.

"Holy shit, that stinks," I yelled.

The headsets came off. Stan and Steven were removing my bonds and covering as fast as possible. They had freed me from my bindings in a matter of seconds. They had freed me from everything, except for the lingering odor. That, I was sure I would never get that smell out of my sinuses.

"What the hell was that?" I asked.

Bill, smiling, said, "Well the darkness and noise didn't seem to bother him that much. I guess he was getting used to it. Lucky for you this milk in the refrigerator went sour. He wasn't counting on dealing with your sense of smell."

I wanted to hear more, but now we had to move fast. Time was critical. I asked Steven to get ready to contact Ari, then I stopped him. They turned to look at me. I knew they were wondering if I had changed my mind. I hadn't; I was ready, ready as I could be. That wasn't it.

I just couldn't let Ari come without warning them one last time. I took a minute, knowing time was of the essence, to remind them of my experience and prepare them for what they would see, when Ari arrived in person. I had to let them know if anyone wanted out, now was the time, and I would understand. If not, we had to do it now!

There was no hesitation, nobody second guessing what they were doing. Steven smiled and typed, "Now." Again I felt that familiar sensation. I had wondered if it would take longer to travel the universe then it did to get to Jupiter. My answer came immediately. It didn't seem to take any longer. I was there. All I had to do now was prepare myself for the images I had in my head.

35

Chapter 5

The sensations from the exchange passed. I sat for a moment, preparing myself when I heard a voice.

"Marc, Marc, are you all right?"

That was Bill's voice. I opened my eyes. I had kept them closed. Still not sure how ready I would be to see Gera's race, especially with them awake and moving around. Hearing Bill's voice was almost as much a shock to me as seeing him. I was sitting in my house. Right where I started, Bill was standing in front of me, showing obvious concern. Stan was standing off to the side. Everything was the same, except for Steven. Where was Steven? He was standing there just a second ago.

"What happened?" I asked, "Didn't it work"?

"Yes."

That answer confused me even further. Bill continued to talk as my mind tried to absorb what he was saying.

"You're here."

"Here, I know I'm here, but why?"

Pulling up a chair, Bill sat in front of me. "Marc, you're here, here on Rikiel."

Now I was really confused. First I thought *why is Bill screwing with me?* But as I looked around, I remembered Steven.

"Where's Steven?" I asked.

36

The Alien's Gift

• • • • • • • • •

"Steven is still on your planet," Bill said.

Bill put his hand on my arm to calm me as he spoke. "Let me explain what's happening."

"I was just about to let you do that," I said sarcastically. I sat back and, with my full attention on Bill, I said, "Explain away."

Bill took a deep breath and started to explain what was going on. "First you're now on Rikiel, Your friends are on Earth with Ari."

I was ready to just sit and listen, but somehow sitting here having Bill tell me I was talking to him from the other side of the universe was too much. I knew Bill wouldn't play with my mind, not now, not at a time like this.

"Then—then who are you?" I asked, not sure I really wanted to know.

"I" he started, "We're the watchers."

Lení, I learned, was the name of the person in front of me. Lení was not only, not Bill, that much I was starting to understand. Lení was also a… she.

Bill was a she? My mind played with that thought for just a moment. *Oh! Bill, I can't wait till I see you.* My mind snapped back to Lení. She had been talking. I apologized and ask her to start over. Patiently, she went back to the beginning. I was on the planet Rikiel. She and the Stan looking guy over there were watchers. It seems from what she was saying that some species have difficulty with the exchange. The watchers are there for both the safety of Ari's body and, in this case, mine.

I didn't ask what could go wrong or what they did when it went wrong. I wasn't sure I wanted to really know the answer to that one either. I had a few million other questions running through my mind instead. For now I sat and continued to listen as she explained the setting was for my benefit.

"Having a familiar setting and surrounding helps with new species exchanges."

I'm not sure I like being called a species, I thought, almost laughing to myself.

Now that she had decided "the new species" seemed to handle the exchange well, Lení allowed me to move around.

Well, it's my house anyway, I thought whimsically.

Now it was my turn, and Lení was answering my questions one by one. Her answers always seemed to be quite candid, showing great patience with me, when needed. The other "Stan" never said a word. He just sat watching us during our conversation. The "Rikien," that's what they called their *species*, a little species revenge in my thought as I mulled that over. The Rikien are capable of taking on shapes and forms. "Shape shifters," that's what they were called in the science fiction movies.

The Rikien, however, were far more than that. They seemed to be able to

37

manipulate energy. Not just the energy that goes into making up their form. The energy that makes up their surroundings can also be manipulated. Again, the sci-fi movies came to my mind. This was like a holographic chamber, except they didn't need the chamber. I started to ask to see her as she really looked, then, remembering Gera, I passed. I was sure she was beautiful from a Rikien's point of view, but then, I was another "species."

It only seemed like a few minutes had passed when Lenî notified me it was time to return. I moved back over to the chair. As I did I thought, *I probably didn't need to, but hey I'm new at this*. I felt the exchange begin. Then I realized I hadn't even thought to see what Ari's body looked like. My eyes went quickly to his hands as I felt myself being transported across the universe again. I felt Ari as we passed. We mentally nodded to each other, and I thought now that's a nice guy to exchange with. A lot nicer than Gera, that's for sure.

My eyes opened and there was Bill sitting in front of me.

"You're Bill?"

I looked around this time, seeing Stan and Steven. Bill looked at me strangely.

"You haven't been gone that long," he said.

I laughed, saying I would explain that later, adding, "You're going to love it."

First I wanted to make sure everything went alright. As I looked around, everything seemed to be status quo. Stan was at the table writing away, Steven was on his computer.

Bill just kind of nodded in their direction. "You know those two. Stan and his notes, Steven is looking up things after Ari's visit."

Bill wanted to know about my adventure and wasn't about to let me move until he heard everything. I waited for Stan and Steven to finish what they were doing and join us. Once everyone was seated, I began to tell them about my experience on Rikiel.

I had saved the part about Leni till the end. That was too special to waste. As I had expected, we had a great deal of pleasure with the fact that Bill was the spitting image of this girl named Lenî on planet Rikiel. Bill took it well.

Over the next few minutes I told them all I learned from the limited time I was there. I was about to ask what had taken place in my absence when I felt the exchange with Gera begin.

"Now." That was all I could say before I was off across the cosmos once more. We had decided that was the "word," and I hoped the guys weren't caught off guard too far.

I passed Gera. He seemed to be paying much more attention to me as we moved by each other this time. I think he was aware of the challenge he was starting to face. I could feel him reach into my mind for information. Fortunately the only thing that was going through my mind was my concern for the guys, they were unprepared. He couldn't have had enough time to get anything from me. Or could he?

I could only hope he didn't, but for now, I was in the capsule. You know this is a place you could get used to—if you were in a coma. What made it worse, this time; I wasn't sure how long I would be here. We had been caught by surprise; the guys didn't have time to set up a formal greeting for Gera. I tried not to worry. They had dealt with Gera before. I turned my attention to looking for Jupiter instead. I was getting good at moving around in the gel. I moved over to the wall.

The capsule was shimmering more now. I knew why, and that thought gave me reason to pause. *A month* I hope Ari was talking about earth time when he said that. I was also hoping he was good at math. I kept the thought, *the capsule would hold together for another month.* Meanwhile Jupiter was outside, and all I could see was a dark mass, huge in the distance. Distance, I wondered. How far I was from the planet? With not much to see out there, I touched the wall, examining it maybe, testing it for what? The wall went solid again as my, rather, Gera's fingers came into contact.

That was reassuring. I watched the wall now, counting off the seconds in my mind. *How long would it stay that way before returning to the shimmering state again?* Forty-three, forty-four, forty-five, the wall started to shimmer again. *Forty-five seconds, is that good?* That was a question for Ari. I was on to my next experiment when I felt myself going home.

I was having trouble breathing. *What was wrong?* When I opened my eyes I saw Bill sitting on my chest. He had his knees pinning my arms to the floor. As soon as Bill knew it was me, he got up. Stan and Steven had been holding my legs. They released me on Bill's command. As I got up, I felt my jaw. It hurt like hell.

"Yeah, sorry about that," Bill said as he watched me stroke my chin.

It seemed Gera's arrival had caught them off guard, and Bill, true to his word, "Kicked my ass." Bill had been sitting right in front of me when Gera arrived, he started to explain. They hadn't been ready and, when Gera stood, Bill jumped up and hit him—me in the jaw.

"When he went down, I jumped him."

Stan and Steven moved to assist once Gera—I was down. Gera struggled for several minutes, then it just seemed he gave up and left. We had been caught off guard. We could let that happen again. I was still stroking my jaw as I seconded that amendment. Bill offered me a cup of coffee. Almost as a peace offering, he was still feeling bad about what happened. *A little remorse,* I was glad to see that. I told him to let it go.

"With any luck I might have to kick your ass soon."

Bill smiled, "Good luck."

With that, it was put into the past. Not the too distant past, I hoped. While we were talking, Stan and Steven had returned to their respective computer and paperwork, Bill made the comment that if they didn't do it, they'll just go nuts. I laughed at that. *Why would two guys, who were fighting an alien, that was trying to inhabit one of their friends go nuts?* Putting the thought aside, I took another sip of coffee and sat back listening as Bill filled me in on what had happened when Ari arrived.

Bill told me as soon as Ari had gotten here they took him to the equipment. There, he would point to something, Stan and Steven would assemble it, with Ari directing every move. It seemed he was quite specific in details as to what part did what. That, Bill explained, is why you got the Wright Brothers over there doing their thing. I wanted to look at it, but Bill said Ari was quite adamant about not letting me.

Holding my jaw, I asked, "Just how adamant?"

Bill laughed. "Well, I don't know if we need all that, but Ari said you didn't want to have the image in your mind when you met up with Gera."

That made sense. My mind returned to the extra probing Gera had attempted as we passed. Now I didn't even want to know any details about the equipment for the same reason. Gera was already starting to suspect something. I knew we were running out of time. I changed the subject.

"When is Ari coming back?" I asked.

Bill jumped up "Damn, now, we're supposed to tell him when you got back. I forgot after having to…well, after the excitement." Looking toward Steven, Bill hollered, "Now, Steven, now."

Steven didn't even look up as his fingers danced across the keyboard. Then he and Stan were on their way to the other room. Bill stayed to keep me company as they went to greet Ari. It seemed the stage was set. I hoped Ari would take a form that was acceptable by Earth standards.

I didn't have long to wait. Without sound or fanfare, Ari had arrived and, with Stan and Steven in tow, he was walking into the kitchen. Bill and I froze. This wasn't a human form. Ari walked across the kitchen straight toward me like a man, or rather, a Rikien on a mission. Ari's focus was on me alone as he crossed the room. He was also moving fast, almost too fast.

Bill was the first to move, jumping in front of me in an attempt to block Ari's advance. At the same time, Steven and Stan started to move in from the rear. Me—I started to panic. With a raise of his hand Ari froze the room. Now the only thing moving was him and, he was still heading straight for me. Ten feet, five, then he was there. He put his hands on my shoulders and tilted his head to mine. I felt a strange calming sensation run though me as

The Alien's Gift

he did. Ari held me like that, foreheads touching for several seconds before releasing me.

The room was free again, Bill continuing to jump in front of me, Stan and Steven again closing in from behind. They met each other in the middle of the kitchen. Ari, having already moved past the point of contact, was standing beside me. We both watched as my gallant knights came to my defense, only to arrive late at the party. I would have been amused if I wasn't so overwhelmed. They had been trying to defend me.

"You have good friends," Ari said as he looked at me.

The guys were feeling rather foolish as they tried to get untangled from each other. They turned to see Ari as he stood by my side, now realizing there had been no attack. The excitement passed. We turned our attention to Ari. Ari didn't look human, not really. He didn't look like Gera either or at least what I believed Gera to look like. *Were my senses that off?* I wondered.

Ari pointed toward the kitchen table, saying, "Gentlemen please, if you would."

With so gracious an invitation, we all sat, anxious to learn more about everything—hell, more about anything. We were actually sitting at my table in my kitchen with a being from the other side of the universe. It was taking a moment to absorb the reality of it. Bill and I looked at each other, then at Stan and Steven. This was actually happening. Ari, expecting exactly this reaction, was waiting patiently, giving us time to adjust. Once the questions started, they started from every direction at the same time. Ari spoke.

"First, we must move. I must stay close to the room we prepared."

Once we had relocated and settled back in, the questions started. Ari was again bombarded with questions from everyone at once.

Ari actually laughed. "Gentleman, I'm of an advanced race, it's true, however, still I'm only capable of answering one question at a time."

First Ari wanted to explain why we had relocated. "If Gera comes, this door will have to be closed immediately." He reminded me I would have to stay out of that room, along with Stan and Steven. We had to make sure Gera wasn't aware of Ari's presence. The brothers would stay with me to guard me. That being said out loud, Bill jumped up, coming back in a moment with the flashlight, the zapper, restraining straps, and the good old radio.

"Don't want to have to kick your ass again," he said as he sat back down.

I thanked him for that. Ari went on to explain he had installed a force field around the room he was in, preventing Gera from sensing his presence.

I had a question, probably not as important as several other questions that needed to be asked. But I needed to ask it nevertheless. Ari was, for the lack of any other description, almost angelic in shape and form. His being,

41

although nothing like a human, had all the same features as ours. He was, however, beautiful. Gera, on the other hand, was nothing short of demonic. I had to know why. Ari explained his race was a race of energy and matter, the same as ours, however his had evolved to pure energy. Then centuries ago they had retaken physical form for reasons he didn't go into.

Their form was now made up of manipulated energy, where as the energy that created Human matter was formed by nature. Confused? So was I. He went on to explain that Gera's energy was damaged, and that damage was being reflected in his being. He also explained that the infra-red light in the capsule was due to effects caused by the gel, but were easily overcome by simply adjusting the spectrum in the eyes. I smiled as I thought *now why hadn't I thought of that? Just adjust the spectrum to your eyes, stupid.*

"Gera, he'll know you're here," I shouted almost too loud. "He can probe my mind." I thought we blew it. I hadn't thought about that.

"No, he won't," Ari answered in a calm voice. He went on to explain that the contact he made on his arrival was to reinforce my energy, my mind. Gera wouldn't be able to probe my mind as it was now. Mine was now as strong, if not stronger, than his was in its injured state.

Ari went on to caution me, "Make sure you let him have access to your thoughts. Just control them. We don't want him aware that you're stronger, not yet. If Gera realized he couldn't control you, he might look for another transferee. If that should happen…"

I had turned into myself as Ari continued to speak. I was looking for the new super powers I possessed, the conversation continuing on without me.

Ari advised my friends to alter their tactics with Gera. Telling them to, "Make it less of an assault and more like you're trying to negotiate. We don't want him jumping ship now."

As if on cue, I announced, "Gera's coming."

I was able to sense him much sooner. We had time to move to a more suitable location before the enveloping sensation came over me. I was secured to the chair with Bill and the guys standing over me before I was off. Gera was probing me again on his way by. I tried to project dismay, the thought of wanting to know why he was doing this, of what was he doing in my mind.

Then I was up to my neck in gel again. I didn't seem to mind it as much, maybe because I knew this time it was voluntary and I could leave at will. At least I thought I could. Not wanting to try, *that would surely blow our cover,* I thought. I turned my attention to Jupiter. I moved to the wall of the capsule. *Okay, Mark, adjust the spectrum,* that was the thought, now. *How do I do that?* The image in front of me was shifting, I don't know how I was doing it, but the image of Jupiter was coming into focus. It was huge, magnificent.

I had seen pictures; everyone has. I have seen every NASA fly by photo and film taken, but there was nothing, absolutely nothing, that could compare to what I was looking at. I was actually in space staring at the largest planet in our solar system. It encompassed my entire field of view. I've never seen anything so massive so—so—there just wasn't an adjective good enough for what I was seeing. I was giggling like a school boy. I might have cried if…was Gera was even capable of that? Have to check with Ari on that; can Rikiens cry?

I'm not sure how long I was there this time. I didn't even care. The sight was magnificent. Too soon, I felt myself going back. As Gera and I passed, the contact with him erased the joy I was feeling from seeing the universe, like I had never even dreamed possible. Gera filled my mind again, the coldness, the arrogance.

He felt he had regained control. With it and the evil he possessed, he reached out to punish me. My mind, strengthened by Ari, controlled his assault easily enough. However, I did let him think he had succeeded. It seemed to please him. My ruse worked. I found myself sitting in the chair. No lights, no horns, bells, or whistles, all a pleasant relief.

"I saw Jupiter." I blurted it out before anyone could even speak.

I felt like a school boy. I had to tell someone. I wanted to tell everyone, but except for present company the words would have been that of a mad man. Ari came walking out as I was telling them about Jupiter, my words tripping over each other in the attempt to get them out of my mouth. He smiled the smile you would see on an adult as he watched a child tell his friends about his trip to Disney. I smiled back, the smile of a child looking at the parent who just took him there.

Realizing we had a job to do, I came back to the moment at hand. "How did it go here?" I asked.

"Lucky you didn't get your ass kicked again while you were gone," Bill replied. Before going on to describe what happened during Gera's latest visit.

He had felt in control again, that's for sure. Bill said they tried doing a *please leave Mark alone* and a *why are you doing this* act with him. They hoped to prevail on his better side. From Bill's reaction I could tell that didn't work, Gera didn't have a better side.

"Arrogant asshole, I should have slapped the crap out of him." Bill's comment kind of summed it up in a nut shell.

Ari, like a patient parent with his children, reminded us once again that Gera was ill. He went on to explain what kind of person Gera had been before. As I listened, I started to feel different toward Gera. For the first time I felt sorrow. The emotion made me cringe even as I had it. He was so evil, so cold, how can I feel sympathy for him? Ari's story, however, had calmed the moment. Everyone had started to settle back down. Now we waited for him to tell us the next move.

Ari told us he needed to see NASA. Not pictures, not films; he needed to be at the actual site. He didn't explain why. Saying only, in order to move onto the next stage, it would have to happen. When I told him how lucky that was, explaining that I lived close to NASA, Ari informed me it wasn't luck at all. It was, in fact, one of the reasons Gera had chosen me. I had never thought to wonder why I was the one chosen. It made me feel a little less important hearing it, though. I just happen to live at the right address. I wasn't a perfect specimen, a prime example of my species or anything cool like that. I just happened to fall into the ten mile or less radius category, great.

We made arrangements to go the following day. "After all, I live close anyhow," I commented. Okay, so my feelings were still a little hurt.

Before he left, Ari looked at each of us and smiled. "You'll be a good addition to the universe one day."

He was talking about our species we knew. It made us proud and at the same time humbled. After all, he did say "will." We're still young and foolish children. I was starting to understand that a lot better than I would have last week. With that statement he was gone.

Stan had been looking down as he spoke and didn't see him leave. "Where did he go?"

"Back to Rikiel…I guess," was my response.

We had the day to rest, and the pool seemed like a good place to do it. Steven went to get lunch; the rest of us headed to the patio. When I walked outside, I was assaulted by the pups. They had been ignored during most of this time. I spent the next hour lavishing some much overdue attention on both.

Later, as we sat eating lunch, the conversation migrated from Ari to Jupiter, to that asshole, Bill's new nickname for Gera. We never stopped on any topic for long. Later that afternoon Stan went to his notes, Steven to his computer. Bill and I decided on the pool.

The day turned into night. An evening too nice to be ignored, we ate on the patio. The discussion at dinner revolved around tomorrow and what the day might bring. Each of us had a different idea as to what Ari might have planned.

Gera would come up from time to time. We hadn't heard from him for hours, for some reason, that was disquieting. What was he up to? We were about to retire for the night when Gera finally decided to visit again. I was getting good at this. I told everyone he was coming, got up, and moved to the chair in the house. The guys got the restraints. Everyone was in place before the move.

As I passed Gera, I sent out the thought of fear. He seemed to enjoy that. I fought hard to keep from mentally slapping the jerk. The moment passed, and I was in the capsule again. I turned my attention to Jupiter. Wow Is a word not good enough, but the one that came to my mind. I could also see a couple of its moons. One of the moons so close, for a moment I was concerned for the capsule. Then I realized the capsule was in an orbit along with the moons. The orbit was degrading…I'm not sure how I knew. But it was one more reason we had to move fast.

I had been here a long time and started to wonder just how much trouble Gera was causing. I was trying to figure out how I could help. I turned inward, looking for the parts of Gera that were still here with me. When I did, I pinched him with my mind. That's the best way I can describe it. I pinched his being. It worked. I was on my way back, fast. Hatred poured from Gera as he passed me. Hatred, for sure; there was no lack of that, but also concern. He didn't know what happened, or how, or even if I might have done it. However you look at it, I got him with that pinch.

I smiled, waiting till I cleared his mind before I let my thoughts loose, *serves you right, you bastard.*

I had been right. He was a problem. Bill said he thought I might not make it back this time. He said Gera was now promising to destroy them all once he gained full control. According to the guys, he was quite explicit on how he would seek his revenge. The only specific they would give me was to say he had a good imagination. Whatever it was, I knew it wasn't a pretty one. I figured that out a little later, when we decided to turn in for the night. I made the suggestion that I be secured. I was a little surprised at just how quickly they all agreed.

Must have been one hell of an imagination, I thought.

Chapter 6

The evening passed without any further incident. When I woke in the morning, Stan was sitting over me. I wasn't surprised. Somebody was with me at all times now. It had been his watch. I smiled at Stan, before asking if he would undo my bindings. Once free, I got up and got a cup of coffee. Everyone else was still sleeping, so with the dogs at my side, I headed for the patio. For awhile I could believe it was like any other morning. The dogs headed out across the yard on their patrol. I sat sipping my coffee and thinking about how much my life had changed. *Had it only been a few days?* Just three days ago my life was normal.

It was only a few minutes later when Bill came walking out. The dogs stopped long enough to see who it was before continuing their patrol. We sat enjoying our coffee, not talking, just watching the dogs as they ran from scent to scent.

As I watched the pups I realized I had one more detail to cover. "Bill, will you take care of the dogs if anything happens?"

Bill started to go into the *nothing would happen* speech, but stopped. He knew it was something I had to ask, something I had to know.

His answer was short and simple "Yeah," then he sipped his coffee before adding, "They've always liked me best anyway."

I just smiled. I could always count on Bill to be there when needed and to say the right thing at the right time.

I sat for a moment before I answered, "Not on your best day."

It was my way to let him know thank you and thank you. That said, we sat watching the pups play in silence. The patrol complete, they trotted back to the patio and laid down at the sides of my chair. Bill watched them as they took their positions beside me.

"Yes," he said again. This time it was just a whisper.

It was a little after eight when we called our offices. We needed to clear our schedules for the next few days. Once that was completed, it was time to call the guest of honor. Ari appeared as I was about to speak the words. At least I thought it was Ari. The man standing in front of me was human. He saw my look of confusion as I spoke his name. He smiled and confirmed his identity. Smiling again, he seemed to be doing a lot of that.

"I had to dress for the occasion. I believe that's the correct term."

We were ready. I asked him about Gera, reminding him about his tendency to drop in uninvited. Ari placed his hand on my head for several seconds, then said, "He shouldn't bother you now. If he tries to exchange, he'll think you're under the influence of alcohol."

From the look on my face he knew I needed more reassurance than that.

"Gera won't want to waste his energy with your body in an altered state. He'll wait."

With that out of the way, we left for the center. The drive was uneventful, except for Stan. He kept pointing out sights to Ari. The rest of us thought that was pretty funny. Okay, Ari was technically a tourist, that much is true. It just seems when you're able to traverse the universe with little more than a thought, Disney being only x miles away, well, it just didn't seem that important. We kept quiet, except for the snickering, and Stan kept pointing out sights. The tour ended as we pulled into NASA. We were here, but I still didn't see how the tourist park at NASA could help Ari. As for Ari, he seemed pleased with the progress. Once in the park, we moved to the shuttle bus at his request and were off.

The tour consisted of multiple stops. Each stop had something different about the space program and its facilities. At one of the stops there were posters being sold. One of the posters had pictures of the astronauts flying the next mission. Ari asked if I would acquire it for him. I just smiled, thinking *tourists* as I "acquired" one for him.

The bus was leaving, but Ari held us back. There was nothing unusual about missing a bus. They ran one after another, and people would move from bus to bus during the day. However, Ari had a special reason for stopping us. He explained that he wanted me to stay with him and for the rest of the group to keep on with the tour and wait for us at the main park.

47

Bill didn't like that idea, and after ten minutes of debate, Ari conceded. Bill was coming. Stan and Steven were also attempting to debate the issue. Ari stopped them immediately, he was already concerned that adding Bill would put pressure on the plan. Ari explained that if they tried to come, the plan would fail. There could only be three no more. Steven and Stan finally agreed and moved off with the crowd onto the next shuttle.

We watched them leave before I turned to ask Ari what the next move would be. He was gone. I looked at Bill. We both started looking for him, but Ari was nowhere to be found. We were about to get on the next shuttle when I heard my name called. There was a man standing in a doorway waving at me. Bill and I started walking toward him. As we got closer I recognized him, it was Colonel Hyett, the command module pilot. He had just called me and waved me over. There was only one problem with this. I didn't know Colonel Hyett..

When we reached the Colonel, I asked, somewhat dumbfounded, "You know me?"

"It's me, Ari."

Looking at Bill, I said, "Well, now I know how he's getting in."

Motioning for us to follow, Ari led us through the building. Emerging on the other side where we grabbed a shuttle. Not a tourist shuttle this time, this one was an official shuttle. We rode it until we arrived at the shuttle bay. There was less than a week left before the shuttle launch. The shuttle craft had been rolled into the bay to have the solid boosters set in place. As we walked toward the entrance, Bill and I kept looking at the guard, both of us wondering how this was going to work. Colonel Hyett here was going to get in, but we were pretty sure they didn't allow tourists.

As we approached, the guard snapped to attention.

"Colonel Hyett, Commander Boil, and Lt. Smalls," he said with a smile. "Can't get enough of this place can you, Sirs."

Not sure what the guard was talking about, I turned to Bill to see his reaction. Now my reaction was the one that had to be controlled. I turned to look at Bill, but I saw Commander Boil. Commander Boil was walking right beside me in Bill's place, right down to his name tag, picture and all. I stumbled slightly as we passed through the door.

An hour later we were walking out of the building. Ari had gathered all the information he would require. From there it was off to the Command Center. While we were there Bill and I stayed busy receiving a lot of good lucks on the mission from the ground teams. We were the distraction while Ari was busy doing whatever it was he needed to do. Finally we were back on the shuttle again. Better still, Ari was done. Bill and I were about at the end of our nerves.

As Colonel Hyett, he looked at us and said, "Let's give the tourists a surprise visit."

The shuttle driver smiled. He had no problem with the Colonel's request. He drove us straight over to the park. We got out and walked into the terminal building, emerging the building on the other side looking like Bill, Mark, and the guy I had driven over with this morning. Stan and Steven joined us as we walked toward the front gate. Stan was asking how it went. Bill and I just looked at each other, never slowing our pace.

"Tell you later. Let's just go," was all I could say.

It wasn't until we got five miles between us and the park, before Bill and I were finally able to breathe. Both of us were still pretty sure the police would pull us over any second for breaching security at NASA.

"What the hell happened back there?" Bill asked, getting the words out before I could.

"Rikien magic," Ari said, smiling.

Okay, Rikiens have a sense of humor. But what happened? How did that happen? I looked at Bill, wondering, *did that just happen?*

Ari explained he used the picture to change his structure to match the Colonel.

"What about us?" I asked. "Did you change our structure, too?"

Ari said he couldn't do that, reminding us that he was an energy being that recreated matter for a body. We weren't. For us, he had manipulated the matter in front of our face and body to mimic the rest of the crew members.

Yeah! Whatever, I thought, before going on. "What about the crew? What if they had shown up?"

Again Ari explained he had found the crew with his mind. They were at rest time, and he just made sure they slept till after we had left the building.

Gera had attempted to exchange with me twice while at NASA. I felt the probing just before the exchange would normally take place. Ari was right, sensing I was intoxicated; Gera just seemed to pull back and conserve his energy. I wondered how long the effect would last. We still had a little over an hour before getting home. Now wouldn't be a good time for him to show up.

We had decided earlier that I couldn't drive just in case Gera decided to experience intoxication. I was sitting in the back seat. Ari was sitting in the front seat, right in front of me. It had been a long morning. *How much longer would he hold off*? I let the thought go. Ari hadn't let us down yet. I didn't think he would let a detail like this ruin his plans. Still, I have to admit I'd be much more at peace once we got home.

Bill pulled the car into the driveway. We had made it. With a sense of great relief, we entered the house. Ari went straight to the room that had been set up for him. He was working with the data he had and sending it back to

Rikiel. We felt pretty sure he wasn't going to need our help, so the rest of us headed out to the patio. It had been a long morning, and I knew Stan and Steven were going to want all the details.

They were a little more the curious about what happened after they left. I, for one, was hoping Bill had the answers. Frankly I didn't know. All I could really say was, we went into the control room, we went into the shuttle, and Ari took pictures with the camera he had brought along. I had spent most of the time waiting for security to grab me by the arm and ask what the hell I was doing there.

A few minutes later we were all sitting at the patio table sipping hot coffee. As I had predicted Stan and Steven started to ask about the morning. I gave Bill a palm up, indicating it was his story to tell.

Bill's response was remarkably like mine. "I don't know what the hell we just did."

He had spent most of the time waiting to be arrested the same as me. Now, with no facts to deal with, we did what any red blooded American male would do, we speculated. It wasn't productive, but it did kill time until Ari could fill in the facts. Bill and I were interested in hearing them ourselves, that and I wondered about the camera. I don't remember seeing it as we left. What the hell happened to the camera? I hoped he didn't leave it by mistake. That would blow everything. I decided to keep quiet about it until I could ask Ari. I didn't want to get everyone upset about it, especially if it turned out to be nothing. Maybe he had it and I just didn't see it.

We had been talking about fifteen minutes or so when I felt Gera. I felt surprisingly calm about it. I let the guys know he was coming, then I walked into the house and prepared for the exchange. Moments later I was passing Gera. He was irritated, I could sense it. I guess he didn't like me taking a vacation. *I hope the guys are ready. He is not in a good mood,* I thought, and for Gera, that's a bad day for sure.

Once again I was in the capsule. I didn't mind that in itself; the sights of Jupiter had me spellbound. I had figured out the moon I was trailing must be Europa. I hadn't realized it the last time, probably because at the time I thought I might be crashing into it. Now I was looking at it closely, the ice covered surface full of cracks. Scientists say it's from the upwelling of an ocean below the surface. I wondered if there was life under the ice.

Life in the universe; I would have laughed if Gera's body was capable of it. Here I was in a capsule orbiting Jupiter inside an alien body. This week I had traveled to the planet Rikiel and met up with a different "Species." Oh! On the other side of the universe, I might add. Still, I'm wondering if there's life out here.

My mind snapped back to reality. As much as I was enjoying myself in the capsule, I was starting to get concerned about the guys. What the hell was going on back there? I wondered if I should tweak Gera again. I thought about it for a moment before deciding against it. I didn't want him to realize I have as much control as I do. *But what can I do?* As the thought formulated, I was being pulled back. I passed Gera. His mind was almost psychotic, the rage surpassing anything I had sensed from him in the past. I felt sure he would have damaged my mind if it hadn't been strengthened by Ari. I buffered the brunt of his anger. Even with that, he still shook me to my core.

Finally I was back. Pain was shooting through my entire body. It felt like bolts of electricity were discharging in every cell. My body was curled up in a fetal position on the floor, and I was unable to control it. My mind struggled trying to figure out what was wrong. Had something gone wrong on the exchange this time? Was I unable to reconnect with my own body completely? Gradually, I felt the contractions subside. I was starting to regain control of my muscles. I let my body totally relax, not wanting to re-contract muscles that had been overwhelmed just seconds before. I remained totally collapsed on the floor for several more minutes before I attempted to move. I didn't even want to talk, for fear it would cause the pain to return.

When I finally felt I could move again, Steven and Stan lifted me back into the chair. As I mentioned they're both big boys, and I was more than happy for that fact. They lifted me and set me down in the chair.

"What the hell happened?"

Stan and Steven moved back. They planned on letting Bill tell the story. It seemed that Gera was in fine form when he arrived. That much I had known already. Bill was telling me how they tried to calm him, negotiate with him. None of it was working. In the end he just wasn't going to leave.

"So I zapped him," Bill said.

"You what?" My eyes opened wide.

"We zapped him. It worked"

Bill made the statement in a matter of fact tone, followed by a much delayed, "Sorry."

I needed to let the moment pass. Changing the subject, I asked about Ari. Stan said he had left sometime during Gera's visit. I got up slowly and started to move around, testing my body and making sure I didn't overwork muscles that were already strained to a breaking point, when Ari appeared. We discussed what had just taken place while Gera was here. As he listened we were only confirming what he had suspected—we were running out of time. Ari reminded us that now, in his damaged state, Gera was unable to pull his entire essence when he was entering my body. That is why he was still unable to control my body's reactions to sight, sound, and pain. He went on to say that would change once Gera gained full control. Time was running out—my time.

51

Chapter 7

My mind was still pondering the thought of *time running out,* as Ari had begun to explain the next phase of the plan. I had to stop him and ask him to repeat what he had said. Showing great patience with me, he started over from the beginning, filling me in on the details I had missed. The shuttle launch was in two days. Everything would start off normally. The shuttle was scheduled to launch early in the morning. The astronauts would first ensure the shuttle obtained a proper orbit. Then they would check all systems. During that time the doctors at command center would be running basic tests of their life monitoring systems.

Ari had acquired the flight schedule and was going through most of the morning of day one. The important time for us took place four hours into the mission. During that time the entire team was scheduled for two hours of rest, which would also be mission down time.

I stopped him. "What's down time?"

"Down time," Ari explained, "two hours without testing or experiments."

Ari tried to explain that during that time there would be no data recording of any kind, with one exception—their medical scan. Other than that, the astronauts would rest. I wasn't sure how that was significant, but I didn't want to interrupt him anymore. Ari went on to explain that during that time he and three Rikiens would then transfer with the crew.

As much as I hated to, once again I had to stop him. "That's four, and the crew is five."

"Yes, you're the fifth."

Ari looked at me as he said it. Without cracking a smile to indicate he was joking, he continued with other details. All of which I missed, my mind was stuck on the phrase, "you're the fifth." I seemed to do that a lot when Ari was talking. I'm the fifth! Did he say I was the fifth? Why am I the fifth? What am I going to do on a shuttle? He did say I was the fifth.

Ari, unaware that my mind had stalled on his last statement, had continued to explain the details of the mission. Again, I felt stupid, would that be again or some more? Either way I had to apologize once again and say I hadn't been following the conversation. Ari showed more patience than one could ask for, then told me he would be sitting with me to go over everything in greater detail and not to worry.

Worry? Why should I worry? Holding that thought, I tried to follow the details as Ari finished. He went on for several more minutes going over the plan in general, stopping only to answer a question here and there as they were asked. I'm happy to say that I didn't have to interrupt him again. Sad to say, only because I had no idea what he was talking about. It would seem I was still busy not worrying.

He then assigned some tasks to Steven. Stan joined his brother, wanting to help in any way he could. I was about to get a one-on-one with Ari to insure I understood all the details as he was laying them out. Well, not a one-on-one actually. Bill stuck tight to me, the plan was concerning him. He wasn't about to let it go till he got all the details.

Ari touched my head. "This will give us a little time. Gera won't bother us for awhile."

Bill and I cringed as he said those words. We both remembered the price I had paid for locking Gera out the last time. We sat down, and Ari went over each detail again, stopping to explain anytime Bill or I would question something. It seems I was going to visit Rikiel again, only this time not in an exchange, but straight teleporting as Ari had been doing.

"Are there any problems involved in teleporting that may affect some species?" I asked. I was remembering Lenî's words concerning the exchange. This was one of those questions I hated to ask.

Without giving any details as to what he meant, Ari simply said, "Sometimes."

I knew I wasn't going to be happy with the answer.

The conversation returned to the last exchange that took place with Gera. Ari was quite concerned at the speed in which Gera was progressing. That had been one of the reasons for deciding I was to be the fifth astronaut.

They needed to have me on board, that way if Gera managed to take full control, the Rikien would know it. Hearing Ari say "full control" alarmed me considerably. Then Ari reminded me, I could now regain control. That thought was just starting to calm me down.

Then Ari went on to say, "However, at that point Gera would be strong enough to exchange with someone else."

I was alarmed again. This time because it had become my battle, I didn't want to lose it, and I didn't want someone else to pay if I failed. This was becoming personal.

Ari, hearing my objection to the last option, calmed me again by saying, "We just have to make sure that doesn't happen."

At that point I had to interrupt the conversation. Gera was on his way. Ari was surprised by this event; he had believed "the touch" would hold Gera at bay. I moved to the chair hollering out to Stan and Steven the now way too familiar "Now." I saw Ari pass something to Bill, then he was gone. I followed shortly after.

Passing Gera was truly an event this time. I hoped the guys had me hog tied before he arrived. In the capsule I didn't attempt to move to the wall. I hadn't gotten over the fantastic view of Jupiter or even Europa, for that matter. It was just my concern about Gera. He was in rare form as I passed him. I decided I would take the chance and tweak him again to pull him back. I turned my mind into the body looking for signs of him. I was surprised at how hard it was. The first time it was easy, his essences seeming to be everywhere. Now he was scarce and difficult to find. He was getting closer; we had to move fast. I was just starting to tweak him when I felt myself drawn back.

I hadn't done a thing yet, so why was I returning so fast?

My pleasure at being back in my body without having any pain was overshadowed by my concern for the guys. What might have happened? Bill's smiling face greeted me on my arrival. Stan and Steven were laughing so hard I was concerned they might wet themselves. I started to laugh with them, not really knowing why. It felt good, and I didn't ruin it by wondering, not yet. It was several minutes before everyone settled down.

Freed from my bonds, I just sat there knowing I would find out once Bill returned to normal. That was the first time I realized I was sitting in the tub full of water. I looked up at the guys, my expression caused a second round of laughter. Once again I was drawn into the hysteria. I soon found out Rikiens aren't fond of water. At least Gera wasn't. Bill tried to describe the terror that Gera showed when they lowered his—my body into the water. I wanted to know how they thought of it.

Bill said, "Ari told me, actually he passed me a note. It said, "Give Gera a bath," so we did."

They were all still laughing as they left the room. I got cleaned up before re-joining the guys in the living room. They were still talking about the look on Gera's face. I was happy for them. For the first time in a long while they had won, and it was way overdue. Moments later Ari joined us. He sat and listened as the guys relived their experience, punctuated by fits of laughter. Once they were done, Ari stood and said it was time for us to go to Rikiel. The launch was still a day off, but he wanted me to go through a dry run, a rehearsal, not sure what you want to call it, I was going. I don't know why I was so nervous. I had been flung across the solar system and even the universe already, but this time it would be different. This time I wasn't exchanging minds; this time I was going. How? I forgot to ask that the other day. You can't transport something as complicated as a person without the machine. Ari had told me that himself.

The time was now. Ari had made that clear. What he didn't clarify was the how. I was going to have to ask. I hate asking, especially when I don't really think I want to know the answer. This was another of those times. Ari's answer confirmed my thoughts.

"Just use your mind."

My mind, I thought. Oh! You're going to have to do better than that. I must be out of my mind. Amend that. You must be out of *yours.*

There had been a lot of laughing and snickering going on in the room. The guys were still talking about Gera and the tub. All of that stopped abruptly. Ari had gotten everyone's attention with that last statement. I looked at Ari to see if maybe that Rikien humor was showing again. He showed no signs of it being a joke. I thought I would remind him that I was a different "Species," and "my species" doesn't have that power.

Calmly, as if teaching a child a new lesson, Ari said, "Your species' minds don't have that power. On that you're correct. But yours does." He went on to explain that the exchanges with Gera along with the contacts with his mind had altered mine. I was now capable of much more than I realized.

As Ari was explaining, I remembered how I had adjusted the light in the capsule after he told me I could. Okay, I did that. I adjusted the light spectrum with just a thought. So I adjust my vision some; hell, I can do that with glasses. From there, you want me to just flash across the universe?

"I don't know how to do that," I said.

Ari told me to focus on him. "I will go before you; you just focus on my mind."

"Why wouldn't that just cause us to change bodies like it always does?" I asked.

He simply said, "I won't let you." Then he smiled and was gone.

I looked at Bill. His concern was as great as mine. I could see it on his face. I was wavering.

"Guy's, I don't know if I can do this."

Bill spoke up first, "You don't have to."

He was afraid for me, I could see that. They all were. Funny, that offer to back out was what gave me the strength to go on. I readied myself, smiled, weakly I admit, but I smiled. I let my mind reach out to find Ari. It was easy, almost as if he was right beside me. I could almost see him standing there. I started to reach out to pull to him. I hesitated for just a moment. My eyes caught Bill's, I whispered, "the dogs." Seeing him nod, I pulled.

I felt myself flashing across space, then it stopped. I held my eyes closed tight during the trip and was reluctant to open them now. I took a mental survey of my body. It all felt right to me. The only thing left to do is open my eyes and see. Almost like a kid on Christmas morning I allowed my eyes to pry apart ever so slowly. Things were blurry at first, mainly because I was still squinting. Finally I just opened my eyes. I was in the shuttle.

I was in the shuttle! My mind reeled. What went wrong? How could this even happen? I looked around. No doubt—I was inside the space shuttle. I could see the earth outside the window as we circled it. I felt my body floating in the weightless environment.

Oh! Boy! You screwed this one up, Marc, I thought.

I was trying to figure out how I was going to fix this. I let my mind reach out to Ari ready to try again, wanting to get out of here before I was seen.

Ari's thoughts touched me. *Calm down, you did it.*

No, I didn't, I thought back. Oh boy! Did I not do it.

Then I heard Ari speak, not in my mind, but from behind me. I turned and Colonel Hyett was standing there. I was just about to try and explain—explain? How do I explain this?

"It's me, Marc, Ari, and you know Lení."

Those words came from the Colonel's mouth. My knees buckled. I would have fallen to the ground if the law of gravity had been in effect. Lení was by my side now, asking if I felt better. I wondered why she was here, then I thought, *naturally she was the watcher.*

"I should have known you would be here, Lení. How's my species doing? Hey, you don't look like Bill," I blurted out loud, not meaning to.

"There's no reason to this time, Marc," she said with a smile.

I looked at her. She was beautiful. No, that was the wrong word, too inadequate, way to inadequate. Like Ari had been in his natural form, she was angelic, only better. I couldn't pull my eyes from her for several moments. She was busy telling me that my species seems to adapt well, and I should have no problems. I would have thanked her, but I was afraid I couldn't speak when she was looking at me. Ari came to my rescue. Reaching out, he pulled me to the window at the front of the shuttle.

"You have a pretty planet, too, Marc."

I think he said it as a Rikien joke. Judging by the way I had reacted to Lení. I was grateful for it. I had already made a spectacle out of myself on arrival, and I was still embarrassed.

Then my eyes focused on the view in front of me. Earth, what a beautiful planet we had, of that there was no doubt. I remembered my awe at seeing Jupiter and its moons. They were magnificent, to say the least. However, nothing compared to the sight before me now. We truly had the gem of the universe. I corrected myself; at least the solar system. Realizing I hadn't seen anything of the universe yet. I wondered now if I ever would. Maybe I could amend that thought and eliminate the word yet.

Earth, but it's not supposed to be out there, not yet. What mistake had I made?

"Did I do something wrong? Did I jump to the future?" The launch wasn't today, I knew that.

Ari laughed before letting me know I hadn't jumped into the future. This was a mock up, a hologram. The one the astronauts would be in tomorrow, when we did the real shift. I was in fact in the middle of a stage rehearsal. He explained that tomorrow when we took over the shuttle, the astronauts would be here in this one. The hologram would simulate down to the minutest details of the actual flight as it should happen.

The Rikiens were busy going over every aspect of the illusion they had developed, insuring all was exactly as it should be. My only job would be to practice teleporting. Ari wanted me to practice till it was perfect. We got right to the business at hand. He explained that until now, all exchanges I had done were initiated by the other party. What I needed to do was learn how to do the exchange myself. That was something we would practice while I was on Rikiel. He would explain why in detail later, after I practiced. For now, he just wanted me to get good at it, real good. So he gave me his motivational speech. It was short, but to the point.

"Your life may depend on it."

I was motivated by that speech. He's good—real good.

I might have been lost in that statement, however, Ari had kept the best for last. I was to practice the exchange with Lení. I have to admit I flushed like a school boy at the thought of contact with her in any way. After making sure that this would be alright with her, I set out to make the attempt. Lení wouldn't try to block me. If she were to block, I wouldn't have a chance. Her energy force was much more powerful than mine. With the ground rules in place, we started. I reached out to her mind, ready to pull myself across the gap between us.

That was when I found myself in a position of extreme embarrassment once again. As I touched her mind, I pulled hard. But the exchange didn't quite go off like it should. I did manage to zap myself to her form. However...I didn't pull her essence out in the process. What I did manage to do was mix us both, in her body, at the same time. The sensation was indescribable. Her mind was like touching clouds, cashmere. It was perfect. But I knew it was wrong. I zapped myself back to my own body almost as fast as I left. I looked at LenÍ. Was she blushing?

Ari was looking at me with amusement. He bowed apologetically to LenÍ. Then he walked me off to the side to explain what happened.

"I did something wrong. I know it didn't work," I said. I was pretty sure I had screwed it up. I just hadn't realized how bad.

"Depends on what you were trying to do," Ari said, barely able to contain his grin. He then went on to explain I had just mated with LenÍ. I could feel the blood run from my face. I looked over at LenÍ. She was looking at us as Ari explained exactly what I did wrong.

I started to stutter, to apologize I was lost for a moment. *What do I do now? How do I?*

"Oh, LenÍ, please forgive, I didn't, I wasn't," I couldn't finish a sentence.

LenÍ walked to me and told me she knew that I hadn't done it on purpose, I didn't even know how it was done and she was aware of that. It was totally accidental. Then to relieve my guilt she looked at me and winked.

"Not bad...for your species."

I had to try and put that behind me, I would have to attempt the exchange again. Still somewhat embarrassed I told her I could practice with someone else if she preferred.

LenÍ started to smile, "The rest of the Rikien are male. I'm not sure they would trust you, Marc." She gave me a kiss, human style. "Relax. Just pay closer attention next time."

I did. I reached out again, not pulling on the physical form. I made sure I was only in contact with her mind this time. You have to feel and separate the mind from the form, almost like pulling meat from a lobster. Believing I had it right this time, I pulled.

I was looking at me, my own body across the shuttle. When I saw that smile, I knew I had done it. I was tempted to let my mind sink into LenÍ's body, to look for any trace of her essence. The thought shamed me. I had already violated her once. Somehow that seemed to be an even greater breach of trust. I reached out, found her again, and pulled. I was back in my body.

Success at last, but with a price. I blushed. We practice several more times. Each time Lenĺ would increase her will making it tougher for me to extract her during the exchange. Finally Ari announced he was satisfied with my progress.

It was time to go home and rest. Tomorrow was the big day. I apologized to Lenĺ once more, and once more she assured me that she hadn't been insulted by the events of the day. Ari took me to the side and told me he would join me soon, saying he still had to go over the final details. I wondered why he hadn't already. Finally deciding it was because I had so much to learn in such a short time, he was telling me things as I needed to know. Okay, I was going home.

"Um, how do I do that?" Embarrassment seemed to be my natural state today.

Ari told me to focus on something at the house, hold the image, then project. I did. I was standing on the patio. The dogs were surprised for a moment, but recovered fast and were all over me. They were acting as if they hadn't seen me in forever. I was down on the ground with them, having the same feelings. Hearing the commotion, Bill walked out to see what was going on.

The reunion expanded from there. It was a true reunion. Nobody had said it out loud earlier, but none of us were sure if we'd ever be together again. The relief showed. It became a party. Stan fired up the barbeque. Steven got the booze, Bill was grabbing the mix, and I went after the cigars. Everyone headed out to the patio for a celebration. On the way out I spotted the restraints. I slid them in my pocket. The celebration was premature, and I knew it. We hadn't won the war yet, but we had won a battle. Besides, we all deserved the moment. The fire was going, my drink in my hand, I lit up a cigarette. Sitting down, I looked at my friends around the table. Then I turned my head down and both pups were at the sides of my chair sound asleep. The saying may be trite, but I felt I was a rich man.

The mini party was in gear. I had my third drink and was pretty sure old Gera wasn't going to want any part of this body for the rest of the evening. We were discussing the day. There had been a lot of laughter, at my expense I might add. I was happy about that. I had brought these guys into my nightmare and was grateful I could give them a laugh. I hadn't told them everything about Lenĺ. That was something I held to my own thoughts, and I must admit the thought kept me smiling.

We laughed about everything that had taken place from the sightseeing trip to Gera's bath. Laughing till our faces hurt, till breathing was hard. Then the restraints dropped from my pocket. We all watched as they fell to the ground, reality hit hard. We just sat staring at them as they lay on the ground. Their purpose and why I had them, pulling us back to reality. The party ended. We have almost made it, but not yet. Everyone said good night; Stan and Steven went off to bed. Bill stayed behind. Bill was my keeper for the first shift. He sat back in the chair staring at me for a moment.

"Good to see you," he said and nodded as if to confirm the words. "Damn good."

Chapter 8

The next morning I woke early. This was "D" day. Like a kid on Saturday morning, my mind just wouldn't allow sleeping in. I turned to see my keeper—surprise! It was Bill. Actually I wasn't surprised at all. He had sat there the entire night. It was the "last shift." Seeing I was awake, he came over and undid my restraints. *When did he put those on*? I wondered. I had fallen asleep without them. We grabbed a cup of coffee on our way out to the patio.

Bill was becoming part of our morning ritual. We sat down watching as the dogs ran into the yard. It seemed just like any other day. To the pups, it was like any other. Bill and I sat quietly. It wasn't any other day, and we both knew it. I looked at the sky, with no moon the stars were out in force. I could see the outline of the trees in the night sky. There was a cool breeze and the smell of jasmine in the air. Looking around, it was hard to believe the events of the last few days were real. Bill reached out and passed me a cigarette.

I looked at him. "You get on me for smoking, always have. What's with this?"

"Today is your last day of smoking again, that's why. No reason to after today."

Taking the cigarette, I thought *no more after today*. Bill stopped as he passed it to me not releasing it at first.

"You're quitting tomorrow, that's why." It was almost a command. He was telling me to make sure I come home.

We sat quietly after that. The dogs finished their patrol scampered up and took up their usual spots. Him to the left, her to the right; *Always the same,* I thought. I reached down and scratched their heads as they settled. Bill had gone to get us another cup. He was just getting back as the pups were settling. He stood smiling as he watched. He seemed to be enjoying the moment as much as I was. Then as if to announce his return he spoke up as he sat down.

"Still early. Looks like it's going to be a good day, though."

I didn't answer. He didn't expect one.

More than an hour passed before the dynamic duo came out. Bill and I had almost finished the better part of a pot without having said another word. The brothers seemed to fall right into our silence. Both just sat, leaned back, and sipped their coffee with no more than a nod. It was getting just a little too quiet for me. I figured I would start what we were all thinking.

"Never thought you guys would have coffee with an astronaut, did you?"

It broke the ice. Now everyone was talking. First it was mostly banter, but gradually it turned real. It had to get real. Like it or not, today it was. Today we would meet and beat Gera, or… The sentence didn't need to be finished. We all knew.

Ari arrived earlier than I had expected. The shuttle wasn't due to launch for another hour. Then we had another four more before we would rendezvous. I hadn't expected him for a couple or more hours. It seemed it was time for him to give me the final details. The details he alluded to yesterday.

It was true that we were at the home stretch. But we all knew the race hadn't been won yet. Ari made that point quite clear again. He also wanted to remind me that Gera was regaining his strength fast. He was very concerned that Gera might make the exchange sooner than they had been anticipating. Indeed the reason I had to go on the shuttle was in the event Gera transferred while they were in route. If I wasn't with them and he succeeded during that time, they would lose him. The only thing they would find when they got to the pod would be Gera's body, with me inside. The thought sent a chill up my spine.

The plan for today was to borrow the shuttle. I already knew how that was going to be done. Really it was quite simple once you knew Rikiens' abilities. Then we would just fly the shuttle to Jupiter. Okay, that one was still a mystery to me. I was sure it would become obvious when the time came. The shuttle was going to have another capsule in the loading bay. I had to admit that one had stumped me until Ari informed me he already had a receiver set on the shuttle. He had placed it there when we were on board.

That was what happened to the camera, I thought.

Once there, Gera's body would be transferred and re-secured in a new pod. The new pod would then be sent back to Rikiel. They would teleport it I guessed, or whatever they do, so that it was back in orbit. All of this was to take place within the two-hour window. Okay, so that's another detail I found hard to understand, yet. One thing I have learned is never underestimate the Rikien. The plan was simple enough, simple for me. So far I had nothing to do. What was my part? That's what was concerning me? What might I be doing that could blow this whole plan was a better way of putting it.

I was the bait, the prize, the worm. If Gera were to switch during the flight, I had to be with the Rikiens so they could contain him. Ari assured me they could do that without harming my body. However, if the exchange did take place, I would have to stay in the capsule until they arrived. Ari explained once in contact with Gera they couldn't let him go back to his own body. He would flee in another direction, taking another humans' form and life in the process. If that should happen, the power driven by his rage would be devastating to the population of earth.

Gera would literally be a walking demon. His abilities would make him invincible to anything earth could muster against him. As he spoke I understood, I would have to stay in the pod, there was no debate. I couldn't allow that to happen. It gets tricky from here. When the shuttle arrived, the Rikien would prepare to teleport Gera's body into the new pod. At the instant of transport, Ari would contact me. I would have to exchange with Gera as his body was being teleported into the new pod. Too soon and he might escape; too slow and I'll be the guest of the new pod. Now, this was the part I didn't want to hear. I knew because Ari got real somber as he spoke.

"Marc, if you're in the pod when it seals, you'll stay in it for the next three thousand years. They are tamper proof, even by us."

That'll wake you up in the morning, I thought. No wonder he waited till now to tell me. I would have been so nervous, I couldn't have concentrated. I sat back; this was a lot to take in. Ari sat watching me. He was giving me time I needed to absorb what he had just said. I could see in his face how much he regretted having to give me this information.

"There's no other way?" I asked.

I already knew the answer. If there had been another way, Ari wouldn't have been talking to me now. I knew that. I wanted a drink, but knew better. If I ever had to have my wits about me, today was the day. Ari left me alone to gather my thoughts. I sat on the patio, wondering if I could do it. The dogs had taken off across the yard, chasing an unseen intruder. I thought about the planet with Gera loose, the mayhem that evil mind could cause. I knew the first to pay would be those close to me, those who had helped me, against him. He would not forget, and he was incapable of forgiveness. Bill, Stan, Steven would be the first to pay; that thought angered me.

The pups came running over to me. They seemed to sense my anger and frustration. I was their alpha, the one in their life. They would give their life to protect me, I knew that. He would destroy them also. I was furious in the thought. My resolve now became absolute. *You're mine you, Bastard,* I thought. I would bring him down one way or the other. *You will come down.*

The door to the house opened, and the guys came rushing out. Ari had felt it necessary to inform them of the latest detail. They all thought the idea stunk. Just give them a little time and they would think of a much better one. Who are these Rikien that we have to solve their problems? Let them take care of it themselves; get someone else to do it. One after the other their objections came out. All I heard was friends' concern for another friend. We all knew there was no one else.

This isn't a hero story. I didn't volunteer. Gera picked me; he made it my battle. That was the bottom line, and we all knew it. Either I met and beat him out there or he comes here and we lose. The only thing that made me feel bad as I looked at each of their faces was the fact they didn't have a better gladiator.

Ari came walking back out. It was time. We had to leave. He didn't say it. He didn't have to. I stood and thanked each man in turn. Stan and Steven were friends men spoke about on the battlefield. They had indeed joined me in one. Bill; there was nothing I could say to Bill. Nothing he didn't know already. I just smiled—he returned it, our story passing between us in that moment.

Ari said, "Marc, I'll see you on Rikiel. Gentlemen, we'll both see you later tonight."

He was gone. I walked to the dogs, playing with each for a moment. They could sense my distress, so I went inside quickly. I was gone. I wanted—had to leave before they came in.

The shuttle had launched and was coming up to the second hour of the mission. We were ready for the transfer. I was given the picture of the section for my arrival. Ari told me to focus on that when I jumped. The down time arrived and as one, like a navy seal team storming a hostage house, we went. The astronauts were now on Rikiel, safe in their replicated world.

They had been induced to sleep insuring the down time wouldn't be interrupted. We didn't want them awake and looking at each other. Their minds were all in Rikien bodies except for Commander Boil. I hadn't transferred. I had to teleport. The Rikiens switched with the astronauts. All except for Commander Boil. He was teleported. My body was the one at stake, not his.

The shuttle's orbit was being maintained on NASA screens just as if it was there. It had been, till now. That changed after we arrived. LenÍ moved to the rear of the shuttle cabin along with two others. Ari was in the pilot seat. The shuttle turned. I could no longer see earth below us. There were no shudders, no shimmy, no burst of speed. It was just a moment, and there was Jupiter coming at us fast.

Ari walked back to speak with me as we closed in. I was watching the shuttle as it now slowed rapidly.

"How are you doing this? Jupiter! How?" I asked.

"We've created a small fold in the universe, barely a crease for this jump," Ari explained.

I could feel Gera. We were so close to him I could feel his essence in the air. I told Ari. He had been concerned about just this. With all the contact we had, Ari felt the closer we got, the stronger the connection would be.

The walls of the shuttle started to shimmer. No, it wasn't the shuttle. I was in the capsule. Gera had felt me just as I had him. Feeling that strong connection Gera had jumped. I hadn't had time to warn Ari. With my mind I screamed out, hoping to reach him, warn him. He was standing beside Gera and might not even know. For a moment I started to panic. *We had lost. So close, and we had lost.* I was starting to sink into total despair. Then the thought hit me, *Ari hadn't been caught short on anything yet. Maybe he hadn't this time either.* I tried to relax. I needed to settle down, I wasn't about to give up yet.

I lay quietly in the capsule. I would just have to wait for the call from Ari. Trying to remain calm, remembering the timing had to be precise. Only then could we defeat Gera. Defeat Gera? I just realized we weren't fighting Gera, not really. Ari had tried to tell me more than once Gera was a good man—"Rikien," and this was a disease. One that could destroy my planet if we let him escape, I admit, but a disease none the less. I wasn't fighting a being. For the first time I felt true compassion for Gera. I had seen the beauty of his race in both body and mind. What kind of damage had caused Gera to become the beast he had become, again in both body and mind? I hoped we still had a chance. This time I was hoping to save us all, including Gera.

***

As I had moved into the capsule, another battle was taking place on the shuttle. Gera had indeed caught Ari by surprise, as I had feared. His mind hadn't been strong enough to hurt Ari, but his body—my body was. Before Ari could respond to Gera's presence, Gera hit him, hit him hard. It seemed like Gera knew what was waiting for him and was planning on our arrival. Ari went down, knocked unconscious from the blow. Gera then turned his attention to the Rikien at the front of the craft, and within moments subdued him as well.

Gera then moved toward the back of the ship. He was going after Lenĺ and the other Rikiens. That was when he made his first mistake. He was too far away, realizing he couldn't reach them in time he reached out with his mind. He was trying to eliminate Lenĺ. He had chosen her, thinking she was the weakest and easiest to overcome. That would leave him with only two to defeat. Two to one odds, I grant you, but much better than five to one.

What Gera didn't know was that Lenĺ had been practicing. She'd been working with me all day the day before. Because of that, her senses were sharp and on high alert. Lenĺ felt his attack immediately. When he struck, she struck back, hard. Gera was caught by surprise. He hadn't planned on that nor had he braced for a counter assault.

To use an earth term, Gera went down hard. Lenĺ's mind defenses took him out at the knees. She had retaliated so hard she even felt regret for her action. The results were that Gera was unconscious. She was rushing to his aid, starting to move toward him even as her mind had countered his. By this time Ari was up and moving again. He stopped her. He would attend to Gera. She was needed in back. Timing was critical; she had to be at the loading bay.

***

I lay quite still, not aware of how close I was to being encapsulated for the next three thousand years. My mind trying to stay sharp, *I had a split second against three thousand years.* I had to drop that thought; very distracting, that thought. "NOW" Ari had chosen to use the term we had adopted at the house, believing the familiarity of the word would help in my response. It worked. My mind was wandering all around the universe, thinking thousands of thoughts. Three thousand of them, to be precise. Hearing "Now," I pulled. I was passing Gera. He was unconscious, I realized, as we passed. *Heal well, my friend. I wish I could have known you. The person you were and hopefully will be again.*

I was in the shuttle. Ari looked at me, smiling. We had done it. The Rikien at the front of the shuttle was still unconscious, and I noticed a bruise on Ari's forehead. That was when I first realized something serious had taken place. I was standing here, so we must have won. I congratulated Ari on a battle well fought.

He smiled, saying, "Thanks, but I lost."

I was confused by his statement. "Well, who, how—did we win?"

He smiled looking back toward Lenĺ. Lenĺ looked at me. She had almost a sheepish grin.

I smiled "You, all that beauty and a heroine, too."

"You trained me" was all she said.

The Alien's Gift

I looked at Ari; he was as confused by her statement as I was. With Gera safely in his healing chamber, we turned for Earth. Seconds later the pod was teleported to its orbit around Rikiel's moon, and the astronauts were back in the real shuttle. I found myself sitting on Rikiel with Ari not really believing it was done. Was it less than a week ago my life was normal? Over the last few days the world was at stake, I had traveled across the universe, met with an alien race, seen Jupiter and its moons. Now it was all over. My life would return to normal again. *Could I live a normal life again?*

Either way, it was over. Ari smiled and said, "Go, see your friends, they worry. I'll join you soon."

I focused on my patio. Oh! I love that patio. The dogs were the first to spot me. I had only been gone a few hours, but you know dogs. I had surprised them, appearing out of nowhere like that. They recovered fast and were all over me. My response to them was as if I hadn't seen them in days. The noise we created alerted the house. Stan and Steven were out the door in a flash. I was picked up by one only to be put down and picked up by the other over and over.

Finally I begged them to stop while I could still walk. As I've said a few times, they're big boys. Bill walked out last, and walked out the slowest. He was walking like an old man. I could see the last few hours had taken a lot from him. I think I knew why. Men will sometimes die for other men, of that there's no doubt. It may only be because we can't handle the idea of seeing the other die. This time no one had died. Bill looked at me and we nodded. That was enough.

True to his word, Ari arrived soon after. He happily informed everyone that Gera was safely in orbit, and that the healing process was once again underway. He also took a moment to thank us all personally. Gera had been a close friend of Ari. To watch what had become of him was to watch the destruction of his own soul. He thanked us for all we did to bring his friend back and vowed to tell Gera one day all we had done for him. I looked at Bill as he spoke those words thinking *they aren't as different as one would believe.* Ari asked if he could bring company. I was intrigued. Who could Ari have invited to my house? I told Ari on Earth we have a saying among friends. For you, my friend, it goes, "My house is your house."

Ari thanked me for the honor. He whispered, and Lení was standing there. My heart skipped a beat when I saw her. Her beauty wasn't lost on the guys either. To describe her would be an injustice. Lení can't be put into words. I couldn't believe she was standing on my patio. She walked to me, pulling me into her arms, and gave me a kiss that men have conquered nations for. Then she stepped back and smiled. Her smile lit up the sky.

67

Ari explained that Lení needed to thank me also. "Gera is Lení's father."

I heard Ari speaking, but the words didn't register yet, my mind still reeling from her kiss.

"I heard you as you exchanged with my father. Thank you for the kindness you showed, thank you for the compassion and seeing through to the goodness lost to his illness." Tears were welling in her eyes as she spoke.

Ari spoke again, "I will tell my friend of the kindness and compassion you showed him during his hours of weakness."

"You did all that?" Bill said. It was his way of keeping my head from swelling.

He turned and looked at Lení.

"I was worried about you, and you were with her!"

With that, the laughter started. The tensions of the last few days, tensions I now realized involved two worlds, were released. It also seemed to strengthen Bill once again. We spent the rest of the day enjoying each other's company. It was good to be home.

Later that night Bill and I sat on the patio. Steven and Stan had returned to their homes. Our lives were going back to normal. I thanked Bill, not for what he'd done, but for who he was. He told me it was a shame, he really wanted the dogs and they did seem to like him best.

There was no way to thank Bill.

"Have another drink and shut up," I said.

Chapter 9

A new morning, I opened my eyes feeling refreshed. For the first time in days I had slept a deep and restful sleep. My mind and body felt re-invigorated. Getting out of bed, I felt ten years younger. The pups must have noticed the difference. Instead of my normal walk out of the bedroom, this morning I was accompanied by two dogs springing around as if they were on pogo sticks.

I have to admit it's a little unnerving to have two hundred pounds of puppies bouncing around your body as you're trying to walk across a room. After attempting to settle them down for a second, I realized it was of no use. So I plowed through to the kitchen. I quickly grabbed a cup of coffee and headed for the patio. Once outside, I was finally relieved of my escort as they shot off into the yard. It was down to business for them now as they took off on their morning patrol.

I stood for a second just enjoying the morning, I took in a deep breath. *Nature always replenishes herself during the night.* I thought that most mornings, but this morning was a little different. This morning just seemed a little nicer. Nature had outdone herself today. I sat down and leaned back in my chair, ready to enjoy the start of this new day. As I sat there, I let my mind run through the last few days, but only lightly, ending with Bill and me sitting in this exact spot last night. Bill had left early, around nine. Both of us had full days today. Both of us had to get ready to resume normal lives.

Normal life: I was just wondering about that when the dogs pulled me out of my thoughts. They had found something that wasn't supposed to be in their domain. They were running across the yard to confront it. I looked into the yard attempting to see what it was they might be after. I had done this a thousand times, and a thousand times I had failed, never being able to see what had aroused their interest in the dim light. This morning was different.

As I focused into the yard, it seemed to lighten before me. It was as if a full moon had risen in the sky and lit the entire yard. I could see a flash moving toward the fence, the dogs trailing behind, closing in fast. Then I could see it clearly. It was a small fox. Fortunately he had made the fence and in a single bound was clear of his pursuers. The sight of a fox was not that unusual. Living in the country, I've seen them on several occasions. What was unusual was seeing one in the dead of night. I looked to the sky thinking possibly the moon had been behind clouds and come out in time to light up the chase.

There was no moon. *No moon!* I thought, *but I can see so clear*. I remembered the conversation I'd had with Ari about seeing in the capsule. I remember Ari had said you can adjust your vision; you just have to focus. I thought about that for a moment as I watched the dogs. They were just returning to my chair and seemed quite satisfied with themselves this morning. After all they had driven off the intruder.

This time it was just a poor fox, whose only mistake was crossing though their domain. The excitement was over. It was going to be a good day. I let my vision return to normal. I was missing the silhouettes of the trees and just the hint of glitter of the pool. *Super vision has its drawbacks* I thought amusingly.

Soon enough, the day had started. It wasn't long before I had my morning chores done and had started off to work. As I drove down the street, everything seemed to be just a little sweeter. We were so close to losing so much and I, at least for now, could appreciate what we have. I had seen Earth from a whole new perspective while in the shuttle. *If only everyone could maybe…* I let the thought go. Knowing I couldn't change the world, I decided instead to play with this new ability of seeing in the dark. As I focused in, the world around me brightened. Not a glaring or painful brightening, it was more like a full moon was lighting the night.

I looked at the car beside me. I could see the woman at the wheel. I could see her as clearly as if it were the middle of the day. I could also see her daughter sitting behind her in a baby seat. The little girl was looking my way. I couldn't help but notice the big smile on her face. The joy I saw in this little girl matched my own today. I thought *how lucky I am to be able to experience the joy that's usually only reserved for the very young.*

The Alien's Gift

I had been busy enjoying the sights my new vision was providing when the light changed. The car beside me pulled away as I sat lost in my thoughts. Finally the car behind me tapped on the horn, bringing me back to reality. I started to pull forward, my attention now back on the road in front of me. I could see the car with the mother and little girl. They were already four or five blocks ahead as I left the light.

When I first noticed the truck, it was coming down the side road. I could see it through the breaks in the trees as it sped toward our road. He wasn't going to stop! I knew it. I don't know how I knew. It was just one of those things you know. Maybe his speed was wrong. Maybe he wasn't aware of the stop sign, something told me. *The car, it was going to hit the car,* I thought. The speed and positions of the vehicles left little margin of doubt. They would collide. My mind screamed, out *Go lady*, hoping she would clear the intersection before the truck. She was going to make it.

It must have been at that point she saw the truck. I watched in horror as her brake lights came on. The vehicle broke hard. Now there was no doubt as to the pending crash. I've heard this called the deer in the headlight syndrome. Sometimes drivers will slam on the brakes in a pending accident when if they had only accelerated they could have averted it. This was one of those times. If only she would step on the gas. I watched as the truck raced toward her. I could still see that smile, the face of the little girl in the back seat, so young, too young.

"No," I yelled, "not today. This can't happen today. *NO.*"

As I screamed out with my mind and pushed, I watched the tires on her car smoke as the car lurched forward. The brakes were still on. The wheels locked tight, still fighting back even as the car jerked ahead. The truck clipped the rear bumper as I watched. I saw the car weave slightly from the impact before the truck blocked my view.

"Be alright," I said out loud as I accelerated towards them.

The truck clear, I could see the car again it was fine, only having swerved slightly from the glancing blow. She was slowing and pulling to the side of the road. I pulled in behind her. When I got to the car, the window was up. I tapped on the glass, asking if they were okay. It took her a moment before she rolled down the window. I could see her hands were shaking, but she seemed alright. I looked to the back seat, the little girl looking back at me. She was still smiling.

That little smile calmed me. She was alright and she knew it. Adults get stuck in the "what could have happened" world. Children on the other hand live in the world as it is. I turned my attention back to her mother, using the new perspective provided to me by that little smile. This time I didn't ask, I told her they were both okay, that it was over. She looked at me for the first

71

time. Tears welled up in her eyes. Tears of fear and relief drained from her body.

"They were both alright," she said, almost like it was a question.

I looked up to see the driver of the truck come running toward us. I could see he was still panicked by the near collision. Not wanting him to re-ignite her fears, I caught him before he got to the car.

I waited as the woman called her husband. The driver of the truck sat on the side of the road still needing to regain his composure. They had both just faced death, both looked it dead in the eye. I knew that feeling all too well after this week. I knew that now each was still wondering how they were saved from that event. No one really had an answer. We just had to be happy with the outcome. As I got back in my car I thought of that little smile again, happy in the thought it would be there tomorrow. I knew tomorrow would be a good day for all of them, the mother, the truck driver, and the father of that little smile. Now they would appreciate tomorrow just a bit better, too. A smile returned to my face as I continued on to work.

The rest of the drive was quite uneventful. Traffic was light, nothing to disturb the normal flow of my commute. My mind, having this respite, returned to the incident. *How did that truck miss?* Then I remembered seeing the brake lights come on, the car stopping directly in the path of the truck. My mind screaming out, then I saw the car pull forward. *But the brake lights were still on. I could see the tires smoking as they resisted the cars movement. Could I have?* I let the idea go.

That, my friend, is crazy even for your mind. I let my mind go back to the highway and the rest of my commute. I would have to make one more stop before I got to work. I wanted this day a little nicer for everyone.

I had gotten in early. I was eager to get back to a normal life. I went straight into my office. I got right to work, retrieving the messages that had been piling up on my desk and phone during my absence. There were several, and for the next thirty minutes I was lost in the task of catching up. I was so busy I didn't hear Cindy arrive, only knowing she was in when I heard her as she spotted the small gift I had left on her desk.

My stop was for a flower. Not a bouquet, nothing like that. Cindy and I were friends, nothing more. It was just a flower, one flower to brighten her day, one flower to say thank you for holding down the office while I was gone.

"Marc," she called out my name as she came through the door with the small vase in her hand. That smile told me it had worked. It was nothing really, only a way of saying I appreciated her. She knew what it was and started to tell me I didn't have to do that.

"I know," I said, watching her smile.

Another smile, I thought. *I'm going to like this new day.* We spent a few minutes talking, mostly her asking about my company. For those few minutes I was slightly uncomfortable. I hated not being able to be totally honest about the events of the last few days. But I couldn't tell her the truth for obvious reasons, with one exception, I did go to NASA.

The day was great. Everything was normal. No, everything was wonderful. I couldn't remember a better day. I had caught up on most of the business of the last few days. We even had a few border line contracts sent to us for final approval. I left the office feeling like a kid. On the way home I called Bill to see how he was doing. It seemed Bill had also rediscovered life.

Bill and I chatted awhile longer, neither of us ever mentioning the last few days, only today. I asked if he was up to a barbecue this weekend. Bill, never being one to turn down food, agreed immediately. We agreed on Saturday. I said I'd call Stan and Steven, and the deal was done. As soon as I hung up with Bill I called Stan and left a message on his voice mail, filling him in and asked him to call Steven.

As I hung up I thought *I'm going to need a lot of food for that crew.* As I mentioned before, the brothers are big boys, and Bill...well, let's just say he's never been known to push too hard against a table when there's barbecued food on it. Once again I had to smile. I was enjoying this new habit I seemed to be developing; smiling, that is.

The pups were there to greet me when I got home. For the next hour it was a battle for attention, each maneuvering to position inside the other. Their attention had been long overdue. I think even they seemed to smile today. After our re-union ritual ended, we headed for the kitchen. I was taking their food out when I thought one more smile.

I just might have time for one more smile today. Today had just seemed special. Today was going to be special for everyone. With that, I pulled out some cut beef and a package of smoked pork.

Smoked pork was like Ice cream to them both. *"Yup, special"* I had been right. I could tell by their response. I grabbed a drink and sat down to watch them enjoy their meal.

Another smile, I thought. *I did it.*

After dinner it was patio time. There we would enjoy the last of the day. The sun was low in the sky. The light cast a golden hue over the trees. The pups were running back and forth across the yard, each chasing the other in turn. *Practicing for the fox* I thought with amusement. I couldn't help but think once again about how perfect the day had been.

I was starting to think nothing could possibly make it better when I heard the doorbell. As I walked into the house I wondered who could possibly be here at this time. I live out in the country and didn't get a lot of visitors. The visitors I usually get are friends, knowing I'm on the patio most of the time, they just walk in. I had set that as protocol long ago. My house is your house. If you're here, just walk in.

As I approached the door I could see a man standing there. It was Ari! I almost jerked the door open. I had thought I would never see him again. This was more than a pleasant surprise. I greeted Ari as a long lost friend. I asked him to please come in, telling him I hadn't thought I would ever see him again. Going on about how happy I was for his visit, Ari greeted me with a big smile. I was rambling, going on a mile a minute, not giving him a chance to even say hi.

Finally catching myself or stopping to breathe, I let him get in a word. Ari thanked me for my warm greeting before going on to say he was here to make a request on behalf of a friend. Ari wanted to know if it would be alright if they came to vis, explaining that it was someone who really wanted to meet me. First I was struck with humor at the formality of his request. *You come from the other side of the universe and you're asking if it's alright to bring a guest.* Then without a second thought I said of course he could, anytime.

"If you're in the area, just walk right in," I said.

Ari went on to say that he would also appreciate if Bill, Stan, and Steven were able to attend at the same time. I told him they were coming over the next day for a cook out and that he and his guest were more than welcome to join us.

"Then tomorrow we shall meet," Ari said, thanked me, and left. *That quickly, he came all this way and only stayed a minute.*

As I walked back out to the patio the strangeness of it all made me laugh. First I had to calm the dogs. We had a visitor, and they didn't get to say hi. They hate when they can't say hi and let me know they were upset about it, too. I smiled as I took my seat again.

A visitor, I thought. *Who could he be bringing? Leni' maybe, but he didn't have to ask for her.* Well, tomorrow I would know. I decided to call Bill and let him know about Ari's visit. Bill was as happy to hear Ari came by as I had been. We spent the next thirty minutes speculating about who the guest could possibly be. Over the next hour I spoke to both Stan and Steven, letting them know about Ari's visit and about his special request. They confirmed they would be here.

Chapter 10

After my morning ritual the day really got started. I needed to run to the store. Now that, for me, was a real ritual. I had to get food for the cook out and now, with the added guests, that was more difficult than it might have been. *What do Rikiens eat?* I wondered as I walked through the aisles of the grocery store. I had gotten steaks, hamburgers, hot dogs, and all the things that went with it. Then I got tuna fish, egg salad, macaroni salad, and more vegetables than my house had ever seen.

The girl at the checkout counter kept looking at me. She knew me because I shopped here all the time. Till now she had never seen me buy anything more than the simple basics. What was before her now was half the store. I knew she wondered what had gotten into me or what I was doing. I had things on the counter unheard of, at least for me. Finally, after she looked up at me for the third time. I said, "Company." That seemed to satisfy her curiosity.

It was a little past eight when I got back to the house. Bill was already there. Stan and Steven were pulling in the driveway as I was opening the trunk. Everyone was as excited and as curious about the visitor as I. That was obvious. Well, my job would be a lot easier now that I had all this help. Everyone carried in something and still we went back for more. I had bought a lot.

Bill kept looking at me. *Just like the girl in the store,* I thought. Once in

75

and unpacked, they all kept staring at the spread before them, and then they would look back at me.

"What?" I said, "What would you make for a Rikien?"

That settled, we put everything away before going out to the patio, where we started speculating on who the guest Ari was bringing could be. I was pretty sure we had exhausted every possibility. We even invented a few more that weren't possible.

I went on to tell them about the day before, what a day it had been. I told them about the near accident, most of the time spent talking about that "little smile." I tried to convey how much strength I found in that little smile. The conversation went around the table. It turned out yesterday had been a great day for us all. Everyone had a day that was beyond good. As we all spoke, it had one common thread, the day was special. Life in itself had become a lot more special for each of us. By the time we had finished telling the details of the day and moved on to believing this day might just bring more, the morning had passed.

We were just starting to wonder when Ari and his guest might arrive when the patio door slid open. The sound caught us off guard. We all turned to look. Ari was standing in the doorway looking somewhat apologetic.

"You said just come right in." Even as he made the statement I could tell he wasn't quite sure if he had done the right thing or not.

Recovering from the surprise of the door opening, I stepped forward, quick to let him know he done just the right thing. As Ari moved out onto the patio, Lení came into view in the doorway behind him. If she needed any reassuring, the smile on my face let her know she was more than a welcome guest in my home. I was just about to greet her when a third figure appeared in the doorway.

This must be the guest Ari had asked about, I thought.

He was also Rikien, of that I had no doubt. Their race was, as I had said, angelic in beauty. That he was Rikien was unmistakable. Who was he? Why had Ari brought him here? Those were the questions still to be answered.

Ari started to introduce him, but stopped when the stranger raised his hand, his gesture imparting that he wished for Ari to announce us first. With that cue, Ari turned to introduce us. He announced each name with what seemed like great honor, taking his time to ensure he stated our names clearly. As he said our name we stepped forward. It seemed to be a formal introduction for them, and we acted in kind.

"Stan," Ari announced. Stan stepped forward. The stranger moved to position himself in front of Stan. With his hands placed palm up on his thighs, he bowed, lowering his head in a deep respectful bow. He was honoring and showing respect to Stan, of that there could have been no question.

The Alien's Gift

"Steven," Ari announced next. Steven stepping forward, again the stranger stepped forward to bow, repeating his gesture of respect.

"Bill." There was an added personal respect in Ari's voice as he announced Bill's name.

The stranger also detected it. He had been moving forward. Stopping now, he looked toward Ari for just a moment. He paused once again to look Bill in the eyes before completing the ceremony. Bill looked at me as he stepped back.

I thought, *if you're looking for an answer from me, you're wrong.*

Then my name was called. I stepped forward, my mind trying to figure out what this was all about. I was sure we were being honored. That seemed obvious from the start. The manner of how the introductions were being done left little doubt of that. It was also starting to look as though I was the focal point of this event. Why? I had done nothing except be the object of Gera's escape plan. I hadn't done anything. Bill, Stan, and Steven had been the heroes in my story. LenÍ had actually been the one to save the day. All I had done was… I really hadn't done a thing!

All these thoughts were running through my head as the stranger stepped in front of me. His eyes were now looking deep into mine. I felt like he was looking at my soul. I also felt a respect. I felt an honor coming from him, one that I felt I didn't deserve.

This was all a big mistake, I kept thinking, *and someone is going to be embarrassed once they figure it out.*

Even as that thought was running through my head the stanger bowed. This time Ari and LenÍ both followed in suit, both bowing as they stood behind and to the sides of the man in front of me. I looked at the guys. When they stood, Ari stepped forward. It was time for us to finally meet the man that has just shown us this honor. Ari stood tall, with his hand gesturing to the man standing before us. Then with the respect of someone introducing the President of the United States, Ari spoke."Gentlemen if I may introduce my friend" …Gera."

We all stepped back. I sat down before I fell down. To say shocked would be an understatement. I could have been knocked over with a feather was an accurate assumption. Gera, misunderstanding our reaction, stepped forward and was speaking to us. I hadn't realized it at first until I looked up and saw his lips moving. I focused in on his words as he was saying, "I didn't mean to intrude."

Realizing he was misinterpreting our reaction, I spoke up.

"No, please you're more than welcome in my home. It's indeed an honor."

With that came a flood of questions from us all, all asking at the same

77

time, all asking multiple questions one after another. Gera, stepping back slightly confused, looked toward Ari.

"They're an excitable and curious species," Ari said, smiling.

Ari reminded us neither he nor Gera was capable of answering multiple questions. At once we settled down. I asked the first question. "So, what do Rikiens eat?" It was my lame attempt to make everyone comfortable.

It only caused Gera to look at me in confusion. I realized he had no idea where that question came from, so pointing to the grill, I said, "For the barbecue." They looked to each other, then back to me. That broke the tension, and the cook out began. There would be time for questions, but first we needed to get to know each other.

"Do you guys eat meat?"

Well, I had to start somewhere. They were vegetarians...of course they were. Luckily I had gotten all kinds of those vegetable things. During dinner Lení kept asking the names of the different vegetables as she tasted them. I didn't know what they were most of the time. At other times I would call them by the wrong name. Bill, Stan, or Steven would correct me from time to time. Sometimes none of us would agree on the name. This seemed to amuse and confuse Lení at the same time.

"You don't know the names of your foods?" she asked.

True, I thought, I had just kind of grabbed stuff and had no idea what a lot of it was even called. I spoke up in a vain attempt to salvage some dignity.

"Ours is easy," I told her, "a couple of steaks for Stan and Steven, Bill and I were eating burgers."

I could tell by her laugh that I hadn't succeeded. We just sat around asking questions for the rest of the morning, Lení was gracious enough to avoid any more questions about food. The mood had become more casual. There was one thing I had really wondered about.

Looking at Gera, I asked, "How can you be here? Shouldn't you be in the capsule for three thousand years or something?"

"I was," Gera said with a smile.

His answer stopped me in mid chew. I looked at Ari. I was stunned and slightly confused.

"Correct me if I'm wrong, but didn't we just transfer him to a new capsule?"

Ari tried to explain. He spoke carefully, knowing what he was about to say wouldn't be understood easily. "Only a short time for you, Marc, It's been three thousand years for us."

He went on to explain they had visited us today not just from Rikiel, but from Rikiel's' future. Okay, I admit Rikiens' abilities really confused me most of the time. But I had to get this one straight.

The Alien's Gift

"You're saying you came from three thousand of our years into the future?"

"Yes."

Steven spoke up, "But you don't look a day older."

Ari's answer once more reminded us they were indeed aliens.

"Remember we're energy beings, much more than simple matter. We don't age, not in the way you do."

Lení realized we needed more information to understand.

"Gera, my father is a scientist. He's long believed that time travel was—is possible."

Gera spoke next, knowing the task was difficult. They were trying to help us understand the understandable.

"I had been working on the problem of time travel for centuries. I almost had the answer when I was hurt."

I could see that memory was painful for him. I listened as he continued to explain.

"I spent a great deal of time working on and indeed found the answer while I was in the pod. During the last few hundred years I had been able to rework the experiment in my mind."

He went on to explain that during the first experiment something had gone wrong. A power disturbance altered the energy field. That's what caused the damage to his pattern. Gera said that, once released from the pod, he resumed his experiments. He'd been correct about the power problem and its effect on the equipment. Once that was corrected they just had to test it.

"The experiment proved successful," Gera said with a smile.

"When did you first test it?" Bill asked.

"About three hours ago now, I would say."

"Today." The word exploded from my mouth.

"You mean this is your first attempt at time travel?"

My mind was reeling. *Today, and we're the first people they visit?*

"I—we are honored to be the first." I knew I was starting to ramble.

Gera stopped me.

"Marc, it is I who am honored. Not only did my friend, nodding toward Ari as he spoke, my daughter also told me of the service you did in helping me. You and your friends also are truly special, and it's a rare honor to meet such men."

His compliments were almost too much for us. Guys aren't good with things like this, unless of course it's pure bravado.

Bill spoke up in an effort to relieve our discomfort. "I told you a thousand times what a great guy I am. You didn't want to believe me. So now listen to him."

79

It worked. We were back in our comfort zone again. We started to smile. Gera, now starting to understand our species better, smiled with us. He looked at me and nodded.

Message sent, message received, thank you ran through my mind as we sat. I believe Gera heard me.

We sat and talked for several hours. Most of our questions had no answer, or the answers were something we really didn't understand. Wait! Ari had been here yesterday to arrange the meeting I wondered how that was possible if they hadn't actually traveled through time until today. Ari explained that he hadn't actually traveled through time yesterday. Yesterday they had sent a holographic image through time.

This was another aspect of Gera's experiments. The holographic image would respond exactly the same as a person would. This allowed for probes, it also allowing them to make adjustments to equipment, prior to actually going there. Surprise! Once again I was lost on exactly how it worked.

As the evening progressed, everyone broke off into groups, Rikiens included. *It's the same in all parties,* I thought. Like a good host, I made the rounds. Stan and Steven were sitting with Ari. They were discussing something about computer evolution on Rikiel. I stopped to listen. Ari was saying that in the past his race had interfaced with computers. It seemed they, the computers, were evolving technically faster than his race. Later as the Rikien evolved, they no longer needed that connection. They had once again surpassed the abilities of computers. Steven was transfixed on his every word. Stan was taking notes, *as always.* I just scratched my head and moved on.

LenÍ and Gera were talking, telling Bill they believed that humanity was on the same course of evolution as the Rikiens. They believed that we would one day evolve into beings of pure energy as they had long ago. I smiled as I sat down, their conversation too deep for me to just jump into, I just listened. Gera sat watching me for a minute, then engaged me in some philosophical questions. I was amazed at how often our opinions seemed to match. We were lost to our discussion for the better part of an hour.

The day turned into evening. I was putting the grill to bed when LenÍ walked over. She looked at me as if she didn't really believe what she was about to ask. I could see her trying to assimilate the information. She touched my arm. It was a touch of reverence, respect.

"My father would like the honor of a mind meld with you" she said.

I wasn't sure how to respond to her, not really understanding what she was asking. All I knew was I had been exchanging with Gera too much in the last couple of days and wasn't sure I wanted to do that again. She explained it wasn't like that. That was, exactly as I had stated, an exchange. This is a meld, the two minds join. I looked at her now somewhat embarrassed by what I was about to say.

"You don't mean like I did with you!"

She laughed. "No, that was two minds active in one body."

I was relieved to hear it wasn't that, but I was confused. That led me to ask the next question. "How many mind things do you people have?"

She smiled at that before she went on to explain in more detail. "The mind meld is the connection of two minds in common. It's a way of bonding. Rarely have I heard of it even being done on my planet. It's considered the highest of honors between two people. I've only known my father to do it once."

Her eyes went to Ari as she made that statement. Ari was indeed the one she was referring to. I looked at Gera standing on the other side of the patio, Ari standing with him. They were watching us as we spoke. I knew they were giving me my privacy while Lení explained the request.

"Why?" I asked. "Why me?"

"That's a question only my father could answer for you."

I walked over to the chair and sat, I had to think. *This was an honor—an honor I just don't deserve.*

Ari walked over and sat with me.

"You don't have to do this if you don't want to my friend."

I tried to explain to Ari what I was thinking. I didn't understand. Why should I deserve an honor like this? Ari's answer helped with my decision.

"You deserve this honor because Gera feels in his heart it would be an honor for him. For a man to respect another, that's not something that can be questioned." Ari paused for a second before he said. "You deserve it in my eyes because a man, one who can look for the best in another when he's seeing him at his worst, is truly an honorable man."

I was overwhelmed; this had to be a mistake, a big mistake. Ari could see the look of hesitation still in my eyes. I realize he was misunderstanding me. I told him my true fear.

"What if I do it wrong?"

Ari laughed. It was a loud laugh, the kind that forms from relief, from the release of tension.

Then he said, "You can't."

Standing, Ari motioned for Gera to come. His arms waved wildly in the air. His delight was undeniable. All conversations on the patio had stopped. Something was about to happen, that was obvious. Gera approached me, thanking me for giving him this honor. I told him I was humbled by his request, that the honor was indeed all mine. With that Gera placed his hands palm up on his thighs. Ari had told me to mimic his moves, so I did the same. As he leaned forward I followed suit, hoping I didn't knock his head and screw this up.

Ari and LenÍ moved till they were positioned at our sides. Then, placing their hands on our heads, they slowly touched our foreheads together. I had been standing on the patio surrounded by everyone at the party. Now I was alone with Gera. I knew Gera—I mean I knew Gera, like I knew no one else. I knew his essences. It was amazing, and he was amazing. The contact lasted just moments, seeming like minutes, hours, possibly only seconds. Time didn't seem to count. The exchange is something I won't go into. It was indeed an honor is the only thing I would say about it.

The night was getting late. Stan and Steven were the first to say good night. Gera again bowed as they were leaving. Then it was time for my Rikien friends to depart. I thought, *Hell, look at the time, and you got to get to the other end of the universe still tonight.* I shook Ari's hand realizing I may never see this Ari again. There usually isn't a lot of reason to go back three thousand years in time. LenÍ, I gave a big hug and re-introduced the good old fashion human kiss. Now Gera was special to me.

I had known Gera at his worst. Believe me, there couldn't be worse than what he'd been when we first encountered each other. To have spent the evening with the man I had met tonight had been an honor. The word used a lot during the evening already was an understatement in his case. As we said good night, probably goodbye, Gera stood straight, hands palm up on thighs bowed deeply at the waist.

Knowing it was something he had to do, I stood to receive this honor. As he stood, I carefully placed my hands palms upon my thighs as I had seen him do. Hoping my bow conveyed the same honor to him as his had to me, I bowed deeply at the waist. Standing, I looked him directly in the eyes. Tears had welled up in his eyes, and when he spoke it was with a tight voice.

"Three thousand years ago I encountered a true man. Tonight I had the honor of meeting a true friend."

I was deeply touched by his words. All I could say in response was "My friend." They were gone.

I looked to Bill after they left. He seemed to have something in his eye. Realizing I had the same problem, I walked into the other room for a moment before returning to the patio. Bill was just saying good night to the dogs as I got back outside. He looked up at me as I came out.

"You know your parties are going to be hard to top, my friend."

We laughed, and I promised to start toning it down a little in the future. Then we ended up sitting for a few minutes as we usually did after events of any sort. Bill never once asked about the mind melding. The few minutes turned into a few hours.

Chapter 11

The next morning as I sat on the patio drinking coffee, my thoughts turned to the shuttle. I had actually been on the shuttle. I had been in orbit around Earth, if only for a brief period. I decided to see how they were doing. Trying to find it on the news wasn't going to be that easy. One of the problems of mankind is boredom. When the shuttle was news, they had the interest of the world. After a few launches, we seemed to want more, and the shuttle coverage was reduced to almost nothing.

The news was busy keeping us up to date on the latest killing or movie star scandal. I wondered why we didn't get tired or bored with bad news. *Good news is bad, bad news is good. For the news media at least,* I thought, wondering again why we allowed it, the constant diet of negativity. Then I remembered the NASA channel. It was still available, for the few who still wanted to see how we were doing in space.

With a fresh cup of coffee, I sat watching the shuttle mission. I was in luck. They were live for a space walk. NASA isn't a glitter production by any stretch of the imagination. The visuals, however, are always spectacular. I watched the astronaut outside the shuttle.

Space walk, now there's something I haven't done yet. I kept thinking, I *sure would have liked to have done that.*

I was so intent on it I felt like I was looking through the helmet of the

83

space suit. I was staring at the shuttle just where the astronaut I had been watching was. I lifted my hand—there was a glove, part of the space suit.

Oh! I didn't, I couldn't, I don't know how—I did!

I focused and pulled back, I was back on the couch again. I sat for a moment trying to understand if I had actually just shifted with the astronaut or was it just me daydreaming. I looked up at the television; the astronaut was still on the screen.

Was there anything different? Surely he'll say something to mission control if it happened, I thought. *No, not while on a clear channel, he couldn't. What would he say?*

I looked around the room. Was there anything visible that would trace them to me? *What did I do? How could I explain this?* This can't be explained.

I called Bill. *Boy, is he going to get tired of me fast.* I heard Bill answer.

"We need to talk, and it has to be in person. I can't talk on the phone." Then I hung up. I knew he was going to think I was crazy, but I was afraid my phone would already be tapped. I just knew the government was coming, even as we spoke. Bill didn't question me at all. He just came over as fast as he could. We sat at the now way too familiar table. I told him what had happened, what I had done. I just didn't know how I did it. Maybe I was crazy and I just imagined it. Bill suggested we first see if it could really happen. Could I actually exchange or had I just imagined it?

"How do I do that without them possibly catching me?" I asked.

"Swap with me," Bill said.

"What?" I couldn't believe what I was hearing, mainly because, to me, the swap hadn't been a pleasant experience.

Bill went on to explain the only way we would know if I was truly able to do that was for me to try it again. The only way to do that safely was to exchange with him. He was right. But I couldn't help but think of my experiences with Gera earlier in the week I was uncomfortable doing that to my friend. Bill told me to relax, saying he would actually like to experience what it was like.

"You're the only one who had fun all week," he said sarcastically. Then said he felt he would be fine.

After more convincing, I conceded, it was the only way to know for sure. Bill went out to the patio, and I stayed in the kitchen. I watched him sit in the chair. As he leaned back to relax, I switched.

I was sitting in the chair on the patio. I turned and saw Bill now in my body, looking out the window. He sat up in the chair rather quickly once he realized we had switched.

Snickering to myself, I thought, *that's how it feels, Bill.*

Then to my surprise I heard, Wow! This is wild.

That wasn't my thought.

Bill, I thought.

Yeah, he answered me!

Now I was freaked and reached out and pulled, exchanging back into my own body. I was already on my way out the door even as I re-entered my body. Bill was heading toward me. Both of us were trying to speak at the same time. Each of us had just experienced more than either had expected. For Bill, it was the exchange. It was one thing to know about it and see it. It was quite another to experience it.

With me, well—we were communicating the same as if we were just talking in the same room. He had heard my thoughts and I his.

I realized this was a bigger event for Bill than for me, so I let him speak first. As I had expected, it was way different to experience than to see. Bill went on about looking out the window and seeing himself sitting on the chair. I had to admit it was strange to see your own body during the exchange. I hadn't had that experience before practicing with Lení. I was happy to hear it hadn't rattled him in a bad way. He had actually thought it was pretty cool. His statements were putting my concerns about possessing his body to rest. Bill hadn't felt that at all. He was prepared for that. He just hadn't thought about seeing himself sitting outside. Far from upset, he found it amusing.

"Oh! We could do some party tricks with this one."

I let him run down before I brought up the fact we were talking. That hadn't bothered Bill. He thought that happened all the time and wasn't surprised by it at all. I told him it didn't happen all the time. I had never had any real communications before that. I had only felt or sensed Gera's emotions as we passed. Until now, that is. Then I remembered Ari and the first time in the shuttle. But I still wasn't sure if he was actually talking or not. I was so nervous at the time, I just didn't know, I didn't even care. This was real.

Once we settled down, we turned back to the problem at hand. We proved I could do it, so I didn't imagine it. That would mean I had swapped with the astronaut and we had that problem.

It was real, I hadn't imagined it, I thought.

Bill and I discussed it for several hours, finally concluding there was nothing that could trace the event to me, at least nothing we could think of or see that might give away my identity.

Mission control would know something had happened. But without any real evidence it would remain a mystery. I only hoped they didn't think the astronaut had lost his mind and have him committed. Bill commented he might not push what happened too hard anyhow.

"They don't report it most of the time."

As I listened to Bill, I started to wonder. *Are the sightings real? Never believed it, but now... But the Rikien are on the other side of the universe and have never been here before.* I mentioned that to Bill.

"Yeah, but has anybody else?" he asked.

For the rest of the day we watched the NASA channel to see if anything unusual was happening. We watched to see if any changes were made in the flight plan, listened to see if there was anything extraordinary. Nothing seemed to have changed. We didn't know if there was any communiqué behind the scenes.

Bill gave Steven a call, just asking if he had heard or noticed anything about the shuttle trip this time. He didn't go into what had happened earlier, making it sound like just a follow up from the rescue. Steven always followed the shuttle missions closely. If anyone would notice a difference, it would be him. Bill and I knew that. He hadn't seen anything unusual, adding that they didn't seem to know anything about what had happened earlier in their flight. It has been a normal flight for all intents and purposes.

Normal, if only you knew, I thought.

Just to be sure, we sat watching the NASA channel for the rest of the evening. Finally the astronauts went to sleep and, with that, Bill said good night and headed home to get some sleep himself.

Bill called me when he got to the house. He was still amazed by the "Switch" as he was starting to call it.

"I want to try it from my house."

He wanted to see if I could switch at will or if it can only happen under stress. It was a good point, and I wasn't sure myself. We agreed to try. I told him to have a seat before I hung up the phone. I sat back and focused in on Bill. Sure he would be ready by now, I switched. I was sitting in Bill's living room. I hadn't been surprised at all, having expected to be able to for some reason. I heard Bill in my head.

"Damn, Marc."

"What? Are you alright?" I couldn't help but wonder what had caused that reaction.

"The pool. You could have told me you were in the pool."

I started to laugh. I had been sitting in the pool when we did the exchange. Bill hadn't expected the water. I switched back. I was still laughing when Bill called. He had planned to tell me off for not warning him, but when he heard me laughing he realized his complaint was going to fall on deaf ears. He decided to question what was happening instead.

"How are you able to do this?"

"Gera. Something happened with my contact with Gera."

I had been thinking about it since he had left. It was the only thing

I could think that might have done it. When I mind melded with Gera I somehow received some of the Rikien abilities. We discussed it for awhile, but didn't really know. We were speculating, finally deciding the answer wasn't going to be found tonight. We called it a day. What a day it had been.

The next day was a business day, and after my morning ritual with the pups, I headed out to work. For the most part the day was quiet. The only exception was the unusual amount of calls. Stan and Steven would call to talk about the cook out. I had to admit it was something that you just couldn't let go. Bill would call to talk about the "switch." Sometime during the day we agreed we were going to have to let Stan and Steven know about that. They had been through too much with me, us, to be left out of the latest news. We decided we would all go out to dinner that night so that Bill and I could tell them what had happened.

I got to the restaurant around seven. Stan and Steven had already arrived. We grabbed a booth and were discussing the cookout while we were waiting for Bill to arrive. Once he got there, the conversation started.

"Did you tell them about yesterday?" Bill asked as he sat down.

Stan and Steven looked at me. I hadn't told them anything about it yet. I'd been waiting until Bill arrived. I was planning on letting him tell the story. But now that he was here I could see he was still a little too excited. Not really wanting the entire restaurant to hear what happened, I decided I had better tell them instead.

I took a moment to collect my thoughts. Once again I was thinking, *how do I say this and have them not think I'm crazy?* Funny, even after all we had been through, my mind would still have thoughts like that. Once I started, I told them everything, going through it quickly. I tried to hit all the main points, deferring any questions till later. We agreed any detailed discussion should take place in a more private location. Highlights covered, the subject was then dropped till after dinner.

We went straight to Bill's house from the restaurant. He lived the closest, and the brothers weren't willing to wait much longer, they wanted details. Once we got there I told the story again, this time in detail. They weren't buying it. Both kept laughing and saying they wanted to see this switch Bill kept referring to. Both were pretty sure we were playing with them. How could we prove it? I wondered. Bill was more than ready to prove it and knew exactly how. He had said it would be a great party trick.

Bill got up and went into the other room. He made Steven come as a chaperone. Steven would make sure he wasn't cheating. I stayed in the living room with Stan. Then I had Stan write down a number on a piece of paper. After showing me the number, he folded up the paper and slid it into his back pocket out of sight. Once that was done, I signaled Bill and we switched. Now

I was standing in front of Steven in Bill's body. I told Steven the number that Stan had written on the paper. Then for further proof I told him Stan had put the paper in his right rear pocket. He went in to check with Stan. They were convinced.

The rest of the evening was spent discussing this latest twist to our lives. Steven planned on digging into the astronaut situation in detail. Nice thing about being a computer geek is the inside lines you're able to tap into for information. We agreed it would have to be discreet, making sure we only got information and didn't give away any in the process. I was still more than a little concerned. Had NASA discovered the switch with their astronaut? If they knew and discovered I was the source, I'd be in for more than I'd like. Stan agreed to work with Steven to see what they could find. Bill and I were going to explore more about what was going on with me. Just what abilities had I developed? That was something I had to learn and understand.

In Bill's words, "Let's find out just how much super power you've got there, Batman."

We decided that we'd meet again tomorrow right after work. By the time I got home that night it was pretty late, leaving me little time to play with the pups. I always hated when I lost that time. I decided it wasn't that late, so we played before getting ready for bed. I was just lying down when I looked at the big boy. He was sitting and staring at me. For a moment I thought, *I wonder what it would be like or if I could...*stopping the idea even before it could complete itself in my head. *Way too dangerous.*

Chapter 12

Over the next few days we met each evening at my house. The brothers had nothing to report on about the incident with the astronaut. That it would seem wasn't going to be let out of the tightest circles at NASA. Had the astronaut even mentioned it? I did have some good news, though. It was a Friday night, and I was happy to report I hadn't switched with anyone either on purpose or by mistake all week. Everything seemed to have returned to normal. I was happy about that. I had the ability to switch, but I seemed to be in control of it. A *cute party trick*, nothing more.

The television had been on as we were talking. I keep it on most of the time, more for background sound than anything. On the screen the news was showing a car chase taking place in California. The news helicopter was filming the chase just as they had a million times before.

Bill commented, "Somebody needs to stop that asshole before he kills someone."

I looked at the screen, watching the car as it swerved in and out of traffic, the police cars right behind him. I wondered, could I? I had done it before. I focused on the television for a minute.

I had switched and was looking out the window of the car. I looked down at the speedometer. This clown was doing a hundred and ten miles an hour. Then I realized I had switched without saying anything. This clown was sitting in my living room with my buddies, and they didn't know. I had to act fast. I reached for the keys and shut the car off. Then I threw the keys out the window, switching back as I did. I was sitting on my couch again. As we watched the television, the car slowed down. The driver kept sticking his head out the window. I knew what he was doing. He was looking for the keys. The news commentator was expressing his surprise and wonder at what had just taken place on the camera.

"How's that, Bill?" I said.

"What the hell just happened?" Bill asked.

The guys all turned to look at me before looking back to the television. We watched as the car rolled to a stop. The police were pulling the man from the driver's seat. He was bewildered, still not sure what had just happened. Suddenly I realized I liked this new ability. I was just about to say that, but I was no longer part of the conversation.

They were busy going over things that could be done. Discussing different ways I could be Batman. That was what Bill had called me earlier. Stan had his pad out again, writing notes. Steven wanted his computer, so he could research something. Amused by the scene I began to laugh. It was only then that they seemed to remember I was still in the room. I turned my attention back to the screen. The police were walking the suspect to their car. His head kept turning back to his own car. He was still trying to figure out what had happened.

"Yup, I'm going to like this ability," I said.

It had gotten pretty late. Shortly after the news, the guys left for the night. I was pretty sure nobody was going to get a lot of sleep. Not tonight, they wouldn't. They were still going over the "how could"," what ifs", and "can you" questions as they walked to their cars. Yeah! I was sure. They wouldn't get very much sleep tonight. Me, I planned on getting a great night's sleep. I headed for the bed where I fell into one of the best night's sleep I had had for a week. I woke early the next morning ready for the day. I headed out to the patio like any other morning.

The dogs were off as soon as I opened the door. I sat watching the night sky as I drank my coffee. I wasn't even tempted to focus my vision on the pups as they made their morning patrol. I was enjoying the morning as I had been for the last few years. The gift was great, that was true. But today I needed to enjoy this world. I was doing just that when I heard the door open. I turned and saw Bill coming out. He walked over, coffee in his hand, looked at me, said "Morning" and sat. For the next half hour we sat in silence.

It wasn't until we had both had a second cup of coffee that Bill finally spoke up. "Do you know you've got some kind of super power there?"

It was a question, but more of a statement. I was certainly aware of it. However, I have to admit the full nature of it hadn't really set in. For the moment I was still enjoying the satisfaction of stopping that mad man on the highway and hadn't really taken it any further than that. Bill's words were bringing it into perspective for me. I had been given an enormous gift. *How can I use it?* We were just starting to discuss it when the door slid open again. This time it was Stan and Steven who came walking out.

During the night they had come up with questions. Today we would try and figure out the answers. What was the limit of my ability? It seemed as if distance played little or no part. I had exchanged or "switched," as we called it, with the astronaut while in orbit. I believed I had to know the target location. I had to be able to visualize it in my mind. I had exchanged with Bill without seeing him, but I knew his surroundings and where he was located. The astronaut and the car chase I had been watching on the television. It was true that Gera had exchanged with me without any sort of information, at least as far as we knew. I had no idea how, though, and wasn't sure I was capable of doing that. Not yet anyhow.

Who could I even help with this ability? That still remained to be seen. Should I help? I think a one-on-one judgment call would have to be made at the time. I wasn't sure exactly how I could help a situation without knowing what it was. How would I even know who to help? That was the clincher. Obviously it would have to be a live event, and I would have to be aware of it. This put a damper on the enterprise. Unlike Batman, I had no light in the sky calling. There was no hi-tech system to monitor the world. No way of knowing the movements of the Joker, or any other villain. *Does it have to be a villain all the time?* I wondered.

The last couple seemed to be the most important limitations. I would have to know who, and where as it was happening to even have a chance of helping. They had all thought of that, while I had just slept. I felt maybe I was taking this for granted while they were working hard to help. Maybe it was what they had to do? Either way, they were ready when Bill had brought over a police scanner. Steven had gone online and set up a rotating monitoring system for world news events. The system was set up to flag anything that had the word "live" in the event. I would also need them if or when I could do something. My body would be in the hands of the person I switched with. It had to be protected. Restrained, *again I'd have to be restrained,* I thought, this time, however, for a better reason at least.

Stan was becoming a news junkie, watching the television news going from channel to channel. Everyone wanted to help. Everyone wanted to make a change in something that needed changing, and morale was high. Steven was the first to find something, a story about a man who was going to jump off a building in Texas. I needed more than that to switch.

Stan was going from channel to channel looking for a live feed. Bill's scanner was local, so that was no help. He and Stan were surfing the news stations for something, anything. Steven was busy doing a web search, trying to pull up a picture of the building online. He found it, but it wasn't enough for me to lock into. The news channels hadn't gotten on scene; I had no live feed. Then the news reported the man had jumped. We all sat there totally devastated. We didn't make it. We couldn't help. It was right there, but we didn't have enough. We didn't have enough information to help this poor lost soul, not this time.

We were determined to learn from this. We had to try and figure out a better way. There had to be something, something faster.

"A satellite feed, if only we could have tapped into the defense department's satellite," Stan said.

"How can we do that?" I asked.

"There are a few hackers in the world who could do it without being traced," Steven said, but he wasn't one of them.

"Do you know where we can find one?" Bill asked.

"Of course I do," Steven said and went out to his car. He came back in with a computer geek magazine. Inside was an article about one of the world's foremost computer geniuses.

"This is your guy," he said.

I was reading the article. This guy lived in New York. There wasn't enough information for me to switch, but enough to find him. *Then what?* I thought. *He isn't just going to tell us.* I could hear it now. I would just say, "Excuse me, but we need to tap into a government satellite. Can you help?" Then, of course, he would answer, "Hey, I know how to do that. Here, let me show you." Okay that wouldn't work. Well, first we had to find him, then we could figure that part out. I had his picture and I knew where he lived. It was a start.

I was going to try something new, something I hadn't done yet. But I needed to test something else first. I had communicated with Bill when we switched. Was it because we had switched or could I do telepathy? I walked out onto the patio and put Stan in my mind. Then I called to him mentally.

Stan, can you hear me? I felt confusion, then I heard Stan as clear as if he were standing beside me.

"*Who? What the hell...*" He was totally confused and getting nervous.

Stan, it's me, Marc. I'm talking to you with my mind, I communicated again.

"Was that you? Was that really you? Tell me I'm not going nuts," Stan asked as he came busting through the patio door.

"I'm sorry for doing it like that, but I had to see if I could." I was smiling even as I apologized.

Smiling because now I knew I could. Now I was ready. I had Steven pull up a satellite picture of the hacker's apartment building. I focused on it and reached with my mind. I didn't want to switch, I didn't attempt to switch. I just wanted to find him.

Him, what's his name? I didn't know. I pulled my mind back.

"Steven, what's his name? Real and hacker name both?"

Steven told me his name was Jason and his online nick is The LockMaster. I reached out again. Letting my mind explore, I was looking for his mind. I called his name out mentally. On the third try I felt something, a recognition. I had found a mind that was answering or at least responding to the name. I focused.

"Jason you're the lock master, I found you." I could feel his mind as I transmitted my thoughts, I could sense his fear. Good. I wanted the fear. I needed him to be afraid and confused.

Who are you? It was Jason's mind.

I had established communications. I knew I could take him if I needed to switch. I wouldn't unless I had to.

We want to know how you got in. I was vague. I wanted my message to be obscure at first. I didn't want to go for the information I needed, not until I was sure he wasn't going to mislead me.

Get in what, where? He asked.

He was nervous alright, but there was more, something deeper. I probed his mind.

They found me. They know I know. He tried to block the thoughts.

This man was really scared. They, whoever they were, really had him frightened.

I stored that information in the back of my head, something to look at another time. Now I had business to complete, and I wanted to make sure I finished before I lost the advantage. I went back to my question, hoping I didn't spook him so bad he would freeze up on me.

The defense satellites; how did you hack them without us knowing? I felt he would answer honestly. That wasn't what he feared. It wasn't what he held deep in his thoughts. He started to explain. I had him shaken, and he was telling all. The only problem was I had no idea what he was talking about. I had to stop him. I told him I wanted a print out of what he did. Now he was really confused. *Just do a print-out and put it on your desk,* I said. Then I pulled back.

The guys were all sitting around me as I opened my eyes. They were wondering what was happening, I had no doubt about that. I told Steven I could get him the codes, but they were going to have to prepare for a visitor, and he would be here for awhile. We set up a chair in the closet, got a hood

93

ready, and I sat down, I smiled at Bill and said see you in awhile. I let my mind reach back out to Jason.

Did you finish what I told you? I asked.

Yes.

With that word out of his mouth, I switched. I did it! I found someone I didn't know, in a place I couldn't see. I was in Jason's body, sitting in front of one the fanciest computer set ups I had ever seen. What I was looking for was still sitting on the printer, four pages of coding and whatever. None of it made sense to me. I hoped it did to Steven. I grabbed the papers and put them in an envelope. I would mail the letter to me in Florida. I still needed to get it mailed, so I went for a walk in New York. I found a post office and mailed the envelope. Now I only had one problem. I was so busy looking for the post office I got lost. I had no idea where this guy's apartment was. I was starting to get nervous when I realized I didn't need to know. All I had to do was switch, Jason knew the way. I was in my closet again asking Bill to remove the hood.

"Mission accomplished," I said as I looked at the guys. I went on to tell them how I'd gotten the papers from the printer, mailed them. I started laughing when I told them I had gotten lost.

"How did you find your way back to his apartment?" Bill asked.

"Easy," I said. "I didn't. Old Jason, "the lock master," found himself standing in the middle of the street someplace. I was sure he knew the way."

I told Steven the information he needed should arrive in a day or two. We were busy laughing over what must be going through Jason's mind, first sitting in the dark closet being restrained. Then he finds himself standing in the middle of the street. That's when I remembered about the fear I felt in him earlier. I didn't know who *they* were, but *they* scared him. It was a primal fear, not an "oh no fear." A fear that propelled him to do exactly what he was told and not to question anything that was happening to him fear. I felt a guilt for having renewed that fear.

We spent the rest of the day watching the news, along with monitoring the scanner and computer. This wasn't going to be as easy as we had hoped. The scanner didn't really have anything, a few accidents and simple calls. The computer brought up a few things, but again we were hampered by my inability of not being able to get lock in on anything fast enough. With Jason, I'd had over an hour to find him. Most situations didn't offer that kind of time. Last was the news, most of their stories were after the fact, again not allowing me to be of any assistance. We ended up spending most of our time discussing ways I might be able to use my new gift. I spent a lot of my time wondering what the downfalls of interfering might bring.

It's one thing to be ready to be a hero, another to have that ability. You really have to think seriously about what you're doing. People's lives are affected by your actions, and sometimes simple things aren't that simple. Was there a delay in reactions as I switched with the person? Could that delay somehow cause bystanders to get hurt? When I took over for the car driver, I had been prepared. I was watching the scene before hand and knew exactly what I was stepping into. Without live feed there would be a split second to orient myself and during that time I could cause a larger problem. We would have to watch and make these decisions on a one-to-one basis. The problem was they would have to be made fast.

It was getting late so we called it a night. Bill asked about someone staying with me, but since the switching was under my control, it really wasn't necessary. After they left, I went out to the patio with the pups. They ran off to do a final pass on their yard as I sat and thought about the day. I had a gift, one that could be used to help people, if only just a little. Along with it came a responsibility, the scope of which I had not yet started to comprehend.

Chapter 13

Everyone got to the house around seven the next morning. We were all anxious to put my new ability to use. Steven set up his computer, Stan started to scan the news channels. Bill and I got busy setting up the guest bedroom. We had decided trying to crowd into the closet would get real old real fast. In the guest room we hung blankets over the window to block out any light, pulled the chair out of the corner, and set it in the center of the room.

That allowed Stan and Steven better access if they had to restrain me. The chair was also much more comfortable than the folding chair we had in the closet. On the bed was a hood and wrist restraints in case they were needed. Once we had the room set up, we went out to see how the research team was doing.

Stan was the first to find something. The news was showing a man robbing a bank. He was caught inside the building and had six hostages. A swat team had surrounded the bank. It was a classic standoff. This one was perfect. I had time to work this out. I told the guys to plan on having company with this one. Then I explained my idea. It would take more than a minute or two to complete. I was watching the television, focusing on the bank the entire time I was talking. I had the bank image locked. I didn't have a face, so I would have to find him. Entering the wrong person wouldn't help. We decided to move to the guest room , and the wrist bindings were attached.

The Alien's Gift

Bill closed the door. We were ready. I reached out. Finding the bank was easy, but there were seven minds inside.

Which one is he? I thought. *This could take too long.*

I had to just pick one. I switched. I didn't have the bank robber. That would have been way too easy. I was in the bank, though, and now I had a face. I watched him walking around for a minute. He was nervous, too nervous. I could tell by his eyes he was on the edge. His hands were sweating. He kept swinging the gun around. The way he was pacing up and down, he was close to losing it. These people were in danger, and I knew it. I switched back to my body, returning the now totally confused hostage to theirs. I switched again.

I got him. I was standing now in the middle of the bank. Looking down, I could see I was holding a gun. The hostages were sitting on the floor in front of the counter. I walked over to them, careful not to point the gun in their direction, I didn't want any mistakes.

"Get out of here," I ordered.

They just looked at me, not sure they should move, not sure they wouldn't get shot if they attempted to. I knew from my short view this guy had been close to the edge, and they were all aware of it. I spoke calmly to reassure them, trying to get them to move.

"Please—go. I'm sorry for what I'm doing. I really don't want to hurt anybody."

Then I walked over close to the door, making sure I stayed out of the line of fire before I hollered, "Don't shoot I'm sending out the hostages."

I walked back over to the hostages and again instructed them to leave. This time they started to move, slowly, still not sure if they would get shot for even attempting it. The closer they got to the door, the faster they moved. I knew it was because the closer they got to safety, the more they were sure something might happen.

The first one there was a woman. She opened the door and hollered "Don't shoot" as she exited. The rest followed quickly. I had been unloading the gun as they were leaving. As the last hostage left, I walked to the door. I threw the gun out into the street as far as I could before I walked out. Now timing was everything, but I had gotten good at that. I stepped through the door, my arms behind my neck and switched.

Once I was back in the room, I let them know it was me. Stan removed my restraints, and we all moved to the television to see the finale to my plan. The robber, now back in his body, was totally confused. In the last ten minutes he went from standing in the bank to being tied up in the dark. Then a couple of minutes later he found himself standing outside the bank with his arms behind his head and police moving in on him from every direction. We watched as it unfolded before us on screen.

We watched again and again as the news showed the replay of the police taking him into custody. The look on his face was priceless. I wasn't sure if it was relief or not. After what had just happened to him, I believe jail would feel comfortable, for a while at least. The news moved on to the next story. This one was over, at least for now. I looked around the room. We had done it, made a difference. It felt pretty good.

It had gone off without a hitch. The hostages were released and the bank robber was captured unharmed. Everything went picture perfect. Bill told me the only thing the robber said while he was here was gibberish. He was saying the, who, what, when, where, why's and how's. I described what I had done, telling them about how I went about finding the robber. I had made the switch back and forth fairly quickly. They hadn't even been aware that I had switched twice. Finally we all took turns reliving our view of the robber and the surprised look on his face when he realized he'd surrendered. We were all feeling pretty good about ourselves and decided to go out to dinner as a reward. It had been a long day, and going out for a nice meal to celebrate was in order.

I arrived at the restaurant a little ahead of everyone else. Normally I would have just gone in, gotten a table, and waited for everyone inside. It was too nice a night for that. Besides, I was still feeling pretty great from the day. I decided to stroll around and enjoy the evening while I waited. I walked over to the end of the parking lot. There was a road or an alleyway that led between the buildings, probably for deliveries and trash pickup. I could see some men standing at the end of the alley talking, but I didn't really pay a lot of attention to them.

Bill came walking over, and we stood there chatting. We saw Stan and Steven pulling in and were just about to join them when I heard a man's voice cry out in fear. I turned back to look down the alley again. Three of the men seemed to be moving in on him. Stan and Steven had just walked up. We were four to their three and could have gone in to help, but I had a better idea.

I asked Stan and Steven to grab my arms and hold me tight. They looked at me strange for a moment, but then did as I asked. As soon as they got a good hold on me, I focused on the man in the rear of the group. He was closest to us. I said hold on tight and switched. I was in his body. I could feel the adrenaline still rushing though his system. I would put that to use. I looked around and found a board on the ground, picking it up as I approached the other two. They both had their backs to me, and why not, I had been their ally until a moment ago.

Unfortunately for them, their ally was now watching the entire event from my body. He could only watch as I hit one of his friends across the back with the board. I didn't hit him hard enough to cause serious damage, just enough to knock him down. The other guy turned, surprised as he saw his buddy go down. I hit him, putting him down, too. Then I dropped the board and backed up a step or two. I wanted to give them both time to recover and stand up.

I waited a moment, giving them time to realize they had been attacked by one of their own. I was waiting for just the right moment. I backed up again slowly, still watching, still waiting. I wanted just the right moment. Finally it came. They started to rush me. That was what I had been waiting for and switched. Safe in my own body again, I let Stan and Steven know that it was alright to let me go. We watched as they rushed the gentleman I had just borrowed. He was about to be assaulted by his two buddies, and having watched the whole thing in disbelief, he knew why. He started to run. We stepped out of the way as they passed us.

"My buddy looks like he can run pretty fast," I commented.

We were still laughing as we walked into the restaurant. Stan said dinner was on him. He hadn't had this much fun since high school.

During dinner we went over some of the events of late. We agreed the most fun had been the latest one in the alleyway. That one was priceless, and I got a high five from Steven. Bill hadn't stopped laughing since the guy started running, and Stan, well, he was buying dinner because of it. We went back to some of the earlier events.

We took turns telling and re-telling the stories, embellished them more every time they were retold. The stories were getting funnier every time they were retold, too. Every story, except for Jason's. Something was really going on there, a lot more then we knew. My mind kept teasing me about it but hadn't really locked in on what it was just yet. There was something in the details. Something I felt I would have to address. But for now we were waiting on the mail I had sent from him.

It was late. We were leaving for home when Steven approached me. He wanted to ask a question. I could tell by the way he was acting, but for some reason he was uncomfortable about asking it. He kept starting and stopping, never quite being able to get to the point. I spoke up, hoping to end my friend's discomfort.

"Steven, I owe you my life. Whatever it is you need, ask it, please."

Steven had been dating a girl named Carol for the last three years. Her brother was serving overseas, and they had just learned he'd been captured. Steven was trying to ask if there was any way I could help. He was feeling funny asking for something that was so personal. I let Steven know that personal things, especially my friends' personal things, were important. We would do everything we could for her brother. He thanked me. I told him to come over tomorrow. We would have to plan this out. I wanted to make sure this went right. It had to go right.

I gave Steven a call when I got home. We would need Carol's help. I wanted to emphasize she couldn't know I was involved, for obvious reasons. For starters, I needed to know where he was being held. Any information she had would help. I would have to plan on visiting this place once or twice. I had to know all I could about it, inside and out. Steven was sure that Carol would be getting a lot more information, and he would make certain she knew nothing about me.

Not that she would ever believe what I was about to do was possible, I thought.

I told Steven we'd start tomorrow. Before I hung up I wanted to make sure Steven knew how I felt about this.

"Steven, thank you for coming to me with this" was all I said. It was all I needed to say.

I spent the rest of the evening thinking through the problem. Steven had brought a complicated one to the table for sure. I found myself making a list.

I had to go into a war zone.

Learn my way around a prisoner of war camp.

Find some way of getting her brother out of the camp and in one piece.

Then we had to get out of the country.

All that, plus I didn't speak the language.

How was I going to pull this one off? I had to get this one right. This man needed our help. He was going to get our best, of that there was no doubt. But how I would pull this off? That was the problem. The next day we would begin. Tonight I needed sleep.

Steven came by early. He had the location that her brother was being held. He started by pulling up a picture of the camp on the computer. I didn't know you could just do that. It seems you can pull up a picture of anywhere in the world, if you have the coordinates. Steven had both them and a picture of Robert. I wasn't going to switch with Robert, not yet anyway. I wanted to focus on the camp. I would need someone else for that, someone who wasn't a prisoner. I was ready.

I reached out, my mind moved through the camp until I found someone. I could feel three minds. One was young, too young. The second guy was nervous, too nervous. The third I knew was my target as soon as I felt him, arrogant, self righteous, full of anger. I decided then I would use him when the time came. He wouldn't be challenged. When the time came I would use him to gain more information. I had found him, my inside man. But I needed to know more about this camp location first. I hadn't thought of that. Getting out was one thing, but then what? I need to know the area around this camp, where it was. I pulled back. I needed a lot more information before I tip toed around the camp itself.

When I opened my eyes, Steven wanted to know what had happened.

"Did you do anything?" he asked.

I told him I hadn't yet. I needed to know a lot more about the location. I wanted to learn all the details. Steven was on the computer before I finished speaking. What I needed to know he would find out. I needed to know the location of the camp and any means of transport that might be relevant. In less than a minute Steven had found some of the answers already. He said that the camp was near a train track. It was a good start. He continued looking for more. Steven would spend most of the day doing research. That was a place to begin before I bothered with the camp itself. I knew he was itching to get Robert out. I didn't blame him. I felt the same, maybe more after having touched the mind of that one guard. But we had to move carefully.

The next day at work I was ready to visit the camp. I told Cindy I was going to try and nap through lunch. That would give me the time I needed without being disturbed. I closed the door to my office and sat back in my chair. I went looking for the guard's mind. He was easy to find, I listened to his thoughts quietly for a moment to get a feel for what he might be doing.

He was at lunch with some of the other guards. I focused in on his vision. Most of the time was spent looking at a couple of guards. From time to time he would look up and across the yard. That was what I was hoping for. This was what I came after. I needed to get a feel of the camp. The camp was in a clearing. There was a tree line around fifty yards from the fence. They had kept the area around the fence clear. Still, that was close enough to give me the chance I needed.

I waited patiently, hoping the guard might go into the building Robert was being held in. I could find him on my own when the time came. But that would take time. We would have to move fast when we finally moved. I didn't have the luxury of strolling around the camp. I wanted to know the exact layout of the camp before I moved. Life is slow in a prison camp. Lunch lasted for well over an hour. I was about to give up. I was starting to be concerned about getting back to my office before I raised suspicion or Cindy came in to see if I was alright.

Finally we were moving. We were heading for one of the buildings by the gate. I didn't think Robert would be in there. The building was too close to the entrance. That would be too much to ask for when the time came. I was right. It was the barracks. I counted the cots as we walked across the room. He was headed for a small room on the far side. It was his room. He had the private room; I had lucked out. This guy was their leader. Now I realized why he was so arrogant to the others.

On the way I had counted five cots. That was a total of six men, counting him. I wanted more information, but I was out of time. I jumped back. Once in the office, I started to draw out a layout of what I had found. I worked on it till the end of the day, making sure I drew it as accurately as possible.

Everyone was already at the house when I got home. They had gotten there early. Coffee was made, and they were all sitting on the patio. The dogs came to greet me as I walked out. Sensing there was more going on than usual, they kept it brief and allowed me to sit and work on our plan. I was going to have to continue gathering details again tonight. I didn't plan on switching with the guard unless something went wrong at the camp. We planned for it anyhow. We got into place in the guest room, lighting and sound effects ready. If I had to switch, I wanted the guard as disorientated as possible. Everything in place, I went to the guard.

I was in luck. When I entered his mind he was in the hutch where they were keeping the prisoners. They had five prisoners in this building. I hadn't thought about that. I had been thinking about Robert, not realizing there might be more. Now I wondered if there were more in another building. I would have to find out. I wasn't leaving anyone, not if I could help it. Robert was in here; I had found him. Now all I needed to do was wait for this guard to leave. That way I would know which building we were in.

I didn't have to wait long. A moment later we were standing outside in the night air. The guard house was off to my right. I knew where this hutch was in the yard now. We were walking over to the next building. This was the only other location they could be keeping prisoners, if there were more. I already knew the fourth and last building. It was the mess hall.

As we entered the building it was dark. I waited as he lit the lantern. The light lit up the room—it was storage. That was a relief. Moving five prisoners was going to be tough enough. I had what I needed for now. I had to get back. It was time to make our final plan.

We needed to put this plan in place and fast, I thought as I pulled.

Once I got back we sat down at my drawing, where I quickly filled in the new buildings. Then we put together all the information we had. The guards, I had only seen a total of five each time I was there, counting the general or sergeant, whatever he was. We counted on there being six just to be safe.

The camp was in the middle of nowhere, which made sense. You don't have a prison camp in the middle of a downtown. The one good thing was the train. The tracks ran within a half mile of the camp. We were pretty sure the camp site had been picked for that exact reason. The train was close enough to allow them to move guards or prisoners as needed. It was also conveniently located for re-supplying the camp.

The next day I called into the office and told Cindy I wouldn't be in. I was thankful for the way things had gone at the office despite all the interruptions we'd had. We still had a great couple of weeks. With those new contracts in place taking time off didn't look out of place. Then I went out to check the mail. I had forgotten to the day before. The letter from Jason was there. I opened it immediately and started to look at what he'd sent. It meant nothing to me. I was totally lost in the scribble on the papers before me. Steven would know what to do with them.

I called Steven and told him about the letter. He said he would look at it tonight. First we would go after Robert. We had today to finish up my plan. Things had to go just right for this to work. I had five men to get out. That wasn't going to be as easy as one. Back here these guys were going to have their hands full, too. They would have the general to deal with, and I would be gone for awhile. I spent the rest of the day at the camp. Making sure I had the correct count on the guards. I watched how the other guards reacted to the general as I was with him. He scared them, and they didn't challenge his authority, ever. That would make this much easier.

Steven had said the train stopped each night at the camp zone. It would wait for ten minutes before it resumed. Getting out should be easy if my plan worked. Staying out—that was another question. Once we left the camp it would be a play it by ear thing.

That night Steven arrived first. Carol had been asking him a thousand questions, and he just didn't have any answers for her. I hoped tomorrow we would change that. I was as ready as I felt time would allow for. We would go tonight. I would have loved to plan another day or two, but I was worried about Robert and the others. From what little I had seen on my visits they weren't being treated well. I had to go while I knew they would still be able to travel.

Once everyone got to the house, I sat in the chair. Bill secured me knowing they would have a visitor. Once we were sure everything was ready, I jumped. Finding the guard in charge was lucky for me. I realized the reason was because of his mind. He was in charge, and the minds around him broadcast it. I entered into him, tuning in to see the camp and know if the time was right to move. He was heading to the building that held the prisoners. It was time. I switched thinking as I did. *Good luck, guys, he's all yours.*

As I entered his body I continued to walk. I couldn't help but feel the power of this body. His command was one of authority and strength, I knew that now. I was coming up to the guard at the door. I wondered how I would handle him as I approached. I decided I wouldn't. I didn't think the general here would. I walked past the guard without even giving him a glance.

Inside there was a second guard. I wasn't surprised by that, I knew he w0uld be there. There were two guards on the prisoners at all times. I walked straight up to the cell and, looking at the guard, I snapped my fingers and pointed to the lock. It worked. He responded immediately. Pulling his keys, he unlocked the cell without giving me a second look.

I had hoped this would happen. I couldn't speak the language and was counting on not being questioned, only obeyed. Pointing to the prisoners, I motioned for them to get out of the cell. They all stood and walked out of the cell. The guard kept his weapon on them as they moved into the hall. I had forgotten to pull my pistol. I reached for it quickly, reprimanding myself for the oversight. I had to be more careful. I motioned with my gun for everyone to move out into the yard. The guard outside was caught by surprise as we emerged. He recovered quickly once he saw me. Not sure what was going on, he took a position at the rear of the prisoners. Once he was in place, I started across the yard.

I was leading the group of prisoners straight toward the gate. When we arrived at the gate, I stopped. I stood there for a minute wondering how I would get past this obstacle. Then I remembered it had worked before; why not try it again. I turned to look back at one of the guards. I was waiting, and my look implied I was getting quite impatient. He broke from the rear of the ranks and rushed up to the gate. Removing his keys he looked at me for authorization. I nodded, and he started to unlock the gate. He looked at me a couple of times as he was opening the gate. He still wasn't sure. When I showed my impatience at his delay, he moved quicker. The gate was open, and I was starting to be happy about this general being a demigod.

Leading the group though the gate, I stopped once we all got outside. I motioned for one guard to go back. The other was to come with me and the prisoners. Again I could see the look of confusion on their face. But they never challenged my command. We headed toward the train tracks walking until I was sure we were out of sight of the camp before I stopped the group once again. I wanted to make sure we weren't being followed. I didn't think the general here would be challenged. But I looked just in case the guard might have gotten overly suspicious of my actions, and tried to follow.

Sure now that we were alone I continued to lead the group to the tracks. We waited there another ten minutes before the train finally arrived. The second guard, now adjusting to the situation, was watching over the seated prisoners. Once the train arrived I pulled my pistol out again and motioned for the guard to move the prisoners onto the train. He shuffled them rapidly to the designated car. I was amazed how well this was going.

The Alien's Gift

I couldn't believe I could get this far without having to take out the guard. We climbed into the car and once it was underway I hit the guard on the head from behind, knocking him out cold. Now I could finally speak. As I walked toward Robert, I said his name. It took him a moment to realize I was calling him by name. When I had taken out the guard, they had all gotten a lot more nervous not sure what was going on.

I told him I had been bribed by his government to help them escape. It was a lie, but one that they could believe. I pulled the keys from the guard's pocket and unlocked Robert. Then I passed him the keys and instructed him to unlock the others. Twenty minutes into the ride we jumped from the train. Everything was going perfectly, but we still had to cross five miles of unfriendly land to get to a neutral country. From here they would be the experts. Knowing that, I asked Robert if he felt they could make it on their own from here. I already knew they could. Robert confirmed my belief. It would be up to them from here. But I knew they would be fine now.

I told Robert to continue east until they crossed the river. At that point they should be safe. Then I asked him to shackle and gag me so that I could say I had been taken prisoner. I had hit the guard on the train from behind so the whole thing would look like an escape. They didn't know my real reasoning was to keep the general quiet while they escaped. Once they had me shackled to a tree and gagged, they took off. I watched until they were well out of sight. Then I waited another hour just to make sure before I switched.

I must say I never had anyone so happy to see me when I got back. It would seem the general wasn't a pleasant guest. I had twice the restraints on now as when I left. Once they un-shackled me we headed outside to share our stories. Now it was up to Robert and the rest. I felt pretty good about it, though. They would make it, I knew. It would be another couple of days before Steven came over to tell me Robert and the other prisoners were safe and on a flight back home. He started to say how thankful he was. I stopped him, explaining that I thought he was too big for me to kick his ass. But if he kept that up I would have to try. I asked him to give Carol and her brother my love and told him the conversation was over. He smiled and at the risk of getting his ass kicked said, "Thanks."

Chapter 14

We decided to take the rest of the week off. Time needed to regain our center. It would also give Steven the time he needed to decipher the papers from Jason. Mostly we caught up on work and social obligations. I wasn't seeing anyone special at the time, but the rest of the guys had girlfriends who had been patient with their extremely busy schedules for that last couple of weeks. Social time was in order. Social time was way overdue.

Saturday morning arrived, and we had to return to business. I woke early, having the morning to enjoy with the pups. Bill arrived first. *I think he likes my coffee.* Stan and Steven arrived shortly after, and the day began. Steven started the day off with bad news. The information we got from Jason was way beyond anything he could comprehend. Complicated even more by the fact that it would require a computer he only dreamed of to accomplish. What he was saying in so many words was, we needed Jason.

When I first dealt with Jason it was with an attitude of near distain. I hadn't liked Jason without even knowing him. I had a pre-conceived opinion about hackers. I felt they were arrogant, destructive people. The only thing they seem to do in life was disrupt the hard work of others for no other reason than to be rebellious. Even Jason's nick name seemed arrogant, *The Lock Master.* To me it seemed to say he thought he was above others and would show the world he counted. I always thought they were people who had wasted their abilities and were now only driven by jealousy. But the more I thought about Jason, the more I felt I was wrong. The mind I felt wasn't like that at all.

Jason was a man scared. Not a simple fear, something we might all experience. This fear was deep rooted. It was a fear of something beyond his control. A fear of something he knew, something he wished with all his heart he hadn't found out. I was going to have to approach Jason much differently this time if we were to get his help. Not only did we need his help, but I truly believed he needed ours as well. Together maybe we could combat his demon. I just hoped they wouldn't become our demons in the process. With that in mind I reached out to Jason. I found him in his apartment.

Jason, I called his name out softly, not wanting to unnerve him any more than having a voice in his head would already. He responded immediately. He seemed to be expecting me. I felt like he had anticipated my return. Only this time I could feel a sense of determination. He was willing to fight to the death to stop me.

But why? Why this reaction? True, I had scared him the last time, intimidated him, but never threatened his safety.

I spoke to his mind softly, carefully. I had to assure him I meant no harm. *Jason, I need to talk to you, I need your help.* I hoped in telling him that, he would sense vulnerability in me and listen.

Jason seemed to be expecting me, but he wasn't expecting that. It caught him by surprise. But he wasn't sure if he believed me, I could feel that. I could feel his distrust. There was also that fear...a deep fear. He feared for his life, but there was something more, what? He pushed it back in his mind, and it was deep. I wasn't sure. I thought I could find it if I probed deep enough into his thoughts, but I wouldn't do that. I wasn't going to invade his mind on that level. It seemed immoral to invade a person at so deep a level and whether I could do it or not was unimportant, I refused to try.

I would have to try and calm him and get him to understand. *How do you make someone understand that you're just another human who happens to be telepathic and have the ability to swap minds?* This wasn't going to be easy. Again I sent my thoughts, softly, gently.

Jason, I need your help. I have to get you to trust me.

He answered me carefully, cautiously.

What do you want from me? I never meant to...

He stopped, whatever it was he didn't want to say. I could tell he didn't know if he had already said more than I might know. He didn't want to add to his dilemma. Again I felt the primal fear rising in him. I had to calm him down.

I broke the connection briefly. Opening my eyes, I told the guys I planned on bringing Jason here. I also explained why. We had to show him we weren't some sort of alien force trying to invade his body. That in place, I went back to Jason.

Jason, I called out again with as calm a thought as I could.

When he answered, I told him I was going to switch with him. I explained what that was. Trying to explain to somebody when they open their eyes they will be in another body isn't easy. I didn't tell him our location, not yet, I didn't want him to have too much information about us, just in case this didn't work. He was nervous, very nervous. I talked to him more before I attempted the switch.

Jason, if you don't want me to, I won't. But I have to show you somehow that we need your help.

He agreed to let me. But I still felt he did it out of fear of something worse happening if he refused. For now at least it was a start. I switched.

I didn't let go of his mind during the switch. I needed to make sure everything was going as smooth as possible. This was the point of no return. If this didn't work, I wasn't sure how we could win him over. I knew now we needed him more than I had realized. He knows something—something I believed we had to know. Something we didn't want to know.

I couldn't see what he was seeing, I wasn't even sure I could do that without doing a full switch, but I figured by this time he had to be looking at the guys. I introduced him to them with my mind. They were ready for him. I had been sitting in the guest room. Stan had put away the restrains before I jumped. We wanted to make sure it didn't look like some sort of torture chamber or interrogation room. I felt his mind. He was apprehensive and surprised. I don't think he believed he would see humans when he opened his eyes. *Why?* I let the thought pass. At this point there was too much at stake to deviate from the present.

I explained to Jason that Bill, Stan, and Steven were exactly the same as he was. I was the only one who had the ability to switch and the gift of telepathy. I explained that I wished I could have been there personally to meet him and explain why we needed him, but that was obviously impossible under these conditions. I then left his mind, giving him time to talk to the guys. It was in their hands now. They would have to win his trust.

I spent the next hour looking at computer stuff out of the movies. *This guy is really into computers*, I thought. I had never seen anything like this. He had more screens and cables, cables that were everywhere, miles of them it seemed. There wasn't much else to do while I waited. I didn't want to touch anything. I was afraid if I did I might set off a chain reaction that shut down the city or something. *Still have that hacker mentality going, Marc. If you want him to trust you, trust him.* I caught myself, corrected myself.

The hour passed and I connected with Jason again. He seemed to be much

The Alien's Gift

more relaxed now. At least I hadn't scared him when I contacted him this time. The fear that he held deep was still there. It hadn't diminished in the slightest, but the fear of us, me, seemed to have subsided. There was something else. A new feeling, hope. He was hoping he had allies. I asked if he was ready to switch back. He was. I focused and switched. He was back in his apartment in New York. I was still in contact with him in his mind.

Jason, can I call you on the phone? I think you would be a little more comfortable speaking to me that way.

He said yes and started to give me the number. I stopped him. I had an hour to kill, and the only thing I had to do during that time was get his phone number. I started to break the connection, stopping at the last instant.

Oh! Jason, my name is Marc.

I know, he answered.

I broke the connection. I opened my eyes, everyone sitting around, not up on top of me as usual. They were all spread out in a more casual atmosphere. I was happy to see that. I asked how things had gone on this side. I already felt they had made headway. I could sense that from my contact with Jason in the end. Stan spoke up first. He told me at first it was a little touch and go. He reminded me that he and Steven are big guys, and at first Jason thought they might be there to control him. Bill put that to rest pretty fast. He told Jason that if it would make him more comfortable, he would kick the goons out.

Stan was laughing now. "I think our response to Bill was, 'what Jason needed to do was relax, not see you get your butt kicked.'"

Friendship shows fast in men, and Jason knew they were friends. Bill went on to explain that for the next thirty minutes or so they had answered questions.

"We answered every question he asked," Bill said, adding, "The only restriction we put on questions was personal information. We explained we couldn't do that for obvious reasons, not yet, but hoped we could all be friends in the near future."

Steven finished, adding only "Then we explained why we needed his help."

"Okay," I said, "looks like I have a call to make."

I still needed to take one last precaution first. I jumped into the car and ran over to the drug store to get a portable phone, the type you pre-pay. Jason wasn't one of us yet, and I couldn't take the chance of him knowing exactly who or where we were. Returning to the house, I made the call. I still wasn't totally comfortable. I kept thinking he could probably still trace the call somehow. The equipment in his apartment was imposing, and I had no idea what his capabilities were. I only knew they were impressive.

The phone only rang once before he answered.

109

"Jason?" I said his name to make sure I dialed correctly.

"Marc?"

He answered to confirm it was indeed me he was speaking to. *We were both being overly cautious*, I thought. *That's good.* Once our identities were confirmed, we started to talk. We were both very careful not to discuss anything of substance. We both believed the conversation might not be as private as we would like. The main purpose of the call was for him to hear my voice and get a better feel for me as a person and not just a voice in his head. We spoke for a few minutes. The conversation was quite mundane, a conversation any two friends might have just checking in on each other.

I ended with "I'll be in touch. Are you going to be around later?"

His response was what I hoped for.

"Anytime. I'm always here when you need me."

We hung up. I contacted Jason as soon as the phone clicked.

Jason, it's Marc. Can we talk? I tickled myself as I thought. *Marc, I just told him who I was. Who else would be inside his head*?

Jason was feeling much more comfortable with me now. The caution we'd been showing and the way I had been so casual on the phone must have made him believe we were also concerned about someone listening who shouldn't be. The one thing I really knew from the conversation was that we needed him here. I didn't know how we could do that. Jason's actions led me to believe he was being watched closely. How can you move a mountain of computers and him without drawing massive attention?

Once more, luck was on our side. I hadn't thought about the fact that computer geeks, hackers of his stature made a lot of money. Jason was famous in the computer world. I should have realized it from Steven. Steven had known about him. Hell he had shown me a picture in the magazine. Jason had built a company during the boom and sold it for billions. Billions he had billions, I had tapped into a billionaires mind. Anyway, it seemed that Jason owned a home in Florida, a much nicer home than any of ours, I was betting. He agreed to fly down and contact me when he got here.

For Jason to give us his personal information wasn't really a threat to him. Anybody could, and most geeks probably did know where he lived. He was rich and famous. I gave him the number of the portable phone I bought, suggesting he get one himself. I thanked him for meeting with us and told him I looked forward to meeting him in person soon.

When I pulled back, I filled the guys in on our conversation. Steven couldn't believe I didn't know who Jason was. Stan was also surprised, but then I thought, being an accountant, Stan would know about billionaires. I turned to Bill, my last chance at not looking like I was the only one in the room who was not aware of Jason's identity. Bill was an investment broker. *Okay, just me.* Now that this embarrassing moment was over, we could start making plans. We all knew we couldn't all just drive up to this mansion. If he was under surveillance, a car full of guys might draw a lot of attention. Everyone wanted to meet him it was true. Unfortunately we had to be discreet.

It was decided it would be me. Bill didn't like the idea of course, feeling I was too important to make the initial contact. I reminded him.

"I was the only one he hadn't met, I was the one in his head, I was the only one he wasn't really sure was a human—for obvious reasons."

It was agreed, I would make the contact. It had to be me. It was two days later when I got the call. I knew it was Jason. He was the only person who had this phone number. We talked for a few minutes and set up a meeting. I hung up, then called Cindy into my office. I started to tell her I'd be out the next day for a business meeting. When I mentioned Jason's name, she was all excited. She knew Jason. Everyone knew Jason. *I've got to get out more often*, I thought.

Cindy didn't ask about the details. We were a construction company, and meeting a client wasn't unusual. It would seem meeting a client with this much money, however, was an event. For Cindy it was that obvious. I called Bill to let him know about the meeting. We would get together at the house tonight and go over any last minute detail. This was going to be an important meeting, and I wanted to make sure Jason was on our side.

The next morning I was up early as usual. Coffee in hand we, the pups and I, moved to the patio. The pups being unaware of how important this day could be just ran off into the yard for their morning patrol like any other day. *I guess they don't know who Jason is either*, the thought made me smile. I watched the pups as they patrolled. It was nice to have something that was stable in my life. The rest of my morning was the same as any other, the only change coming when I got on the turnpike. I was going south instead of north. Two hours later I was driving down Jason's road. I listened as the GPS told me every little turn I needed to make.

"You have arrived. Destination on the right."

I pulled up to the gate and pressed the call box. I heard Jason's voice and announced myself. The gate swung open. I have to admit I'm not impressed easily, but this place was something. Jason lived in a community of five acre lots. He owned four combining lots, giving him a total area of twenty acres completely enclosed by a fence with security cameras, I assumed plural, having seen two on the gate.

The house was set deep on the property, out of view until you drove around the bend in the driveway. It wasn't crazy large like something you see in the mansion magazines, maybe five thousand square feet, but comfortable looking. He might be rich but didn't seem lost in it. I felt I was going to like this man.

As I pulled up to the door, Jason came walking out to greet me.

This is it, I thought. *First impressions are always the best.*

When I got out of the car I was totally relieved. The minute I looked Jason in the eyes I knew we'd be friends. It's just something you know. Jason was about my age, in his mid thirties. He carried a natural smile. His greeting was warm, but there was also something else. *Hope, I keep getting that sensation from him,* I thought. Going into the house, we started the beginning of what was going to turn out to be a great friendship. Again it was just something I knew.

We talked till late in the day before going out to get something to eat. We didn't discuss anything of any importance, but rather spent the time learning more about each other instead. Not in the *so what do you do for a living way,* more of a *where do you come from, and what are you made of conversation.* We talked till late in the evening, and Jason invited me to stay. I told him I had already booked a room locally, explaining I had already planned on staying the night. Jason would have no part of that, as I was his guest. The conversation was closed.

The next morning I was up a little after four just as always. I went down to the kitchen to find coffee. Jason was standing there pouring a cup for himself. Jason looked up as I walked in. He was surprised to see me. I was just as surprised to see him. "Not a lot of people get up at four" he said.

"Best part of the day," I answered.

He agreed, then said something that won my heart. I had known the moment we met we would be friends, and now he proved it. Jason opened the door and said, "I usually start the day on the patio. The day is new."

I joined him in the celebration. We sat having coffee, commenting on the silhouettes of the trees in the sky and the way the pool water glittered in the light. I took a chance; I reached out to him with my mind.

Thank you, I thought, then adding *my friend.*

Jason only turned his head my way and nodded. A second later he turned back.

"How do you do that?"

I started to laugh, telling him it was a long story, but one he would learn about for sure. I still had secrets to keep and, when I just touched his mind, I knew so did he. We had become friends overnight for sure, but something in his head was too important to reveal just yet. I didn't mind. I still had my own secrets to keep.

We finished our coffee before we got into a serious conversation. Once we started, I explained to Jason in detail why I wanted to use the defense

The Alien's Gift

satellites. I didn't have a cloak and dagger adventure, no plot to overtake the world. It was just another tool to help find the people who needed help, trying to explain in the same breath that I didn't think I was the savior of the world, just that I had been given a gift.

I was almost embarrassed by my gift, not wanting to sound like I thought I was special. I didn't need to justify it to him. He understood, and he was more than willing to help. There was also that underlying thing. He needed help and, until he was ready to take me, all of us into, his confidence, I would have to wait to find out. For now we were just getting down to planning how to work together.

Later that day Jason blew me away with his proposal. I have to say right up front that I know the ability I have is enough to freak people out. Billionaires have the same power. They think on levels you and I don't even begin to comprehend. Jason was talking about the logistics of working together. His home was two hours south of mine. That was going to cause some problems.

We had discussed the pay-as-you-go phones. Jason was concerned about his residence being monitored. Wireless communication can be detected and monitored. Phones of any sort were a potential security breach. Then I made what I thought was a joke. I told Jason it was a shame the house next door wasn't for sale. I could just move in there. It was a joke, one made by a normal man, not a billionaire.

"That makes the next part of my plan easier," he said. "You can."

I played along with the joke for another second or two, telling him it was too close for a summer home. He wasn't smiling. I got serious explaining to Jason that I couldn't afford to buy something just like that and, besides, I had a business to run. Now it was Jason's turn to speak, and he came hard and fast. He was a lot like me, in this respect. He had thought this through and was ready with answers from any angle.

"I want to buy your business. With the money you make in profit you can buy the house next door. I know you can. I own it."

He said all that and never once smiled. He was serious.

"I can't sell my business," I told him, explaining that I had a lot of people who counted on me every day and, besides, why should he just buy my business and what would he even do with it?

"That's what I do," he said simply, almost like he was buying a pair of shoes. Jason explained his logic to me. "First, to do what you want to do with your power, you can't be trying to run a business."

He was right sooner or later I would run it into the ground through lack of attention. Jason said he bought successful businesses all the time; it wouldn't be unusual for him to buy mine. It would also allow us to work together without drawing any attention.

I was thinking about what he said. If I was getting into the helping people business, it would take time. But I hadn't planned on it being so involved I would start to lose time from my business. I could tell from the way Jason was talking he knew different. He still knew something I didn't know. Then my mind was playing with the idea of my pups having five acres to run in. It was one of those *I won the lotto* thoughts.

My thought was interrupted when Jason asked, "What is your company worth?"

His question caught me by surprise. "I don't know," I said honestly. I had a general idea how we were doing, but had never thought about selling, so didn't pay any attention to its overall worth.

"I'd have to ask Stan," I told him. "Stan is my accountant." I was still stunned, still not sure I wanted to sell.

Later that morning I called Bill and asked him to go by the house and grab the pups and come up to Jason's. He started to ask why and thought maybe not over the phone. I surprised him by answering his half answered question.

"Mr. Fin has made an offer on my business. I will need you, Stan and Steven to come up to work out some details. Mr. Fin was kind enough to open his home up to us and even insisted I bring up the dogs."

There, I'd said it out loud and on the phone. I had done it deliberately in case we were being monitored. If we were, I wanted a legitimate reason for everyone to be at Jason's. This conversation did that.

Bill stuttered for just a second, then, taking his cue from the *Mr. Fin,* I kept dropping, said, "Yes, sir, we can do that right away."

I don't call people Mr. anything unless it's strictly business, and Jason hadn't been business, at least not that kind of business. Bill knew there was more to it and not to question me on the phone.

By six that afternoon everyone had arrived. I was amazed at the good time they made. Each must have run out the door on the call. Stan and Steven had driven up together, and Bill came up with my pups. I owed him for that. Two hours in a car with those two was a trip. Jason and I met them all in the driveway, Jason welcoming them to his home. Me, I just wanted to see my pups. They jumped out of the van and came straight to me. Play time was play time, no matter where they were. Today, however, they didn't play long before realizing they were in new territory, ground they hadn't explored or scented, and off they went. I had just started to call them back, concerned that they might get lost.

Jason stopped me. "The whole place is fenced. They can't get into any trouble."

I wasn't too sure about the getting into trouble part, but then I wasn't sure they would even hear me if I called, so I let them run.

With that settled, we went into the house. Jason was kind enough to take Steven straight to his computer room. I had told him about Steven drooling over what I had described seeing in his New York apartment. I led Bill and Stan out to the patio. While we were waiting for Steven and Jason to return, I started telling them about Jason's offer. Telling Stan I would need him to run up some numbers, explaining that I still wasn't sure it was something I was willing to do, but I had promised Jason we would look at it, so I wanted to get that underway. Stan agreed and said it really wouldn't be that hard, and he could have the number in no time at all once he got on it.

I also let them know about Jasons offered to sell me the house next door. Bill looked around, commenting if it was anything like this, I would be crazy to pass it up. Then the reality hit. Bill and Stan were two of my best friends. I couldn't move and just drop my friends. This idea was crazy, and I was starting to feel that there was no way it would work, when Jason and Steven joined us.

Steven was going on like a school kid talking about the computer room. We really didn't understand half of what he was describing, but we could tell it was cool, at least to Steven it was. Jason was just smiling. He was also a computer geek, so he appreciated what Steven was going through. You tend to take things for granted after awhile, and it's nice to have it put back in perspective. Jason let Steven go on for almost thirty minutes before he interrupted him. He wanted to go into more details on his plan, parts he hadn't gone into with me yet. This part of his plan required their approval as well. He was about to show us billionaire thinking again. Not one to waste time, Jason started.

"Everyone is going to work up here."

I was stunned. We all were. Jason had laid it out short and sweet. We all need to be free to pursue this project, as he put it. He would buy my company, without raising any eyebrows. As for hiring Stan, my business was one of Stan's accounts. Jason used lots of accountants and actually having his own accounting office would help with all the businesses he owned. Steven was easy. Computers were still a major business for Jason. That left Bill, Bill was a financial advisor. Who could use a financial advisor more than a billionaire?

Quite simply he would hire everyone under their present vocations, and we'd all work on the project my gift had offered us. Everyone sat there speechless. This was a lot to grasp. Jason knew it and told us to think on it for a couple of days and in the meantime please be a guest of the house, take time to get to know each other and enjoy.

For the next few days that's just what we did, with work mixed in. Stan was getting the numbers together on my business. Steven became familiar with Jason's computer set up while Bill and I, well, Bill and I played some tennis, went swimming in the pool. We also borrowed Jason's golf cart and drove over to the house next door. It was vacant, and we had the run of it. Mostly we did what Jason suggested.

Chapter 15

It had been a few days since we arrived at Jason's. I promised Jason we'd get together this morning and give him an answer one way or the other before the end of the day. Then I went out to join the guys on the patio. Jason was going into town for something, giving us time to talk on our own. Stan started off the conversation.

"Marc, yours is the biggest decision, so let's start with you. Your business is worth ten million dollars on today's market."

"Dollars? Did you say ten million?" I was stunned. I had no idea. Hell, I lived well, but not that well.

Stan nodded before going on.

"Contracts, equity, buildings, other assets and accounts receivable, along with good will. Ten is a fair market price."

I was still somewhat shocked by the number. I turned to Bill as if to confirm what I'd just been told.

"If I do this, Bill, I'll need a financial advisor more than ever, you know that."

Bill said, "Well if you do it, I'm with you, you know that."

Steven didn't have to be talked into anything. This was a dream of a lifetime for him. We all turned to Stan. It was up to him now. Everything now rested on his decision. We would have all dropped out if Stan wasn't in.

"I guess if Jason likes the numbers, we're moving."

It was done. Stan would get with Jason when he got back and go over the numbers.

Jason got home soon after and he and Stan went in to his office to go over the offer. I decided not to attend the initial meeting. Frankly I was too embarrassed to attend. I was still having trouble believing the company was worth that much. An hour later they called me in. As I sat down, Stan started to speak.

"Marc, Jason doesn't like the deal."

I had to admit I wasn't surprised. I started to tell Jason I didn't mind at all and that I wasn't trying to take advantage of him or anything like that, when Stan interrupted me.

"Marc, what he didn't like was the number. He insists the price is twelve million. He also insists that you retain twenty-five percent of the company."

I almost fell out of my chair. It was too much. I looked at Jason.

"Stan had said it was only worth ten million. Did I just say ten million and the word only in the same sentence?"

Jason started to explain his offer to me.

"Good will comes with the owner, and I want you to remain the president and deal with any serious decisions that come up. The extra two million is so you can buy the house next door. You didn't think I was going to sell it cheap, did you?" He sat back and smiled. The deal was done, and any sane man knew that.

The next few days were filled with paperwork and moving. I went up to the office; I had some things that had to be taken care of and could only be done in person. Telling Cindy was going to be the hardest part. We went to lunch, and I told her about the buyout. Ray would be running the office, so it wasn't going to be a bunch of new people in the. Naturally it was a sad day for us. Cindy had been with me for a long time, and I was going to miss her. I would still be working with her, but not on a day to day basis. I picked up my personal belongings and as I walked out, I made her promise she and her husband would visit. I wasn't that far away.

Today we start on our new adventure, I was a little nervous. When I came in, everyone was in the computer room. Jason had added several television screens to a wall so that multiple sources could be monitored. A chair was put into a small zoned off area fitted with restraints for controlling my body when guests were visiting. This kept things out of view, while giving me a place close during a switch. Now all we needed was something to do. Bill had the first one. He was watching the news when he found a jumper, a man on a bridge. This one was important to me. We had lost the guy on the building, and I needed to save this one. I watched the screen for a moment before moving to the chair. I switched.

The Alien's Gift

· · · · · · · · · ·

I was on the bridge looking down at the water rushing under me. I almost fell when I looked down from vertigo. I turned to get down. *There were no police.* I hadn't realized when I jumped that the police hadn't had time to arrive. Only luck allowed the film crew to be there. They had been on the bridge for a dedication of some sort. I waited. I felt stupid standing there. I was also afraid of falling. I just couldn't get down before the police were here to detain me. If I did and switched back, he would just do it again, so I waited.

When the police got there I still had to wait. If I just got down and gave up, they would have thought this was just a prank to be on television. I had to convince them I needed help. How do I pull this off? I don't need help; well, only help getting out of here, off this bridge. I decided to let them sneak up and grab me while I was distracted. Finally they had me and, with that, I switched.

I looked like an idiot up there. Jason had recording equipment, and anytime I switched to a scene that was being covered, he would record it. This was one of those times, and I looked like an ass standing there. I kept looking around waiting for someone to come grab my dumb ass. Bill was amused. Jason pulled me to the side when it was over.

"Marc, that was incredible. You just saved that man's life. This is worth it all, just this alone."

I corrected him. "*We* just saved that man's life." It had been a joint effort and would always have to be.

The next thing we watched was a forest fire. A helicopter was flying over filming the scene. Through the smoke, the camera caught a glimpse of three people running up the hill, trying to escape the flames. What they didn't know was they were going the wrong way. They would be trapped. If only they could see what we saw. To the left was a break in the fire wall. It had been caused by a pond on the hillside. It was their salvation, but only if they knew and moved fast. The break was closing in on the sides rapidly.

I didn't switch, deciding instead to reach out with my mind. I found the man leading the group. His head was full of turmoil. He didn't know what to do; he just ran out of instinct, fear. I hollered out to him. I attempted to muffle my voice, wanting him to think it was someone calling out over the flames and not a voice in his head. It worked. He stopped and turned toward the pond. We watched as he pointed, calling to the others, and they ran. Seconds later the walls of flame closed in, and they were gone from view.

I searched with my mind and felt him. They were alright; they must have made the water. I still felt the fear, but it was somewhat under control now. It was more than two hours before the news reported that they had miraculously found the pond that saved them. The man told the story of a voice calling out to them, leading them to safety. The firefighters looked for the mystery person who had called out, but never found him. It had been a good day. I was going to like my new job.

Over the next few days we had stopped another car chase, helped a robbery suspect surrender and lose the keys to a bank robbery getaway car. We used the satellite only passively, monitoring a drug boat making a run through some chain islands to escape from the Coast Guard. They seemed to have lost their bearings and put the speed boat into the mangroves. Other than that, we had been using standard news broadcasts and police monitoring devices. Jason had watched us every step of the way, joining in from time to time, but mostly watching to see what my capabilities were. Or at least it seemed. I hadn't really thought about it other than wondering if he was trying to decide if he had gotten his money's worth.

We had called it a day and were all heading out to grab a bite to eat. Steven was staying. He wanted to keep working with the computer systems. He was rapidly becoming quite good with all the new systems he'd been exposed to. Jason was working with him hand in hand and was an excellent tutor. We were about to leave the restaurant when Steven arrived. He was looking pale, like he'd seen a ghost. Stan met him as he was walking to our table.

As they walked back toward us, Steven just kept shaking his head. He sat, called the waiter over, and ordered a drink, looking at us.

"You guys should get one, too."

From the look in his eyes we decided maybe he was right. The waiter left, and we took the opportunity to ask Steven what was wrong. All he would say is we need a drink, then we had to get back to the house to see Jason.

We sat in silence as we finished our drink. Steven didn't seem to want to say anything except Jason would explain. We headed back for the house. Stan drove Steven's car. He still looked a bit shaken, and Stan didn't want him to drive. Bill and I followed in my car. All the way home we were speculating on what it could have taken to spook Steven that much. After everything that had taken place in our lives, what could still cause that reaction was a mystery. By the time we all arrived at the house our curiosity was at its peak.

Jason was sitting in the living room when we got there. As I walked in I could see he was still trying to figure out how to explain whatever Steven had experienced. I could also sense he still wasn't sure how much he was willing to reveal. We sat waiting, giving him time to tell us at his own pace. Jason sat back in his chair and looked at each of us in turn. When he got to me, he stopped. Looking me straight in the eyes, he said, "First I don't want you to think I don't trust you. I wasn't sure at first I admit that, but after…" He paused collecting himself before he continued. "After…I wasn't sure if I wanted to expose you."

I looked at Steven. *What did you see?* I wondered.

Steven was sitting with his head down, still trying to put together in his mind whatever he had learned.

What could Jason expose us to? That we haven't already been exposed to?

We had been with him for more than a couple of weeks already. I realized he had bought my business mostly to have a valid reason for us being here. If he had decided not to trust us, he could have just dismissed us as he would any other business arrangement, and no one would be the wiser. It would have cost him tens of millions, but billionaires spend more than that on boats. At the same time it looked like just a business to anyone watching.

Jason asked us to follow him to the computer room. Inside, he sat down and started working the keys till an image from space was on the screen. He had tapped into a defense satellite. We knew that, having seen the image on several occasions.

"This is what Steven was looking at earlier," he told us.

I had to admit I was confused. *Why would an image from the defense satellite bother Steven?* But Jason wasn't finished; he reached up and turned a dial on one of the connected machines. As he did, the image started to alter and several craft came into view.

Jason waited, giving us time to absorb what we were now seeing on the screen. Several craft were moving around coming and going as if on a business commute. After a moment Jason continued. "This is what Steven saw while we were working."

I looked at Steven as Jason continued.

"When he first saw the craft, the image caught him off guard."

"They're everywhere" was all Steven could say.

Jason turned off the screen before leading us back into the living room. I went for a drink. Steven had been right when he said we needed one.

This was patio thinking, and I headed that way. I do some of my best thinking on the patio. Walking outside, I called my pups. They came running to greet me. Jason had allowed me to keep a gate between our homes open, allowing the dogs the run of both properties. Right now I was thankful for that, I needed my pups close. We were into something big. I wasn't sure what it was, but whatever it was, it was big. Bill came walking out to the patio and sat down beside me. He looked at me for a minute before he spoke. "Adventure seems to find us."

I wasn't sure for a moment if he was upset or not, until I looked at him. The smile was big. Whatever this was, we were in it now, and we knew it. Stan and Steven walked out, each with a drink in their hand, both still trying to process what we had seen. When they sat down, they looked like they had the weight of the world on them. Jason was the last to join us.

121

As Jason started to speak, he didn't look up. He wasn't sure how to explain. He felt guilty for not telling us about what he had found.

"I'm sorry I got you all involved in this."

This conversation was way too familiar to me. The emotions he was going through I knew too well. I had felt the same ones when I first got the guys involved with Gera. My heart was with him.

"Jason," I interrupted him, "you didn't cause this, and you didn't get us involved in it. We did."

Then Bill, the master at breaking a tense moment chimed in. "What, did you think we haven't done this before or something?"

Bill's words started us all laughing, all except Jason. He didn't understand, but then we hadn't told him everything yet either.

I went over to the coffee cart. Rolling it up, I started a fresh pot before turning to the table.

"Well, let's get to work," I said.

Jason started, filling us in on the missing pieces. It would seem, or at least he suspected, our world was being sold a piece at a time. This didn't make sense to us. Why would anyone sell our planet? What good would it do them? What good would the money or power do if the planet was lost?

Jason explained how businesses had done things like that for decades, how they were willing to destroy the world's ecology a piece at a time and for nothing more than money. These people never have enough. They seem to have no concern for tomorrow. As if their money would buy them and their children a tomorrow. The game is played on multiple levels of power. This time it seemed as if the level was being played at the top. The pay off might be unclear; that it was happening was unmistakable to Jason. Was it real? The ships seemed to be. As for the rest, for now we could only listen.

Jason had been observing the process, trying to find out exactly what was going on. Then he'd find a way to expose them to the world. That was one of the reasons he'd been using the defense satellite. He had gone unnoticed until a short while ago.

"Something had happened during the shuttle flight," Jason said.

Until that point Jason had our interest, but now, with those words, he had our total attention. I looked at Bill. Jason caught the look, but continued.

"The shuttle left!"

His words carried his astonishment. He still didn't believe what he was saying could happen. He continued.

"It left, just for a second, then it was back. Don't ask, because I don't know," he said as if to suspend any questions before asked.

I didn't have a question; I had a thought. *It was when that happened, the space ships became visible, only for that instant.* I brought my attention back to Jason.

At that point Jason said security went on high. That's when they might have found someone on the satellite and started to trace the source. Jason wasn't sure if they had found him or not. Being an ex-hacker, his system was set up to echo and re-route though several routers to keep the source from being discovered. He had shut down rapidly once he thought the trace started. Normally he wouldn't have been too concerned, having faith in his own security systems. This being the government with the help of who knows what they are, he just wasn't sure.

I listened as Jason explained. Now I understood the sensations I received from him when I first contacted him. As he spoke it explained the fear I felt in him. I also understood his deep held secret. He was sure he was dealing with another race. We were all pretty sure of that. That made it an unknown power. He had felt he was caught and didn't know what his fate might be. I had inadvertently come at the least opportune time. I was also impressed. Even under those conditions, he had kept his balance. Not giving away any information. He held his secret until he found what they might know. I continued to listen to Jason as he finished telling his story, knowing that once he finished, we had our own confession to give. Our secret would answer some of his questions. The rest of the mystery we would work on together.

Jason was almost gleeful when I told him about Gera and my adventure with the shuttle. It had answered a lot of the questions that he felt might never be answered. First, it went a long way toward explaining my abilities. Which I am sure now were causing him considerable concern. He had to always be wondering if I might be part of what he witnessed flying around in our skies.

I hadn't realized until he said it, but only one time had he asked how I was able to do the things I do. That was only half-hearted. Now that I think of it, that was strange, not to ever ask again. He had also wondered what had happened when the shuttle literally disappeared from the sky for a moment. Jason's account of the shuttle had it missing for just a fraction of a second.

The hologram had worked; however, there had been a slight flicker, one that caught on camera showed it being actually gone for an instant. Now Jason wondered if NASA had noticed it and security was enhanced. Had he just caught a routine sweep of the system? Maybe they didn't know about someone looking. We had to continue, as if they did for our own safety. But maybe they didn't.

We had all shed our secrets. Free from those constraints, we were now able to focus our attention on them, whoever they were. Jason the most relieved, he no longer felt like he had to keep one eye over his shoulder. That gone, plus now that we were aware of the dangers involved, we were making the choice to stay. That released Jason from the strain and guilt he carried, from bringing us into harm's way.

Mostly he knew we were with him. He no longer had to face this adversary alone. I knew that feeling. I know that feeling well. His back was covered, our backs were covered. We had each other. I knew what that felt like already. Jason was just beginning to. We were a team, and we were committed. We didn't know how we could win, yet. We just knew we couldn't lose.

Chapter 16

We had been here before. We knew one of the first things we had to do was to separate what we think from what we know. First the aliens, capable of space flight with the technology to be invisible. Were they alien? Who were they working with, if in fact they were working with anyone? Were they working with the government? If they were human, the technology points toward the military. If they were aliens, they had a technology we didn't understand. We just didn't know.

What we did know was that they were powerful. Their presence, if know by others, was kept secret. They wanted something we felt we couldn't afford to give. That was it, all we had to go on so far. Not much when you have cloaked ships in space. We needed more information, a lot more, and recon was at the top of our list. That had already begun. Jason and Steven were doing things on the computer that I won't even try to explain.

Reconnoitering, that's what they were doing, I just didn't know how. While they did that, Stan was going to look for a money trail. He was looking to see if anyone was getting rich, and how they were doing it. I was going to do some searching myself in my own special way, using my mind as much as possible and switching only when needed. Bill was going to be my body guard, literally. He would have to guard my body, to keep me from getting hurt if I switched. He also had to make sure the person I switched with didn't find out any details about our operation.

125

The first thing I had to do was go to NASA. There was an astronaut there I needed to find. *Had he reported the incident?* I needed to find out. *If he had, what was the response?* If he didn't report it, I need to try and find out why. I asked Jason to locate him for me. It turned out he was quite easy to find. He was working with the flight crew for the next shuttle mission. Jason knew exactly where to find him. He brought up a picture of the building for me to study. I had a good place to start. I memorized the building, and I was ready. I sat in the chair, gave Bill a nod, and reached out. Once at the building, I searched until I felt his mind, then I sat back and listened to his thoughts. The closest I can describe the sensation is that it's almost like eavesdropping.

It was actually quite easy to do. There was only one problem. It wasn't working. I wasn't getting the information I needed. He was too busy working with the next crew on the mission. They were busy working on flight drills. Nothing in his mind dealt with the incident that happened while he was in space. I decided to try something new. I knew he was watching a monitor; I could feel the images flashing through his mind. *Can I manipulate his thoughts and make him see things?* I wondered.

I focused my mind. I was going to try to project an image into his head. I was attempting to change what he saw on the monitor. I kept projecting an image of him in space, with the shuttle in front of him. It was working. He was seeing the shuttle, reigniting the memory of the switch. Just as I had hoped, he was running though it in his mind. He had reported the incident. I could read that thought clearly in his mind now. He had filled out a complete incident report on it.

Nothing from anyone. No calls, no follow up. His thoughts came through so clear.

He was truly confused by the lack of any investigation. I had to wonder why myself. Did that mean the government knew and was trying to bury it? I would need to find out, if I could, but there were no answers here, so I pulled back.

I got back, and we broke for lunch. It was time for and update. It had been agreed earlier that we would have a debriefing every couple of hours. That way, if someone found something, even something that might seem insignificant to them, it could be brought up. It might just be the missing piece of someone else's puzzle.

I didn't have a lot to report. I told them what I had received from the astronaut's mind. He didn't seem to be involved in any cover-up. That meant the craft in space had to have avoided any contact with the shuttle. I believed NASA was unaware of them, at least NASA on his level. I had one other thing to report. It seemed I have the ability to modify someone's vision. To

The Alien's Gift

what extent was still unknown. I would need to test it further before I knew its full potential.

Jason was next, reporting that he had continued to look though NASA's computer banks after he had found my guy. His report seemed to confirm my assumption. Jason said he was unable to find any knowledge referencing the craft in their system. There had been nothing he could find in any of their classified communiqué that would even remotely suggest they were even aware of any alien craft. He had also run a program that performed a word sweep, screening any records that contained the words, craft, space craft and unidentified. None of the hits were even close to what we were looking for.

Stan had only just started on his search of money movements. It was still way too early to have anything to add at this point. Steven had been looking at major social events in the world to see if there was anything to investigate there.

"The world is so screwed up, it'll take time to see if any are significant to us," he said.

It didn't seem like much of a start, but in reality it wasn't that bad. True, we didn't find any smoking guns. All we had come up with was a lot of dead ends. But that in itself was information. We did go a long way toward eliminating NASA. They didn't seem to have any connections with the aliens. We weren't really sure they were aliens and not someone with technology we were unaware of. Bill had raised that point during the earlier meeting. We still had to find that out somehow. Proving or disproving it was a big part of our research.

"This job was just getting easier and easier," I said in an effort to maintain morale.

Lunch over, we headed back to work. Two hours into the afternoon session Stan came to us. He had found money. Not a lot, but the transfer seemed to be odd. It was a consistent flow of money. That was all he knew, and he needed some help looking. Steven picked it up from there and started a search for what might be happening. We all went back to our tasks while Steven looked deeper into it. It didn't take him long to find out what was happening and he called us together. He was laughing as he reported his findings.

"We found a little crook."

As Steven told it, this guy had found a loop hole in bank transfers. He was able to attach a transfer fee. The fee wasn't large enough to even register on the system. He was only extracting one hundredth of a percent each time, and only on small amounts. Over the thousands of transactions a day, the banking industry makes, it was turning into a nice cash flow for him.

We were working on a world problem, true, but we would make time for some down home justice. I asked if it was possible to get this guys address

127

and a picture. I wanted to pay him a visit. I would also need a little coaching on computers. Jason volunteered for that arduous task. Everyone else knew me too well.

Two hours and one break later they had gathered everything I needed. I was about to make a visit. I was also planning on making a withdrawal during the process. I sat in my chair; I was ready. Bill was going to hood me on this one. He wanted to be a bad guy and wanted this guy to be nervous. He said he'd tell me about it later.

Jason was sitting at his computer ready to go. We were going to utilize his particular talents on this one. Once everyone was ready, I switched. As soon as I took over his body I went straight to his computer and turned it on. While it was booting up I contacted Jason. Jason gave me the few key strokes he wanted me to enter, then took over. He really didn't need my help. He had told me that earlier. It was a nice way of saying I needed more than a little coaching before I was ready to play with computers.

It didn't take long for Jason to break his password and enter his bank accounts. This guy had over two hundred thousand dollars in there. *From fractions of a cent* I thought as I read the entries. Jason donated all but a thousand dollars of his balance to charity as I watched. We didn't want to leave him penniless. Okay, Jason didn't want to.

While Jason was working on his accounts, Bill and the brothers were working on our guest. They were playing a game. They didn't play federal agents or anything like that. No, they were the ever notorious bank police, "not ones you ever hear about." Not the kind who carry a badge. More like the kind, that isn't really happy with you, especially if you take their money.

They explained they weren't the type to ask the courts to handle it for them. He seemed to understand what they meant. As this play was happening, Jason was closing the loop hole in the banking program. He wouldn't be able to steal again. I kept thinking *Jason could have made a nice fee for fixing that one.* Once they were done, Jason said it was time to come home. I switched.

We had sidetracked a little, but it was good for morale, at this guy's expense, I might add. Bill was explaining how they played good guys and bad guys, as he termed it.

Explaining to him "it would not be a healthy thing for you, to be taking money anymore."

I might add, Bill has a bad accent. They were surprised my pants were still dry when I returned. I thanked them for that small favor.

Bill laughed, saying, "Don't thank us. We tried."

Stan said the guy never even realized what had happened to him. He was so scared he thought he was still home. He kept asking how we got in. When my turn came, I told them how I watched the balance on the screen change. I watched as Jason moved about one hundred and ninety nine thousand dollars to charity.

During all this time Jason never said a word. He just sat and smiled. For him it was something else. He had hacked again. He had re-entered a past he had tried to put away. It was bothering him a lot more than I realized.

"You did the right thing for the right reason," I said, hoping it would relieve some of his guilt.

His only response was a smile. I knew it was something he would have to work through on his own. We finished the night early. Tomorrow was another day, and we needed the most out of each day. We really didn't know how many we had.

The next morning I woke around four and went downstairs to the kitchen. There had been a lot of chances in my life. Stairs was one of them. I was thinking about that as I walked out onto the patio. That was probably why I was so started when I heard Bill's voice in the dark.

"I thought you'd sleep all day."

I almost jumped out of my skin. I had forgotten Bill was staying at my house until the realtor found something for him. Stan and Steven were staying at Jason's. He had room. Bill had decided to stay at my house, saying he was afraid I'd get lost in it. I was glad he did, I enjoyed his company. I sure had more than enough room, he was right about that. After my heart settled back down, we started to discuss the craft. Bill was wondering how much time we had before something happened. I couldn't answer that. I didn't even know what they were trying to do, never mind how fast they could get it done. None of us did.

We finished our coffee, jumped in the golf cart and headed across the yard to Jason's. The side gate was always left open, mostly for the dogs. I drove to the back by the pool. Jason was sitting on the patio when we arrived. Stan and Steven were still sleeping. Jason started to offer us a cup of coffee. He stopped in mid sentence as he watched us walk straight to the pot. I think it pleased him that we had gotten so much at home with him. As I sat down I started to tell Bill and Jason an idea I had that I wanted to run by them.

Bill knew me well, and when I wanted to run something by someone, it usually meant it's a big something. Jason seemed to pick up on that, too. They both leaned forward, listening intently to what I was about to say. It was a question more than a statement. I wanted to run it by them for their opinion.

"We all agree we need information, and fast. I have an idea, but I don't want to blow this whole thing."

The question was still there to be asked and Bill was getting impatient.

My voice was making him feel uneasy. He knew from the way I sounded this was a big question.

"I was thinking about the ship and its inhabitants. We could learn the quickest from them." I paused to sip my coffee and figure out how to word the question part of my statement.

Jason finished it for me. "You want to switch or try and read their minds."

He had finished my statement for me, only his voice had a *you're out of your mind* tone to it.

Stan and Steven joined us as I was trying to explain my idea. Realizing this was more than just a casual conversation, they sat at the table. Bill was happy to fill them in. The way he told it I wasn't referred to in the finest of light. I seem to remember the words "this ass" was used more than once. I pushed my point despite that show of confidence.

"How much time do we have?" I asked.

Jason countered with "They may be aliens. What if they know you're there?"

Good question, I had to admit. If they could trace me, we were lost, I couldn't argue that point. Bill jumped in right behind him.

"How do you know they aren't like the Rikien and better at mind stuff than you?"

Another good question. I thought about LenÍ, how Ari told me she countered Gera when he attacked her mind. If they were like the Rikien, they would ruin me in an instant. My answer was to the point and presented in an adult manner.

"Well, what else can we try?" *Now that was an intelligent retort*, I thought.

Childish as the question was, it caused us all to spend the next half hour thinking. Each man to himself, the answer wasn't easy and the consequences were big.

It was decided the answer could wait a couple more days. We really didn't know for sure if we had the time. To be honest we didn't even know what was going on yet. Maybe this was nothing; maybe they were just friendly visitors.

If so, why hadn't their presence been announced? Why didn't the world know we had visitors from space? Then again, Bill had said it again and again. "How do we know they're from space?" In the meantime we would try to learn more about them.

I asked Jason to use the satellite link so I could view them. I wanted to use a regular satellite and try and adjust my vision. That way we didn't trigger any response from the defense department. He agreed, believing there was no

The Alien's Gift

risk in trying. We headed to the computer room, and Jason set up a link for me. Now with the live feed on the screen, I focused and let my eyes scan the horizon looking for objects. I couldn't find anything and was about to give up when I got a glitter. I had it, but not quite. Now that I had an idea of its location, I adjusted until it became visible to me.

The craft was in a stationary orbit, allowing me a good view. It seemed to be about the size of a small stadium. There were no means of propulsion I could see. There were no windows. There was a glitter around the ship. I was trying to figure out what that might be. Then I realized it had to be a shield. The ship would be visible if not for that. I went back to looking for more details. There were no obvious openings anywhere on the hull. I had been speaking out loud the entire time, knowing that Stan had his pad and would be taking notes. This allowed me to keep looking without having to stop to contemplate things as I was going. We would have time to go over it later.

There was a smaller craft coming toward the larger ship. It had the same glimmer around the hull. It had to have the same sort of cloaking device. At its approach, the larger ship developed an opening, allowing the craft inside. Moments later an opening formed at another location on the craft. A craft the size of the one I had seen earlier departed. I tried to follow that ship as it descended toward earth but it quickly moved out of the range of the satellite camera.

I pulled my eyes from the screen, letting them refocus on the room. Jason was staring at me. His look was strange and aroused my curiosity.

"What?" I asked.

"I've still got to know how you do that." He said the words as a statement, not a question.

I turned to Stan. "Did you get it all?" That was a question.

Once he confirmed he had, I suggested a trip to the patio. I wanted to explore this information while it was still fresh in my mind. Everyone agreed, and we headed outside.

Sitting at the table, Stan pulled out his notes. We started to go through them point by point.

"First, the ship was the size of a stadium." He read from his list.

That would mean the chance of it being earth born wasn't as likely. It would be one thing to develop space ships in secret, another to develop one of that mass. It was however still in the realm of possibilities.

"Second, it had no openings until ships arrived, no indication of any openings for propulsion or viewing."

How it developed propulsion was out of my league. No one seemed to know how it moved. Steven added that to his research list. Having no windows, on the other hand, gave an indication of the inhabitants. Humans

131

are a visual race. Windows are in everything we ever developed; from the Luna Lander to the space shuttle, we've always had windows. Jason pointed out that monitors could achieve the same results. You would still be able to see and not have the vulnerabilities of windows. Again we put it back on the list for further study. We ran into the same problems with the cloaking, along with the strange openings appearing for the incoming craft. Craft were coming and going to a mother ship. Did that mean they didn't have a home base on earth? Or were they from earth and going to the mother ship for other reasons? Again we had another question that needed to be answered.

We went over all the information point by point with me adding any details I remembered. After compiling everything I had observed about the satellite, only one conclusion could be made. I had to go in. I stated my conclusion, and the table lit up with conversation. A conversation they seemed to have excluded me from. I felt as if I had disappeared.

Every point they discussed was negative. They were still against my attempt to visit the craft. All their objections, everything, seemed to be based around their concern for my welfare. The underlying scenario seemed to be my safety. I waited patiently until their passions died down before I spoke.

"All I've heard from this meeting is a concern for my safety. Gentlemen, I do appreciate the concern, I really do. However, what are the alternatives?" I sat waiting for their responses.

After five minutes of silence I went on.

"If there are no alternatives, and there doesn't seem to be, when do I?"

At that point I felt they needed to deal with the next phase of this mission on their own. I said good night and walked back to the house. I left the golf cart for Bill, for a couple of reasons. One, I really needed the walk, and two, it let him know I wanted him to stay and come up with the answer. I hadn't gotten ten feet from the patio before I was greeted by the pups. They made the walk home a great one. As we strolled across the yard the dogs ran ahead of me only to turn and rejoin me. We hadn't been on a walk together in awhile. The house came much too soon. I sat on the patio letting my mind return to the reality of this mission.

I had been all bravado during my speech, but my doubts where strong. I wasn't dealing with a human being; at least I truly didn't believe that I was. I was convinced they were alien. I wondered how strong they might be mentally. Would I be able to connect to their minds? Could I use their senses or even switch if that was needed? I didn't know and wasn't sure what my fate would be if I tried. My main concern was for the guys. I didn't mind me taking the risk; I did mind putting them in danger.

It was late by the time Bill got home. I had already gone to bed. It wasn't until the next morning I saw him. I was sitting on the patio as he came out.

The Alien's Gift

Bill greeted me with a simple morning as he sat. We sat and watched the dogs until their morning patrol took them too far to see. I remembered how I worried about that for the first few days I was here. The yard was large, and along with Jason's yard attached it meant their morning patrol consisted of twenty-five acres. They had assumed responsibility for it all with glee. I remembered thinking more than once they were lost, only to have them come running in thirty or forty minutes later.

Once they ran out of view Bill started to speak. I had been waiting for him to. I didn't want to influence or interfere with anything he had to say. He was truly concerned about the risk I was taking, but if it was something I believed I had to do, he was in. He wasn't afraid for himself. His fear was for me. We didn't know what, if anything could happen to my mind during the attempt. I knew that and realized once again what a good friend he was.

One down, three to go, I thought. Thinking at the same time, *do I really want to win this debate?*

After coffee we jumped in the cart and headed over to Jason's. The dogs joined us in route and raced along beside us. The morning seemed so serene, I wondered about the day. Jason, Steven, and Stan were sitting on the patio when we arrived. Has it been an early morning or a late night for them? Again I sat in silence, not wanting to lead or direct the conversation. Jason and Steven wanted one more shot before we went for my plan. Stan had agreed with them, thinking their idea was worth a try. I sat and listened to their new plan along with Bill. He was hearing this idea for the first time with me.

They wanted to pull all the stops. They wanted to track the earthbound ships all the way to their destination. It would require they use multiple satellites, all they could, including the defense department satellite. I expressed my concern about the exposure. I was worried it might bring the world down on us. Jason put that concern to rest quickly. They felt his system was capable of shielding any attempt at tracking.

He and Steven had stayed up most of the night building a relay system that would run the signal halfway around the world and back twice before getting to us. In that time we could track the ship all the way down and still break connection before being found. Then he reminded me, even if we were found, we'd be in no worse off a position than my plan had offered. I had to agree, and the decision to give it a try was unanimous.

After breakfast we went to the computer room. Jason began by running me through the procedure. I would be a critical part in the operation. Jason could adjust the image on one of the servers, but not all of them. That would be up to me and my gift. We were going to use multiple receivers if we were to insure tracking the ship to its destination. That meant I would have to watch the monitors. I was the only one who could actually see the craft. I would also be directing Steven on satellite shifts to track it all the way to the ground.

Once I understood what I needed to do, we started to practice. Steven pulled up a satellite image. We were staying away from the defense department satellites for now. He centered in on an object in orbit, then as I instructed him, he swapped satellites trying to follow it on screen. At first we weren't doing very well. Steven wasn't looking at the screen. He was making the adjustments using only my commands of up, down, left, and right. It was the only way to simulate the tracking.

During the real thing Steven wouldn't be able to see the craft. He would have to go by my instructions the entire time. It was a lot trickier than one might think. We practiced several hours before we were finally able to follow the object for a complete orbit. Our first success was celebrated by breaking for lunch.

During lunch it was decided we needed to practice a few more days. We couldn't practice constantly for fear of detection. Once we were on a military satellite we could only stay for thirty minutes. We didn't want to chance being detected. We were going to have to utilize them to complete the sequence. It couldn't be avoided. That meant there had to be a thirty minute shutdown between each attempt. We had to get it right, and with only one success to our credit, we weren't ready.

I suggested practice didn't have to be boring or keep us locked in the house. We could practice Steven's reactions to my commands outside. This drew looks of inquiry from everyone, especially Steven. I was looking out into the back yard when I got the idea. I thought it would be fun, and I wasn't the only kid in the room.

"We have a golf cart and acres to play in," I said.

The smiles went around the table instantly. I was right a room full of kids. Finishing lunch, Steven and I set off to practice. We knew this would only deal with two dimensions, but it was a start and a heck of a lot more fun. Jason and Bill said they would be back, leaving Stan alone to watch the fun.

We blindfolded Steven and started across the yard. We had taken the precaution of moving outside the pool area prior to starting, deciding up front we weren't ready for that much of a challenge. I could say we had a slow start, but I'm not sure you could call the speed the golf cart was moving as slow. It was somewhere a little below that.

Steven was unwilling to actually step on the pedal for more than a second before his own natural defense mechanism caused him to hit the brake. There were other times Stan accused Steven of peeking once or twice, to which Steven confessed. The blindfold wasn't perfect, but we were making some headway and were having fun. By the time Bill and Jason got back we were actually moving.

When they returned, the game took on a whole new level. Steven was about to lose his ability to cheat. They had gotten a real blindfold. They also had several poles and some rolls of ribbon. New rules were set. The poles would be placed out across the grounds in a course. We had to stay to the left of the green ribbon and to the right of the red. We would also be going up some small hills and down on others. This would allow Steven to be aware of the changes even if there were no actual control adjustments to be made. Steven and I returned to the patio as the poles were put in place. Neither of us was allowed to view the field as it was being laid out.

Stan returned to the patio announcing the course was ready. We got into the golf cart, and Steven's new improved peek proof blindfold was installed. Stan placed it over his eyes, with a great deal of glee, I might add. We started out toward the first flag. We were starting to get the hang of it. I was concise in my directions, not adding words to confuse the situation. Steven started to trust my commands and actually kept the cart moving, not fast, but we were improving.

The guys were running around the yard relocating the flags as we passed, increasing the difficulty level as we progressed. We were even negotiating hills, with me telling Steven as we approached "Up" and in some cases "Down." Soon even those changes presented no problems for him. We were starting to speed up. An hour later we had gotten so good Steven was racing through the course. I was extremely impressed with our progress, and his trust. The dogs had joined in the game at one point and, even with the interference caused by their barking, Steven stayed focused. He was maneuvering the field with confidence.

Bill and Stan were running around with the markers leading us to the back end of the property. Ahead I could see they had set the poles out guiding us up a hillside. I told Steven to turn right at the marker and up to make him aware of the incline. As we neared the peak I gave the down command, giving him fair warning of the change as we reached the top. That's when I saw the pond. I hadn't known there was a pond on the property until now.

"STOP!" I screamed, and for good measure, I rolled out of the cart.

When I screamed I startled Steven. He hit the throttle. As I rolled all I could hear were Bill and Stan laughing on the hillside. Steven came to a stop about three feet into the pond. The water wasn't deep. Actually it only came up to the seat cushion. But it was wet, cold, and a big surprise. Oh, and funny, did I mention funny?

Bill and Stan had decided to run back to the house without us for some unknown reason, leaving me to walk back with Steven. He was soaked from the waist down. I tried desperately not to laugh each time I looked at him. But then I would envision him in the pond. It was no use, I was laughing. It didn't take long for Steven to find his sense of humor, and on the second half of our walk we were both laughing. When they were sure Steven had finally found the humor in the situation, Bill and Stan came to pick us up in another cart.

Back at the house Steven went to shower and change, I went to the phone and called the golf cart people to come repair my cart. As I hung up the phone I thought, *I was right. That was fun.*

After a break we returned to practicing. We took Jason's cart this time, as mine was still imitating a boat. Bill and Stan promised to be good for the rest of the day. It didn't take long for Steven to regain his confidence, and we were following the tracks laid out at full speed. Steven was making adjustments perfectly as I instructed him.

During one of our breaks I told Steven I would like to try something, but it would involve me touching his mind. I wouldn't allow myself to do that to him without his approval. He was up for it and was actually rather interested in having the experience. For the next ten minutes, I directed his turns with my mind, no longer calling out commands. Steven turned the wheel as I controlled him mentally; it was as if I was driving myself. We were going though the course perfectly.

Returning to the patio, I started discussing what we had just done. I was excited about the possibilities, thinking this would remove any possible misdirection. I would just control Steven's hands. Jason was interested and wanted to know more. We had never actually had any discussions related to the process. I had switched with Jason long ago, but never controlled him in this manner. I found it hard to put into words; we agreed I would just give him a demonstration. Jason and I went down to the cart. He drove as we started off toward the flags. As we approached the first flag I took over.

Steven wasn't wearing a blindfold. It wasn't needed for the demonstration, so as we approached the first flag, I reversed the procedure. I wanted him to have no doubt that I was driving and he wasn't. I made sure by not moving as he had expected. I went to the left of the green and to the right of the red. On several occasions I had to turn the wheel sharply, waiting until the last moment to perform the maneuver. One of the turns was so sharp I actually had to slow the cart down.

Jason was impressed, although he did admit the experience was quite unnerving. Then he went on to say it wouldn't work. I couldn't understand why; I would have direct control. I thought that would eliminate any possibilities of a misstep. Jason explained that on the cart, everything I had him do, I was able to do. I knew how to drive and knew exactly how to control his hands

The Alien's Gift

in the turns and even his foot to slow the cart down. That was on the cart. I wouldn't be able to once we got on the computer.

I didn't know how to perform the functions needed to manipulate the computer controls. That was why Steven and I had practiced so hard. I might know what I want the computer to do, but I didn't know how to make that happen; Steven did. He was right, I had no idea how to manipulate the computer, and we didn't have time for me to develop the skill. Steven and I were a team. There was no other way.

The next day was spent practicing on the computer. We practiced until we were able to follow an object from one satellite to another flawlessly. We spent the entire day working until we felt ready for the real thing. Tomorrow, we decided was for real. Celebrations weren't in order, but we were ready, and we knew it. What we didn't know was if they were ready for us.

Chapter 17

It was time. We had planned for it, and we had trained for it. Now we had to go for it. The mood was somber during breakfast. Not knowing what the day would bring brought a mixture of excitement and foreboding at the same time. I believed I was feeling the same sensation a warrior has before entering into battle. Today we live or die, that was a possibility. There was winning, not today. We could lose, that was true, but we had no chance of winning. That we knew could not take place, not on this day. Winning would only mean the battle goes for another day. Today we were ready. We had planned each step each obstacle that might arise, covered every aspect we could think of to ensure we didn't expose ourselves, we hoped.

Today we entered a war room. The lights from the computers even seemed to cast an almost ominous glow as we approached. Steven sat at his chair and opened the satellite link that pointed at the mother ship. I focused, and we waited. I had been watching for thirty minutes when Jason ordered the satellite link terminated. We had agreed that even though the ship was in the path of the satellite we wouldn't stay connected longer than that, fearing detection. We went outside for a break. We couldn't afford to get wired too tight, and continuous surveillance was taking its toll on our nerves already. Thirty minutes off, then thirty minutes on, that was the plan. We sat through the second shift; again nothing happened. Our frustration was starting to show during our second break.

Bill had been put in charge of this project. His only job was to monitor us for stress. Bill was the investment broker; he was used to looking at investments objectively. An investment doesn't just have to be just a good one. It does have to be the right investment for that right client at the right time. Knowing your client is crucial. We were Bill's clients, and he knew us well. Bill would be the one to call the session off. Once he felt we were too stressed to think clearly. I only mention this because it was at that point, he did.

"Tomorrow, gentlemen" was all he said.

We knew he was right. We were too frustrated.

The next morning we started with a different outlook. We had expected them to just perform for us yesterday and lead us to the answer. They didn't. Today we were prepared to wait for them, all day and into tomorrow if need be. We took our seats, more relaxed this time, and everyone was ready for a long day. After sitting for a half hour we took our first break. Our new attitude was working. We maintained a level of comfort that hadn't been possible the day before. We were still more than ready as we returned to our second shift.

Finally our luck changed and the mother ship opened. I watched as the craft maneuvered down and to the south, directing Steven as it moved. Luck again was with us, and we only had to change satellites once. I watched as the craft lowered to the ground. We were on a weather satellite of all things. The satellite didn't have zoom capabilities, and we wouldn't have attempted to use them if it did. That would surely draw attention. I did have those abilities, and I used them to follow the craft to the ground. First I pointed to the location, trying to pinpoint the spot for identification.

Once the craft landed, a hatch opened and several people exited the ship. They all looked humanoid at first glance. But then I noticed a glimmer around two of them. They were projecting a field slightly different from the one the ship projected, but it was a field. The image I was seeing wasn't real. I adjusted my eyes, trying to pierce their vial. The image disappeared, the screen went black.

"What happened?" I exclaimed "I lost them, I was just about to find out, and I lost them."

"Thirty minutes." It was Jason.

I started to object, saying I was that close to seeing what they really looked like, when he said it again.

"Thirty minutes."

He was right, and I knew it. I didn't have to like it, but I knew it. I spent the time on break telling everyone what I had seen. Making sure I didn't have the sound of disappointment in my voice as I discussed the shielded beings. I knew Jason had felt bad enough about calling the session, even though he was right in doing so. We were all anxious to get back to the monitor, and the thirty minute break proved to be one of the longest we ever had. As soon as we got back into the room Steven called up the satellite, and I tried to relocate the ship.

I don't know if it had left or if I just couldn't find it. It was one thing to follow it down another when you didn't have the exact location. For whatever reason, I was unable to relocate the craft. Bill, sensing my frustration, suggested we break and collect our data, this time a suggestion not a demand. I agreed Bill was right. It was calling it close. We adjourned to the patio.

Once at our seats, we started to go over what we had. I had pointed out the landing area. However, the shot was from space. Without having a closer view we only knew the general area. I was only able to narrow it down to Washington State. It was a large area to search. Jason said he would be able to tighten the search area up considerably, and we moved on from there. I went to the beings in the craft.

"They have to be alien," I said. "Why else have the shields?"

Bill didn't think it was enough to go on. They had that technology, we agreed. It could just as well be used to disguise a human.

"Maybe they just didn't want the others to know who they were," he said.

He was right, that was a question that still needed to be answered. I was frustrated, to say the least. I was starting to believe this wasn't going to work. Our time window was too short. Thirty minutes wasn't enough time. For security reasons we couldn't extend it. That was true, and we all agreed. Still, it didn't change the facts. We needed more time. We needed to do something different.

"I need to go in mentally," I said.

I was fully expecting to hear a chorus of objections. There were none. Instead I heard conditions.

"You're going to practice and practice a lot before you try," Jason said.

Now we were getting someplace, I thought. I had already thought of that myself. I had moved into minds, but I hadn't really tuned the ability, I needed to move in fast. I wasn't sure if I even could. I had done it several times with the general and others. But all of those times I was able to inch in. I could take all the time I needed. To do what I needed to do now, I would have to be able to jump in fast and not give them a headache in the attempt. I had a dozen questions about what its potential was, and the only way to do that would be testing. I just didn't know how, yet.

We started to figure out our next step. Steven was going to have to continue to try and find the landing area on the computer. Once Jason narrowed his search, Steven would have to work through conventional channels to find what if anything was in that area. Stan was still busy working on following money, which would keep him busy. That left Bill and Jason to work with me.

Teams established we set the ground rules for testing. Bill and Jason would take turns watching me while I tested my capabilities. While one watched my body, the other would be my subject. I wasn't sure if this might cause them any damage, so I insisted we only work in short shifts.

That thought made me wonder what was going on with my body while my mind was off in never-never land. Bill had always watched over me, so I asked.

"Nothing. Your body just goes limp, almost like a rag doll," he said. "You continue breathing, but that was about it."

I was happy to hear that, the breathing part, that is.

"Most of the time your eyes have been open, but they looked lifeless." Bill said, the first time it happened, it scared the crap out of him. He thought I had died. I was only half listening as Bill was speaking.

My mind kept drifting back to my task. I needed to find out if I could share a sense with someone quickly and not just take it over in the process. In other words I had driven the golf cart this morning with Jason, but I controlled it, and he was totally aware of his lack of control. Could I feel the wheel with him as he drove? That was just one of my questions. I had to find out.

It was time to get started. Bill insisted on being first, saying it was only fair, he hadn't tried it yet. That started us with a laugh, and we let him have his way. I told Bill to just sit in the chair watching anything in the yard. I moved into his mind. Bill was aware of me, saying I had barged into his head like a bull in a China shop. I pulled back and tried again, moving delicately, trying to share his vision and not take it over. This time I was better.

Bill was still waiting for me to try again. I already had. I was looking out through his eyes, even as he was. I had to resist controlling him. Surprisingly I had to control myself, too. The desire to look around was almost overwhelming. If I had, he would realize immediately something was wrong. I had to control my yearning to look around. I was just getting used to being a passive observer when Bill turned toward my body.

The sight was shocking. I looked like a zombie, Bill had warned me, but seeing it was something else. I was startled. Bill felt me. I pulled back. As I sat up I looked down at my body, concerned now for my own welfare. I was alright. *Of course I am. Nothing had happened to me—so far.*

It took a minute or two to settle myself down after that experience. In an effort to take my mind off what just happened, we started to go over what progress had been made, and what potential hazards I needed to be aware of.

141

I had to move slowly and gently when moving into a subject, that was evident. Bill felt me instantly the first time. The second time he hadn't realized I was there until I lost my composure. I had to learn to control my reactions. They were a dead giveaway, and we had no idea what I might see or hear during the time I was monitoring someone. *I had to learn to control myself, but how do I do that?*

Jason suggested periodic surprises. Desensitize me, if it were possible. I had to learn to control my reactions. I agreed, it was something that had to be done. We made it part of our training.

The rest of the day was spent working back and forth between Bill and Jason. I practiced using their sight, hearing, touch, and smell. During the day as we practiced they would surprise me periodically. They seemed to take great delight in this part of the training and worked hard to throw the unexpected at me. At one point Bill even sacrificed himself by jumping into the pool. One moment I was watching Jason drinking a soda, the next I found myself underwater looking at the side of the pool. *That one was fun*, I thought, wondering now how I would pay them back for this.

Bill was also the one who poured ice water down Jason's back while I was working with him. Jason had his turn by pouring ice water down my back while I wasn't practicing with anyone, allowing me to have the full sensation on my own. All in all the day went well, except for almost having a heart attack four or five times, but that was "all in the name of desensitizing," they told me. *All in the name of desensitizing.* I thought, I would have to remember that.

Desensitizing over for the day, at least I hoped it was, we got ready for dinner. Stan was still buried in paperwork in the other room. I decided to go get him. I didn't actually walk in; I went to his mind. Everyone had agreed I could practice with them if I chose to. I chose to. I moved in slowly, more like a field test. I was looking at papers with names and numbers all over it. Stan was working on...? I don't know what Stan was working on. Whatever it was, I was looking at it with him and he wasn't aware of it. I touched his mind.

Stan, it's time to eat. Stan hadn't had any desensitizing training.

He jumped five feet in the air. I pulled back and was telling Jason and Bill as he walked in the room. He didn't seem to think it was as funny as we did at first, but joined in on the joke soon enough. We were all still laughing about it when Steven came in. He wanted to know what was so funny.

"Nothing, really. I was just coming to get you." The laughter took over the room again.

During dinner we brought each other up to date on what we had accomplished during the day. Stan was following a lot of monies moving from several unconnected sources, but still hadn't found anything that pointed to a world-shaking event. Steven had almost completed his search on the possible landing zone.

Jason's grid had narrowed the search area down to fifty miles. That still left several developments; none of them seemed to be isolated enough to be our target. There was however a large park that consisted of several hundred acres. It could possibly be the site. It was large enough and fairly isolated. He also found a few estates. Most had been too small, but one, one was over a hundred acres. He was tracing the owner, but so far that hadn't been easy. That narrowed it down to two possibilities. Not bad for a fifty mile area.

We discussed the improvements of my abilities, but it was agreed, I still needed a lot of practice. Stan agreed, but told Steven I was really getting good at it. Steven was confused by the laughter that followed, until Stan filled him in. The laughter had started, it was time to unwind for awhile.

Bill and Jason took turns telling stories about my desensitizing training. I was pretty sure they described each incident—twice. They seemed to take a great deal of delight in the telling. Dinner was on Jason, and the laughs were on me.

The rest of the evening was spent working on our next step. Stan would continue as he had been. We were still pretty sure a money trail would appear someplace. This had to be a big operation on its merit. That meant big money was moving. It was just a matter of time finding it. Steven was digging into the owner of the estate piece by piece. Tomorrow I would practice just eavesdropping on Bill and Jason. I had done that with the astronaut and was interested to see how much I could pick up from their thoughts that way. I believed it was the faintest of all forms of contact. Tomorrow's testing would give us the answer. At that point we called it a day. We needed to just relax.

The next morning Bill and I got an early start. We headed straight over to Jason's. When we arrived, everyone was just sitting down to coffee. It seemed we were all getting an early start today. During coffee, the conversation was optimistic. Everyone just felt like something would break today, and we were all anxious to get started. Steven was the first to move. Finishing the last of his coffee, he excused himself, and he was off. The day had officially started. Stan was right behind him. I asked Bill and Jason if they were ready for me to eavesdrop.

I didn't want to attempt it without either of their permission. I felt this was the most invasive of any of the things I was able to do. For that reason I wouldn't think of trying without their consent. Bill, like the kid he is, shook his hand in the air like a school boy.

He kept yelling, "Me first, me first."

My concerns were gone. I let my mind loose. I hadn't been the only one who thought that was a school boy jester. Bill was thinking that it was, too, *just like he did it in the third grade.* Then his thoughts settled. He was anxious for something to happen. The not knowing was harder on Bill than whatever might happen, I could read that clearly. I started to giggle to myself. Bill's next thought was, *do this well, Marc. Let's get going.* I wondered if my giggle had alerted him to my presence. I returned to my body for a moment so I could ask.

It had gone off without a hitch. Bill never sensed me, even when I was tickled. Well, I won't say without a hitch; that wouldn't be true. Jason was quick to point that out. As I was celebrating the fact that I went unnoticed, Jason reminded me I giggled. He was right. I hadn't controlled my reaction. That was a major slip. Would I ever be able to control them completely? We discussed that problem for several minutes. Finally it was concluded that it would always be one of the risks. Jason put it simply.

"We can't turn you into a cyborg in a day."

The one good thing discovered is the eavesdrop method was the least likely to be detected. Practice was over. I had to do something. We went to the computer room. Steven looked up as he heard the door open. When he saw the three of us walk in, his face lit up. He was ready, too. I watched him roll his chair over to the main console.

"Okay, let's get to work," was all he said, and the monitors came to life.

Pulling up my chair, I focused in on the mother ship. It was only a minute before the ship opened a hatch. Unfortunately it was opening for a craft to enter. Still, I wasn't deterred. *Hell that was something*, I thought. We were working again, and I was happy about it. Thirty minutes passed, and the screen went black. It caught me by surprise. It hadn't felt like we were there for more than ten. We took a break. None of us needed one, but rules are rules. Jason was adamant about it.

Much to my relief, the break seemed just as quick. Before I knew it, we were back at the console. I sat watching the ship. Twenty more minutes had passed, and I was just starting to hope nothing would come now. I knew the time was running out. As luck would have it the ship opened a hatch, and the smaller craft slid through the opening. I wasn't going to have time to follow it to a landing and knew that. In desperation, I reached out with my mind. I knew it was a dangerous move, I just couldn't go another day without something. I would only eavesdrop, that was the least detectable. At least for us.

As I moved into the craft, I felt a human mind to the side. I went for it, feeling that would be the safest. He was concerned he had to give someone bad news. Things weren't going as fast as Mr. Fallen would like. I could read that loud and clear. He wasn't happy about the news he had to deliver. Mr. Fallen, it would seem, was used to having his way. I started to loosen on his mind.

The Alien's Gift

· · · · · · · · · ·

I was tempted to search the rest of the craft. I reminded myself, *prudence is the better part of valor.* I decided not to push it. I had a name, that was a big something. I pulled back to my body.

When I returned, everyone's eyes were on me. I wondered if something had happened to me. I examined my body, but I seemed fine.

Bill spoke, "We were worried. We closed the connection but you were still gone."

I had a lot to explain, I knew, and suggested we take a break. We went to the patio. Once there Jason started saying how they had shut down at the thirty minute mark, and that I had been gone for almost five minutes after that. I reminded them I didn't need the monitor once I was in contact. The monitor was only used to locate a target for me. They had known that. I also knew it hadn't been part of the plan, not yet.

I apologized for breaking protocol and jumping. My heart wasn't in the apology, and everyone could feel it. I was elated. *Finally I had something,* kept running through my head. I blurted out the name.

"Mr. Fallen. Who is Mr. Fallen?"

Jason's head snapped up at the name. He knew him, or of him in any case.

"You saw Mr. Fallen?" he asked.

"No, but the guy on the craft sure didn't want to report to him," I answered.

I wanted to know who this Mr. Fallen was. Mr. Fallen turned out to be one of the richest men in the country. He was a media mogul, maybe "the" media mogul in this country, Jason explained. We had a name, and it was connected to the ship in orbit. Stan now had a target. He would look for anything he could find on this Mr. Fallen. Especially any new investments he might be involved in.

Jason was going to set up one of the computers to research and locate any properties he might own, directly or through shadow companies. Just maybe this Mr. Fallen owns some property in Washington State. Jason said he could have the computer doing the work and would still be free to work with us.

Break over, we went back to work. The day had started positive, but now we were almost too energized. I was aware of that and tried to keep my exuberance to a minimum. I knew Bill was also aware of it and didn't want him to pull the plug, not today. Steven turned the monitor back on, and we went back to our watch. During these times my mind started to run through the little things. Looking for things I might have missed. Did we overlook anything important? It was a habit I developed on my drive to and from work.

That's when the thought hit me. *Defense Department. Why hadn't I thought*

145

of that? I filed it in the back of my brain for discussion on the next break, not wanting to distract us during a monitoring session, the time being too short and valuable as it was. I was right about the time being too short. Right after I had the thought, the screens went down.

During the break I brought my thought up for discussion.

"Why don't I search the defense department?"

"For what?" Stan asked.

"There has to be a top general or something whom all this information would go to. You know, someone who's in charge of a blue book kind of project, only real."

We agreed. If there was such a person, his would be the mind I needed to listen to. It might be risky, but it was worth the chance. We also knew his name wouldn't be part of any public record. Jason would have to tackle this assignment personally.

We decided it was a big enough potential to call the monitoring off for the rest of the day. This would free up Jason. Steven went back to work helping Stan research Mr. Fallen. That left me and Bill free.

"Good thing I have this talent or these guys would have no use for me," I said.

Since we had the day off, Bill invited me to go look at some homes his realtor had lined up for him to see. He gave her a call and we met at her office shortly after. Bill was looking for a home on a lake or at least a canal with access to a lake. The realtor took us to three houses she thought would interest him. Bill wasn't crazy about the first one. The second he really liked, but it was beyond his budget. Realtors always ask you what you want to spend, then show you a home that costs twenty-five percent more. Good sales strategy, actually. After all, we all have to be sold at some point or live in a cave. The last house was closer. It was in his budget, but the lake was a sand pit. The realtor said it was from recent dredging, and it would settle in a few months, she was sure of it. We weren't, so Bill decided to try again another day, thanked her, and asked her to keep looking. We headed back to Jason's.

On the way I asked Bill what his budget had been on the house. It wasn't a question I was embarrassed to ask. Bill and I knew each other way to well for that. I wanted to know just how far over his budget the realtor had tried to take him. He was in the one million dollar range. The house was one point five. *Oh! She was pushing the limit on that one*, I thought.

That was the first time we had spoken of money since Jason made me rich. We were more amazed at how well we were doing rather than thinking of being rich. One million dollars would either of us have ever thought we could buy something for a million dollars ten years ago. We really started to

The Alien's Gift

laugh when Bill said, "Ten years ago, neither of us could even afford the car the realtor was driving."

We were still discussing it as we drove up the driveway. Jason's house looked big again. We had gotten used to it, but our trip down memory lane had put things back in perspective again. We went into the house and found the guys in the dining room eating pizza.

"Well, we still eat the same," I told Bill as I looked at the pizza.

"Just part of a long story," I said, realizing I had drawn everyone's attention, then let the comment drop.

We went back to discussing Bill's house search as we ate. We had made a dinner table rule, no business. Soon we were on "back in the day" stories. Stan picked up on my earlier statement first.

"Pizza, that's what you meant."

Then he one upped me. "We couldn't afford pizza."

The gauntlet was dropped. From that point on the rest of the dinner was walking to school, uphill, in a snowstorm, without shoes, both ways. Jason held his own. It would seem poor was something we all understood.

We moved to the patio after dinner, where the conversation shifted to the news of the day. Stan was first. He started to paint a picture. Mr. Fallen, it seems, was a lot more than a media mogul. He did, however, deserve that title. He owned over one hundred and fifty radio stations across the country. That was just the beginning. He also owned or controlled over one hundred newspapers and periodical publications, along with major holdings in most of the major networks' and one of the largest cable companies in the country. Together, that added up to the fact that he redefined the term mogul.

It didn't stop there. He was also a founding member of the Trenton Group. Stan explained that was a business group made up of some of the most powerful people in the world today. The political and financial influence they wielded was immense. They were in major business dealings spanning the gamut from the military industrial complex to fresh water rights around the world.

I was stunned. *How could one group of people obtain so much power?* I wondered. After Stan finished his summary, I wasn't sure I was ready for Jason and Steven. I got up, signaling I needed a break. I needed time to absorb what Stan had just reported. I walked over to the bar. I needed a drink. Bill joined me first, then everyone did. It was hard to believe our lives were under so much control by just a handful of people. I couldn't help but wonder, *how did we get into this*? I kept trying to put some sense into what I had just heard. I looked at Jason.

Tell me something good, I thought. I don't know if I projected my thoughts

147

or not, but Jason started to tell me about the General—Lieutenant General Baset. My mind soared as I listen to his words.

"Lieutenant General Baset, you found him," I interrupted.

I needed good news, any good news. Finding the general would do. Yes, it would do nicely. Jason went on. The General works at the Pentagon. He's the man in charge of all extraterrestrial activities for the Pentagon.

"I didn't know we had a department for extraterrestrial activities," I said.

"We don't," Jason said, smiling. "At least not a legitimate, the country knows about it, kind of department."

What I did know, tomorrow I was going to the pentagon. Tomorrow I would enter one of the most highly secure areas of the nation. *If only they knew.*

It was only four in the morning, and I had been on the patio more than half an hour already. Sleep was getting harder to do these days. Bill came walking out carrying two cups of coffee. I looked at him, wondering why he had two.

"Heard you get up earlier, figured you needed time to yourself and by now another cup of coffee," Bill said as if reading my mind.

I smiled as he set the cup down. We talked for almost an hour before heading over to Jason's to meet the guys. Sitting around the table, we planned the day. It no longer seemed important about who might own the property in Washington. It may not even be where the ship had landed. Plus, now that we had a name, it was no longer that important. Steven's time would be better used elsewhere.

Stan was turning his attention from Mr. Fallen to the Trenton Group, following its latest business ventures to see if that could shed any light on what the aliens were doing. They may be terrestrial, but my gut said no. I had high hopes that Lieutenant General Baset would shed light on that for me. But it was way too early to visit the General.

Until then we were going to the monitors. Steven turned on the screens, and I watched for some action. It was getting pretty boring, but at least I had a chance of seeing something. If nothing else I got to look at this mother ship. Steven, Jason and Bill could only watch space, a clock, and me. I stopped complaining to myself about nothing happening. For me, at least, there was a chance. For them, nothing ever changed. I thought I would use the time to describe the mother ship out loud so they would have some idea of what I saw.

Without any doors or windows, it was hard to describe for half an hour. I gave it my best, though. During break, Bill, showing that he appreciated my effort, said "So that's all you see, really? You must be bored to tears."

The laugh was good for all of us. We needed all the laughter we could get. When the opportunity arose, we took it every chance we could. Soon enough, we settled down and watched the monitor for most of the morning. Bill kept an eye on the clock for me and soon enough he spoke up.

"It's almost nine, and time for you to visit the Pentagon."

Jason pulled up a picture on the screen for me and pointed to the section of the building the general's office was located. Bill commented he wished he could go.

"Always wanted to see the building," he commented.

I explained to Bill I don't really see the places when I go there. It was hard to explain.

"I just see them in my mind and I go. I don't really see them; I feel them." With that brief explanation, I went.

I was at the Pentagon. I felt it just like I had told Bill. Funny, now that he said it, I wished I could see the building myself. The only way to do that would be to use someone's eyes, and I didn't want to chance that. Not now, there was too much at stake. I felt for the general or any sign of his essence. I was in his office, I knew that. But he wasn't there. I felt a mind in the room so I eavesdropped. It was his assistant. He was relieved that the General wouldn't be here for another hour. I was about to go back when he thought, *thank God he's at his morning briefing.*

That's why he wouldn't be there. I thought he had to be close, if only I knew where. I had to chance it. I let myself move deeper into the aide's mind. Slowly, gently I looked through his eyes. I needed him to look at his desk. There had to be a calendar. He kept looking at the clock. I hoped we wouldn't do that till the general got there. My patience was at a straining point when he finally went back to work. His head now on his desk, he shuffled through some papers before stopping on the General's calendar for the day. I had it nine am morning briefing, but where? There was a room number, but that did me no good. I couldn't see the numbers without entering someone else. I was getting frustrated, so I pulled back.

I was back in the computer room. I was so annoyed with myself for failing.

"I should have planned it better. Going to the Pentagon and no plan, no map, no idea what I was doing." I was furious with myself.

Jason and Bill worked to calm me down. It didn't have to happen in one day, and we had learned our lesson. I tried to console myself with that fact.

"I had entered the aid and used his eyes. That wasn't planned," I said, annoyed with once again.

Bill put me straight. "Marc, we can't plan it all. There will be times you have to make a decision and go with it. You knew that. You did and you pulled it off. He didn't know you were there, did he?"

"No." He didn't, that was true.

Bill was right, I was being too hard on myself. I had tried to make the best out of a plan that went bust. I didn't blow it. Tomorrow was another day. We were pretty sure attending the briefing was the thing to do.

I spent the rest of the day watching the mother ship. Following the thirty minute rule. The day passed with no luck. It just wasn't going to be my day. Thankfully I had reached the point of laughing it off. I thought, *Sometimes you're the bug, sometimes you're the windshield.* I just hope nobody turned on the wipers. It was around three, and I decided to call it. Not doing anything for thirty minutes, then taking a break might sound easy—it's not. The day and I were both done.

Besides, this afternoon I had something I needed to do. I excused myself, saying I needed to go over to the house for awhile. Once I was alone, I called Bill's realtor and told her I wanted her to make an offer to the owner on the home Bill wanted.

"Tell him if he sells for one million flat I'll give him three hundred thousand cash on the side."

I wanted this deal for Bill and knew he wouldn't take the money. I asked her to let me know if they were willing to make the deal. Bill was not to know. She started to laugh.

I have to admit it was a little unnerving. I had just made an offer for a large amount of money, and she was laughing. Maybe she thought I was joking? I assured her I was quite serious in my offer. She apologized for laughing, explaining that she didn't mean to make me think she didn't believe me. What she hadn't believed was that this was the second time today she had gotten this call.

Jason had called her earlier in the day with the same proposal, with one exception; he had offered two hundred and fifty thousand. She had already presented the deal to the seller, and he agreed. She went on to say how she would like to have a couple of friends like Bill had. I thanked her for her time before I hung up.

When I got back to Jason's, the party was in full swing. Bill saw me pulling up and ran out the patio doors to meet me. He was ecstatic.

"You're not going to believe this."

He went on to tell me a story about the house he wanted. How the guy had some kind of business deal go bad and needed money now. If he agreed today to the offer, he could get it for a mill clean. I listened to him as he told me the story. He was like a kid ready to jump out of his skin.

The Alien's Gift

I admit to being disappointed that I hadn't done this for him. I covered it well, and keeping a straight face, asked if he took the deal.

"Took it? Did I take it?" and he was off again.

I was over it, his joy overtaking me. We celebrated. His realtor showed up about an hour later with some papers.

Bill took her to Jason's office so they could go over them. Jason and I walked out to the patio. Once we were alone I told Jason that I appreciated what he did for Bill, but that I would be glad to refund the money. I explained how I had found out so that he realized my offer was genuine. Jason smiled at me.

"Marc, you're a millionaire, that's true. But I'm a billionaire. B comes before M in the alphabet."

I couldn't argue that with him, I did explain that I would love to cover it Bill was my friend. Jason got a serious look and asked me to go for a ride in the cart. We drove out away from the house. Jason had something he wanted me to hear. What he had to say, he had to say to me alone.

"Marc, when I first met all of you, I was a man scared. Not for my life. I was afraid something bad was happening and I had no power to stop it. Totally helpless, that's real fear."

He went on to say how when we all got together he felt like he had a chance to beat this.

"You, Bill, Steven, and Stan helped me to beat my fear. You all allowed me to fight back. Bill is my friend. You're my friend. Steven and Stan are my friends. Please let me do this."

I realized at that point that I wasn't the only lucky man in this world. We drove back, and I never made the offer again.

Bill was on his way out of Jason's office just as we got back to the house. Karen, I believe was the realtors name, smiled as Bill introduced everyone. Bill started to walk her to her car. Jason asked him if he could have the honor. Bill smiled and stepped back. As they walked out Bill turned to me saying it looked like they wanted to more than talk. Smiling, I agreed. We went back to the celebration, with me not feeling so disappointed.

When Jason returned, Bill commented he looked light on his toes. I thought, *about a quarter of a million lighter.* Looking at Jason, I knew the money was nothing to him. He had the opportunity to do something for a friend. That meant something—something I understood.

We didn't start till late the next morning. The party lasted till midnight so we all slept a little late. It was around eight when I got to Jason's. We ate light and chatted for a bit more before going into the computer room. Jason had pulled up a layout of the Pentagon. It had the room I needed to find the general. I wondered where he got this layout. Surely you don't get a tour of

151

the Pentagon brochure. Jason didn't say, I didn't ask. I got prepared and just before nine I jumped.

Once in the general area of the meeting room I reached to find someone thinking about the general. Surely someone was walking down the hall needing to attend this briefing. I hit pay dirt. I found the general himself. I was about to pat myself on the back until I remembered the day before. *Don't get cocky*, I thought. I started to eavesdrop. To be honest I was a little surprised. Most of the briefing was pretty boring. I thought they lived a more exciting life in the Pentagon.

I was about to write it off as a total loss when the general thought what about the space ship. Bingo, he knew about the ship. His thoughts retraced the sequence of events. I realize he didn't really know anything. Only once, they spotted something once. Why couldn't they find it again? Was it gone? Was it real? The ship was a mystery to them. I stayed till the briefing was over. Nothing more of interest was said or thought. The meeting ended along with my connection.

Back at the house I wasted no time bringing everyone up to date on what I had just learned. Nobody in the government was aware of the craft. Well, NASA and the defense department weren't anyway. That's not entirely true. The defense department or the extraterrestrial department suspected something, but had no evidence. Mr. Fallen, it would seem, was our only lead. *Him and the mother ship*, I thought.

Once again we adjourned to the patio. It was one of the places of privacy. Jason had a cook and a housekeeper. Both managed to stay out of sight most of the time. We always made sure they were out of ear shot when we met. It all came down to having two sources to investigate, Mr. Fallen and the mother craft. As the guys were discussing options and planning strategies, I was busy thinking the unthinkable.

I needed to be alone for awhile. I apologized again for needing to leave. When I got back to the house I got in my car and went for a drive. Being out on the road felt good. I hadn't been out with the exception of house hunting. Now I was out and driving alone for the first time since we had started. I headed toward the beach. I usually did my best thinking at the beach. That wasn't my reason today.

I have to admit getting out for a drive was something I missed. I decided I would enjoy it for just awhile longer. On the drive I kept thinking, *I should buy that sports car Bill is always talking about.* When I finally got to the beach, I pulled into a parking space and fed the meter for a three hour stay. I hadn't planned on being here that long, but wanted to cover myself in case time got away from me. Then I grabbed a towel from the car and walked out to the sand. I stretched out, lying on my back and then put sunglasses on, just like

I had a thousand times before. This time was to be different. I focused on the mother ship and jumped.

My mind wandered inside the ship, still not willing to test touching anyone. I lingered for several minutes building up my courage. This was a big move. This might be a stupid move. I knew that. I just had to find out who or what they were. I took every safety precaution I could to protect the guys. I had moved myself to a neutral location. Another precaution I took just in case they were able to trace me. It was now or never. I let myself feel their minds. I found one and eavesdropped.

After awhile I returned and went back to my car. Checking my watch, I had only been gone a little over thirty minutes. Driving back, my mind went over the experience. My mind also went over the thought of having to tell the guys what I had just done. I felt guilty. I had done something on my own without their agreement. I endangered myself, which jeopardized the mission, and I knew it. There was no excuse I could offer. I got home and went straight over to Jason's. The mood was light when I pulled up to the patio. We didn't have enough good times. I didn't like putting a damper on one of them.

Bill was the first to spot me. He knew when he saw me something was wrong. He seemed to trigger everyone. I became the center of attention. There was no other way to do this. I just said it. "I went to the mother ship."

The room was dead silent. I knew I had gone outside our plan. I didn't blame them if they were upset. *Upset, what a small word.* I had endangered the whole group. Bill was the first to speak.

"I don't know about these guys, but for me it's about time. I don't know how you resisted for so long."

I looked Bill in the eye, trying to determine if he truly meant what he said. Was he just trying to relieve me of my guilt? He was serious. I was still looking at Bill when Jason spoke out.

"Marc, you did break the plan, that's true. But we knew you would have to at some point."

Steven spoke next. "We figured that was exactly what you were doing."

I couldn't believe everyone agreed it had to be done. Stan finished.

"We knew the danger in this for you. It was a decision you had to make for yourself. We wouldn't have been able to tell you to do it."

That simple then, they were behind me. I couldn't believe it I was so... Jason broke my thoughts saying.

"Well, what did you find?"

Bill said, "Yeah, you're here. That's a good start. But did anything go wrong?"

I walked to the bar. I needed a drink. This was taking time to absorb. That and how did I explain the mother ship? I still didn't know how to tell them that. As I mixed myself a drink the bar filled in around me. I was the center of attention, and I knew it. I just didn't know how to tell them what I knew.

Bill got me started. "Marc, if you don't say something soon I'm going to hit you with this chair."

He was right. I wasn't sure how to say it, but I had to at least try.

"First I need to explain how I find a mind," I spoke slowly, trying to make it clear.

I went on to describe how I look for an area, then it just seems to be there. I go where I think. Once there, I look for a mind. The best way to describe it would be how a dog follows a scent. The scent leaves a trail, and you sweep as you move along it. It gets stronger the closer you get to the source. That's about the best analogy I could give. I find the mind, then move toward the signal, it gets stronger the closer I get. They seemed to follow me so far.

"They aren't human," I said.

It came out without any build up, without any kind of lead in. The words just jumped out of my mouth. The impact they had on the room was noticeable. We had all suspected they weren't humans. It was one thing to suspect it and another to know it.

Everyone sat quietly for several minutes. I let them digest what I had just told them. I was still dealing with the fact myself. I let my mind drift back to that moment.

Bill regained my attention. "Marc."

My mind came back to the room and my story.

"When I find a mind, there's a steady smooth stream to follow. They aren't like that."

I tried to explain what I felt on the ship. It wasn't difficult, just alien to me. They don't think in a smooth continuous flow. Their thoughts pulse. There was always a steady underflow. Only they had strong pulses from time to time. I tried to explain.

"Think of an orchestra. The violins holding a note. With so many violins the note is a continuous sound. Now add a base drum. Not with any steady beat, just coming in whenever it chose to. That's what I followed." I stopped and took a drink.

This was the part I didn't want to say. I had deliberately embellished the story to this point, stalling. I had taken a big chance, and it was for nothing. How do I tell them? *Just saying it,* I thought.

"I don't know what they're thinking." It was out, I told them.

"I took the chance, and it was for nothing. I couldn't understand their thoughts."

Jason spoke first. Not to me. Not to anyone in the room.

"Telepathy," he said, half to himself.

He looked up, seeing us all looking at him.

"Telepathy, they use telepathy. That was the pulse. It has to be."

I felt a chill run up my spine as I listened to his words. I thought, *they knew I was there.* They were all busy discussing Jason's theory when I stated my fear.

"They must have known I was there," I said. "What if they followed me back?"

Had I led them to my friends? All the precautions I had taken for nothing? Jason broke my thoughts.

"I don't think so."

I grasped at his words for hope, listening as he explained his theory. Jason believed if they used telepathy to communicate with each other, they must be used to others in their mind. Al-though he agreed they would notice a mind as foreign to them as a humans might be, he didn't think they would have noticed anything as soft as my eavesdrop. I clung to that theory with some hope. However, I still carried the fear. *I had betrayed my friends* still lingered in the back of my mind.

We knew our enemies now. Not well, I admit. But they were out in the open. We had targets to focus on for information. The aliens would be a problem. We had to figure out a way to know their plan. I didn't speak Venetian or whatever they were. It wasn't a lot yet, but it was a start. We took our small victory and enjoyed the remainder of the evening. I admit, I spent most of the time looking over my mind's shoulder.

Chapter 18

I had made the first move. We knew it hadn't been enough. I would have to find out more. What did they want? Why were human beings willing to help them? Were they helping them willingly, or had their actions been controlled by some means? We were only starting to scratch the surface. I needed to learn a lot more information. That wasn't going to happen by playing it safe. I would have to be better if I was to have any chance. Jason had made the comment

"It's too bad you're the only one who can eavesdrop. We would be able to gather a lot more information, and a lot faster if they could."

He was right. The problem was there was only one of me. The solution: I had to be better at what I did.

As much as I hated to say it, I had to practice more, a lot more. *I hate practice*, I thought, even as I was thinking it. I knew I needed to be faster, much faster. I needed to be able to move from person to person rapidly. I was going to need everyone's help with this. That said, I laid out a plan. I was going to jump from one to the other throughout the day. First I would practice eavesdropping.

Gradually, as I got better and faster, I would progress to more complicated tasks. Try to listen, see, and if needed, feel what they were experiencing. The only good part of this practice session was it wouldn't interfere with what they had to do. I wanted them to go about their normal assignments. I would just do what I do. Every two hours we would report back to the table.

We were set. The last thing I asked was that if anyone felt my presence they had to let me know immediately. I could then make adjustments throughout the day. At the break they were to tell me if they had thought I was there, but weren't sure. Ground rules in place, we went to work. I sat in the computer room with Bill as my watcher. I had requested that. After seeing the way my body looked when I wasn't with it, I didn't want to be left unattended. Even though today was a safe day and I wouldn't be visiting any hostiles, I still wanted him there. I leaned back and relaxed.

I moved to Stan first, only because he was the furthest from me. I eased into his thoughts, moving much faster than I had been. Until now I had eased in to someone's mind like a person moving into a cold pool, an inch at a time. Now I was just going in. I wasn't doing a cannon ball mind you. I just slid into his thoughts. I was there, and he hadn't felt my presence. He was still wondering if I would eavesdrop on him. Then his thought shifted to *I wonder if he is now?* For a second I had thought, *he felt me.* The thought never went further. He hadn't. It was just a thought, pure speculation. I was in and hadn't been noticed.

The drill was to try and move quickly and visit several minds as fast as feasible. I only stayed long enough to insure success. I jumped again, this time to Bill. I slid into his mind as easy as I had Stan's. His thoughts were disturbing. He was watching me as I entered. I wasn't using his eyes; this was a drill on eavesdropping. I couldn't see "me." I have to admit I wasn't upset about that having already had the experience. Bill, however, was watching me. He was thinking I looked more like a zombie than a person.

Those thoughts were disturbing, and I was ready to move. I had done the connection, which was the goal. I jumped. Jason was my next target. I slid into his mind. It felt as smooth as the others.

Jason thought, *Hi Marc.*

It caught me by surprise. I wondered if he felt me or was just thinking to startle me if I was there.

Marc, I can feel you.

It was a statement not a guess he knew I was there. I pulled. Once back in my body, I called for a debriefing. I had to know what went wrong. We all met at the table, and I asked Jason to speak first. I knew he had felt my presence, but how or why? It was a big question for me. It was a big question for us all. Jason started off by saying he could feel an uneasiness in his mind. Nothing he could put his finger on; it just didn't feel right.

Jason said, "It's like when you walk down a dark alley." In his mind something wasn't right.

He did admit that I was at a big disadvantage in this test. We are all aware of what you are doing and aside from the exact moment, when you're doing it. Anything that was felt, even just a slight uneasiness, could be and would be attributed to me. That wouldn't be the case, or at least we didn't believe for someone totally unaware of the situation.

Bill agreed, saying, "It's not like they're expecting people to jump in and out of their head."

I disagreed. "The aliens would. They're telepathic." My comment was sobering.

What had gone wrong? That question still needed to be answered. We started to review everything. Starting right at the beginning, I walked through each contact as I had made them. Even going over the thoughts they were having. How Stan had wondered if I was there, Bill thinking I looked like a zombie. Steven jumped in on that.

He said, "Bill's thoughts, that's what shook you."

I wanted to brush the statement off. *Was it my vanity?* This was too serious for that. So we—I had to look at it closely.

"Do you really think I'm just being vain?" I asked. I really didn't want to believe that was the case.

Steven explained, that wasn't what he'd been trying to say.

"The other day when you saw your body, it shocked you, scared you. You expressed your concern, and you examined yourself once back in it, remember?"

I couldn't deny what he was saying. I had been quite disturbed at the image I had of seeing myself. What Steven was saying was true. He believed that Bill's comment about being a zombie weighed heavy on my mind. That could have been what caused me to lose some of the finesse I had been showing before.

Bill apologized for disrupting the exercise. He was also deeply upset about the zombie thought. He didn't feel I deserved that and was embarrassed for even thinking it. I tried to put it all in perspective and hoped I could put his concern at ease at the same time. I looked around the table as I spoke.

"We were practicing, and disruptions are something I have to overcome. As for the zombie comment, he was right."

The bottom line, I had to control my emotions better. I needed to drop my fears and, as much as I hated to admit it, my ego.

There was a bright side to the debriefing. Jason had looked at his watch to time when he had felt me. I had been in that session for almost fifteen minutes. During that time I had jumped three times. Okay, only two of the times I was successful. The thing was, I did it in just under fifteen minutes. I could slide in faster, and I was just getting started. I would get better. That

I promised myself. I would get better. The debriefing was over, we went back to work.

Bill and I sat down ready to start again. Bill wanted to tell me again he was sorry and would control his dumb thoughts better. I told him not to worry about it and reminded him it wasn't his thought that caused me to be caught. It was mine. I promised him I would control my dumb thoughts. That was something I had to settle in me personally. That said, I sat back and we went back to practice. I stared with Stan again. It was a guessing game to me.

Would Stan be looking for me, thinking I started with him the last time so I probably would again? If so, he would be looking for me. That's just what I wanted him to be doing. I slipped into Stan's mind. I was right. He had already been searching to see if he could feel me in his thoughts. I pushed just a bit and went to his eyes. I was looking at the window. Stan hadn't started working. He was spending all his energy trying to discover me. It tickled me. I was looking at Stan's reflection in the window as he was looking for me. The irony of the situation was comical. I controlled my mind as I felt myself sniggering. It worked; I didn't pass my thoughts to Stan as I was reading his.

I had waited until the moment passed before leaving Stan. I did it as more of a self control exercise for myself. I jumped to Bill. I went to Bill again for the same reason I had failed the last time. I was going to use his eyes. I needed to come to grips with my own image when I was in that state. I also knew it would be just as disturbing as the last time. I had to control those feelings and not allow them to leak into my host. My image was disturbing to me, just as much as the first time I had witnessed it. Bill was right. I looked like a zombie. The only good thing I could say was at least I wasn't drooling.

That thought did it for me. I tickled myself with that thought. I looked to see if Bill caught me. No, I was safe. He hadn't detected my presence. I seemed to be able to put a barrier around my thoughts. I discovered that with Stan. At least it felt like I had. I could almost feel a wall going up screening me. I could hear their thoughts and block mine. When I jumped to Jason this time I was sure he wouldn't detect my presence—he didn't.

I spent the day practicing. Everyone else worked as usual. The day was deemed a total success. The only detection all day had been the one with Jason that morning. My wall seemed to work. I had gotten my speed to the point I could visit everyone in less than five minutes. I wouldn't have to shift that fast we knew. I was in each mind so little I couldn't really gather more than a thought or two. What it did do was develop my ability to enter rapidly, undetected. I had also been able to move into sharing eyes, ears, and touch with the same success. Through it all I was never detected. It had been a good day.

Bill was on the patio the next morning when I came out. I was going to miss having Bill here once he moved into his own house. His new house would only be a few miles from me. It would just be different not seeing his face over coffee in the morning. The puppies and I had gotten used to him being around. I asked about the house as I sat down. I wondered if he had heard anything more from the realtor. Bill said the closing would be in two days. I could tell from his response he was going to miss the morning coffee, too.

For some reason neither of us were in a hurry this morning. We sat and had a second cup of coffee together before starting the day. Jason and Steven were sitting in the dining room when we arrived. Stan had left early to head back to his office. We had moved on pretty short notice, and he still had some business that he had to attend to. As we sat at the table I started to discuss going to the mother ship again. I wanted to try once more. I had to try and learn more about them. Maybe there was something I had missed.

I told them I was going to head back to the beach after our morning meeting. It was a precaution I felt was needed. Everyone agreed it was a good idea. However Bill insisted on going with me this time. I knew shortly after the debate started he was going. Bill was a stubborn man. When he finally mentioned the fact my body would be unguarded, he won. He cheated, but he was right, I conceded. We went back to the house to get the car.

I drove for over an hour before we found a beach that wasn't crowded. This beach was more sea grapes than sand. That explained the shortage of bathers, but it was exactly what I wanted. I laid out a blanket, put my sunglasses on, and prepared to jump. Bill just smiled and told me he'd wait for me there. I jumped.

In the craft I could feel several minds. I felt the same pulsing sensation as I had the last time. This time I tried to find a pattern in it. There was a steady stream of background thoughts accented by the pulsing. Telepathy that's what Jason thought this was. *Was it? How could I tell?* I realized at that point that the pulsing thoughts had varying distances. When I find a mind I can tell how close I am to it by its strength. Some of the pulses were much closer and stronger than others. The stream seemed to be the same from everyone. I was unable to tell the difference in the stream. They were from different sources. I could tell that. The minds close to me would pulse from time to time, overriding their smooth stream. Jason was right. Telepaths, their thoughts while communicating were resonating in the minds around me.

I had to enter one of their minds again. I took a moment to collect myself. I needed to be careful, I knew that. Ready now I slid into the mind closest to me. The thoughts were as foreign to my mind as they had been the last time. I wasn't going to gain any information from them. Not this way. I was about to pull back. But that last thought stuck in my head. *Not this way.* It was at

The Alien's Gift

that point I made my decision. Coming here was a risk, a big one, and we all knew it. I was here. I had to go for it. Slowly I let my mind focus through its eyes. I put my wall in place as I had learned to do during practice, taking every precaution I could think of. I kept thinking, *telepaths. I was doing this to a telepath.*

At first I couldn't make sense of what I was seeing. I had started to believe this wasn't going to give me any more information. When he finally lifted his head. I could see the inside of the craft. Their light seemed the same as ours. At least I had no trouble making out what I was seeing. Not that I could tell you what any of it was.

There were no aliens, people, whatever they were, in his field of view. I fought the urge to rotate his head. Finally he turned, bringing someone into view. I was looking at a creature not of this earth. They were reptilian. Not scary looking lizards, like people only reptile. They were humanoid in appearance.

I felt its mind speak. I still couldn't tell you what was said. What I could feel was the strength of its mind pulse as it sent a signal. I wondered if it felt me and was warning them. Fear started to grow in me as I had those thoughts. I slowly eased myself back out of his mind. I jumped.

When I opened my eyes I looked over saw Bill still sitting right there. He wasn't aware I had returned. My zombie eyes had been covered by dark glasses. As I watched him he was looking back and forth sweeping the horizon. *Always on guard,* I thought. I knew my body was as safe with him as was humanly possible. The thought gave me comfort. I sat up, and Bill almost jumped out of his skin.

I apologized as soon as I had finished laughing. I knew it wasn't right to laugh. He had been on guard for any danger, his focus intent, when I just jumped up from the dead. Maybe it was the relief of being out of that ship. I don't really know why, but I laughed for a long time. Bill didn't really seem to mind. I think he knew. Besides, he needed to practice desensitizing. On the way back to the house I filled him in on what had happened and what I had seen. I had confirmed they were aliens; now I knew for sure.

The meeting began as soon as we got back to Jason's. Everyone had been sitting around all morning, waiting. To say they were anxious would have been an understatement. I couldn't say I blamed anyone either. I wasted no time in relaying my story. I was tempted to just blurt out "they're aliens" at first. I decided instead to tell it as it happened. Stan was taking notes. The only way to be sure I didn't miss something would be to document it step by step. That would allow us to analyze it for any details I might have overlooked. For that reason alone, I started from the beginning.

Thirty minutes later, I had finished telling everyone every detail I could recall. There hadn't been a sound in the room the entire time I spoke. Not a question, no interruptions of any kind. I had their total attention. They focused in on every word, making sure not to miss any detail. Now that I was finished, they were still quiet, each trying to process what they had just heard. Stan spoke first, the word just blurting from his mouth. He only said the one word.

"Stenonychosaurus."

We all looked at him when he said it. Stan had been looking down at his notes. I don't believe he even realized he had said the word out loud.

"What's a Stenonychosaurus?" I asked.

Stan looked up, surprised by my question. I was right. By his reaction, he hadn't realized he had even said it. Hell, I wasn't sure I had just said it, correctly anyhow.

"Stenonychosaurus was a dinosaur."

Stan was an amateur Paleontologist and to be honest the only one in the room who had any idea what the hell a Steno-whatever was. We all listened as he explained. Saurians, as they are also called, lived over sixty-four millions years ago. Some Paleontologists believed that if they hadn't been wiped out during the great disaster, they might well be the intelligent life on earth instead of man. At the time of their extinction they had been considered the most intelligent of dinosaurs on the planet. Way ahead of mammals on the evolutionary scale. Stenonychosaurus were already walking up right, and using their hands and arms. They did all that, before we even reached the evolutionary stage of rat. They also hunted mammals.

He went on to explain that at that time mammals came out at dusk and after sunset to feed. The saurian found his niche feeding on them. This meant that they hunted after the sun went down. I wasn't sure how they did that. I thought dinosaurs were reptiles and needed the sun for warmth to move. I didn't ask. Stan was too excited. He would have answered in great detail, and I was still working on Stenonychosaurus. Even with that, when he finished, I had to ask.

"You think these creatures are Saurian?"

Stan said he didn't know and wasn't trying to say they were. He was just pointing out that if they were the same species they just have sixty-four millions years of evolution on us. I wasn't sure of that. I was sure they had a ship in orbit bigger than the Queen Mary.

So, Saurians—we had a name for them. Now we knew both sides or at least we knew parts of both sides of the equation. What they wanted and what they might be doing was still a question. We were still going over the conversation when Steven asked if I was sure I hadn't been detected. I hadn't thought so, but I guess I really didn't know. We went to the computer room to find out if there were any reactions showing on the monitor. Steven pulled it up, and I watched for the next half an hour. Everything seemed to be just as it had been. No flurry of ships going in or out. There was nothing pointing to them believing they had been compromised. We felt secure in the belief I went undetected. The risk had paid off.

The following day was closing day for Bill's new home. We decided to take the day off. Jason had called for a limo. We were going to the closing in style. Stan and Steven said they would have to pass, claiming they had lots to catch up on from the day before. Bill was like a kid, saying it wasn't everyday he bought a million dollar house. At the closing we met with Karen before going in. It took a few minutes while we waited for the prior owner to arrive. Bill and Karen went into the office, and we excused ourselves, choosing to have coffee instead. Buying a house isn't that interesting to watch. You get to see someone sign papers for thirty minutes. Brokers pass checks across the table, then ending with a set of keys. Once we thought of that, Jason and I decided coffee was a better idea. We would meet them later.

We got back just as the meeting had come to an end. Our timing was perfect. Bill was talking to Karen when he saw us coming. He had more news and wasn't willing to wait till we got to him, he started moving to meet us. He was still a kid, only now a kid with a bigger story to tell.

"You remember the furniture in the house?" he started to say, even before he reached us.

"He gave it to me."

The joy on his face was priceless. When Bill and I had looked at the house, he couldn't believe how much he liked it. Even the furniture, he would love to have taken it just as it was. Everything had been perfect to him. Karen joined us about then, and Bill started talking to her again. He was so busy going on with Karen he didn't notice the look Jason gave me.

It took awhile before we got Bill to touch back down to earth. We might still be there if Jason hadn't spoken up.

"Well, let's go see your house."

That was all it took. We were off in the limo. The only true way to celebrate a new place is with friends and food, lots of food. So on the ride over, Jason and I made Bill promise to have a cook out just as soon as possible.

Bill agreed, "As soon as possible."

We got to the house, and the limo pulled into the driveway. Bill's car was parked in front of the garage along with Stan's. While we were at the closing, they had gone to get food for the cook out. As soon as Bill saw the cars he knew he had been had. We were having a cook out, and we were going to have it today. The party went on till late in the evening. We congratulated Bill one last time, before we piled into Stan's car and headed home.

Later that night when we were alone Jason turned to me and commented.

"You bought the furniture, didn't you."

I laughed, "B might be before it, but M was still in the alphabet." Then I thanked him. Because of you I could do what I did for Bill. Jason smiled. We never spoke of it again.

I woke late the next morning, not getting up till quarter past five. I walked to the kitchen, poured myself a cup of coffee, and, with dogs in tow, headed to the patio. When I opened the door Bill was sitting at the table.

"About time," he said as I walked out.

He scared the crap out of me, again. I had been thinking this would be a strange morning. I was used to having Bill's company at coffee. Well, it wouldn't be a strange morning after all, not today at least. As we sat having coffee Bill was telling me how he couldn't get over all the good things that had happened to him.

"Karma" was all I said.

We finished our coffee and headed to Jason's. It was time to go back to work.

Chapter 19

The day started just a little different. Today we had a specific agenda. Now we were aware of the Saurians. We also knew they were involved with Mr. Fallen, probably the Trenton Group, somehow. Why? We needed to know why, what did the Saurians want? What was Mr. Fallen's involvement with them? What was he getting? What might be an even more important question, what were they getting in return? The questions were on the table; the answers still had to be found.

Steven had been doing some more background on Mr. Fallen. He seemed to own several homes and moved around the world extensively. Most of his travels seemed to revolve around business for The Trenton Group. The Trenton Group is involved in several areas that might be of interest to the Saurians. I needed to find Mr. Fallen. We still had a mystery to unlock, and I believed he was the key.

It turned out that finding Mr. Fallen wasn't as easy as you might expect. Fortunately I had a good team working on it, by noon Steven had found him. He was on business in the south of France. I had to believe that wherever Mr. Fallen was, it would involve business. From what little I learned about this man, greed and power seemed to be his main motivators.

He was staying at a private residence. Probably one of his own, but seeing it was only an earth watch picture away. Steven had that for me in no time. I studied the location for a minute or so before I jumped. The security around

165

this home was impressive. I could feel their minds everywhere. Each one I touched was dead serious. These men were professionals, there was no doubt about that. I don't think any man could get in to see Mr. Fallen without permission. Well, almost any man, I was here, and I would find him.

Now that I was here, I had to do just that, locate him. I started to look for a lead in the thoughts around me. After moving through several minds I finally found one who was thinking of Mr. Fallen. It wasn't him, but I was closer. I slid into this mind to get more details. He was thinking of Mr. Fallen for good reason. He was at a meeting with him. I let myself move to his vision.

Mr. Fallen, I thought. *Glad to finally meet you in person.*

I was looking straight at him. The man I was sharing vision with let his eyes scan the table, allowing me to see who else had attended the meeting. When he turned back to Mr. Fallen, I moved to listen. Mr. Fallen was upset with product shipments. Schedules were not being kept. He was showing his displeasure. However, I detected some insincerity in his manner.

On a hunch I jumped to his mind. I was right. He was upset, but not for reasons you might think. It was about his power. It would seem that if Mr. Fallen said something would happen, than it had damn well better. His anger was more about his pride and reputation, not over any concern for the client. He didn't like to have to answer to those "*lizard bastards*." His thoughts, not mine. He was pretty sure they needed him more than he needed them. His arrogance was palatable. The only thing good about this man was I'd be able to find him again anywhere. His mind was truly unique and not in a pleasant manner.

The rest of the meeting consisted of him expressing his displeasure. He was quite upset because his orders weren't being carried out to the letter. I was forced to listen as he ranted about the consequences if things didn't improve. He wanted a complete update on the shipping status before his meeting the next day. As he spoke he kept looking down at his calendar. *This was a man of schedules*, I thought, as I read tomorrow's schedule, meeting at four pm. Having about as much as I could take of this man in one sitting, I pulled.

"That guy is a piece of work," I said as I re-entered my body.

My mind needed to say the words out loud. Bill jumped at my sudden animation. I apologized for scaring him like that and made a mental note, *I would have to stop doing that.* I had been gone for more than an hour this time. Everyone had been waiting for my return. We headed to the patio, I was happy to get some much needed fresh air after having been in the man's head for so long.

As soon as I sat down the meeting started. Stan had been checking into Mr. Fallen's latest investments. Nothing unusual had shown up. He had

The Alien's Gift

purchased a new island home. Actually he had purchased an island, with a home on it. According to Stan, it was a cute little summer place, around thirty thousand square feet under air. The island itself was almost a mile long and half a mile wide. Stan didn't think it really meant anything. He just wanted to give us some idea of the stature of the man we were dealing with.

I had met the man, in a sense, and didn't need to learn much more than I knew. He was a man of power, too much power and for too long. His arrogance and self righteousness showed that. I told them about the meeting set for tomorrow. I found it hard to believe the curious distain he seemed to have for the "clients." For a moment I wondered why anyone would do business with someone who felt that way. Then I remembered the man. Power and money were his only impetus, nothing else. I was also curious to see if the clients were indeed the Saurian or not. My gut feeling was they were. I would have to wait and see.

Waiting wasn't one of my strong points. The first part of the day was never a problem. I always enjoy the patio in the morning. The pups had now gotten in the habit of only checking the immediate surroundings in the morning. This allowed time for our morning get together. When I left for Jason's house, they ran along with the golf cart. It was only after I got to Jason's house that they resumed their complete patrol of the property. It was a big job, but they were happy to do it, and I was happy they could.

Jason was already on his patio when I arrived. We kept our conversation light this morning. We were both deliberately avoiding mentioning the meeting. I was pretty sure it was the only thing that was really on our minds. We both knew that with luck, this meeting might tell us what the aliens were after. We needed a lot of luck. First, we weren't sure the meeting was even with the Saurians. Mr. Fallen only said "meeting the clients" in his conversation. My second and the bigger problem was how I would know what their real motivation was? What was being delivered? Would they be discussing that in depth or just referring to it as the shipment again?

It wasn't until after nine when Bill asked if we were sure the meeting was going to be the same place as I had been the day before. Jason and I looked at each other. We were both moving even before Bill had finished his sentence, heading for the computer room. All the way there I was busy kicking myself in the behind. *Why hadn't I thought about that?* Our only hope was that they were going to meet at the home I was at yesterday. We wouldn't have time to locate Mr. Fallen in time for the meeting if it wasn't. That would mean we missed the only opportunity we had.

I went to my chair as soon as I entered the room. Jason and Steven headed straight to their computers. If Mr. Fallen had relocated with any luck they might be able to find him. I wasted no time. Sitting in the chair, I jumped to the home in south France. It was almost nine-thirty when I left. It would be three-thirty in France. We had only thirty minutes to find him.

I started to look for signs of Mr. Fallen's mind as soon as I got there. If he was still here I would have no problem finding him. As I said before, his mind was loud and arrogant. I was right. He was easy to find, and more important, I was lucky. The meeting was in this location. I found Mr. Fallen and moved in to eavesdrop. I hadn't planned on spending this much time with him. His mind was difficult to take. I was here, I would live with it. Now that I thought of it, I might actually get some valuable information. I was sure he would be getting a briefing prior to his meeting.

I thought about the guys back at the house. Realizing they were just as concerned as I had been, I had to let them know. I decided Mr. Fallen could hold for one more minute, and I jumped. At the house I opened my eyes, only long enough to let Bill know, I had found Mr. Fallen. That done, I smiled, nodded to Bill, and jumped.

Once I was back, I prepared to settle in for the long term. I truly had to brace myself prior to entering Mr. Fallen's mind. I wasn't concerned about him knowing I was there. I believed I had gotten too good at this to worry about that. My problem was his mind. He was hard to take.

Mr. Fallen was indeed receiving a briefing. I tuned into his hearing so I could follow the conversation. The first thing reported to Mr. Fallen was that the shipments were back on schedule. There was a great deal of relief in the voice of the man reporting that. Fallen, true to his nature, took the information with a "damn well better be" attitude. I really didn't like this man.

One of his assistants came in to inform him that the clients would be arriving any moment. A car was there to bring them to the house as soon as they landed. Hearing that gave me hope. If they needed to be picked up, did that mean they came in a craft of some sort? Otherwise they could have just driven to the front door. Then I realized the car could just be picking them up at the local airport. I needed to relax and wait to find out.

Fallen got up and started out of the room. I tuned back in to his thoughts to find out where we were going. I had thought the meeting was supposed to take place in this room. It was. Mr. Fallen, it seemed, planned on making an entrance. He was also planning on keeping the clients waiting for a few minutes before he made it. He wanted to be sure they knew how important he was. All I could think was *I needed strength to get through this. Fallen is obnoxious.* We waited in a room down the hall.

While we waited, Fallen went into his briefcase and pulled out a plain folder. I tuned into his eyes as he opened it and started to read. It was some waste reports from power plants. *So much for glamour,* I thought as he read down through the numbers on the sheet. I didn't think anymore about it at the time. I was only interested in learning more about the clients. They had arrived. One of Fallen's aids had just informed him. We waited another five minutes before he got up and made his entrance.

Mr. Fallen managed to irritate me still again as we entered the room. His eyes didn't look at the clients as he entered, preferring to keep his attention on a piece of paper he carried instead. I could feel in his mind it was just another way of showing them just how important he was. It wasn't until after he actually sat down his head came up, and he made eye contact with the clients. They were human. At least they looked human.

I thought about the glimmer. I had seen it when I was looking from the satellite. It made me wonder if they were really human or screened. I wasn't sure I could focus Fallen's eyes to adjust. It was a moot point. If I could then, Fallen would have seen them along with me. I tuned in, having to be content with listening. The conversation was vague, mostly they were discussing produce shipment schedules.

This meeting wasn't going to yield much information, I decided. I would take a chance. I had to at least try to find out if they were Saurians. I let my mind withdraw from Fallen. The relief was palatable. Then I entered one of the men at the table. As he spoke his thoughts were in English. I started to withdraw. I was beginning to feel the trip wasn't what we had hoped, when I felt the Saurian thoughts in his mind as he translated to himself.

Never having learned a second language, I wasn't sure how that worked in someone's mind. I've been told by some, that, you think in your own language, then translate it to the foreign language in your head. That seemed to be what this Saurian was doing. He was thinking in Saurian, then translating it to English. I had a way of understanding them. I almost jumped right out of him in my excitement before I caught myself. Regaining my composure, I settled in.

The Saurian wasn't fooled by Mr. Fallen in the slightest. He didn't have words for that in his mind. But there was no doubt about the feeling. Some things are just universal. He was speaking to Mr. Fallen.

"Will you be able to complete phase one of our deal within the month?"

He was also communicating to someone else as he spoke to Fallen. I could feel the pulses in his mind. There were a lot more people involved in this meeting than Fallen would ever realize. I was letting my thoughts drift. I turned my attention back to the meeting. Fallen was telling him they should have no problem with the schedule. They had just completed the acquisition of a new facility. Future delivery schedules should increase within the week.

With that, the meeting was drawn to a close. There was no fanfare, no shaking of hands and wish you well speeches. It just ended.

As the Saurians left, I decided to travel with them. We got into the car and drove to the edge of the tree line on the rear of the property. The Saurians left the car and walked to the edge of the tree line. As we approached, a ship appeared. It had been screened to hide its location. As soon as we entered the craft, the Saurian in front of me returned to his natural state. From that point on they never thought in English again. At this point I would only be on for the ride. However, never having been on a flight into space, not like this, I stayed for the experience.

The lift off and acceleration was so smooth I wouldn't have known we launched if not for the view. View! I could see out a window. But the craft didn't have windows. In a matter of seconds we were pulling up to the mother ship. I watched the opening appear, and the craft maneuvered inside. My ride was over. I switched.

Bill was watching me when I opened my eyes. I wondered how he could stare at my lifeless form for so long without it bothering him. I knew he would, though. It was his job. His eyes never left me. I smiled, Bill and I got up and started for the patio? Jason followed and Steven went to get Stan. Once everyone was seated, I filled them in on what I had learned. I really didn't have much information other than confirming the Saurians were the clients. So, thinking I would give them some color commentary to make the meeting interesting, I went over all the trivial details. I was telling them about Fallen. Spending a great deal of time explaining what an ass I thought he was. Then almost as a joke I told them about the waste report. I had been amused that someone of his supposed power was in the trash business. I laughed as I told them. I thought he even classified the information to keep it a secret, to make sure nobody knew he was a junk man.

What I had thought was just a funny anecdote was serious to Stan. He jumped on it immediately. He had been putting together what I had said. The combination of increased deliveries because of a new acquisition plus the waste report meant a lot. Stan told us that The Trenton Group had just closed a contract for removing the nuclear waste from power plants in France.

Okay, so he was a high class garbage collector, I thought.

Jason spoke out, only saying one word. But it was a big one.

"Plutonium." One word—but it carried a lot of weight.

I might not be a scientist, but I did know Plutonium. Growing up during the cold war, I was aware of plutonium. I knew weapons grade wasn't nice. I didn't know if they were going to make it that or if they even needed it to be. I did know one thing. The word sent a chill up my spine. Looking around the table, I could tell I wasn't the only one.

The Alien's Gift

Now we knew what the Saurians were after. We still didn't know why, and what they were giving in trade? Those questions became paramount. We would have to find out a lot more about Plutonium. Steven had already started. There was a lap top on the patio, and Steven went to one of the best sources, Google. While he was gathering the basics, the rest of us tried to figure out the best way to discover what Fallen was getting out of the deal. I was going to have to visit with him a lot more. The thought of it didn't please me in the slightest. The thought of the Plutonium scared me enough to do it. We had a lot to try and figure out during the day. It was going to be a long day. I could hardly wait for it to end. I needed a drink. We all did.

Meetings were suspended for the rest of the day. Steven was going to try and gather enough information as possible on Plutonium. I was going to visit Fallen as much as I could handle for the rest of the day. Stan was trying to find out just how many plants the Trenton Group handled waste disposal for. Jason was working with both of them. Bill had to watch the zombie all day. We worked until a little after five before calling it a day. I had visited with Fallen for more than three hours during the day. Bill spent the same amount of time with the zombie. The other guys had been looking at screens and numbers until they were half blind. At dinner we just talked about everything but... We needed a mental break.

We were all sitting in the living room, chatting about mundane things and having a drink. The television was on in the background. Jason seemed to have the some of the same quirks as me. I was listening to Bill tell some kind of tall tale that would always end completely opposite from what you expected. Something on the television caught my eye. It was the man on the screen—he was shimmering. I almost dropped my drink. I interrupted Bill's story.

"That's a Saurian," I blurted out.

All eyes turned to the screen. Jason turned the sound up. The Saurian I was looking at was the leader of a Middle Eastern country. Jason asked, "Are you sure?"

I wished I could have told him I was wrong. But he was shimmering. "He isn't human," I said.

He was talking about war. Ranting like most dictators, he announced, his country had attacked the infidels who tried to invade his country. We listened to his war chant till the news moved on to another world crisis. Jason turned off the set.

Jason was the first to speak. "Oil, the Trenton Group wants the oil."

I was confused by his statement. How was going to war going to help Trenton Group? Jason looked at me as he tried to gather his thoughts. It would seem Trenton Group would win on multiple levels. They were a key player in the military industrial complex. War = money. They were also in energy, oil,

171

gas, you name it. I understood all that, but I still didn't see the connection to oil on this one. Jason spent the next hour explaining about corporations the size of Trenton Group.

These companies had more money than most nations. They could well afford to form one of the largest military forces in the world. Not to mention they are part of the military complex, so arming them would not only be easier, it would be cheaper. However, they don't need to do that. For them, there was a much better, and believe it or not, more profitable way. They spent less money gaining controlling governments and then use their military. That way they can make money selling the armaments and also reap gains from the booty. All that made sense with the exception of the oil. I didn't understand how it worked.

War would disrupt the flow of oil in the short term, and it could be years before they got control of the additional supply, Jason explained.

"That's a win-win for these companies."

He went on to explain that oil was rapidly becoming a scarce commodity. If the flow is disrupted temporarily the price increases dramatically. The short term effect would be an increase in their profits tenfold. Then, in a few years, after the existing supplies have dwindled, they would then have control over the new source.

"Supply and demand. You control the supply and you increase the cost. They do it with diamonds; they have for years. Why wouldn't they repeat it with oil? Lesson learned and lesson used."

I tried to think of what kind of a person would condemn so many people to death for nothing more than their own gain. How could they believe the cost to life was worth it? Just so they could live in a luxury beyond anything imaginable. I was just about to reject that theory as being beyond belief when I remembered Mr. Fallen.

People meant nothing to him. He was superior to normal people. He felt that with every fiber of his being. Slavery to him would have been the natural order. I had heard a question asked long ago. "What man would agree to slavery? If he were told he was the one who would become that slave." I don't think Mr. Fallen ever heard that question asked. If he did, he didn't think about it long. We knew the motivation for both sides now. They were using the Saurians to take nations to war, and they were paying them with Plutonium.

Chapter 20

Five men found themselves in the position of trying to counter this assault, somehow. It wasn't clear whether we were fighting for our freedom or for our existence. It was definitely an attack on our lifestyle and freedom, to say the least. The Saurians were in place and pushing countries into wars for profit. Were they only after the Plutonium? Would the wars they created just weaken us and set us up for the final fall, at their hands? It was an old plan, but still a good one. One we planned on stopping, somehow.

Jason was going to become a hacker again. That wasn't a choice he entered back into lightly. It was something he had to do. Stan was looking into money deep now. We needed any financial information that could be used against the Trenton Group. Steven, he would be back on the satellite monitors, assisting me.

I was going after the Saurians. I had to figure out a way to expose them. So far I only had one idea, one thing I could try. I would have to do it from here, and I needed the monitor. I wasn't sure if my plan would even work, but tomorrow I would try. Bill would be back on zombie watch. We decided to get started the first thing in the morning. Then we called it for the night.

I headed back to the house. A few minutes later I saw lights in my driveway. I had no idea who might be coming by at this time of the night. I walked to the front door to see, Bill met me there. We went to the patio to talk.

173

Bill had started home. He knew whatever I had planned wasn't going to be easy. He had to know what it was, and he wasn't leaving till he found out. I had known Bill long enough to realize he wouldn't sleep until he got this off his mind. So I told him.

"I was going to try and control a Saurian."

"How would that do any good?" he asked. Even if you're able to, and I'm not too sure you can."

"I'm going to attempt to crash one of the craft into the mother ship. When it makes its final approach, I'll take him over and steer the ship into the hull."

Bill spent the next few minutes explaining all the potential flaws in my plan, and there were many. I might not be able to control them at all. If I could and the ship goes astray, the mother ship could just take control of it and bring it in safely. If I do take control and, if the mother ship isn't able to regain control of it, the shielding may just cause it to bounce off like a balloon. I knew all these things. I had thought about them and more. But I let Bill have his say.

"You'll also have to wait until the moment of impact to pull out or they'll just avert it at the last moment." When Bill finished, he was almost out of breath. He had run through reason after reason so fast he didn't stop to breathe.

Now finished, he said, "Okay, I'm going to bed," and walked into the guest room.

He knew I was going to do what I had to do, but he had his say. I smiled and went to mine.

The next morning I headed for the patio as usual. I knew Bill would already be there. I knew that because it was Bill. Bill was sitting there sipping his coffee when I walked out. He didn't lift his head. I took my seat and waited. Bill would speak first, I knew that. He still had to finish from last night. I didn't have to wait long.

"What do you think they'll do when the ship crashes?" he asked.

It was Bill's way of saying if we're in this, we're in it together. I smiled into my cup.

"Probably make an accident report and call their insurance company."

He had my back in this, and it seemed to help. I wondered how I was lucky enough to meet such people. The rest of the morning consisted of one smart ass remark after another. It was our way of dealing with the tension.

This morning I spent a little more time with the dogs than usual. I didn't really have a feeling of apprehension, not for a second. I was casting my net to sea and had no second thoughts about that. I did have concern for the pups. What if this didn't work? If something goes wrong, what will happen to them?

The Alien's Gift

Who'll take care of them? We were launching an attack on a race that flew across the galaxy. Bill and the rest of the guys might be caught up in it. Who could I call at this time of the morning and what could I possibly say? The thought lingered in my head as we drove over to Jason's. I watched the dogs running along with the cart. I really did enjoy watching them run.

It was about six when we got to Jason's. The conversation was upbeat and full of bravado. We were going to kick some ass today for sure. Inside we were all hoping the ass that got kicked wasn't going to be ours. It was during breakfast that the thought came to me. When we got ready to start, I told Stan that I needed him to take my car and the dogs and go to Bill's house. That got strange looks. I knew I would have to explain.

I was concerned for the dogs. If anything went wrong, it could come back here. Stan could work from Bill's house with no problem. The dogs will be fine over there…and have someone to take care of them. Stan just nodded. He understood what I meant. Everyone else just went back to eating. They all knew what I was saying. When Stan got ready to leave, I met him at the car. I looked at Stan.

"Make sure you take good care of them."

"Promise." He said, smiling.

I was ready. We headed for the war room. I pulled my chair out and sat it in front of the monitor. I wasn't planning on jumping, but really didn't know. Security wasn't a concern anymore. If the enemy found me, there was a good chance they found us all. Steven turned on the computer and we began. We still planned on thirty minute shifts. We couldn't take the chance of the defense department finding out about us and doing something that might disrupt our plans. Weak as the plan might be, it was all we had.

We were on the second shift when I spotted a craft leaving the mother ship. Together with Steven, we followed it all the way down. It had landed at the same point as the last time. Once it had landed, I called for a break. We went outside, and Steven wanted to know why. Why now when we had them? He was concerned we would lose our chance. I didn't think so. I was pretty sure we had at least fifteen minutes while they loaded the craft. I wanted to wait until it loaded, that much I knew. I also wanted to make sure I was on top of my reflexes, so I decided to turn from the monitor until it was closer to time.

I had found a pack of cigarettes in my car the night before. I pulled one out now and lit it. Bill looked at me and commented.

"I guess you're just going to smoke one of those every time you do something like this, aren't you?"

I smiled, drank my coffee, and smoked that cigarette. I was ready now. We headed back down. We had left the monitor on the craft. It was a weather

175

satellite, so we weren't worried about being observed. I had been right. The craft was still on the ground. It was another fifteen minutes before it took off. As it left the ground, I moved to the craft. I eased into the mind inside. There was only one saurian in the craft, so knew I had the pilot.

The craft maneuvered with a joy stick just like a jet fighter. I had watched them flying it on the last trip. I eased into his vision, and I could feel the stick in his hand. He hadn't noticed my presence. I was in place and ready to take over when the time came. I watched as the mother ship got closer and the hatch opened. I waited until we got close, then pulled the controller to the side.

It moved, but he pulled it back before the ship could even veer. I could feel the panic rise up in him. He knew something was happening. I needed more control. Pushing hard into his mind, I pulled the stick over again. I don't know if I caught him by surprise or it was just sheer will, but the craft veered.

I watched as the mother ship came closer and closer holding right up until we started to impact the craft. I held, I could see the front of the hull start to crumble. There was no stopping the impact now. I jumped.

I was watching the screen as the craft disintegrated into the mother ship. The explosion was almost blinding. When the flash cleared, the craft was gone, but the mother ship looked unharmed.

"That should alert the defense department," I said.

I was stunned when they asked what I was talking about. They hadn't seen it? They didn't see a thing. The explosion had been contained within their shield and not seen. I had hoped to alert the defense department with the explosion. Steven said he didn't see a thing change on the monitor the entire time. Bill had been watching me, so he wouldn't have seen it anyway. I watched the screen to see what the response would be from the mother ship. The hatch closed. I watched for another fifteen minutes before we had to shut down. Nothing—there had been no reaction at all.

We went outside for a break. I explained to them what had happened and how I had to fight for control over the craft, almost losing the battle in the process. It was decided that I wouldn't attempt to return to the ship today. They had to be on heightened alert, and we were afraid I might be found. That plan a total loss, I asked Jason how he was doing. He said he was working his way into The Trenton Group system. It would still be several days before he was ready to launch any kind of assault on the group.

I decided not to call Stan back here yet. I wasn't sure if they were aware of us. They might just show up at the door. I didn't want my pups here if they did. If the pilot had died in the crash, they wouldn't know about me. I hadn't heard him transmit any thoughts during our struggle. He was mostly caught by surprise as he wrestled me for the controls. The day was still young. Stan could stay where he was for a few more hours.

Steven went to look for Mr. Fallen after the break was over. Jason went back onto his computer to continue his work. Bill and I sat on the patio. Once everyone left, Bill looked at me and asked, "How close did you come?"

I couldn't deceive Bill and get away with it, so I told him, "I rode it in."

He just sat back for a moment before he spoke again. "How many times can you pull this off Marc?"

It was an important question. It was also a question I didn't know the answer to. I didn't even try to answer. Bill wasn't expecting one anyway. Steven broke the moment when he came out to tell me he had found Fallen. It was time to go back to work.

We pulled the chair back behind the screen before I sat down. I wasn't dealing with aliens this time. If I had to switch, the less they knew would still be better. Fallen was back in the U.S., New York City to be exact. Steven had shown me the building. He was in the Trenton building. Fallen's office was in the penthouse. I wasn't surprised. I moved to my chair, winked at Bill, and was off. I moved through the penthouse until I found Fallen. He was upset about something, and I wasn't really surprised. This wasn't a happy man. For all his money and power, he was one of the most miserable people I had ever known. I eased into his mind, reluctantly I admit.

Just as the first time that I had been with Mr. Fallen, it wasn't an enjoyable experience. I had expected that. He was at a meeting with several people. I tuned to his hearing so I could follow the conversation. The Saurians needed a shipment replaced. It seemed they had some sort of incident that caused the loss of the last one. Fallen personally could care less, thinking it wasn't his loss. They had delivered the shipment on time and wouldn't just jump to replace it. He didn't like the pressure put on him, feeling it was his fault it had been lost.

I decided to see who was in the meeting and tuned into Fallen's sight. He was looking at one of his flunkies as he continued to release his wrath. It wasn't until he turned his head, sweeping the table to insure everyone was suitably nervous, that I saw him. The shimmer, a Saurian, was sitting at the table. They had infiltrated his inner core. I almost chuckled. I knew they hadn't trusted him anymore then I had. Fallen asked him what had happened to the shipment. Realizing the potential of learning something, I jumped to him.

He was forming the answer in his mind in English. Because of that, he was thinking in English. They didn't know exactly what had happened. I got that clearly in his thoughts. He didn't know, none of them knew. It was almost astonishment he felt when he thought of the actual incident. It just couldn't happen. Fallen had turned his attention back to the first flunky.

177

"Tell them we'll do what we can." Then he barked at them to get out.

I jumped back to Fallen as they were leaving. A moment later the door opened and Jim Blanchard—President Jim Blanchard, retired to be exact—came walking in. He was also a member of the Group. I hadn't voted for him when he ran for office. I was especially happy about that once I discovered what this group was about. I didn't trust him when he was in office; it seems my instincts were right. Fallen greeted him warmly as he walked in. For the first time, Fallen was in the presence of an equal. I could feel it in his mind.

President Blanchard was talking about the Middle Eastern stand in.

"With any luck, the lizard head will have them to war in a week," he was telling Fallen.

My respect for him fell even lower as I listened to him speak. He went on to brag about armament sales already having picked up in the region. It seems they were already making money. I hoped Jason was doing something about that. The conversation drifted into a discussion about their power and riches. They were starting to make me nauseous. I had enough, so I jumped.

When I opened my eyes, Bill was there. He was a good sight to see after having been in the presence of those two men for that long. Jason and Steven were already done for the day. I had spent two hours with Fallen. We got up to walk out to the patio. I had my phone in my hand calling Stan as we walked. We didn't have any visitors by now, I didn't think we would. Bill's house was only a few miles away, and it wasn't ten minutes before my pups were home. Homecoming was especially exciting today. The pups are used to seeing me constantly throughout the day. Being gone for several hours was a lifetime to them. It always was. Today I agreed. I was happy to have them back.

After dinner I told the guys about the alien infiltrator in Fallen's group. I don't think they thought for a minute that someone had infiltrated them. I don't think they contemplated it even being possible. That was a plus for our side. Arrogance and sense of superiority would work in our favor.

Over the next few days we would try and whip that mental smirk from their face. I wasn't sure if we would win or not. But now I knew they would know we were in the fight either way. Steven and I would be working on a new assignment. Tomorrow we would start looking at all the leaders in the world we could find. I wanted a list of the imposters. I would find them one by one. Then we would take the fight to them.

Bill had decided to stay the night. It was the end game, and he wasn't going to be out of my sight long during it. I wasn't sure what he could do if they caught my mind. I didn't even know if that could even be done. Can you catch a mind? Well, if they did, I bet Bill would try and crawl in my head and come get me. I took comfort in that thought. Even if I knew that it couldn't be done.

The Alien's Gift

Jason came over to my house that evening. I was surprised by his visit. I had seen Jason every minute of every day. There had never been a reason for him to come over. Bill and I were sitting on the patio when we saw his cart pull up. Jason sat down without saying a word. I didn't know Jason as well as Bill. I was amazed most of the time how much alike we all were, though.

Bill knew it, too. He just looked at me, and we waited. Both of us knew he would talk in his own time. Jason cleared his throat before he spoke. That wasn't something he did normally. When he spoke, his voice was tight, full of emotion. I might have mentioned before, guys are not good with emotion. When we do have it, we find it uncomfortable. Jason was uncomfortable. Bill and I sat quietly.

"I just wanted to say thank you to both of you."

Jason paused after getting those words out. He wasn't done, and we knew it.

"You both know as well as I do, we might not make it through this. That's a fact I've dealt with for a long time. I didn't think I would make it."

I remembered the fear I felt in Jason when I first touched his mind. That was what he was referring to.

"I just wanted to say, if we don't make it, it's been a great privilege to have known you both." We knew what he was doing. Bill and I had done it the day before. If we didn't make it, he just wanted us to know. He had said essentially what he had to say. I tried to turn the conversation and end it on an upbeat note. I told him I had too many good friends around me to go anywhere. Bill jumped in saying he just got a new house, so he wasn't planning on moving.

It was our way of saying we knew, and we felt the same. We sat and talked about nothing for awhile before calling it a night. I didn't think we would lose. The idea of winning was close to insanity, I know. I just kept the belief we would. If not, it would end with valiant men at my side, and that's not a bad way to leave. I slept well that night.

The next morning we got to Jason's early. Jason was sitting outside and already had our coffee on the table as we walked up. For a moment I wondered how he knew we'd be there that early. Then I realized he had to have seen the cart lights as we drove over. Mysteries usually have a simple answer.

The pups had come up to lay by my chair. They hadn't moved far from me for long since they came back from Bill's. I was kind of surprised that they would be that spooked over being away for such a short time. After all they had spent all day home alone at the old house. Bill and Jason even commented about their behavior. Later when we started into the computer room they even tried to follow me in. They're allowed in the house, they're allowed almost anywhere. I spoil them, I admit that completely. I didn't want

179

them in the computer room for other reasons. I didn't want them seeing me during the times I was gone.

Steven and I spent the day finding people of power. We wanted to know how many of them "shimmered." I was happy to see most of them were who they were supposed to be. I did find three Saurians. Two were other world leaders, and the third was the Captain of a military vessel. All of them concerned me. At least the world leaders weren't involved in any conflicts. Not yet, that is. We spent the day looking. I had to see them broadcast live in order to see the shimmer. I was pretty sure of that; not positive, but pretty sure.

Later in the day I decided to learn more about the Middle Eastern leader. Steven found him for me, and I jumped to his location. As I eased into his mind I tuned into his sight and hearing. I wanted to spend some time with him so I could observe what was taking place around him. See who was with him. No matter what he was doing there was always one man who stayed with him. Suspicious of him, I move to his mind. He was a Saurian also. They communicated constantly telepathically. I was unable to understand any of their thoughts, but I stayed with them anyway, in the hope I could learn something. It was when they were alone that I found the thing I was looking for. Their weakness, the way I could expose them to the world.

They always seemed to drop their shield when they were in private. I wasn't sure if it was for comfort or conserving power. I didn't see how they did it the first couple of times. It wasn't until the third time I spotted the pen in their pockets. They would click it, and the shield would turn on or off. That's what I had been looking for. I decided to call it a day and head home. I jumped. As soon as I got back I headed for the patio and my pups. They met me at the door.

We discussed the future during dinner. We were breaking a rule. But time was getting short. Besides, it was looking bright. Jason was only a couple of days from finishing his plan. He was going to attack Trenton Groups' funds. Jason planned on spreading they're money so far and thin, it would take years to find. At the same time inside documents would be made public, exposing the company's involvement with the Saurians.

Once he was ready, we would follow up by exposing the Saurian imposters we had discovered. Exposing the aliens and destroying The Trenton Group was the combined goal. Jason was sure the Group wouldn't be totally destroyed, but knew it would be put it in a difficult position at least. We were almost there and starting to believe the battle was ours to win. I had been sleeping well, but I'd be sleeping better tonight.

The next morning I started to get out of bed. As I stood to get up, my legs collapsed from under me. I was flat on the floor. The pups were as startled as I was, and they came to me immediately. I tried to stand, but my legs didn't seem to want to respond. Sensing something wrong, the pups started to howl. I tried to calm them even as the fear grew in me. They weren't about to be quieted. Bill came running into the room. He thought the aliens had arrived, and I was in a fight for my life. What he found was me lying on the floor, unable to get up. He called for an ambulance.

Jason and the brothers were at the hospital even before the doctor came in to talk to me. The doctor told me they needed to run a few tests. The x-rays found several tumors. They were all throughout my body. He had never seen anything like this, and his concern was obvious. It took just over two days for the doctors to give me their final diagnosis. I was dying. More than that, they didn't know why I wasn't dead already. I had tumors throughout my body. They hadn't finished running the tests on all of them, but the test they had completed were cancerous. The doctor in charge said he couldn't even give me a time, again saying he wasn't sure how I was still alive as we spoke. I had Bill bring me home.

Later when I was on the patio I wondered what had happened and why now. I had always had a stoic outlook on life, felt like I was an old soul. You know, having always felt I had kind of been there and done that thing. Death never bothered me, death had never scared me. When it came, it came. It was part of life. It just couldn't happen now. We were too close. I couldn't die, not now, not yet. They needed me. We couldn't do it without me. How could I help? I wouldn't be here to do it. I thought of Ari.

ARI, I screamed his name out in my mind.

Chapter 21

I had been sitting on the patio for over an hour now. Bill kept coming in and out checking to see if I needed anything. I smiled at him telling him, I was okay and still capable of handling myself. I had tried to get him to go home, saying that I would be alright. He wasn't buying that. He was here, and I'd better get used to it. The dogs hadn't moved from my side long enough to do anything since I had gotten back home.

Jason and the guys had been at my house more in the last day than since I moved in. Everyone was here. Everyone except for one person, the one person I really needed...Ari. Why hadn't I been able to reach him? I didn't feel that weak. True, I had bad moments, but I was calling him with my mind. Why couldn't I reach him?

It wasn't working. I kept calling out more in desperation than anything else now. Had I lost my gift? Had the cancer taken that from me, too? Was Ari just too far away to hear my calls? I didn't know and was beginning to just give up hope. Then it hit me. I was calling Ari. I kept yelling out in my mind calling his name. I would try and jump to him. Could I? Could I jump across the universe to find his mind? I knew of a location. I knew the room where I had first met Lenί and the watchers. It was still clear in my head.

I would need to have Bill watch me, more now than ever. I called out to him, and everyone came. Bill, Jason, Stan, and Steven came busting out the door onto the patio. They scared the crap out of me. I realized this was just

182

The Alien's Gift

as hard for them as it was for me. Maybe in some ways it was even harder for them. Trying to ease the atmosphere, I started to laugh. Now they were confused. But I preferred confusion to fear.

Since they had all come out, I asked them to sit down. I figured I would tell them what I was about to do. I explained that I had been trying to reach Ari since we found out the news. It hadn't worked. Now I was going to try something else. I was going to jump to Rikiel and find him myself. Bill didn't like that idea at all. Jason was one step behind him. I was going to try and jump across the universe. What if I missed? What might happen to my mind in the middle of nowhere?

They were good questions, but as much as I appreciate their concern. They wouldn't stop me from trying. The rest of the conversation was even more difficult. I had to explain that even though I appreciated their concern, the reality was I was dying. From what the doctors had said, I should already be dead. I had nothing to lose. But they did. They needed help with the Saurians and, for that, they needed Ari. I wasn't sure the Rikiens would even help, but I had to try. This was my last battle, and I didn't want to lose. I needed them to watch me while I was gone.

Finally they agreed. They knew there didn't seem to be much choice in the matter. Bill was the last to let it go, but he wanted to talk to me before I tried it. Looking at the guys, he asked if he could speak in private. They turned to walk into the house. Jason stopped at the door, turning to say, "Call us before you leave."

It seemed that I was going to have four watchers on this trip. Once we were alone, Bill sat down, his legs just giving under pressure. He seemed to be carrying the weight of the world on his shoulders.

"You come back, you hear me?" It was almost a command.

I could see the pain in his eyes as he spoke. Bill was my best friend and had been for years. If I could do anything for anyone, it would be for him. I didn't know if I could do this one, but I agreed. Bill couldn't let it go yet. He saw it in my face; now he knew he might be saying goodbye.

"Don't you die out there. Not alone."

We sat silent for several minutes before Bill called the guys back out.

I smiled as I looked at my friends by my side. I told them to cheer up. I would see them again in just a few minutes. I wasn't sure if that was true. Bill had known I wasn't, that was why he couldn't just let me go. As my eyes caught theirs, I said goodbye to each of them mentally. I didn't project the thought. This was my goodbye. I didn't want them to know that. I leaned back in the chair and closed my eyes. I focused hard on the room on Rikiel and jumped.

It was dark. I felt nothing. Had I missed? Was I dead? Was this death, my mind just no place? I couldn't believe that. Your mind can't just wake up in nothing when you die. That made no sense at all. I reached out. I had to keep looking for Ari. I couldn't feel him. I couldn't even feel a stream I could travel to find him. I had failed. I didn't die; at least I don't think I did. But I couldn't feel Ari. I wondered what happened to him and Lení.

Marc! Marc, is that you?

It was Lení. I had found her. I don't know why I had been looking so hard for Ari and had only thought her name for a moment.

Leni, I called out in my mind like a man grabbing for a life raft in choppy seas.

Marc, how did you...

She stopped in mid-thought.

Marc, you're damaged. I can feel it in your mind. It was a statement, and she was right.

I need Ari, I told her, still not able to close the distance I felt between our minds.

She seemed to be far from me, I couldn't find her. My mind reached out in every direction.

Marc!

That was Ari. I had found him.

Ari, I called out to him. *I need your help.*

Ari's words were short and sharp.

Go back to your body. I'll come to you. He was giving me a command.

I started to explain why I needed him. When his mind barked back at me. *NOW!*

I jumped.

I opened my eyes. I was back, sitting on the patio. Everyone was still sitting there, watching me. Jason, Steven, and Stan sat up to greet me immediately. When I opened my eyes, their relief was obvious. Bill just stood and walked off the patio. He walked out into the yard. He needed to be alone for a moment or two. My heart reached out to him. I think the worst part of dying was the pain it was going to bring to my friends.

The others wanted to know if I'd had any luck finding Ari. It was only when I said yes that Bill turned. I was about to tell them how I found Ari, when he spoke in my mind. I told them he was with me and went silent. I focused on Ari. *I need your help. We need your help, and fast.* I only hoped he would.

Ari spoke to me almost as soon as I left Rikiel. He didn't understand how I did what I did.

"How could you have reached across the universe and made contact?"

I told him it was from my connection with Gera. He still seemed confused. My connections with Gera would have strengthened my mind. He had known that. He had actually told me that himself. But this, this ability, was way beyond that. That minor contact couldn't have caused this much of a change.

I realized he didn't know about the mind melding. Of course he didn't. That was in his future. I started to tell him, but he stopped me before I could explain, telling me instead that he felt serious damage in me and needed to come to see what was happening. He asked if I still had the equipment he had sent to us back at the old house. Naturally I had brought it up here with me. I wasn't about to leave alien technology like that just sitting at the old house with me here. When I told him that, he instructed me to set it up. He finished, saying he would contact me again soon.

He was gone, just that fast. I brought my attention to the patio. I let them know what Ari had said and about the equipment. As soon as I mentioned the equipment, Stan and Steven took off, almost breaking the door down getting back into the house. The equipment had been stored in a closet. They knew exactly where it was. They were the ones who had put it away for me. I started to laugh.

"I guess Steven and Stan are going to re-assemble the machine," I said.

Jason asked what was going on. I told him Ari was coming. Jason had never seen a Rikien and was excited to hear the news. Bill had sat there quietly the entire time all this was going on. Excited about the visit, Jason got up to go see the machine and to help them prepare for Ari's arrival. Once we were alone, Bill asked, "Can he help you?"

"I didn't ask."

I explained that once he realized it was me, he ordered me back immediately, insisting he come to me instead.

"Guess we should get prepared to meet our guest," I said as I got up.

Bill was at my side before I made it to my feet. I could walk alright now. Nobody was sure why. He didn't care. His hand on my shoulder, we started to walk in.

"Welcome home" was all he said.

We sat in my living room for another ten minutes waiting for Ari to contact me again. Once he did, I confirmed the equipment was set up and ready for his arrival. Moments later he was standing in front of me. He turned to Jason, not sure who he might be. I took a moment to introduce him. Jason was more than impressed, to say the least. A Rikien is something to see. Ari greeted Jason as a friend. He was among friends and accepted him on that alone. *The friend of my friend is my friend seemed to be a universal concept.* I thought as I watched them greet each other.

I had just finished introducing Ari to Jason when Lení appeared. This was indeed an unexpected pleasure. I pulled her to the side, spending a little time with her alone. Ari was still busy greeting the rest of the guys. I felt close with LenÍ, maybe because of the event during our practice switching, or maybe because I had mind melded with her father. I didn't know why, I just knew it was a close bond.

Greetings and introductions over Ari turned his attention to me. By that time I had already sat down. My body was no longer able to handle the exertion of standing for very long. Ari sat before me. He wanted to know how I had done what I had done. I started to explain to him—them. LenÍ had to know as well. I believed it was with my connection with Gera. Again Ari expressed his dismay at the contact having that much effect on my mind.

Now I was able to take the time to explain about the mind melding with Gera. Then it was Ari and LenÍ's turn to sit down. This news caught them both completely off guard. They sat quietly as I told them of everything that had transpired between us and the future Gera. This seemed to answer one question for Ari. Now he understood how I had connected with LenÍ. My mind having melded with Gera gave me an exceptionally strong connection to her. She was his daughter and a huge part of him.

Bill jumped into the conversation. He had been sitting listening patiently as I explained everything to Ari and LenÍ. I had finished bringing Ari up to date on the future contact. Now it was Bill's turn to speak. He was angry, there was no denying that. You could hear it in his voice. He wanted to know why the future Ari and Gera hadn't been aware of my illness and come to help. Ari listened to Bill patiently. He knew why Bill was mad, and Ari waited for him to release some of his frustrations and fear before he answered.

When he finally did, his answer came in the form of a question. I think he did it for two reasons. He wanted Bill to understand why it was possible, and at the same time highly unlikely. He also wanted Bill to realize that this wasn't anyone's fault, including Bill himself.

"I learned about a thing you called the lotto last time I was here, Bill. Do you know of it?" Ari asked him.

Bill told him he did, but didn't know what that had to do with what he was asking.

"What was the last set of winning numbers" Ari asked.

Bill said he didn't know.

"Why don't you know?" Ari asked.

Bill was starting to get annoyed with this line of questioning.

"I didn't look. Why should I?" The words spat from his lips.

Ari waited, watching Bill. He was waiting for him to find the answer himself.

Bill stood for a moment, waiting. Finally he realized Ari wasn't going to answer. Then he understood, Ari *had* answered. He sat down putting his face in his hands.

Lení walked over and placed her hand on his shoulder. "There's nobody to blame for this, Bill. Not Ari, not my father, not me...not you."

It was at that moment I understood just how much blame Bill had taken on himself for my illness. I should have known it. How could I have been so stupid? Bill had been in charge of watching me all those times. Every time I had left he was the one responsible for watching me. And now I was dying. He was carrying that, and without realizing it, I had let him. If they could do nothing more, I owed Lení and Ari, relieving that burden. I looked at Lení, my eyes thanking her. She smiled back at me. Bill would be alright, we knew that now. He just needed a little time.

Ari brought his attention back to me. Both he and Lení had felt the weakness in me during our contact. He wanted to know more about what was happening to my body. Not being a human, the word cancer had no meaning to him. He had no background about it to draw on. It was true he could read about it and learn the clinical information in no time. However, I was dying from it. He wanted to switch with me. Explaining that would help give him the information he needed. I told him I had no problem with that. I sat back and relaxed, Ari switched. I was now in Ari's body.

I hadn't realized how much pain I was in, not until now, it was gone. I was concerned now for Ari in my body. It didn't look like it was bothering him. He seemed to be doing an examination from the inside out with his mind. You could see the way his eyes were moving, almost as if he was looking at different parts of my body. His eyes would roll up or to the side, following as his mind searched.

Moments later I was back in my body, and the pain returned. I wasn't really prepared for that, I almost let out a yell, but controlled it. Ari had completed his exam. He was amazed at what he had discovered. To him, the cancer was like my body had lost control over itself. The individual cells had gone astray. They had lost their natural pattern. He was taking a DNA sample with him for study. Ari was a physician, I knew that, but I wasn't a Rikien.

That was when Bill asked if he could put me in one of those pods. He'd been thinking about it for awhile. The words came out hard. For Bill, the pod would almost be the same as if I had died. They would never see me again, he knew. But as he looked at me, he said, "At least we'll know you're alive."

Ari looked at Bill, wanting to give him the answer he knew he wanted or needed to hear. He just couldn't. His answer was short.

"Our pods and their composition are for Rikiens." He didn't go on. He didn't need to. A moment later Ari said, "I will study the DNA Bill, give me a chance."

Bill looked at Ari for a moment before he answered, "I have to. You're our only chance." Then Bill walked out of the room.

I told Ari we still needed to talk, but not right now, I couldn't keep talking; the words were stuck. Ari knew I had to see a friend and said he would come back later. I thanked him and Lení. Then I went to find my friend.

It was a little more than an hour before Ari returned. We were still in the living room and more than ready to find out if he had learned anything. He didn't have much to tell us yet. He was still interested in how something like this could happen. He had researched earth's records on cancer, and the one thing that struck him as odd was the extent of the cancer. It seemed to be everywhere at once in my body. He wanted to figure out why.

I was more interested in a bigger problem. I wanted to live. I couldn't debate that point. But I was more concerned with our other problem. I tried to explain what had been taking place. Telling him how close we had been, when this. Well, he knew the rest, and as much as I hoped he could do something about that, I needed to find out if we could get their help on the bigger problem, in case.

When I was explaining what we had learned, I told him how I would jump and eavesdrop. I saw something in his eyes when I said that. He questioned me about the procedure I'd been using. He focused in on my eavesdropping, as opposed to when I switched. He started to explain why, when I had gone to Rikiel he had been so concerned. I had pulled with every bit of concentration I could muster. He asked me if I was doing the same thing when I would do what I referred to as eavesdropping. I told him I jumped the same all the time. That was the missing link for Ari. It seemed to answer the question that he needed to have answered.

Ari sat for a moment absorbing the information he just received. Before he explained what he believed to be the reason for my cancer, referring to a conversation we had long ago. He reminded me how he said the mind looks over the body. I remembered, although I didn't understand what he was talking about at the time, not really, how the mind is separate, but not really.

He was trying to explain that, when I pulled, I seemed to draw most of my mind with me. I only left enough of my mind to keep the autonomic parts of my body functional. That I did unconsciously, probably due to a survival instinct. I had done it so often, each time leaving my body without the mind to watch over it. Without that control, the cancer developed.

I did it to myself, I thought.

As he was talking, I thought of the first time I had seen myself when I was out of my body. I remembered that zombie look that scared me. My own subconscious was trying to tell me. I remember how each time I came back,

I would check myself. How I wanted to make sure I was never left alone in that state again. I needed someone to watch me I was right in that. But that someone, it was supposed to be me. I hadn't left enough of me to watch over my own body. I could have avoided it all by just keeping more in control of my body when I jumped. Ari explained there wasn't that problem when I switched. When I switched, another mind was in my body. A mind controls the body it's in. While I was gone, the mind I switched with would watch over my body automatically, just as if it were its own.

Bill spoke up again.

"Well, now you know, so in the future tell Gera not to mind meld. Marc won't get the ability. Then he won't have cancer."

"The paradox already exists," Ari shook his head sadly as he said the words.

We were confused. Ari could see that so he tried to explain. This is the way I understood it. I had to have cancer. Ari wouldn't be here now if I didn't. The only way he could tell Gera not to meld was to know about the cancer. Now it gets sticky. If he told Gera and a mind meld didn't happen, I wouldn't have gotten cancer. If I didn't have cancer, Ari wouldn't be here now. Gera would perform the mind meld. Catch twenty-two.

I was developing a headache, I knew that. There was still a bigger problem than my mortality as far as I was concerned. I turned my attention to that. I explained the problem to Ari again. Ari listened patiently as I ran through all the details of what we had discovered. I was about to go into details on what we had been about to do when Ari stopped me, explaining that he was primarily a doctor. That at least was the closest word in our language for what he was.

He said he would return to Rikiel and present our case, but that he would continue to study this cancer, as we called it. He was going to try and find an answer for it. Ari walked over and touched his hand to my head. He said he was giving me life force. It would do nothing to correct the damage. It was only to give me strength. Maybe give me a little more time, that was all. I thanked him for that. Then he was gone.

I felt better after his touch. I was ready to move out of this house for some fresh air. I headed for the patio, the pups following close, just as they had been doing since before I had gone to the hospital. When we got outside I decided they needed some exercise, and I could use a change of scenery. I invited myself over to Jason's house for the rest of the day. It doesn't sound like much; it wasn't really. It was just a short golf cart ride between two yards. But for me it was out. So Bill and I jumped into one of the carts. Jason and the guys got in the other.

There were two golf carts, a large yard, and a group of kids. You know we challenged them to a race. The carts shot off across the yard toward the gate that separated our properties. I watched as the dogs pulled away from us. How I loved to watch them run. Their grace and power as they ran was always thrilling for me to see. I was going to miss that.

Bill and I came in second in the race. We were beaten out by the dogs by only a few feet. Actually the dogs had run twice as far as we had gone. I laughed as I watched them run ahead, only to turn and run back past the carts, before turning to lead the way again. Jason, being the driver of the losing team, had to pour the drinks. That night we had pizzas and beer. I wanted the night to be one that was remembered. Every night had to be, from now till...

Ari had lifted a lot of weight off all our shoulders that day. He hadn't fixed the problem with the aliens. He didn't cure my cancer. He gave me a little hope these guys might have help. He gave me a little strength, not a lot, but enough to enjoy the day. It wasn't much, but it seemed to make the day better for us all. We used it well.

It was almost nine when we called it an evening. Bill and I got into the cart and were ready to head back to the house. Jason came running out to stop us. He was very excited and told us we needed to come into the house. When I asked what was up, all he would say was you've got company. Bill and I looked at each other as we got out of the cart.

What company could I have tonight? Why would they have come to Jason's house? There was only one way to find out the answers to the question. We headed for the house. On the way in Jason couldn't contain his excitement. I had no idea who it might be. But Jason sure seemed to be happy. No, happy wasn't the word. Ecstatic is the best description for what I saw.

I was walking toward the living room when I saw Ari though the door. I was happy to see him again, but thought it was strange that he was here. He had only left a few hours earlier, and I doubted he had answers this fast. Never-the-less it was always good to see him. As I walked into the room, Gera came into view. Now I was excited. Jason had known how happy I would be about seeing him. That was what the kid excitement I saw in him was about. He was thrilled for me.

I resisted the urge to run and grab Gera up in my arms. It wasn't the way to great a Rikien. Besides, I wasn't that strong. Instead, I walked up to Gera and, as he turned, I placed my hands palms up on my thighs, looked him straight in the eyes, and bowed deeply at the waist. I had hoped I had done it correctly. As I rose back up, the look in Gera's eyes told me it was good enough. I had done it their way, now I would do it mu way. I wrapped my arms around Gera and gave him a hug for just a moment.

Once I released Gera from my grasp he stepped back, placed his hands

The Alien's Gift

palm up on his thighs, looked me in the eye and returned the bow. I felt bad thinking that I had just interrupted the ceremony. As he straightened up he looked at me a moment. Then with a smile spreading across his face he stepped forward and wrapped his arms around me returning the hug, just as I had done. I hadn't disrupted it; I had only altered it.

Gera released me and stepped back. LenÍ stepped forward. I hadn't seen her when I came in. She started to place her hands on her thighs, changing her mind as she threw her arms around me and gave me a warm embrace instead. She also remembered to throw in the kiss I had taught her.

After our greetings were over I introduced Jason to Gera. Jason had been watching Gera since his arrival. Gera was the Santa whom Jason had been excited about. He was aware what this Rikien meant to me personally from conversations we had. Jason stood in front of Gera his smile warm and genuine. Then he placed his hands palms up on his thighs, looked Gera in the eyes and said, "If I may" then he proceeded to bow. As he stood, he looked at Gera. Suddenly he wondered if he had done the right thing, had he been too presumptuous.

Gera looked at me a moment, then back to Jason before saying, "I am honored."

The smile on Jason's face lifted me just that much more. In honoring Gera, Jason had been honoring me.

Gera came over and asked me to walk with him for awhile. I led him out onto the patio. Gera apologized for not having come sooner. He explained that he has just found out about what was happening to me. He kept trying to tell me how sorry he was for what he had brought into my life, going on to say, "If had only known."

As he was talking I couldn't help but remember how earlier in the evening LenÍ had released a good friend from a burden he was carrying. It was an unjust burden, one that was not his to bear. I only hoped now I could do as well with my friend—LenÍ's father.

I explained to Gera that this wasn't his fault. It was no one's fault. How could he have known this would happen? If I had known it wouldn't have happened, I would have controlled what I was doing. If I were to blame him for this, I would have to blame myself. Responsibility for an illness can't be born. He wasn't the blame for his, I wasn't going to take blame for mine. Diseases are not ours to own. Illness is its own evil. I wouldn't let the honor he bestowed upon me be overshadowed by it. Gera was looking at me as I spoke.

"Marc, once again you've honored me by your friendship."

His words embarrassed me. I responded as eloquently as I was capable. "My friend, the honor has been mine."

191

Ari was watching us as we walked in. His attention focused on Gera. I hadn't realized earlier how much stress Ari himself was under. Seeing Gera now seemed to release a lot of it, but not all. I understood why his friend had been carrying that burden, and Ari felt the weight pressing down just as I had with Bill. I walked into the room behind Gera. He was walking over toward Lenĺ and Jason. Bill and Ari were coming toward me.

Ari had come over to apologize for what he'd to put everyone through. He had been the only one who had carried the burden of knowledge for the last three thousand years. He had just told Gera and Lenĺ a short time ago.

Bill asked, "Why?"

"The paradox," Ari said as he looked at Bill.

"I explained that to you. It was because of that I couldn't tell Gera or Lenĺ. Not until after I had been told in your time."

I couldn't help but think about how many burdens were carried by so many. I hoped we had finally been able to release the last of them. Ari, although knowing he had a paradox that had to run its course, still had a burden, one he had carried alone, for over three thousand years. He couldn't even chance telling Lenĺ. He didn't want her to have to bear it nor chance her letting it slip to Gera early. The stakes were too high.

Bill still wanted one more question answered. As he asked he drew the attention of the room. "So, is it over? Marc, is he all right, or will he…did you…can you cure him?"

Ari was looking at Bill while he was asking his question. As Bill was speaking everyone in the room had moved in. They were now standing in front of Ari, waiting to hear his answer.

His eyes went from one person to the next. He knew we all wanted the answer. He also knew I was the one who wanted to know the most. His eyes settled on me as he spoke. "I don't know yet."

How was that for irony? The one man who knew I was dying for the last three thousand years didn't know. He went on to explain it had taken him almost three months to work out the changes in the pod to repair a human. Jason interrupted this time.

"Wait, you knew how to cure him that long ago. So why don't you know now?"

Ari took a deep breath, preparing to answer. He looked at me, hoping I could handle what he was about to say.

"By the time I found the answer, it was too late."

It took a minute for what he just said to sink in. Bill was the first to find his voice. "What do you mean, too late?"

Ari looked at me as he started to speak. The pain I felt in his eyes tore deep into my being. "Marc, you died before I found the answer."

He told us when he had finally found the answer he had come back to look for me. But my mind was missing. The paradox had begun for Ari. That was the point he had to decide if any future were going to change, it had to be at this point in time. Now, tonight.

I had sat down and wasn't following much more at this point. There's something about being told you die in just a week or two that takes your legs out from under you. Jason had walked to the other side of the room, no longer part of the conversation. Bill had walked out to the patio and was sitting with the pups. Steven and Stan were still listening to Ari.

"Well, you got the pod now, right? Marc will be okay now, right?" Steven asked.

I looked up as I heard Steven. Jason turned from the far side of the room. Bill was standing in the door. We had all heard the question. We all knew that my life depended on his answer.

I looked at Gera and Lenĩ searching their faces for a clue. They were both solemn. That wasn't reassuring to me. Ari finally found his voice again and was answering.

"I don't know."

The answer was simple and honest. *Of course he can't know for sure*, I thought. *Not until we try it. I climb in the pod go to sleep for oh three thousand years, then I wake up or don't.* How could he know? We had to find out. Tonight was when we would find out or at least start too. *I would either wake up or I wouldn't*, I thought, *in three thousand years*. Either way, tonight would be the last time I saw my friends. To them, tonight I would die. I debated at that point. Do I go to the pod and live? What do I live for? My pups, my friends would all be gone. Do I stay and die in the next two weeks or go and die now? Hell of a choice.

Chapter 22

Ari had been watching me as he had given his answer. He was a wise man and knew I needed to be given some time. Gera was the one who spoke the words. "You need time to absorb all you've learned. We'll come back in an hour."

I was pretty numb, but as Gera spoke I stood, I walked to my friend and, placing my palms on my thighs, I bowed. Gera returned the honor. Lenİ, I gave a hug. Ari, how do I thank this man? If not for this man, I had no choice to make. I could only honor him as I had Gera. Facing him, I turned my hands palms up on my thighs, and bowed, thanking him as I stood. Ari was moved and thanked me as they slid from out of sight.

"Well, I don't know about you guys, but I'm ready for the patio and a drink."

I was trying to keep my voice as cheerful as possible when I spoke. Moments later we were sitting around the table sipping our drinks when Jason spoke, "You have to go, Marc."

Stan and Steven joined in, saying they agreed it was the only thing to do. Bill was the last to speak.

"Going to miss you, bud."

His was a simple statement, but the one that put it in perspective. This would be the last time I saw any of them. It was that or I stayed here for a couple more days before I die. To be honest, I hadn't really decided which

The Alien's Gift

was best. Not yet. I didn't know if I could say goodbye. I told them that. I believed my choice was to lose them all now or in a week, maybe two. Bill gave me the only answer.

"You know how much you mean to me, to all of us. The thought of not seeing you again hurts. But you won't be dead. We'll know you're not dead, just gone. The other way we know. We watch you die, and soon."

It was almost time for Ari to return. Everyone headed back into the living room. I lingered for a moment longer with the pups. They were the only ones I wouldn't be able to make understand. As I stood to walk in, my eyes were filled with tears. Bill had been standing in the door watching. He knew this would be the hardest part for me. He walked over to join me.

"I won't let you down," he said. He reached down scratching them on the heads as he spoke.

I knew he wouldn't, still hearing it helped. We went inside and joined the guys. Ari arrived right on time, showing up just as I had sat down. I told him I was ready, but I needed to know if the Rikiens were going to be able to help with our other problem. Ari began by saying that the Rikiens were a non violent race. For that reason they couldn't do anything to harm another race.

Ari finished by saying that he and Gera might be able to lend some assistance, for me not to worry because things always find a way to work themselves out. I wasn't comforted by his answer and was about to change my mind. Jason stopped me before I could. My being here and dying would only distract them. It wasn't a good answer, but I had no rebuttal.

That was it then, I had finished my goodbyes, the mood was pretty somber. Finally, in an attempt to lighten up the moment, Ari said, "Cheer up, guys, I'm not that bad a doctor."

Bill told him he had no doubt that Ari would save me. It was just that they wouldn't be able to hang around long enough to appreciate his work. It wasn't until that point when Ari realized he left out one important detail. Now slightly embarrassed, he said, "Marc will be back in a month."

The response to his statement was quick and in unison.

"What?"

Ari started to explain and apologize all in the same sentence. First he reminded me that I wasn't a Rikien. That, combined with three thousand years of advanced technology, I was only going to be in the pod thirty days, not three thousand years.

Once again, Ari caused me to sit down. They were going to kill me with this stuff before the cancer could, I swear. Bill wanted to make sure he had heard it right. He made Ari say it over word for word. Steven and Stan were holding each other and jumping up and down like kids. Jason sat down beside

195

me, his legs were weak, too. Bill had a problem with something in his eye again. He was walking back out to the patio.

I had to say goodbye to my pups one more time. This time it wouldn't be goodbye. This time I could tell them I would be back soon and to be good for Bill. When I walked back in, Bill was making Ari say it again. Word for word, stopping him in-between each word to make sure they all understood him correctly.

Once that was settled, I said, "See you guys later." I had already vowed when I was outside never to say goodbye to any of them again for as long as I lived.

Ari walked up beside me, asked if I was ready. I nodded, and we were gone. I was looking at Lení. I have to admit she's nice to see on arrival. Gera was standing next to her. Behind him was the pod. It was open and waiting for me. Ari said I would have to undergo some treatments prior to entering the pod. He also wanted to go over some changes that would take place during and after the pod. Ari wanted to go over those with me in detail, but later.

Nothing he said had sounded threatening, so I wasn't bothered by it at all. All I kept thinking is one month and I'll be back. One month and we'll be able to kick some ass. I had learned my lesson. I'd be sure and leave enough of my mind to control my body next time. No more letting myself go. I almost chuckled at my own pun. I was so happy knowing I would see my friends again soon. I could have chuckled about anything.

Getting ready for the pod actually took several days. I knew it was adding to my time away from home. But in the end it would all be worth it. Besides that, Rikiel was a beautiful planet, and it gave me a chance to see some of it. The grass, I guess that's what you could call it, was a soft yellow and wispy. The texture was like a feather, it was so fine. Walking through it was like nothing I could even describe.

The trees, well, we would call them trees, how do I describe them? I guess you could say they would be a mixture between a Banyan tree and bamboo. It twisted and branched in every direction. It seemed to have the massive strength of the Banyan, but it was light and waved in the wind like bamboo. The sound the wind made passing over the branches and leaves was almost musical.

Their sky was blue like Earth's on a day when the sky is pastel in its hue. Their sky carried three moons. Lení had told me that once every year they all come into their full moon phase at the same time. She promised to invite me back to witness it. The air was clean and full. How do I describe full? It felt like it was rich with oxygen, and lacked the pollutants ours carries. Tasting the air made me sad. We didn't know how nice air tastes. Only after experiencing

The Alien's Gift

• • • • • • • • • • •

it did I realize that our generation never had the pleasure of breathing a clean atmosphere.

I spent days seeing different sights. At first I hadn't cared much about sightseeing. I wanted to get the treatment underway and get home. LenÍ explained that I had to wait for the final adjustments to be made to the pod. I had no choice, so I might as well enjoy it. I stopped feeling guilty about not getting home and enjoyed the time I had on Rikiel. Spending the time with LenÍ didn't hurt either.

It wasn't that long before the pod was ready. LenÍ had picked me up that morning and, when I asked what was planned for the day, She told me the pod. I have to admit, much as I was enjoying both her and Rikiel, I was more than ready to get back home. As beautiful as Rikiel was, it wasn't Earth. I might be prejudiced but Earth was hard to beat.

We got to the lab; Ari was there to meet me. He had been making some final adjustments on the pod. He explained that they were adjustments he couldn't make until the final moments. They had to put the gel in the pod. Ari told me the gel was organic and therefore would act organically with my system. I didn't understand what that meant. Ari told me I would before we started. Today was the day I would learn what I was in for. Ari led me into the lab. Gera wasn't there yet, but Ari said he hoped to make it before I was encapsulated. He didn't go into details as to why he was absent, only that he would make it if at all possible.

The briefing started with Ari explaining the gel. It was an organic compound. It was more than that. It was actually an intelligent life form. Symbiotic in nature, it would meld with me. Ari had feed it the data on my original unaltered biological status. According to LenÍ, this meant before cancer. She was explaining what Ari said to me in "English." Okay that means she used smaller words. Ari continued with the briefing. The gel would absorb the cancer as sustenance and regenerate my biological system back to its original state. He went on to explain the reason it would only take a month was because my species. There was that word again, so simple to repair.

I wasn't sure, but I think we just got insulted again. Our species, that is, us—that means you, too. Once he finished, the gist of it was that I would be a perfectly normal human. It all sounded good to me. I was ready. Then it hit me. He said, "Perfectly normal."

"What about the abilities I have?"

This had been what he was waiting till the last minute to tell me. Ari said they would be gone. I would lose those abilities when the symbiot rebuilt me. They weren't part of my natural biological make up. I would have backed out if there were any other choice but dying. The reality was there was no choice.

197

As I climbed into the pod I was saddened by the loss of my gift. My only option was the loss of everything, so it wasn't debatable. I settled into the gel, the sensation was familiar to me. I reached out with my mind to find Gera. I wouldn't have done what I was about to do if Gera and I hadn't melded. I knew Gera, heart, mind, and soul. Because of that, I knew he understood me and all my strangeness.

I found him. He told me he was sorry he couldn't make it, but circumstances just didn't allow it. I let him know that I understood and told him I just wanted to know if he wanted to switch or anything for the next month. If so, I'd be fine with it. I heard his mind laughing. I was right he knew me. I said see you soon, then I watched as the pod closed.

It was my understanding that the pod would now be projected into orbit. Something about the gel junk worked better there. It liked the energy patterns or something. I settled in, comforted in the fact that I would be home soon. At least I hoped I would be home soon. I had a great deal of trust in Ari. Besides, I had some puppies to get back to. My friends, that went without saying. Before I knew it, I was sleeping. For the first couple of weeks I would have no awareness. That's what Ari told me during my briefing.

When I woke, or I thought I had awakened, I was still in the pod. My mind was active at least. I tried to reach out to touch someone. I wasn't able to. *Had it taken that from me already?* I wondered. That was when the reality hit me. My thoughts; I was thinking, I'm alive or I will be once the symbiot was finished. I turned my attention inward. Not into my inner self, but to the symbiot, the gel. I wanted my memories of Gera. Losing the gift was something I didn't like, but losing what I had gained with my connection with Gera was another thing. I wanted to plead my case. I didn't want to lose Gera's touch. I begged, not sure I was even being heard. My mind drifted back into obscurity in the process. I forced my attention on the gel right up until I lost consciousness.

The pod was being opened. I could see light, my mind coming into focus. Ari and Lení were standing over me as the pod split open. I had only been here for a few moments. I thought something had gone wrong, and they had canceled the treatment. I remembered waking up, but now I thought that had just been a dream, and it hadn't worked. Then I heard Ari welcome me back. *Welcome back,* I thought. *I made it.* Lení was smiling at me as I stepped out of the pod. I needed a shower to wash the gel from my body. I was taken to a place to clean up and dress before I was brought back to Ari.

I was ready to go home. Ari wasn't ready for me to, not yet. He had tests to run. Let me amend that statement, he had *lots* of tests to run. I was a different species. That word again. Because of it, he wanted to run a complete scan to ensure everything was okay. Fortunately he wasn't wasting any time getting started. He started running tests and taking DNA samples as soon as I got back in the room. The only good part about the testing was now that he had his samples, he didn't need me. That meant now Lení and I could go sightseeing again. I asked about Gera, wondering when I could see him again. Lení said he should be back on Rikiel the next day.

Gera was on schedule, and the next morning he joined me for breakfast. I realized I had maintained all my memories of him, including our meld. I could tell he wasn't sure if they had remained intact. It was obvious during breakfast. Gera was slightly uncomfortable. He was keeping his questions vague, not sure what I might remember. Once I realized where he was coming from, I put an end to his concerns. I let him know I remembered our meld and everything from it. I was pleased by his reaction. Again, I won't go into what happened during the meld. But the loss could and would be felt by one or both. My not remembering would be as painful to Gera as losing part of himself. I was more than happy to inform him—I remember. We could both enjoy our breakfast that morning.

As we were eating Gera informed me that today he was taking me home. I was delighted to hear the news. I wasn't sure how it was going to happen. I couldn't focus in with my mind and go to it anymore. It was true that the machine was there, but that was just to facilitate bringing my complete body. I still needed to use my mind, the gift. Didn't I? I decided I wasn't going to bother worrying about it. The Rikien were the experts and I was sure if Gera said I was going home, I was.

Gera and I finished our breakfast and started to Ari's lab. Gera seemed as excited as I was about my trip home. Maybe it was that sharing such a deep part of me he understood what this meant more than anyone else could.

We were at Ari's lab for hours while final checks on my body were made. Head to toe, every cell seemed to be normal. I felt better than I had in years and was ready to get back home. With each test result I thought I'd be leaving only to have Ari needing to do one more. I was pretty sure Ari was more like doctors on Earth now than ever. Like the doctors' offices on earth, I didn't think I would ever get out of there. Finally we were done, and I was ready to leave. It was time to say goodbye. I had vowed to never say that again, but... I looked to Ari and asked if I would ever see him again. From what I knew now, I hadn't seen the other Ari for three thousand years. Were we in fact saying goodbye? His answer was philosophical, "We can't know the future Marc. I can only say I hope we do."

I wondered where Lení was. I hadn't seen her. I found myself trying to delay leaving. Where could she be? I couldn't leave without saying goodbye. Lení and I had spent a lot of time together during my stay on Rikiel. She had been my official tour guide. I felt close to her, close enough I wished she didn't live on the other side of the universe.

It was time, Gera was motioning for me to follow. I kept looking. *She wasn't going to make it*, I thought. I had just asked Gera how I was going to get back home. Gera smiled, but as he started to answer, Lenĺ walked in. I wasn't sure if he had answered my question or not after that. My face lit up as she entered the room. I was telling her that I just would have hated to leave without seeing her, when she stopped me.

"You couldn't leave before I got here, Marc," she said smiling.

I thought she was being rhetorical. I was about to find out she wasn't.

I turned back to Gera again. I had turned my attention to Lenĺ as he had been speaking to me. I apologized and asked him to please continue. His smile was even bigger now than it had been all day. He told me that he wasn't upset over my attention being drawn to Lenĺ at all. That would just make what he was about to say even easier. It was true I couldn't go home without seeing Lenĺ, he told me.

"Lenĺ is taking you home."

I was confused I thought, wait.

"Gera, didn't you say you were the one that was going to accompany me home?"

"I am," Gera stated. "Lenĺ is the one who will actually take you."

I was confused. I kept looking at Gera, then to Lenĺ. I needed help on this one, and Lenĺ explained it to me.

"Marc, you know that your body can't get back unless the mind focuses on the receiver and pulls it there."

It was a statement, and I knew that. It had been one of the concerns I had. I knew that the Rikiens would have an answer, so I didn't think hard on it. Lenĺ continued. "Your mind can no longer do that. You'll need my mind to take you."

I still didn't understand. *I couldn't, but she could, but it was my body, and she had to...* I stopped in mid-thought. Gera had walked to the side of the room, giving us some privacy. The sheepish look on her face told me. "You mean" I couldn't finish the sentence.

Lenĺ was going to occupy my body with me. But wasn't that their form of...

She smiled as I stumbled with the reality of what was going to take place. Then she teased me about it.

"Why, don't you like me anymore? Is it because I'm too old?"

I was stumbling now. I wasn't sure how I could answer this. Gera saved me when he walked back over and said, "Well are you going home or not."

I smiled and said, "I guess I am."

Lení sat in a chair provided as a watcher entered. Even on Rikiel it seems they never leave the body unattended. She entered my mind. Gera asked Lení if she were ready to take me home. She told him we were set. I was thinking *I'm going home in style, first class all the way.* Lení's mind responded.

Thank you.

Mentally I was blushing. I forgot she was listening.

I had asked if I could return to the front of my property. I wanted to walk back to the house. There was just something about going home on foot that I needed. Gera had made sure that small consideration was met. The receiver was inside my property a few hundred feet from my house.

We arrived. I had to tell Lení that I thought the trip was much too fast. Being with her was something not to be described in this story. She said it was a trip she, too, will always remember. I did notice she lingered after we arrived. She could have jumped and returned to her body once I had materialized. She didn't. I felt her mental kiss. Sadly, she left, leaving me standing in my yard. Gera at my side.

Chapter 23

The pups were the first to discover me. I had figured they would. They were the reason I had asked Gera if this would be possible. I knew it was going to be emotional and preferred our reunion to be in private. Gera and I were walking across the yard when they spotted us and came running. At first they seemed to be responding to strangers, and the sounds coming from their throats were not inviting.

Recognition set in as they got closer. They were still too far away for me to actually see the change. It showed in their sound and speed. They were coming faster now. *Much too fast,* I was starting to think. Maybe now is a good time to remind you, my pups are a little more than two hundred pounds combined. Two hundred and sixteen pounds, to be exact and moving fast.

I half turned my body bracing for the onslaught. I had puppies everywhere. It didn't take long for them to have me on the ground. Their excitement was all I knew it would be. I had one in my arms, only to have the other push its way in. I had been right, I was emotional, too. I was wrong about it being private, though. There were several minutes of wrestling, that and dealing with them as they maneuvered for the position closest to me. Things finally settled down. We started to walk toward the house. When I looked up I saw Bill standing on the porch. He had watched the dogs greet me and patiently waited until they had finished their welcome. Now he stepped off the porch and started toward us.

The Alien's Gift

We stopped just short of each other. Bill kept looking at me, then turned to Gera. He knew the answer, but I think it was just something he had to hear out loud. "You're alright now?"

Not waiting, or maybe not willing to take my word for it, he directed a second question to Gera before I could answer. "He's alright now?"

It was only when Gera and I both smiled and nodded he finally let his guard down. It was good to see Bill. We embraced for a moment before Bill pulled back saying.

"I suppose you're going to want the dogs back."

We started to smile, then laugh. We had to before we got something in our eye.

Gera was about to leave. I told him I couldn't allow him to unless he promised to return. I wanted a proper goodbye not knowing if it would be the last. Hellos and goodbyes don't go well at the same moment in time.

He agreed saying, "Be with your friends and reunite. I'll see you again, my friend, have no fear of that." Then he was gone.

Bill and I walked into the house. I kept going not stopping till I reached the patio. I walked out and sat in my chair. I spent the next few moments just looking out over the yard. It was nice to be home. A minute later Bill walked out carrying two cups of coffee. He set one of the cups down in front of me. He made the comment, "You just don't look right without this."

He was right; now it was perfect. We sat without talking for the next fifteen minutes. We just sat and enjoyed our coffee.

Once we had finished our coffee it was time to jump in the cart. I was actually excited. I couldn't wait to see everyone again. Even driving the cart again was exhilarating. It was one of those little things. As I got in I thought about just before I left for my treatment. Then I hadn't been able to drive it. Bill or one of the other guys had to. For that reason driving the cart was as satisfying as running a marathon.

We shot off toward Jason's house. The dogs ran ahead. Once more I could appreciate their grace and beauty. They won the race, again. I recalled watching them before I left thinking I might never see that again. They were beautiful, especially so when they ran. Everything was beautiful. Jason's patio came into sight. I could see him sitting outside as we drove up. He was still drinking his morning coffee.

He was reading as we pulled up, and didn't lift his head when he heard the cart pull up, assuming it was Bill coming by. Bill had stayed at my place the entire time I was gone. He didn't want to uproot the dogs, thinking it was going to be enough change with my being gone. It wasn't until I spoke up, protesting the terrible hospitality I was being shown that he finally lifted his head. He almost jumped off the patio, meeting me half way. He looked

203

me over the same as Bill had. He was walking around me as he looked me up and down. I asked if he was checking to see if I had grown a new arm or something while on Rikiel.

Looking at Bill he asked, "He's alright now."

I laughed and wondered why I wasn't allowed to answer that question anymore. I just stood quietly while Bill gave him a full report. *After all, he had been told by Gera.*

Once Bill had certified me healthy, Jason grabbed me, lifting me off my feet, welcoming me home. When he finally put me down we went up to have a seat. Jason went to get me coffee. Bill went over to put some pastries on a dish for me. I was being waited on hand and foot. I was about to tell them I was healthy again, and Gera could validate that for me, too. Then I thought, *well, maybe not just yet.* After everyone had settled down, I asked about Steven and Stan. Jason told me they had gone back up to the Cape two weeks ago.

I was a little disappointed I had hoped to see everyone. I would fix that soon enough. I asked Jason if I could borrow his phone. Moments later I heard Stan answer. I decided I didn't need an introduction, so I just asked a simple question. "Hey, I'm going to be having a barbeque today. Can you make it?"

It took Stan about one second to know who it was. "Marc!" shouting my name so loud, I didn't need the phone to hear him.

The next couple of minutes went between him wanting to talk and wanting to get Steven and head down. Finally I ended the call knowing he just didn't know how to hang up. As I passed Jason his phone back, I asked if he knew he was having a cook out today.

Smiling, as I said, "Stan just told me."

"He's normal." That time it came from Bill and Jason's mouths simultaneously, but, I knew that. *Gera told me.*

Two hours later Stan and Steven were pulling into Jason's drive. There had to have been some speeding involved in that trip. Now with all my friends here, the true party was started. Well, not until Steven and Stan asked Bill and Jason if I was alright. I wondered if I would get to answer that for myself ever again. The night was one of the best nights of my life. I hadn't been gone that long, it was true. It had just been a little over six weeks in all. Still in other ways it was also a lifetime, literally.

I had to tell them about Rikiel, all the things I had seen. After that, we discussed life in general for hours. I deliberately stayed away from any questions concerning the aliens or the Trenton Group all night. I wanted to know, but I was still feeling guilty. I wasn't been able to help anymore. I hadn't told them about that. I wasn't sure what might have taken place. I

The Alien's Gift

• • • • • • • • • •

remembered Ari saying the Rikien were non-aggressive, so I didn't think I wanted to know. Not yet, not tonight.

It was after twelve before we finally called it a night. None of us really wanted the night to end. Bill and I jumped in the cart and headed back to the house. When we arrived, Bill headed straight to bed. I decided to sit on the patio for just awhile. I needed some time before going to bed. It had been a long day, but I just wasn't ready for it to end. The pups came over and curled up by my chair. They went right off to sleep. I guess it had been a long day for them, too. I looked down at them as they slept. It was good to be home.

I must have sat there about twenty minutes when Bill came back out. He hadn't been able to sleep either. We just sat and talked awhile, mostly about mundane things. It felt like old times. We both needed it.

The following morning the sun was up before me. That didn't happen often, but then again I didn't stay up till after two very often either. As I walked into the kitchen I saw Bill coming in from the other side. He looked up, seeing me at the same time. We were both tired, but the kid in us didn't care. It was a race to the coffee. I won. It was a minor detail that I was closer to the pot right from the start. Luck put my bedroom on the right side. I didn't care. I won, and I spent the first ten minutes on the patio reminding Bill of that fact.

We had just started to drink our coffee when I saw Jason and the guys on their way across the yard. It was pretty late, they had started to wonder what happened to us. They wouldn't admit it, but I think they were worried. When I told them Bill and I had stayed up half the night talking, it seemed to put them at ease.

We were all still sitting around having coffee. I was telling everyone how I had beaten Bill in the coffee race this morning when Gera showed up. He was glad to see we were all here together. He wanted to talk to us about tomorrow. He started by explaining that tomorrow he'd be back, and when he arrived, everyone had to be ready. If you start your conversation off like that, you can get everyone's attention. He had ours. He had wanted to make sure of just that result. Tomorrow was an important day.

Gera would have to complete the last phase of the paradox. He went on to explain that after taking me to Rikiel for treatment, Gera started to question Ari more about his long years of silence. What he wanted to do was discover how long it had taken Ari to get the pod prepared. He had to find out what day it was that Ari had returned, all those years ago. That day was tomorrow. I hated paradoxes and didn't think I would ever develop a liking or understanding of one, nor did I really want to. But I gathered this one was important. It was.

Gera was explaining to me, us, but me mostly, what we had to do and why. Tomorrow Ari would be coming to Earth to look for me. He was referring to the Ari of my time. The Ari who assumed I had died. Yeah, I know. It was right about here I started to get a headache, too. Nevertheless Gera continued, explaining that had to remain the same or the paradox would form a circle again. The future or the now in this case would no longer take place as it had. My present was part of Ari's future, because of his past. Okay, I was done with trying to understand.

All I wanted to know was what he wanted me to do. As Gera tried to explain, I realized that he needed me to understand for a reason. There was more to this than showed on the surface. He told me that when Ari had come back and wasn't able to find me, he looked for my mind. This part was easy to follow. I had done that myself, when I still had my gift. When Ari was unable to locate me, he assumed that I had died. He might have known if he had entered anyone else's mind, but he would never have done that. To do that without permission is considered taboo to a Rikien. I saw the look on his face as he said those words. He was remembering the pod. I sat silently. We had cleared that air long ago. This was just a memory that would always be there. After a slight pause he continued to explain. Ari couldn't find my mind that was imperative.

As Gera was talking, I wondered if he was planning on bringing me back to Rikiel. The thought of going back got me thinking about LenÍ having to take me both ways. I started to blush just thinking about it. I was a little ashamed of myself for the thought. But I kept thinking, *if you got to go, you got to go.* I pulled my thoughts back in time to discover that wasn't it. I didn't have to go. I was slightly disappointed and a little ashamed for having the thought. Instead of going to Rikiel, Gera was going to cloak me. Okay, now my mind was back on him completely.

Cloak me; just what was cloaking me supposed to mean? I listened as he explained.

I was happy to hear it didn't involve being buried under a mountain or anything like that. The procedure in itself disturbed me slightly. I didn't think there would be any problem with it myself. I was more concerned for Gera. Now I was starting to understand.

He was going to cover my mind with his. I could see the thoughts of the pod going through his head again.

That was why that memory had been so close to the surface earlier, I thought.

He was thinking he would have to repeat something so close to what he had done. For Gera, the wound was still open. The memory was still raw. He had my forgiveness, but not his own, not yet.

Gera went on to explain that he would also be cloaking himself from Ari

The Alien's Gift

• • • • • • • • • •

at the same. He wanted to prepare me for what that would be like. Cloaking was like going into a nothingness.

"You'll be totally lost. Remember, I *will be* with you during that time. Remember."

I could tell he wasn't happy about having to do this cloaking thing. I got the idea I wasn't going to be too thrilled about it myself. But he would have to. Ari would feel the mind of another Rikien on Earth. Gera's would be obvious. By doing this, Ari wouldn't know that Gera was here, and we'd bring the entire paradox to a close. What had happened, would happen.

After he finished explaining the plan, I asked Gera if he would walk with me. We strolled across the yard. I reminded Gera that he knew me better than any man alive. At the same time I also knew him; we were a shared mind. Mine was part of his now; just as his was part of mine. He agreed with me, stating that was why he had to cloak himself as well. Then he told me, "Ari would feel my mind even inside of his own. We, Ari and I, are also a shared mind."

Ari would know himself if he felt Gera. That was indeed going to make his task all the harder. I was glad he had thought this so far through. I hoped what I had to say would make the task easier.

I couldn't help but see the pain in his face when he said he would have to enter my mind to cloak me. The old wound hadn't healed completely, I knew that now. We had discussed this more than once. Each time Gera climbed higher, releasing some of the guilt he carried. I wanted to, needed him to let it go completely. This was my chance. At this point he was so focused on the meaning and strengths of the meld, maybe I could.

I started by asking Gera to look into my mind. Then I asked if he could find any hate, fear, distrust or anything negative in me concerning him or what we had been through together. Before he could answer, I told him I had done just that.

"I've looked inside you, that part that is within me."

Now Gera stopped walking. He looked at me as I spoke.

"I found a man that warranted my upmost trust and respect. I know you like no other. Gera, my friend, you're incapable of offending or doing any injustice to me."

I felt I was reaching him. I could see him searching his soul, our souls.

"Hear my words, listen to my thoughts, then…trust in yourself once again, my friend."

When I received my answer, it came in the form that answered a second question. The first question, I had wondered about long ago. One, that had been forgotten, never asked. The answer…Rikiens can cry.

We returned to the house, and Gera said his farewells for the day. He would see us again tomorrow. Most of us that was Stan and Steven had to get back to the Cape to close out last minute details on things they were on. Gera said that wouldn't be a problem. Ari wouldn't be looking for them anyhow. They promised to be back in a couple of days. I told them they had better. The way I saw it, this homecoming party wasn't over yet. After everyone had left, Jason and Bill and I spent the rest of the day playing. I was going to ask about the Saurians, but I thought, one more day. I want one more day before I pick up that weight again.

We went looking for a new car instead. I thought if the world comes to an end, I'm going out driving a sports car. Finally Bill had won me over, and living in Palm Beach we had lots of places to look, lots of sports cars to choose from. We had looked at several before I finally settled on a Lamborghini. After all, I was rich now. I'm not sure why I actually wanted it. I was way beyond needing flashy cars like in my younger years, and I wasn't a big spender. I hadn't really spent money on anything aside from the house since the sale of the business. But it was a Lamborghini, and I was alive.

Jason and Bill spent most of the time laughing at me as I was car shopping. No, they didn't really laugh at me, they laughed *with* me. They both understood what was going on. They were caught up in my celebration. Jason kept asking me why I was getting the red one.

Little to flashy, he thought. Overkill was another term he used.

At the same time Bill was commenting he thought it was kind of understated. He thought the car I got should have a little more pizzazz. Their banter kept the salesman nervous. I could see he was worried they might end up ruining his sale. Finally Jason said if I wasn't going to show good taste and buy the blue one, he would. The salesman stopped worrying then. I could see him light up as Jason spoke. The game had begun, and now I was in for the full ride.

I kept noticing the joy in Bill's eyes. They never left the cars as Jason and I were playing with the salesman. Jason and I were buying the car of his dreams, and he had put us up to it. That was when I knew I had to go for it.

"If we go with red and blue, all we need is white to be patriotic. Bill should get a white one."

My words were over the top for the salesman. He was starting to think we were just playing with him. Bill, still thinking we were teasing the salesman, quickly declined, saying he couldn't get one. If he got one, Stan and Steven would feel left out. That was it for the sales guy. He was sure now it was a game. We were going to lose him, and I didn't want that. I wanted this man to have the ride of his life today. I was celebrating my life today. Now it looked like we all were.

So in honor of the day I bought mine—and Bill's. Jason followed by getting the blue one. Then Jason ordered the yellow and metallic ones to be delivered. We had just bought five Lamborghini Murcielagos at a cost of more than two million dollars. I admit the game got out of hand. But we did get the sales guy. His mind was completely blown away as we went to pay. I had just pulled out my check book, telling him I would pay for the red and white one. Bill wasn't far behind the sales guy now. Til this moment he had thought this was a joke, too.

Jason won the day. He had started the game with the salesman, I had followed suit getting Bill. Jason finished by getting us all. I passed the check to the sales guy. Jason told him if he took that check, the other three sales were off. The salesman kept looking at Jason, then back at the check in my hand. I almost watched a grown man cry. He didn't know what to do. He was looking at a check for just under a million dollars and was afraid to touch it. I was looking at Jason, wondering why he had done that. I might have started off playing and, sure the game got out of hand, but boys will be boys and now I really wanted these cars.

Jason told the guy either he took his check for the five or he would back out completely. This led to a debate between Jason and me over the cars. Bill and the sales guy watched in dismay. Jason reminded me about the B thing. I countered with I wanted to do this for myself and Bill. Jason was walking me off to the side as we talked. I was ready for a stiff debate. Jason knew me well enough to know that. What I wasn't ready for was Jason.

Jason got real serious as he started to speak.

"I almost lost one of my best friends a little while ago. I'm happy to say that didn't happen." He smiled his warm smile as he continued. "Not only is he my friend, through him I was introduced to four of the best men I've ever had the pleasure to meet in my life. They, too, became my friends." Jason paused again for a moment. His voice started to tighten up. Emotions were setting in. Did I tell you guys don't like emotions?

"You did that for me. Welcome home and shut up."

He walked to the salesman and passed him a check. Then he instructed him to have the other cars delivered and the paperwork sent to his office for completion. Three sets of keys later, we were racing toward the house. I had the red one, Oh! On the race, I was first.

I had to admit the joke had gone further than I planned. True enough, I had seriously planned on the sports car. Although looking at the Lamborghini had been Bill's idea. We had looked at several cars, and I hadn't been impressed. Bill had always called it a dream car. That's why we went there. He was right, it was a dream car. I planned on getting Bill's right after walking through the door and seeing his eyes. Jason getting one surprised me. He was like me, fairly simple in taste most of the time. I guess my madness was contagious.

We had as much fun once we got back to the house. Discussing the salesman's reactions, we relived every moment. The best part was when he called Jason's bank confirming the funds. Bill said he could hear the guy's heart while he waited. The drive home and the look on Bill's face as he kept turning to look at his new car was the most enjoyable part of the day. What had started out as a lark ended in a great day. What I haven't figured out is why it didn't cost me a thing. I was going to have to get with Jason on this paying for stuff later on.

The fun lasted us well into the night. Right after dinner Bill decided to head home. He'd been staying at my house since before I had left, and it was time he saw his own. I think he just wanted to drive his car. Either way, we walked him out to say good night. Mostly we walked out to watch his face again when he looked at his car. Jason and I stood on the porch till he was out of sight before going back in. I turned to him as we walked in.

"You know we have to talk."

Jason laughed. He knew this would come. I stared out by thanking him for what he did, then I told him even though I did appreciate his generosity, he should really let me pay for the cars. He stood his ground saying, one, he meant every word he said earlier, and two, he was the billionaire. Okay, we were being light-hearted about it, but I reminded him if he kept spending his money like that, it wouldn't be long before he was just a millionaire himself. The conversation was insane to me even as I was having it. It got more so when Jason answered. Jason told me not to be concerned with that, explaining to me that the word billionaire was also plural. I'm not sure if I just shut up then, or if I just couldn't speak. Either way, the conversation ended.

Bill was at the house bright and early the next morning. I teased him a bit asking if he made it home or had he just driven all night. He assured me he had gotten home within a couple of hours of leaving here. I reminded him he only lived three miles away. He informed me he had found a new way home, and it only took an hour or so. The next few minutes were spent talking about new cars. We were still at it when Jason arrived. He had come over to my place this morning knowing that Gera would be arriving. I was having a great time telling him how Bill had found a short cut home. Bill was telling Jason in the same breath that his gift was way out of line.

Jason told us how he had been poor most of his life. He had never had any money until fifteen years earlier. That was when his company took off. Shortly after that he was bought out. That was when he became what he referred to as crazy rich. In all that time he had never done anything crazy. He was actually thanking us for finally being able to. Bill, true to his nature, said, "Well since you put it that way you're welcome."

That kept us laughing until Gera arrived. It was just after ten when Gera

The Alien's Gift

got there. Ari would be here in just about an hour. He went back over what was going to happen with me, making sure I was ready when the time came to do this. I was, I had prepared myself for whatever Gera had to do. I wasn't sure exactly what it would be like, but I felt I could handle it. There were so many ways the Rikiens could do these things. I had experienced many myself. I had eavesdropped. That was like sitting on someone's shoulder. You barely touch their mind. I had tuned into their senses. That was more in depth, but still so light they had no idea of any presence. Switching was a complete shift leaving no doubt that something took place.

Then there had been my experience with Lenĺ again, not something that can be done without the other's knowledge. Melding with Gera, truly one of my most memorable experiences of my life. Complete awareness not only of it happening but the person you meld with. You become one with them. What else could there be? I was ready.

The time was getting close. Bill and Jason decided to head over to his house. It wasn't a distance thing for them. It would just be normal if Ari looked at all. Gera waited for them to drive off before we went inside. Gera told me he was going to leave and, once he got back to Rikiel, he would connect with me. In the meantime I would sit in my lounge chair and await his return.

It wasn't long before I felt the effect. I must admit my heart almost skipped a beat. I was being engulfed. I hadn't felt that since the beginning when Gera first invaded. I was being enveloped, but Gera's mind wasn't with me. He was cloaked so I was in a state of nothing. I had never felt like this in all the times and all the ways I've experienced. None had been a "nothing feeling." Ari would never find me. I could barely find myself. We stayed like that for almost an hour. Gera was making sure Ari had come and not found me before he could pull back.

Finally I was free again. Gera was in my living room almost as fast as he had left. I could see he was concerned. He wanted to know how I had handled the experience. It had been like nothing he'd actually ever done before. It seemed he found it personally nerve racking, which made him even more worried about how well I had done. Actually I was alright. Other than the initial engulfing sensation which set off an old memory, I did fairly well with the experience. I actually used the time to look deeper inside myself. Gera had covered the paradox, and now the future was clear. At least I hoped he had. I asked Gera how we could know for sure. Gera was laughing.

"That's easy, I would have known already, for a long time."

I stopped asking questions. I hate paradoxes.

Chapter 24

Gera had left, returning to the future. I already knew I never would or could see the Ari of my time again. If I had, then he would have known I was alive now. I was starting to get the hang of that paradox thing. Okay, not really. That was about the extent of what I understood. I would never see the Ari of today again. I didn't know about the Ari of tomorrow. My friend Gera, him I would see again. His parting comment rang true, although we cannot read the future.

"When two minds walk the same path, they're bound to meet from time to time." I hoped his words were true.

Lení, I can only hope to see you again, I thought, as I turned toward Jason.

I went straight to Jason's house after Gera left. This phase of life was finished, I think. Now we could get back to work, well, soon. Stan and Steven weren't due back until tomorrow. For that reason I decided I could leave the subject of work closed for at least one more day. Bill and Jason hadn't brought it up, so I thought that was the way everyone had wanted it. I still didn't know what good I would be to the team anymore. I never had anything to offer aside from the gift. Well, tomorrow we'd decide the future. Besides that, the cars were supposed to arrive shortly. I hoped they were on time; I was excited about seeing them. When I got to the house I told Bill and Jason that Gera gave his best and had returned to Rikiel, leaving Ari in the past with a secret to keep for three thousand years. I figure anyone who understood paradoxes would understand that.

We went out to sit on the front porch. The cars were due and, like kids, we couldn't wait to see them. Fortunately, we didn't have long to wait before Jason got a call on his phone. They were at the front gate. The cars had arrived. Jason hit a key on his phone that I guess opened the gate because soon after I saw the first truck turning the bend on its way to the house. The truck was carrying the yellow Lamborghini and Jason's old car. Jason had left it at the dealership, choosing to drive the new one home. The second truck was right behind him.

The driver pulled up into the drive and backed up to the garage entrance. We went out to greet him and watch as he unloaded the cars. He pulled Jason's car off first. Jason pulled it into the garage. The yellow Lamborghini came off next. It sat on the driveway like a stallion. The metallic one joined it soon after. They were magnificent cars, and we were like kids. Now we could hardly wait for the guys to see them.

Tomorrow couldn't come fast enough for any of us. Jason was the biggest kid of all. He was getting so much pleasure out of the surprise. I was beginning to get worried he might just go buy more. We stayed outside looking at them for another twenty minutes before finally going back in. The rest of the day was spent trying to figure out the best way to blow their minds. Bill and I came to the conclusion that was Jason's decision to make. Not because he bought them. He was just as excited now that they were here as if he were receiving one. We couldn't take it away from him. It had to be his game.

That night we sat on the patio and listened to his plan. Actually we listened to four of his plans. No sooner would he get done with one when he thought of another. I looked at Bill halfway through the evening. We were glad we left it up to Jason. I had never seen him this happy.

By the time I got up the next morning it was already after eight. Jason had been going over one plan after the other for most of the night. Neither Bill nor I had the heart to stop him. It was just as well. The guys wouldn't get here until after ten. I wasn't sure I could have waited that long to see their faces. This gave us just enough time to figure out which of the three thousand two hundred plans Jason was going to use. I was about to call Bill and see if he had awakened yet when I heard the purr of his car pulling up. He usually came to my house, but today we planned on it. We didn't want his car in view, not until the final surprise. He came walking outside, not stopping for coffee. Like me, he was planning on getting to Jason's right away.

On the way over he was bragging that he found a new way to my house, and it only took an hour and a half. I laughed, not because it was funny. I laughed because I knew it was true. When we got to Jason's, he was on the patio. Just as wired up as he had been the night before. He was drinking a cup of coffee, but I didn't think he needed it. I asked if he had been to sleep at all. He swore he had just gotten up, but he never actually said what time he went to bed. While we waited, Jason gave us the final rundown on the plan. All we could do now was just sit and wait.

When Stan and Steven got here, they would naturally see the cars. It would be hard to miss something like that in front of the garage. Jason was going to tell them the story about how he and I had both gotten Lamborghinis. Sometime during the story-telling, Bill and I would excuse ourselves one at a time. That would allow us time to bring our cars into Jason's drive way. Once all five cars were outside, Jason could spring his surprise.

The brothers arrived early. It was nine thirty. I could tell by the looks on Jason and Bill's faces I wasn't the only one happy about it either. I wasn't sure we would have made it much longer. Actually Jason walked out to meet them as they pulled up. Bill and I had stayed on the patio. After all it was only a couple of cars, not really a big thing. Yeah! Right! Somehow they seemed to notice the two Lamborghinis parked in front of Jason's garage. Jason joined them while they climbed all over them. Bill and I just sat patiently on the patio. Finally they all came out to the patio to join us. Jason and I played the game. We were trying to be casual as we explained we just decided to get ourselves a toy.

Bill used our 'casual we got Lamborghinis time' to get his and pull it up in front of Jason's garage. A few minutes after he got back, I excused myself and moved mine over. Now all we needed was Jason, and his was easy. He just pulled it out of the garage. Finally after almost thirty minutes of maneuvering, the front of Jason's garage was adorned with five Lamborghinis. We had our cars parked side by side on an angle. It was an impressive display. Once I got back and sat down, Jason was ready.

Jason started to act impatient. Grabbing the brothers by the arm, he walked them outside and around the side of the house to the garage. Stan and Steven were shocked when they saw the five cars. There had only been two when they had arrived. I could see they were confused. Never in their wildest dream could they imagine what Jason was about to say. Bill and I stood back watching like two school kids.

Now in front of the cars, Jason started, "The red one is Marc's. He will take it home in a minute. The white one is Bill's. He already said he would put it over at Marc's house for today. The problem is the blue one it's mine, and I can't pull it out, not until you two get your cars moved."

Once he had finished his story, he turned, holding keys in both hands and held them up to the brothers. Just to close the deal, he said, "Now get your damn cars out of my way."

The Alien's Gift

Jason passed them the keys as he walked by them on his way to join Bill and me. They both just stood there with the keys in their hands. They kept looking at the cars, then at each other. Steven was the first to figure out what Jason had just said. He started to jump up and down and did a thing that might be called a dance. Well it might be, if he had been more graceful. Then it was Stan's turn to lose it.

"NO, no way, tell me you're not kidding. You can't kid about," He turned to look back at us.

We were wondering if there would be a debate on which one was whose. Jason had already made allowances for changing them to different colors if they didn't like those anyway. Stan wanted the yellow one. Steven didn't care, so that worked out. The next hour was crazy. Jason almost got hurt as he was lifted and lowered, only to be lifted again. I had been there and was happy it wasn't me. Okay, I was just happy.

My homecoming party was on again. It ended up being a great day that lasted into the night. The sun was starting to go down when it was decided we should go out to eat. For some reason everyone thought it would be the best if we all drove separately. We had five guys and five cars that sure looked like they needed to be driven. It only took long enough to pick the restaurant before we were on our way.

Jason and I had stayed till last. We wanted to watch as each of them got into their car and drove away. After the last car pulled out I looked at Jason. I told him I wouldn't argue about this. This dinner was on me. He agreed, but only if I got there first. We had a running start race. One rule, speed limit obeyed. Know your way, you get to pay. We were off.

The conversation over dinner was naturally centered on Lamborghinis. It was almost an hour before the conversation started to shift. When it did shift, it shifted fast. Steven was the one who spearheaded the change in subject. As he was thanking Jason for the fifteenth time, he asked if this was a pre-celebration. That comment caught my interest, and I asked what event he was referring to. Steven answered he thought that meant we were a go on the plan. I had avoided this conversation for the last couple of days, not wanting to remind myself that I was no longer of use to the team. Now it was time to face it.

I looked at Jason and asked the question I had been avoiding. "Do you have a plan you think will work?"

Jason looked at me for a moment before he answered. "No, we have a plan I *know* will work."

I was excited to hear about it now. Knowing we couldn't have that conversation at the restaurant, I held my tongue. I would bide my time till we got home. I was more excited than anyone. I think it showed. Jason

215

would look at me from time to time at the table. I would catch him and Bill exchanging glances and smiling. I didn't know what it was, but it was a good plan. I knew it was.

I got back to the house before Bill. I hoped he hadn't taken one of his hour short cuts. I was anxious to get to Jason's to hear what they had come up with. I wasn't kept long. Bill could tell my patience was almost tapped by the time we left the restaurant and was only a moment behind me. We jumped into the cart, and by the time we reached Jason's, everyone was in place.

Jason started by telling me that they had gathered enough information to bury the Trenton Group. It hadn't been easy, but then again Jason was at one time "The Lock Master." The plan was to release files to the news media across the world. Jason knew that Fallen's control of his own media empire would keep the files from reaching the light of day easily, but the world was a big place and news, particularly news of corruption of this magnitude, was major.

Jason went on to tell me how they had everything set up to just a few key strokes. Codes would be sent to various locations to unlock Trenton Group files. Others files would just send releases to news associations. Stan had found corruption in military contracts on a magnitude that approached treason. Steven had listed every alien imposter in a position of power. He had also uncovered a plot to replace the President of the United States.

I wasn't surprise to find out that Ex President Blanchard was involved in that. I asked how they were planning on dealing with the Saurians. That was a problem that a computer wouldn't fix. At least I didn't think it could. How had they accomplished so much? If the stakes weren't so high, I might have been jealous. I had to know.

Jason explained that was where the Rikiens came into play. I was confused. I had thought Ari told us they wouldn't interfere. Bill said that was true. The Rikiens were a non aggressive race. Gera, however, felt he needed to stand in for you. He told me when a brother isn't able to do what he feels he must, another steps in. Besides, he wasn't untrue to his morals. In Gera's words, there was nothing wrong with scientific study. He was a scientist, after all. He was nice enough to sit with Bill and explain how he knew this one was a Saurian and that one wasn't. Gera was just answering Bill's "scientific" questions. During that process, Stan was making a list.

I smiled, thinking of Gera as he helped Bill study "science." My friend, he stepped in to cover for me. The guilt I was feeling washed from me as I listened. Bill was explaining that it was a rather simple cloaking device the Saurians used to look like humans. According to what Gera had discovered in his research of them, they couldn't alter molecular structure. They were projecting an image.

The Alien's Gift

Bill was quite animated now as he grabbed a device Jason had carried out earlier. "For instance, did you know their cloak can be dissolved by just projecting this simple little device?"

I started to ask how, but decided I wouldn't test Bill's "scientific" ability too far. Besides I still didn't understand how we'd be able to handle the mother ship. Jason answered that. They weren't going to handle any of them. All they were going to do is reveal things including the mother ship. The power of the world would deal with them once they were aware.

They still hadn't answered my question about the mother ship. "Was the machine going to expose it also?"

Bill spoke up. Again I remembered he was the "scientific" expert here. The idea of that amused me, but I listened carefully. I knew Bill's information came from a reliable source.

Bill explained that the shielding on the mother ship was different. Plutonium was the fuel the ship used for space travel. It was the main power source of the ship, and they believed it not only powered the ship, but also its shields. He went on to explain that we use Plutonium in our own space missions. Gera though that was how the Saurians found us to begin with. Our signature in space was large, according to Gera. Plutonium is rare in nature, but we produced it and used it extensively in space.

I was getting the picture of how we were discovered by the aliens. I could also understand that they used it as fuel. After all, that was our purpose for it also. I still didn't understand how this information could help us. How could we expose them? I was still unsure. Maybe I was misunderstanding what Bill was saying. I asked again if the machine would expose it.

This time Bill said quite simply, "No!"

"How are we going to do that?" I was truly lost at this point.

"We aren't going to, Gera will," Bill said with a smile.

I was lost now. Gera was gone. Besides, how could he do that? He wasn't allowed to interfere with the Saurians. Jason corrected me, "He isn't allowed to do them any harm. With our plan ... he won't."

I was still concerned. How did we contact Gera? I hadn't told them yet I had lost the gift. I would have to say something. I was about to. When Bill said, "Gera had been checking in every day to see if we were ready."

That fact almost stopped me in my shoes. *How come I hadn't seen him?* I wondered. "Why would he come without me even knowing?"

"We were waiting for you to be ready," Bill said. "You just went through a lot, we knew that. We couldn't start till you were ready to continue."

I was confused. I no longer had the gift. I wasn't able to do anything to help. Why were they waiting for me?

Then Jason spoke, "You're still the leader of all this. You started it, and if

217

it hadn't been for you, none of this would be happening. We couldn't begin until you say go."

I was moved by Jason's words. I looked from man to man as they sat around the table. Their looks told me they agreed with Jason to the man. I was humbled, more than that. Now I had to tell them.

The word choked in my thought as I said, "I've lost my gift, I can't help much anymore. But I'd do anything they asked."

Jason smiled, "There's nothing left to do, but start. Give the word and we push some buttons, that's all."

I couldn't believe what I had just heard. It was that simple. We push some buttons. "Push" was all I said. It was all I could say.

Jason and Steven lead us into the computer room, I watched as they turned on their equipment, and the screens all sprung to life. Jason and Steven were typing in some commands.

Then Jason pointed to the send key as he looked at me and said, "Push".

I did. The end had started. With that simple push, files concerning The Trenton Group's shady business deals were being released to the news media around the world. That was it, that simple! I looked at Jason. His smile said it was done. I turned to each man in the room.

"Now we wait."

Tomorrow the information would be on desks and computers around the world. Tomorrow the questions would begin to demand some hard answers. Tomorrow Mr. Fallen would have a bad day. I smiled as I pushed that button. We had come a long way. The night was ours. I released the button. I was ready for a drink. We spent the rest of the night celebrating the fact we were finally revealing them to the world. All we could do now was wait and see how the world responded.

Chapter 25

I woke around four the next morning. This morning I chose to just lie in bed for a couple of minutes. I was looking forward to this day, and I wanted to savor it from its inception. I might have stayed longer except for the pups. They knew I was awake. Once that happened, I knew staying in bed was out of the question for much longer. I got up, reluctantly, and headed downstairs to the kitchen. For some reason the dogs were anxious this morning, rushing me to get my coffee and open the door. Once we walked out, they were off on their adventure. Whatever it was, they were sure fired up this morning. I had no idea what it might be, but it seemed important, that was for sure. I watched them disappear from sight before I sat down.

I had been outside over an hour when Bill finally arrived. He usually got here around four-thirty, but had been running late since he'd gotten the new car. Sometimes I wondered if he got up even earlier just to have enough time to make it a longer drive. I thought I'd check, so I asked if he found a better short cut as he was sitting down. I was a little surprised when he said he came right here this morning. I realized he was as ready for today as I was. We all were. Bill finished his coffee, and we jumped in the cart and headed over to Jason's.

The morning was filled with anticipation. We were all ready, but it would still be several hours before we would even begin to see how the plan was going. The home stretch was going to be the hardest part. Waiting always was. The new cars helped to pass the time. It was a tossup between the three of them as to who talked the most. Not that Jason and I didn't jump in on more than one occasion. The cars were a trip for all of us. That can't be denied. Before we realized it, it was time to start checking. We headed to the computer room.

The walls and tables in the computer room were now covered with monitors and television screens. Each was on, and we were all searching for news. Most of our focus was on overseas news cast. We didn't expect to see much coverage in this country yet. We were pretty sure Mr. Fallen would do what he could to block that. Jason spoke French and was monitoring their broadcast. I was watching the Australian news. Bill watched England. Steven and Stan were monitoring the Spanish news. Each had something about the Trenton Group.

So far they were still calling them allegations. That was understandable. They needed to validate the data, and there hadn't been enough time to confirm information yet. Most of the reports were discussing the military contracts and dealing with unfriendly nation reports. Members of the media were looking for members of the Trenton Group for any comments. So far they had been unsuccessful. We watched the entire broadcast and that was it. Only superficial so far, but we knew it was just the beginning. It was a good start, better than we had hoped for.

We took turns watching the news most of the morning. After each report was over we would sit down and be briefed on what was said. Bill's report turned out to be the most interesting of the day. It seemed that the U.S. Congress was more than interested in the military allegations. Congressional staff members had jumped fast on the data Jason had made available to them. From the way it sounded, they were meeting this afternoon and setting up a full investigation committee. We knew that would draw in the national media in this country, despite Mr. Fallen being the owner. We would find out just how independent the news was.

Later that day Gera arrived. Jason told him we were ready to go. It was only then that he finally came to see me. I asked why he hadn't just come in the beginning. He restated exactly what the others had said, "I knew you would be ready soon."

He, too, had just been waiting for me to call the time. When I thanked him for his help, he just smiled a coy smile before telling me he wasn't doing anything except showing us some basic science. He didn't stay long. We all knew we were going to have our hands full and didn't believe his assistance would be needed for another day at least. Wishing us luck, Gera said he'd be here when we needed him, and was gone.

We went back to watching the news. By the five o'clock news reports the

The Alien's Gift

story had become the lead-in story in most nations. Only one national news organization seemed to be lacking coverage...ours. The information leaked or compromised up to this point had affected nations around the world. Their interests were personal. Their governments' interests were personal.

Calls came out from around the world for members of the Trenton Group to respond to these charges. Earlier in the day Jason had launched the second volley of attacks. With a key stroke he had released more information. They were the ones who would shock the world. Jason had deliberately waited. He knew we needed them to start to doubt the Trenton Group before showing them phase two. They were ready now.

In phase two the alien connection was being released. Jason knew that most news organizations would pass it by, not paying it a second bit of attention. For that reason Jason hadn't released it directly to the media. Jason had sent that information to military leaders around the world, sure they would take more interest, or at least we hoped they would. We knew that the United States had suspicions about the possibility of aliens in our midst. We knew that at the least Lieutenant General Baset did anyhow. We wanted their attention. That way any information pertaining to aliens would leak out only from the highest military levels.

I was beginning to appreciate Jason's talents. He knew what he was doing and just how to go about doing it. We called it a day, deciding we'd let the pot stew for the rest of the day. Tomorrow was going to be better. We had started. Phase one and two were now underway, but we were nowhere finished with them, not yet.

The next morning as I sat on my patio I swore the air was even cleaner and sweeter than it had been the day before. Bill had just gotten there, and we sat and sipped our coffee talking about the previous day and getting excited about what today would bring. When we finished our coffee, Bill got up to head for the cart. He was ready to head to Jason's the same as we always did. This morning I had a different plan. There would be nothing to do for the next couple of hours, and we all knew that. I had a different plan for this morning. I had already let Jason know we would be coming over late.

I called Bill back, saying I wanted to go for a ride in his new car. I knew he would jump at the chance to go riding again. I knew it would help kill the time, and to be honest, I did want to go for a ride in it. I had never actually just ridden in one, only driven. The ride would be fun. Besides, it would be a chance for Bill to be able to show off his car.

The ride was all I thought it would be and more. The sensation of acceleration was insane. When you're not the one to step on the accelerator, you don't see it coming. You get caught more by surprise as a passenger. Bill was also a running narration of the performance of the car every inch of the

221

way. His excitement was contagious. I truly believed I liked riding with him in his better then actually driving mine myself. We got back in just a little over an hour. During my ride with Bill I realized why he kept looking for those long short cuts. The ride seemed to only last minutes. It ended with me promising myself to do this again.

Gera had already arrived by the time we got back to the house. I greeted him as we walked in. I was rather amazed at how normal it seemed to see an alien sitting in the living room. Maybe it was because I already knew he was going to be here today. *Or was I just getting used to seeing aliens?* Either way, the thought tickled me. The answer came to me in the next moment when Ari and Lení walked into the room. They caught me off guard. Okay, maybe I wasn't getting used to aliens. Then again, maybe I just wasn't expecting them to be there.

"It seems that a lot of Rikiens are willing to teach basic science," I said as I looked at Bill.

Lení was quick to let me know that her father wasn't the only one who cared. Before going on to say that not only were they concerned for us, but had great concern for our species as well. I appreciated her words so much I even let the species thing go by without a second thought. Well, not too much of a second thought.

They joined us in the computer room where we watched the latest reports. By now even the news media in this country had picked up on the reports. However the coverage didn't seem to be as aggressive yet. I had to keep in mind that Fallen was their boss, so they weren't as quick to call him a traitor or worse. Other nations weren't being as nice to the Trenton Group.

Once the information started to come out, members of different companies owned by Trenton were more than happy to become whistle blowers. The congress had subpoenaed all of the board members of the Trenton Group, up to and including Mr. Fallen and President Blanchard. Nations around the world were speaking at the U.N. wanting to have full investigations into their energy and arms trade interests. Everything seemed to be happening at once.

I asked Steven to bring up the mother ship so that Gera could let us know if there had been any change. As Steven started to turn on the equipment, Gera informed us that wouldn't be necessary. The mother ship was exactly where it had been. It had maintained the same synchronized orbit, sure that it would stay undiscovered. Gera was pretty sure they wouldn't move. He was sure they would wait until the last available Plutonium was loaded aboard. Gera said that even as we spoke the smaller craft were shuttling the Plutonium to the mother ship as quickly as possible. The Trenton Group hadn't been allowed to pick up any new loads of Plutonium for the last two days, but we knew they had a substantial quantity already in the system ready for shipping.

I was still thinking we should be doing something about that when I remembered we hadn't tuned into the satellite. Gera hadn't needed it, I had to ask. "Gera, how did you see the mother ship without the satellite image?"

He reminded me he was, after all, a Rikien, and not human. Rikiens could do things that our species was incapable of, even me when I had been… Gera stopped in mid sentence, remembering at that point the fact that I no longer had the gift. Well, serves me right, I did ask.

I turned my attention to Jason and the Plutonium. I kept wondering when we were going to have to cut off the flow. I couldn't understand why I was the only one concerned. I kept thinking the longer we waited, the more Plutonium the Saurians would get. Jason was surprisingly calm. Actually they all were. Almost as if it were a concession to me and my impatient nature, Jason agreed it was time to show the alien connection to the Trenton Group. The military had not leaked the information, at least not as much as we had hoped. Now Jason was releasing the third phase of his plan. He was sending information to the news media that would expose the alien connection, at the same time sending more files to congress. In those, Jason had included the information about the plot to replace the President with an imposter, showing information that proved the Trenton Groups' main purpose was to facilitate business for both the aliens and themselves.

All of that was done with a simple stroke of the keys. From this point it was a waiting game. The rest of the day we watched information leaking out slowly as facts were verified. As the day progressed, more and more governments were up in arms as they uncovered internal dealings involving the Trenton Group. Things were unraveling slowly.

I still wasn't sure what the Rikiens' part of the plan was, other than it involved "teaching science." Whatever they were going to do, that time had not yet arrived. I knew that. I don't know how I knew that, but I did. My belief was confirmed when they announced they were going back to Rikiel, saying they would return again in the morning. I still wasn't sure when that was supposed to happen. I had never really asked in great detail, maybe because I was still feeling that I didn't have much to offer. Maybe they were just waiting until I asked? I would be sure to…if I knew when the time came. I tried not to let it concern me. They knew what they were doing.

All in all it was another good day. I didn't get to see Mr. Fallen squirm yet, but I was betting that wherever he was now, he wasn't being quite so arrogant. On the plus side I got to see Gera along with Ari, and Lení. That makes any day a good day. It wasn't long after they left that we decided to call it a day ourselves. It was time to eat, I suggested we go out. I told Bill I would go with him, then called out shotgun to make sure he knew who was driving.

The next morning I was up and out on the patio by four. Again the air tasted just a bit better to me than the day before. I watched the pups as they took off across the yard, their morning patrol underway. That was the one thing I missed about the old house. The yard, although large, was nothing compared to this. The dogs would patrol and be back in fifteen minutes or so unless they found something of interest.

Here with so much property to survey, they were usually out, coming in only to run with the golf cart as I headed for Jason's. I took comfort in thinking that soon I would have the time to sit and wait for their patrol to end and have them rejoin me in the mornings. That day would come soon, but it wasn't here yet. For now today would start the same. How it would end was another story. I was looking forward to finding out.

Bill came walking out and joined me as I was finishing my thought. We sat and had our morning coffee before joining Jason for breakfast. When Gera arrived we were all sitting on the patio. He had gotten there early saying that Ari and Lení would be here soon. Gera was starting to come and drink coffee with us from time to time. I think he enjoyed the morning get together. I know we all enjoyed his company.

Once breakfast was over, we headed into the computer room. Jason turned on the televisions and monitors. What we saw surprised us. Front page wasn't the word for it. The alien story was everywhere. You couldn't turn to anything that wasn't news talking about the Trenton Group, the aliens, or a combination of both. Each newscast team had taken on a different theme. On one network their banner read, *The Trenton Group conspiring to overthrow the planet with aliens.* We changed the channel only to see the next banner, *Trenton Group traitors of the Planet.* Each news station tried to say it louder and with more indignation then the other.

Ari and Lení had walked in while we were watching the broadcasts. Finally some of the reporters had caught up with Mr. Fallen. They had him and his entourages cornered and were busy asking him questions. This one was one I wanted to watch. I was going to take great pleasure in watching him squirm. I was disappointed. Fallen didn't show the slightest bit of concern. He was standing there on the screen denying all of it. "This is all so absurd, including this alien thing, it's laughable."

That's when I spotted the man standing beside him. The one the Saurians planted. I asked Gera if he saw the shielding, he confirmed it. I remembered the machine Bill had told me about. Turning to Bill I said, "Expose that alien, right here right now, in front of everyone."

Bill turned on the machine, but nothing happened. We looked at Gera for an explanation. Bill wasn't sure if he did something wrong or the machine was failing. Gera looked at us with amusement. He explained the machine had to be in the vicinity of the individual to have an effect. Then he turned to Ari. "Ari, what do you think of this image on the screen?"

Ari commented that there seemed to be some sort of disturbance in the broadcast. However he was pretty sure he could compensate for it. With only a thought, the shield dropped. Now exposed to the cameras with the world watching, the man standing next to Mr. Fallen turned into a Saurian. For the first time in his adult life Mr. Fallen was without words. I saw the panic on his face as he rushed back into the building. That was what I had wanted to see. Fallen's face when he first realized he was ruined. The news group had backed away in fear once the Saurian was exposed, allowing him to escape. I didn't think anyone would try to capture him anyway.

I looked at Ari my appreciation showed. He caught my look and denied doing anything.

"What! All I did was clean up some interference in the transmission there's nothing wrong with that."

He was right, nothing wrong with that at all. It was only the beginning, it was far from over. Bill called our attention to another report. The Washington press had caught up with President Blanchard. Their questions were coming hard and fast. The reporters were now showing little, if any, respect for his former office. They asked what he knew about the attempt to replace the President.

"The idea was preposterous." President Blanchard was giving the only answer he could under these conditions, and he kept saying it over and over.

Unfortunately for him one of the aids standing with him was also shimmering. LenÍ spotted him first. She repaired the problem. The image was now clear of any distortion, both ours and theirs. President Blanchard was standing beside a Saurian. I assumed he was the one that was about to take the place of our current President. Blanchard collapsed as the Saurian came into clear view beside him.

Gera seemed quite pleased with Ari and LenÍ performances. They had managed to do what was needed to assist us. They also did it without any acts of aggression. There was no direct intervention made on the Saurians. After all in reality all they had done was show us some simple "science," clearing up broadcast signals, to be exact. Nothing hostile, but in the process…

They were exposed, and there was no longer any doubt of their existence. The media had seen and broadcast their presence around the world. Still, I was concerned about the mother ship. It sat out there, and we hadn't disrupted the shipments of Plutonium. What was to stop them from taking it? I was talking out loud as the words ran through my mind.

Gera turned. "That brings up an interesting question I have been meaning to ask."

He went on to ask about the Plutonium, wanting to know if the Trenton Group was the legal owner. This one was Steven's to answer. "No they were contracted to dispose of it safely. But that didn't give them ownership."

"So if he understood this correctly, the Plutonium was the responsibility of the government," Gera asked. We agreed with that assessment. He nodded before he continued with his line of logic.

"Again, if I'm not mistaken," Gera said, "they were contacted to make it safe, is that correct?"

Again we all found ourselves agreeing with his assessment.

"In this country the people are the government, is that not correct?"

I confirmed that was indeed correct, the people are the government in this country.

"Perfect," he said. Gera now had a big smile.

I still didn't know what he was getting at. Gera said that if he understood correctly, the government or, to put it in other words, the people, were the true owners of the Plutonium. Once again we all confirmed his assessment was correct.

"That would mean the Saurians did not possess it legally," he said.

Once again I had to agree. He was leading somewhere, and I could hardly wait for him to arrive.

"Then since the plutonium is yours, with your permission, may I demonstrate to you that if you change the base element, it will no longer be a contaminant."

"What?" He was confusing me.

Bill said, "He wants to change the plutonium into something else."

I was still confused, "What would you change it into?" I asked Gera.

"Does it matter?"

He was right. I shut up. Gera went on to explain. Plutonium was a fuel, although, according to Gera, a rather crude and primitive form of fuel. Once you change the elemental structure, it would be useless for that purpose, reduced to pure junk, not much more use then a rock. *Change it,* I thought *Ari had told me they couldn't do that to atoms that had already formed into an object.* Gera seemed to be reading my mind and finished my thought out loud, "It was changed without being destroyed."

I hadn't understood before. They can manipulate any atom. That made sense. If you can, you can. The problem was you destroy what it was in the process. Rikiens would not destroy a living thing. Plutonium wasn't a living thing. I was starting to understand. It would still *be,* just not *be* plutonium anymore. The question was simple. I looked at the guys.

The Alien's Gift

"We don't really need plutonium, do we?"

Everyone shook their heads no. It was unanimous. Turning to Gera once again, I said, "All the representatives of my planet present agreed. We didn't need nor want Plutonium."

He could change it. Gera focused a moment. An instant later the mother ship came into view. Several smaller craft in the area around it came into view at the same time. Gera said he left enough of the Plutonium to allow the ship's life support and basic propulsion. The rest of the Plutonium was gone.

I was staring at the defense satellite monitor, watching as the ships came into view. I was pretty sure someone would be speaking to General Baset any minute now. The Rikiens had done their part. They hadn't hurt anyone in the process, just showed us a little science the results of which left the alien craft out in the open, able to be seen. The enemy was exposed.

Chapter 26

We had done it. We'd exposed the enemies to our planet. Ironically, we had done it with a team that was also comprised of two species, alien and Earth born alike. The Rikiens had done their part. Now it was up to us, but this time it was all of us. The world now knew what, until now, only a handful of men had been aware of.

We were watching the Defense satellite, the mother ship now exposed to the world. On the television news, teams were reporting as fighter squadrons were taking to the air, the military acting swiftly, they were on the job. On every channel and frequency the voice of General Baset could be heard. "Please respond or we will assume you to be hostile and open fire."

I watched as our air power took to the air. I wondered if we could do anything against their armament. The mother ship was in orbit. Could we even get to them? Two minutes later I had my answer. After hearing the General give one last warning, the first missile was fired.

We watched on the defense satellite monitor as the missile impacted the side of the ship. The ship took the hit well, but it did show some damage. I think that surprised the Saurians. They were already starting to climb out of orbit as the second missile impacted rocking the craft. They had made no attempt prior to the impacts. Smaller alien craft were converging on the mother ship from all angles. They were pulling back. The success of the missiles against their craft seemed to catch them off guard.

Gera said the Plutonium must have also operated their defensive shield as well as the cloaking shield. He didn't think they had been aware that the Plutonium was no longer effective. They did now.

"You can bet they're examining the Plutonium as we speak," I said.

We were so engrossed in the scene as it was unfolding, we almost didn't hear Gera when he said they had to return to Rikiel, but would be back in the morning to see how everything was progressing. Then they left without any further fanfare. We turned our attention back to watching as the mother ship continued to pull away from our planet. She was still moving slowly. I believed that was because they were loading the smaller craft. We watched as more craft kept approaching. The defense satellite was rotating around to follow the mother ship's every move.

We continued to watch until the mother ship got out of range. Once it was out of sight we turned our attention back to other news coverage. The aliens' retreat was having its effects. Leaders from around the world had suddenly gone missing, interestingly enough only those who were involved in questionable conflicts. Most of them were now believed to be aliens who were impersonating the true leaders. No information was available yet on what might have actually happened to the real leaders. We went from channel to channel. The world was uniting against the invasion. From what we were seeing so far, the Trenton Group plan was all unraveling fast.

It had once been said that the one thing that would unite mankind would be an alien invasion. It would seem that they were right. Wars seemed to end simultaneously all over the world. Their problems now seemed to be petty squabbles. The planet was united now that we had a common enemy. Worst of all, we had been betrayed from within. Now the world was responding as one. Political and Military leaders were meeting together for the first time as one.

As for The Trenton Group, their assets were seized around the world, pending investigations by those countries. The corporation continued to operate under restrictions. However, Mr. Fallen was arrested, along with the rest of the principles from the Trenton Group. President Blanchard was being held on charges of treason. The world was shutting down their entire operation at a rate I wouldn't have thought possible.

Over the next few days information about the dealings between the Trenton Group and the Saurians filtered out piece by piece. The Saurians worked with and helped the Trenton Group disrupt the nations of the world. That helped drive up the prices of oil and increased sales for the Trenton Group military interest. The aliens received Plutonium in trade. The Trenton Group falsified records to hide the missing material.

As for the Saurians, they seemed to have vanished completely. Nothing of them had been seen since the mother ship exited from earth's orbit. The planet's entire military network was keeping a watch on the skies. They seemed to have just completely vanished. I was pretty sure that General Basset was watching.

Later that night we went out for dinner. It was the first time we could discuss the aliens and Trenton Group in public. It was the main conversation at every table in the restaurant. We spent most of our time eavesdropping on other tables, amusing ourselves on the different theories people had. The one thing everyone seemed to have right was Mr. Fallen and President Blanchard. The common opinion was that they were power hungry, greedy individuals, not worth the air they breathed. I felt their opinion was fairly accurate, too. The aliens covered the gambit from lizard people that eat children to demons directly from hell. Only they were in a space ship.

We still couldn't celebrate total victory. The Saurians were still out there. Would they return? Now that they had been attacked, would they come back in strength? They hadn't returned any fire when fired upon. We wondered why? Surely a race capable of traversing the cosmos was capable of more than just defending themselves. Yet they hadn't fired a single shot. Why had they chosen to just leave instead? We all hoped it was permanent. We just didn't know. We still had Plutonium, and they still wanted it. I wondered personally if they were already back. I kept that thought to myself.

Chapter 27

It had been over a week since everything had broken loose and the Saurian ship left our air space. Every day there was something new about the Trenton Group. Charges were still coming in, not only from nations around the world, but also other corporations. Trenton Group was destroyed. Fallen was penniless, and unless some sort of miracle took place, would be going to jail for the rest of his life. President Blanchard's life would only be spared out of respect for the office he once held. Although many had cried out for his execution, for the same exact reason, the office he once held. Me, my mornings were cleaner and fresher now than I could ever remember.

I was sitting on my patio, and it was just one of those mornings. I had just sat down with my coffee. The pups were off in a flash. Something was there. An intruder was on their property, one who didn't belong. I didn't feel threatened in the slightest by it. I was pretty sure there was no invasion taking place in my yard. Not unless you counted rabbits or possibly a possum. I looked at my watch. It was almost six. Bill would probably be here soon. He was running a little late. He seemed to take longer and longer to get here since he'd gotten that car. There really wasn't a lot to do. We spent most of our time just keeping up with the news events.

Mostly we were waiting on the Rikiens' return. We had expected to have seen them by now. Stan and Steven needed to go back up to the Cape. They kept putting it off while we awaited their return. They were working for Jason, so it wasn't like they would get in any trouble. I think they actually got more work done here than they would in the Cape anyhow.

For the most part our world was filled with a lot of waiting. We were enjoying the break in the action, but I wasn't too sure how long I could take the easy life. Not having to work is a lot different than not having any work to do. *Maybe today*, I thought, as my mind wandered to Gera. I missed not being able to just reach out and talk to him. Not that I ever could, really. Gera could reach out through time and speak with me. He seemed to have to originate it. My mind was never strong enough to break through the barrier of time and space that separated us.

Gera had been the last of the Rikiens I would ever speak with on a routine basis. Ari, I already know, never contacted me again. I should say the Ari of today. As for the future Ari and LenÍ I missed them as you miss close friends, but Gera had been more than a close friend. Gera and I had melded. I'm saddened to report the realization that the connection, that one mind we shared, was fading for me since the pod. I was losing the memories, slowly but losing them nonetheless.

Just as I was about finished depressing myself, Bill arrived. I was happy to see his smiling face. I needed it, just to counter my own thoughts. If anyone could do that in a hurry, he was the man. As he sat down, his magic was already in practice.

"You know the coffee here sucks. I only come because it's cheap."

That was what I needed this morning. Bill always seemed to say the right things when I needed them. We sat chatting about the past for the next hour. Our lives had changed dramatically in the last couple of months. We were reflecting back on the times when I still had the gift. Bill liked the first one, the guy in the police chase. He laughed just as hard today when he would mention the guy's face as he had originally.

I thought of losing that gift. I lost the ability to do so much. All I had to have done was pay closer attention to my body, and I would still be fine. It felt like such a waste. I tried to let the thought go. After all, I had lived most of my life without any gift. I would make it through the rest of it without it.

It was a little after eight when we got to Jason's house. We might not have any work to do, but we still had a free breakfast coming. It was also one of the best parts of the day. I always enjoyed our get together for breakfast. The conversation was usually light and casual. We had decided long ago the combination of the weight of the world and breakfast never went together well. Besides, we knew there was always time for the day to suck later. This morning was no different. Today the conversation rotated around just how much Steven can eat. Steven suggested he was the older brother and was setting an example. The morning was going to stay that way.

We were just finishing breakfast as Gera arrived. It goes without saying that the day just got a lot better for us all. The morning turned out to have a lot of good surprises. Not only had we been awaiting Gera's return, he told us he had great news to report besides. We turned around and sat back down. Gera looked at the coffee pot. I knew he was wondering if he had arrived too late. It was almost funny. The man was a genius with abilities beyond belief. Still, one of his greatest pleasures was sitting on a patio with a bunch of fools drinking coffee. I got up and poured him out a cup, thinking I would always have not only time, but coffee for him.

Once everyone got comfortable again, and Gera had a chance to sip at his coffee a bit, he started to speak, starting first with the Saurians. He had followed their movements after they pulled out of orbit. He, too, had been concerned about their future plans. Gera found out that the ship that was here wasn't part of any invasion fleet or even a military craft, for that matter. It was nothing that exotic at all. They were a simple salvage ship. *That explained the lack of return fire*, I thought. It made sense now. He was also able to understand their thoughts better than I. Go figure. The Saurians believed the Plutonium to be inferior, a problem unique to our planet. That and they also thought they might have been cheated. Either way, they had no intention of returning to Earth.

To say he had good news would be an understatement. The relief in the room was immense. My only regret was that I couldn't pass this information on to General Baset. I'm sure he would have slept much easier knowing what I now knew. Gera spent the rest of the hour just filling us in on general information. Our meeting ended on a high note. Tonight we knew we would celebrate. The morning was indeed full of good news. I could see that Gera enjoyed giving us the good news. He kept watching me as everyone was going on about what we had just been told. I had lost most of my connection with Gera, it was true, but there was something else, something.

After we broke from the table Gera asked if he could speak to me in private. I wasn't surprised. I knew there was something. I asked if he would like to go for a ride in the golf cart. Gera seemed to enjoy not only riding in it, but driving it. That had been the main reason I suggested it. He referred to it as our low pollutant vehicle, stating it wasn't totally pollutant free. The batteries were still a problem for him. Pollutant or not, he loved it and was in the driver's seat before I had a chance to offer to let him. We drove out across the property. Gera had wanted the conversation to be totally private.

It was almost an hour before we returned to the house. Bill had gone for a ride with Stan, surprise. Jason and Steven were in the computer room working on business. They stopped long enough to come out and say goodbye to Gera, telling him to be sure and come see us again soon. Gera promised, admitting he had no excuse not to. After all he had all the time in the world. As he got ready to depart he turned to me. "Marc I shall *speak* to you soon."

I smiled and told him I'd be looking forward to *hearing* from him. I placed my hands palms up on my thighs and looked at my friend. He was already bowing in return. As we stood he simply said "My friend" and he was gone.

Dinner that night was the celebration we had waited for. Bill and Stan were a little down at first, having missed Gera's goodbye. They had only gone to the store and missed him by a minute or two. I tried to cheer them up. Telling them, Gera would always be a lot closer than they knew.

From that point on it was just a party. It wasn't late when we got home, but it had indeed been a long day. Bill and I headed over to the house. Not ready to sleep yet, I turned on the television. The news was on. For the first time in forever, something other than the aliens or the Trenton Group was on. We were watching a good old car chase in California. I looked at Bill. "Now that's different." I said.

We laughed about it for a second. I sat back and watched the car as it zipped in and out of traffic. As I sat back in my seat, I smiled, I had waited long enough. Bill had to be the first to know. I had waited all during the celebration. As we watched the car zip through traffic, I thought now is a perfect time. Without taking my eyes off the screen, I thought, *what do you think Bill. Should we?*

Bill's head snapped up. As he sat up, he turned toward me with a big smile on his face. Now that was a knowing smile. I smiled back, then, I jumped.